MURDER IN AN
ITALIAN
VILLAGE

MURDER IN AN
ITALIAN
VILLAGE

A Bria Bartolucci Mystery

MICHAEL FALCO

KENSINGTON PUBLISHING CORP.
www.kensingtonbooks.com

KENSINGTON BOOKS are published by

Kensington Publishing Corp.
119 West 40th Street
New York, NY 10018

All Kensington titles, imprints, and distributed lines are available at special quantity discounts for bulk purchases for sales promotion, premiums, fund-raising, educational, or institutional use. Special book excerpts or customized printings can also be created to fit specific needs. For details, write or phone the office of the Kensington Special Sales Manager: Attn. Special Sales Department. Kensington Publishing Corp, 119 West 40th Street, New York, NY 10018. Phone: 1-800-221-2647.

Library of Congress Control Number: 2023938829

ISBN: 978-1-4967-4213-1

First Kensington Hardcover Edition: October 2023

ISBN: 978-1-4967-4215-5 (ebook)

10 9 8 7 6 5 4 3 2 1

Printed in the United States of America

This book is dedicated to Cab for making me feel like Bria—a little off kilter, but thrilled to be embarking on a new journey.

As always, big thanks to my agent, Evan Marshall, my editor, John Scognamiglio, and the whole Kensington team. And a special thank you to the beautiful village of Positano for welcoming me with an open heart and opening my eyes to one of the greatest wonders of the world.

Una donna italiana è come un villaggio.
Entrambi forniscono sicurezza, comfort e,
soprattutto, mistero.

An Italian woman is like a village.
They both provide safety, comfort
and, above all else, mystery.

Prologue

Welcome to Positano

Early May in Positano meant anticipation, *la quiete prima della tempesta*, the quiet before the storm. It meant a few more weeks until the official start of summer and the tourist season in this glorious village on the Amalfi Coast, the one that John Steinbeck famously called "a dream place that isn't quite real." In a few short weeks the steep, narrow streets and the pebble beaches would be overflowing with visitors, the many shops and cafés would be bustling with crowds, the streets pulsating with life, and the energy would be palpable. Until then there was time. Time to breathe, time to reflect, and time to take in the almost surreal beauty of this enchanted piece of the world.

Standing on the small balcony outside her bedroom, Bria Bartolucci took in the view, which still took her breath away. If there was a more beautiful place on the planet, she didn't know where it existed. She couldn't imagine anyplace else looking, sounding, or smelling as radiant. She knew she was biased because Positano was now her home, but from the little she knew of the world, she also knew she was right. The English translation of Positano is "a place to stop," and who wouldn't want to stop in paradise?

At this time of day, right before sunrise, it was as if she was watching the village come alive. From her perch about two hundred feet above the ground, Bria could see a large swath of the coastline, pristine and untouched, like it must have looked before the earliest inhabitants discovered the land and made it their home in the first century B.C. She inhaled deeply and allowed the scent of orange blossoms to envelop her; she took another breath, and the sea salt added to the perfume. The fragrances were as familiar and comforting as the smell of her mother's skin.

The air was tranquil and quiet, making it easier to hear the early morning sounds of the many varieties of birds that populated the area. The colorful European bee-eater's high-pitched, elongated *prrreep* blended with the seagull's quick caws and the almost prehistoric staccato call of the alpine swift to create a lazy soundscape. It was the perfect complement to the soft whooshing sounds the waves made as they rolled onto the shore and then retreated to the sea, matching the rhythm of Bria's own breathing. All around her the land was gently being lured from its sleep.

Bria loved this time of day because she felt that it stripped Positano to its core. It proved that it wasn't just beautiful to look at, but also beautiful to experience with all the senses. The hazy glow of dawn cast a shadow over the landscape, like a piece of cloth that had been draped over a painting to cover it from view. She remembered a quote from one of her art professors: "If beauty is always witnessed, it can be taken for granted. To be truly treasured, beauty must sometimes be hidden."

That was how Bria felt anyway, most likely because she wasn't born here, nor did she grow up in Positano. She had lived here for the past year, and according to *i locali*, Bria was not yet one of them—a local—but *un ospite*, a guest. Not the fleeting, temporary status given to a *turista*, but also not the permanent rank of a certified member of the village. She smiled at the thought, intrinsically knowing that was the Italian way. If you weren't born into a community, you needed to earn your place.

Bria grew up with her family in Ravello, a mountaintop village nestled above the town of Amalfi, about an hour away from the Positano beach. Despite the fact that both villages were part of the province of Salerno and located in the Campania region, to the Positanesi, it was as if Bria were a citizen of Australia or the States. So close and yet so far.

Because Italy was much longer than it was wide, with many countries sharing its borders or separated from it only by the narrow Adriatic Sea, the culture of each region had been influenced and shaped by outside forces. Some differences were obvious, like when comparing Milan to Sicily. The Swiss-Franco Milanese in the north were culturally distant from the Sicilians in the southernmost region of Italy, whose traditions reflected their close proximity to North Africa. Less extreme examples could be found all throughout the country.

Positano was one of the thirteen municipalities that made up the Amalfi Coast. For the most part, each one flowed into the next, each one also fiercely maintained its own individuality. Don't ever make the mistake of saying Vietri sul Mare was the same as Conca dei Marini; this was a surefire way to be handed a one-way ticket back home. That was why even though Bria had grown up a short drive away, she was going to have to prove that she deserved to be part of their community.

A year ago, her husband, Carlo, surprised her when he announced that they were moving to Positano. They had discussed relocating closer to the sea, which was a lifelong dream of Carlo's, but they hadn't shifted the conversation from speculation to action. Carlo being Carlo, he couldn't resist purchasing a bed-and-breakfast that Bria's best friend, Rosalie, had mentioned was about to go on the market. He took part of his inheritance, paid for the two-story house in cash, signed all the papers, and then shared the news with Bria. Before she could protest, Carlo wrapped his arms around her and kissed her deeply. He always did know the best way to silence his wife.

By the time Bria regained the ability to speak, she was completely on board with this new adventure. It wasn't because she shared Carlo's desire to run a bed-and-breakfast; it was because of what she saw in Carlo's eyes. His spirit. He possessed a childlike wonder, a natural joy that saw beauty in the mundane, a boy's curiosity trapped inside a man's mind.

His energy, however, wasn't suffocating or overbearing; it was infectious and irresistible. He wasn't one of those annoyingly happy, offbeat people who consciously attempted to defy societal norms to appear unique. Carlo was unique without trying. He was impulsive, passionate, a little bit reckless, but he also understood the importance of being a husband and a father and embraced those roles, never disappointing either his wife or their son, Marco. He simply had the soul of a dreamer.

When Bria saw the house that he had bought, she knew why Carlo had made such an impetuous decision. Perched on the side of the mountain facing the sea, the two-story building was nearly identical to most of the properties in the village. Rectangular, flat roof, and an entrance that was less than two feet from Viale Pasitea, the main street in the village. Two arched windows flanked the front door, and twice as many ran the length of the second floor, with the windows on opposite ends opening up to private balconies. What set the house apart and made it stand out was that while most of the buildings in the village were white, tan, or a muted color that had faded after spending decades in the relentless Positano sun, this one had been painted bright pink. It was as if it were saying, "Come live inside me and I promise you a lifetime of fun and adventure." She understood why Carlo couldn't resist.

The inside of the house was just as inviting. The first floor had a large open space that was separated into a dining area and living room, where the guests could eat and then relax after a long day. There was a kitchen, bathroom, and two bedrooms toward the back, which would be their private quarters, and upstairs were four bedrooms, each with its own bathroom. The master bedroom had its own private balcony, and the back door in the kitchen opened to a small backyard.

Because all the buildings in Positano were built into the side of the Lattari Mountains, the landscape was unusual, to say the least. Viale Pasitea, with its winding descent and hairpin turns, was one way to get from mountaintop to shoreline, but a quicker, though much more strenuous, way was to take the many steps and paths that had been created by resourceful residents more than a century ago. One set of stairs passed by the backyard, and every once in a while, Bria would see a local or a bemused—and panting—tourist climbing up or down the nearly four hundred steps. A locked gate prevented any passerby from entering the backyard. It was odd to know that strangers were walking so close to private property, but this was common and the way of life in Positano.

The other thing that made the house the envy of its neighbors was that it was detached from the structures on either side. Real estate space was in short supply in the village, and most houses and shops were attached to each other. Having even an ounce of breathing room was a luxury. It meant there were two small alleys on either side of the B and B, one that could house Bria's Vespa and one that led to another set of public stairs.

It was the perfect bed-and-breakfast and the perfect place to start their new life. Bria wanted to call it Una Nuova Vita, A New Life, because that was what they were starting together as a family, but Carlo wouldn't hear of it. The house was christened Bella Bella, the nickname Carlo had for Bria because he said she was twice as beautiful as any woman he had ever met. Bria scolded Carlo for exaggerating, but she scolded him even louder if he forgot to use the moniker.

Six months later their dream of opening the bed-and-breakfast and welcoming guests from all over the world to this enchanted place was shattered when Carlo was killed in a plane crash. He was on a flight to Zurich in a private plane to handle some family business that his late father had put in his name when an unforeseen storm took the plane off course and forced the pilot to crash-land in the Alps. Their dream came to an abrupt halt, but not to an end. It took Bria some time to re-group, but after a while she found the strength to move for-ward and work toward fulfilling what she and Carlo had set out to do. She was going to open Bella Bella on the last week-end in May as planned and operate the B and B herself. How hard could it be? She was raising an eight-year-old boy and his faithful canine companion, Bravo, all on her own; a bed-and-breakfast would be easy in comparison.

She shook her head and laughed to herself. *Chi stai cercando di prendere in giro, Bria?* Who was she trying to kid? She was petrified. She was nervous. She was anxious, and she thought she might be making the biggest mistake of her life and should crawl back to the safety of her parents' home. But then she re-membered she was the woman Carlo Bartolucci had chosen to marry, and the woman Marco Bartolucci loved in the way only a young boy could love his mother.

Standing in her backyard Bria looked down at the village she now called home and felt ripples of energy flow through her body. She was strong, she was clever, and she had a thirst for adventure. She was no fragile damsel in distress. She was Bria Nicoletta Faustina D'Abruzzo Bartolucci for heaven's sake and she was going to make Bella Bella everything she and

Carlo had dreamed it could be. First, however, she had to let Bravo outside so he could do his morning business.

Bria roared with laughter because once again she was reminded of a piece of wisdom her mother had shared with her when she was a young girl: A woman's work was truly never done.

CHAPTER 1

The sun had started its daily climb, and Bria had started her daily routine. She was having her first coffee of the day—Lavazza's Arabica-Robusta with steamed milk—Bravo was eating, and Marco was putting on his school uniform. Fully dressed, Marco ran into the kitchen.

"*Giorno, Mamma*," Marco cried.

"Morning, *mi cucciolo*," Bria said.

Like they did every morning, Marco ran into his mother's waiting arms, and Bria kissed her son's cheeks and then the top of his head. She mussed up his thick black hair with her nose, making Marco giggle and then attempt, unsuccessfully, to put it back in place. When she looked into her son's eyes, a lighter shade of blue than her husband's, Bria saw the past, present, and future all at once. It was a sight that never failed to take her breath away.

Marco grabbed his bowl of fruit and slices of bread topped with generous portions of Nutella and sat next to Bravo. The two ate noisily, both content in each other's company like the best friends they were.

Bravo was a Segugio Italiano breed. At two years old, he was still a puppy but was incredibly well trained, with a lean body, long legs, and a smooth tan coat. His most obvious feature was his long ears, which would have looked more appropriate on a bloodhound, and his best trait was that he was loving and protective and Marco's devoted companion.

When Bravo was finished eating, he rested his chin on Marco's leg, not as a way to coax some more food out of him, but just to let Marco know he was there. Bria quizzed Marco on a spelling bee he was going to have that day in school, and her heart burst when he whizzed through *lampadario*, *universo*, and *tabernacolo*. His teacher was right; Marco was one of the brightest second graders at St. Cecilia's.

Bria quickly changed out of her pajamas and put on cropped-length, off-white linen pants, a ruffled sleeveless top in dark green, which perfectly matched her eyes, and slipped into some espadrilles a shade darker than her pants and with a slightly wedged heel, which made walking up the steep Positano streets much less of a chore. She grabbed her oversized tortoiseshell sunglasses from her dresser, and when she saw herself in the mirror, she made the quick decision to let her wavy mass of black hair fall free on her shoulders instead of trying to tame it by pulling it back into a ponytail. It wasn't vanity; it was practicality. She knew such an exercise could take several minutes, and she needed to get Marco to school before the church bells rang.

When she returned to the main room, she witnessed Marco and Bravo playing tug-of-war with one of Marco's soccer banners. Once again, she marveled at how closely her son resembled her husband. Black hair, blue eyes, and an expression of fierce determination that could barely conceal the sheer joy that lay underneath. Even though Bria considered her son to be beautiful, she also knew he was loud and annoying.

"Mamma!" Marco yelled. "Bravo's cheating!"

"*Basta con il tiro alla fune!*" Bria exclaimed, deliberately making her voice sound even deeper than usual as a way to convey her authority over the household. It didn't work, and she had to repeat herself twice before they followed her command.

"Sorry, Mamma," Marco replied. "Bravo started it."

Bravo barked, the sound rougher than one would expect from a dog so young, and it was clear to Bria that Bravo disagreed with Marco's statement.

"Remember, you're going to have to be quiet in the morning when the guests start to arrive," Bria said.

"I know that, Mamma," Marco replied, slipping his backpack onto his shoulders. "But you may want to remind Bravo."

The three of them walked the route they took every morning from Bella Bella to St. Cecilia's, the *scuola primaria* Marco attended. With Bravo in the lead, looking back every few steps to make sure Marco was right behind him, and Bria bringing up the rear, they walked down the narrow, zigzagging road and into the hub of the village, comprised mainly of stores and cafés. The village was quieter than usual this morning, and Bria assumed the business owners were taking advantage and sleeping in before the tourist season truly began and they'd have to work almost around the clock to satisfy the crowds.

"*Buongiorno*, Signore Taglieri!" Marco shouted.

"*Buongiorno*, Signorino Bartolucci!"

Enrico Taglieri was a local, born and raised in Positano. He was also what her mother would describe as *una canaglia*, a rapscallion. While her mother's description was most likely accurate, Bria found Enrico delightful and harmless.

He tipped his sun-faded straw fedora and gave the world a glimpse of his bald head. "Bria, you look so beautiful, you'll make my flowers wilt in shame. Have mercy on them, *per favore*!"

"*Buongiorno*, Enrico," Bria said. *"Grazie."*

Enrico said almost the same thing to Bria every morning; some Italian men couldn't simply say hello and leave it at that. Even though she knew that he greeted every woman he met in a similar way, she was still flattered by his fawning. As were all the other women Enrico greeted, which was why the potbellied, bald, sixty-three-year-old owner of Flowers by Enrico was known as Romeo to the locals.

"Enrico," Bria said, "when is the new wine and cheese store going to open?"

Before replying, he shrugged and raised his eyebrows dramatically. "I thought it would have opened already. The crowds are about to descend on our little village."

"Maybe they're having problems with permits," Bria suggested. "Have you met the owner?"

"No, but I saw a man go in there once, after he bought a bouquet of petunias from me," Enrico said. "I went to introduce myself later in the afternoon, but no one was there."

"I hope he opens up soon. I want to see if he sells Robiola Piemonte," Bria said. "I have a recipe for a delicious pesto with nuts and vegetables, but I don't have a recipe if I can't get the Robiola."

"*Delizioso*," Enrico said, bringing his fingers to his lips and kissing them. In response Bravo tried to imitate the sound but succeeded only in letting out a bark in a slightly higher pitch than usual. "You like cheese, too, Bravo?"

"Bravo likes everything," Marco replied.

"*Addio*, Enrico," Bria said. "Come on, *figlio mio*. We don't want to be late."

They continued walking and picked up their speed, not breaking their stride even when they passed La Casa Felice, one of Bria's favorite stores, which sold ceramics and houseware items that were both practical and masterfully crafted. She wanted to pick up a bowl decorated in *carciofi*, artichokes, because even though he could spell it in English, Marco pronounced it *heartichokes*, so Bria thought the bowl would be a fun addition to her kitchen. She would have to stop on her way back. They were running late, and it looked like Paloma, the shop owner, was in the middle of cleaning up a mess.

"*Buongiorno*, Paloma," Bria cried without stopping.

"*Giorno*, Bria," Paloma replied, washing her hands in the outdoor sink in front of the shop. "It's been a hectic morning already. I dropped a plant, dirt all over, and I have to try and salvage a potted lemon tree."

Paloma Speranza never failed to impress Bria. She was always cheery, efficient, and handled the pitfalls of being a small business owner with ease. Broken tiles and clumps of dirt littered the floor, but there wasn't a stain on her yellow peasant skirt or her bare feet. Bria made a mental note to remember to act like Paloma when the inevitable crisis arose after her grand opening.

"If I know you, Paloma, you'll make it look better than before," Bria said.

"*Grazie*," Paloma replied. "*Buona giornata.*"

They made it to the gate of St. Cecilia's just as the church bells started to chime, and they were greeted, as always, by Sister Benedicta. The nun's name, to Bria, conjured up an image of an old, grim-faced woman who enforced strict rules with a foot-long ruler that was permanently attached to her hand, ready to strike it across the bottom of an unruly child. That couldn't be further from the truth. Sister Benedicta, who took her name from the Benedictine monks who came to Positano in the first century, was fresh faced and a few years younger than Bria, and she greeted each child with kindness and a smile. In return, she was affectionately called Sister B by her students. The only one who gave the nun a warmer greeting was Bravo.

"*Buongiorno*, Signorino Bravo," Sister Benedicta said.

Like he did every weekday morning, Bravo raced over to the nun, sat perfectly still at her side, and waited for her to pet his head with her left hand. When she bent over, she lowered her right hand, and Bravo scooped up the treat with an eager tongue. It was a silly game they played, but one that never failed to amuse Marco.

"Sister B thinks we don't know that she's feeding Bravo," Marco whispered to Bria.

"Let's keep it our secret," Bria whispered back.

"Inside, children," Sister Benedicta said. "Let's start this glorious day off right."

Marco gave Bria a quick kiss on the cheek, nuzzled noses with Bravo, and then ran to greet the few other children who were straggling into the school. Bria wondered if she'd ever be one of those mothers who got their child to school early, and then realized that was a foolish thought. She knew such a goal was never going to be achieved.

"Come on, Bravo," Bria said. "Let's get on with *our* glorious day."

On the way back home, Bravo became preoccupied with trying to cavort with a small family of salamanders who slithered this way and that and who viewed the large tan beast as foe rather than friend, despite Bravo's gentle curiosity. After Bria got Bravo to give up on establishing any type of relationship with the lizard-like creatures, they continued on their way until they reached Paloma's store. Bria was not surprised to see that the mess from earlier in the morning had been cleaned up or that the chicest store owner in the village was once again wearing her trademark red pumps. High heels were rarely worn in the village, since getting to most places required a trek down uneven steps or a hike up a hill. Even Paloma, who was the type of woman who considered being fashionable more important than being comfortable, wore her heels only when working at the store. When she had to run errands throughout the village, she donned a pair of espadrilles like Bria was wearing.

"I hope Marco enjoys the new *heartichoke* bowl," Paloma said, placing the item into a bag and handing it to Bria. "If only they could stay that age forever."

"Every little boy has to grow up to be a man and break his mamma's heart," Bria replied.

"And the heart of some unsuspecting woman, too," Paloma added.

"*Molto vero*," Bria said, agreeing with her. "*Addio.*"

Just as Bria turned to leave, she saw Paloma rub her ankle against her other leg. Band-Aids peeked out from the back of her red leather pumps, and Bria stifled a laugh.

What do you know? Bria thought. *Even the most fashionable can't be saved from becoming a fashion victim.*

Once home, Bria gave the bowl a quick rinse in the sink and dried it off before laying it on the dining room table, where she had placed some fruit and flowers earlier. She was experimenting with different table settings trying to choose between a floral arrangement in a large vase and a bowl of fruit or both. She was in search of the perfect look, but one that wouldn't appear to look too perfect. She wanted the décor to create a casual and relaxing atmosphere for her guests. Bravo, who was upstairs, had other ideas.

"*Silenzio!*" Bria cried.

Bravo ignored her, which was unusual, and kept barking.

Trying a different tactic, Bria cooed, "Come down, *amore mio*, and I'll give you a treat."

Bravo ignored the invitation to eat, which was even more unusual, and continued to bark, sounding more urgent now.

What kind of mess have you gotten yourself into? Bria thought. *Ah,* beh, *only one way to find out.*

Bria went upstairs and expected to find Bravo in the middle of a pile of laundry or playing with a chewed-up book. Instead, she found her dog standing in front of one of the closed bedroom doors. When Bravo saw Bria, he gave out one more rough bark and then stopped.

"Why are you making such noise, bambino?" Bria asked.

She looked around for something that might have triggered Bravo's vocal frenzy but saw nothing. There was some dirt on the floor and down the steps, which Bravo must have tracked in from the outside. Bria had been so focused on finding out why Bravo was barking, she hadn't seen it on the way up.

"What did you do?" Bria asked.

In response Bravo looked at the bedroom door and started barking again. Whatever had gotten Bravo so excited was inside the bedroom. Could someone be in there? Of course. Why hadn't she thought of that?

"Giovanni," Bria called out. "Is that you?"

Giovanni Monteverdi was the local she had hired to be a handyman, sous-chef, and maid for the summer season, but he wasn't supposed to show up for another hour. Maybe he was trying to make a good impression and had arrived early to fix something in the bedroom that Bria didn't know needed fixing. There was only one way to find out if she was right.

When she opened the bedroom door, she did find a man inside, but he wasn't making a repair. He was taking a nap.

"*Salve*," Bria said hesitantly.

Normally, Bria had a deep voice, not gruff and smoky, but a rich alto. The voice she heard speak sounded nothing like that and was high-pitched and thin. Perhaps that was why the only response she received was Bravo's renewed barking.

"*Salve, signor*," Bria said. "*Scusi, signore*. Are you all right?"

She couldn't see the man's face. He was turned on his side and facing the wall, but he was fully dressed in a suit and dress shoes. He appeared to be tall and lean, kind of like a human version of Bravo.

"I'm sorry, sir, but you need to get up," Bria said. "I'm not ready for any guests."

Bravo barked again, as if willing the man to respond to Bria's command, but the man ignored them both. If he didn't respond to Bria's voice, maybe he'd respond to her touch.

She tugged on the cuff of the man's pants and then shook his ankle back and forth in an attempt to rouse him from his sleep. He didn't wake up, but he did roll over. When he did, Bria's scream was even louder than Bravo's barking. The man's shirt was covered in blood, and his face was pale and ghostlike. The man wasn't sleeping; he was dead.

"*Uffa!*" Bria cried.

It wasn't going to be a glorious day in Positano, after all.

CHAPTER 2

Bria had spent hours educating herself on how to deal with all types of potential guests. Rude guests, drunk guests, guests who didn't pay their bill, guests who broke the rules, every kind of guest she could imagine. Except a dead one. This was one situation she had not imagined she would find herself in, but it was one situation she desperately needed to find a way out of.

The grand opening of Bella Bella was a few weeks away. If word got out that her bed-and-breakfast was doubling as a funeral parlor, she'd have to put up a FOR SALE sign before popping open a bottle of champagne to celebrate this turning point in her life. Who'd want to sleep in a bed that was last occupied by a dead man? But maybe he wasn't dead? Maybe this was an incredibly unfunny practical joke someone was playing on the newest business owner in the village? Italy was filled with strange customs. Why not the arrival of an unexpected corpse as a "welcome to the neighborhood" gift?

Bria took a few steps forward until she was only inches from the man's face. He still hadn't moved, and Bria thought if the man wasn't a real corpse, he was doing a terrific imitation. Bravo nuzzled against her right leg, but was he acting as her protector or seeking protection? Bria couldn't be sure.

"Let's find out if this man is really dead," Bria said.

Just as Bria reached out to grab the man's wrist to check for a pulse, gravity intervened. His right arm, which had been resting on his thigh, slipped and dangled off the edge of the bed.

Once again, Bria screamed and Bravo howled; the man remained silent and completely still. There was no further movement, and when Bria touched the man's wrist with two fingers, no pulse could be found. The stranger in her home was definitely dead.

When Bria heard another noise, this one coming from downstairs, she realized there could be two strangers in her home.

She looked at Bravo and placed her index finger to her lips. Bria could tell that Bravo was fighting the urge to bark, but he was such a well-trained dog that he knew Bria was telling him to be quiet. Obediently, he stayed put. Until Bria started to walk toward the door.

Bravo growled and started to follow her, but Bria turned and raised her right-hand palm up in front of him. It was the universal command for *stay*, and fighting every primitive instinct in his body, Bravo proved yet again what a well-trained dog he was and stood still. He continued to growl but remained motionless, and he didn't follow Bria when she left the room.

Standing at the top of the stairs, Bria looked over the railing and didn't see anyone. There wasn't a piece of furniture out of place, and everything looked normal. As she descended the staircase, she was grateful she was wearing her espadrilles. Thanks to the soft, cushiony soles of her shoes, she made it to the bottom of the staircase without making a sound.

Slowly she ventured toward the bathroom, and she could see Bravo's snout peeking out from between the balusters, but this time she didn't put her finger to her mouth because she didn't know if she was going to find someone hiding and would need Bravo to bark for help. Once inside the bathroom she held her breath and pulled back the white terry cloth shower curtain, prepared to scream if someone was behind it. The shower was empty.

She entered the main room and paused to survey the area before going into the kitchen and saw that the front door was open. Keeping her eyes on the door, Bria whispered to her dog, "I know I shut the door behind me, Bravo. I always do."

At the sound of his name, the dog could no longer remain silent and barked his approval.

Bria went to the door and stepped outside but didn't see anyone on the street. Where were the tourists when you needed them? Bria looked at her watch and saw that it wasn't even 8:00 a.m. It was still early, and while Positano wasn't a sleepy village by any means, it was a village where people liked to sleep in when they could.

Bria came back in the house, and after closing the door behind her, ran up the stairs to the bedroom that currently housed a dead man. She felt a flicker of disappointment when she saw that the man looked the same as he had a few moments ago. Was he supposed to get up, wipe the blood off his shirt, and leave? Bria thought. She then chided herself. *Don't be una rimbambita, Bria. Think logically.*

She was faced with an emergency, and she needed help. Who was the best person to call when in a precarious situation? Her mother? Her father? Her mother-in-law? No, no, and definitely no with a capital *N-O*. If Carlo were alive, she'd call him, but he was dead, which she thought, a tad inappropriately, was incredibly unhelpful of him. There was really only one person she could call for help, the same person who had helped her during every crisis she had ever faced since she was a teenager.

"Rosalie!" Bria shouted into her cell phone. "I need you!"

Rosalie Vivaldi had been Bria's best friend since the eighth grade, when they both had had a crush on the same boy, Alphonso Del Trente. Each girl had done her best to make Alphonso like her more than he liked soccer, but they both had failed. Afterward, they'd realized they liked each other more than they liked Alphonso. Neither had gained a boyfriend, but they had each gained a best friend.

They had stayed best friends throughout college, Bria's marriage, and through all Rosalie's many ill-fated love affairs. They hadn't always lived in the same town—Rosalie having moved to Positano immediately after college, while Bria and Carlo had bounced from Ravello to Rome to Angri—but they had always been in each other's lives, constantly texting, FaceTiming, and e-mailing. Now they once again shared the same postal code.

Rosalie lived on *La Vie en Rosalie*, one of two boats she owned, in the marina where she ran her touring business. She was only seven minutes from Bria's bed-and-breakfast if she rode her bright orange Piaggio MP3 three-wheeled scooter, and she could even make the ride when it rained since the scooter had a removable roof. Ever since Carlo had died and Bria had taken full responsibility for getting the place into shape for house guests, Rosalie had made the trek from the marina many times, at all hours of the day and night. She loved Bria like a sister, but she was growing ever so weary of being the person Bria called to solve every minor problem she faced.

"*Amore mio*, you're not having another home decorating dilemma, are you?" Rosalie asked, sitting on a lounge chair on the deck of her boat, having her morning espresso.

"No," Bria replied. "This is serious."

"Picking out the right couch was also serious," Rosalie quipped.

"It's the focal point of the main room!"

"And the wallpaper in the guest bathroom."

"*Piantala*! The pattern needs to be inviting, not overwhelming."

"Bria, you better not be asking me to look at another paint sample," Rosalie groused. "I've told you a million times already, white is white, no matter what you call it!"

"Rosalie, this isn't about the house. It's about a man."

The second Rosalie heard the word *man*, her attitude shifted. It shifted again when she realized the person talking about a man was Bria. Rosalie didn't think men were something Bria was interested in, since she'd been widowed for only six months, and Carlo had been the love of her life. Could Bria already be thinking about moving on with someone new? Rosalie was hardly an expert on romance, having never been married and her longest relationship having lasted less than a year, but she knew Bria better than anyone, and hearing that she wanted to have a serious conversation about a man was surprising.

"What man are you talking about?" Rosalie asked.

"A stranger," Bria replied.

The conversation had just moved from surprising to shocking.

"This is about a *strange* man?"

"*Uffa*! I don't know if he's strange, but he's definitely a stranger."

"Is he with you now?" Rosalie asked, growing worried by the anxious tone she heard in Bria's voice. "Bria, are you in trouble? Do you need to use our safeword?"

"What safeword?"

"The word we chose in high school to use if we were ever in trouble and needed the other's help but couldn't just ask for it, because someone might be pointing a gun to our head," Rosalie explained. "*Dio mio*! Is a man pointing a gun to your head?"

"No!" Bria replied. "And I don't remember us ever having a safeword."

"Mussolini!"

Suddenly Bria forgot about the dead man in her home and

remembered the poorly chosen word she and Rosalie had picked as a means to get them badly needed help if ever such a time arose.

"I cannot believe we chose that as our safeword."

"History class with Signor Lagusso, remember?" Rosalie asked. "He told us all about Mussolini, and we thought he was the worst."

"Signor Lagusso wasn't the *best* teacher we ever had, but I don't think I'd call him the *worst*."

"Not Signor Lagusso. Signor Mussolini!" Rosalie cried. "We thought he was second to Hitler, so we chose his name as our safeword in case we were ever in serious trouble and were looking into the face of evil."

"I'm not looking at evil, Rosalie, and I don't have a gun to my head," Bria said. "But this is serious trouble."

"Bria, you're making me nervous. What is going on?"

"Come over here and I'll show you."

"Why can't you just tell me?"

"Because you have to see this with your own eyes," Bria said.

"I'm on my way."

"Sbrigati!"

When Rosalie burst through Bria's front door twelve minutes later, it was obvious that she had run the entire way. Her chin-length reddish-brown curly hair had frizzed to about twice its normal size, and she was sweating through her Carla Bruni T-shirt. Rosalie fished out her inhaler from the pocket of her sweatpants and put it in her mouth. She pressed down twice to allow two pumps of asthma medicine to help restore her frantic gasps of air into something resembling normal breathing.

"Rosalie, you know you shouldn't be running."

"You told me to hurry," Rosalie gasped.

"I did, but why didn't you take the scooter?"

"Mariana's using it to pick up some supplies in Praiano," Rosalie explained. "Where's the trouble?"

"What?"

"The man!"

"Right, yes, the man."

"Yes! The reason I rushed here and I'm about to pass out," Rosalie said. "Where is he?"

Bria looked up to the closed bedroom door behind her. Rosalie followed her gaze and immediately started to march up the stairs.

"Rosalie, wait!" Bria cried.

"No man is going to hurt my friend and get away with it," Rosalie said, breathing deeply. "You stay downstairs and let me take care of this."

Two seconds after Rosalie entered the bedroom, she let out a scream that was even louder than Bria's had been earlier. She came out of the bedroom, clutched the banister, and shoved the inhaler back into her mouth to take another puff.

"There's a dead man in your bed!" Rosalie cried.

"I know! That's why I called you for help."

"You said you needed help with a man, not a *dead* man. Those are two very different things, *amica mia*."

"You have to help me figure out what to do," Bria said, racing up the stairs. "I open in a few weeks. I can't have people finding out about this."

"It's even worse for him," Rosalie said, looking through the open door at the dead man. "*Ah! Gesù, Maria, e San Giuseppe! Ti prego . . .* Did you kill him?"

"*Sei fuor di testai*!" Bria shouted.

"I haven't lost my mind, but you have some explaining to do, Bria!" Rosalie cried. "Why is there a dead man in your bed . . . covered in lots and lots of blood?"

"It isn't *lots and lots* of blood," Bria replied. "Why must you always exaggerate?"

"You don't think that's a lot of blood?" Rosalie asked, pointing toward the corpse.

"Of course it's a lot of blood," Bria admitted. "But not *lots and lots*. There's more when Marco has a bloody nose."

"Well, then, maybe the man died from a bloody nose!" Rosalie cried.

"He didn't die from a bloody nose, and you know that!" Bria yelled. "Now stop yelling and start helping me!"

Rosalie shook her head in frustration and paced the hallway floor a few times before being able to speak. "Start from the beginning. What happened?"

"I don't know! I found him that way when I came home after taking Marco to school."

"How long were you gone? St. Cecilia's is only a few minutes away."

"We stopped to talk to Enrico for a bit, and then Sister Benedicta had to give Bravo a treat, like she does every morning," Bria explained. "And then on the way back, we stopped because a family of salamanders caught Bravo's eye, and I bought this cute little bowl with artichokes on it from Paloma."

"How long were you gabbing with Paloma?" Rosalie asked.

"Not too long. She was in the middle of a hundred things, as usual," Bria replied. "We were gone for thirty, thirty-five minutes at the most."

"And during that time, some strange man who I've never seen before, have you?"

"Never."

"Comes into your home, goes into one of your bedrooms, collapses on the bed, and dies."

"*Questo è corretto*," Bria said.

Rosalie ventured into the bedroom to look closer at the body and grimaced. "I think the poor guy may have had some help."

"This man has been murdered, hasn't he?" Bria said, joining Rosalie in the bedroom.

"Without a doubt," Rosalie replied. "If he'd fallen accidentally, there'd be blood on his head, or he'd have a bruise somewhere. He wouldn't be flat on his back."

"When I first found him, he was on his side."

"What?"

"I thought he was a vagrant taking a nap," Bria explained. "I shook his ankle, and he rolled over."

"He was alive?"

"No, the movement made him roll over. He was definitely dead," Bria said. "I checked his pulse to make sure, and then I called you."

Rosalie shook her head and looked even more upset than when Bria had made her look at seventeen different paint samples in varying shades of white.

"Rosalie, what's wrong?"

"This is very bad, Bria."

"I know it's bad. That's why I called you for help."

"This is way above my pay grade. I'm your best friend, not your attorney."

"You think I need an attorney?"

"This room is no longer a room in a quaint little B and B by the sea," Rosalie said. "It's a crime scene, and you're the prime suspect."

"Me?" Bria cried. "I just found the body. I had nothing to do with how it got here."

"I believe you, your family will believe you, but will a jury of your peers?"

"Rosalie Vivaldi, *basta*! This isn't funny. This is deadly serious!"

"I'm glad you finally realize that," Rosalie said, "because it's time we called my brother."

Bria knew that was what she should have done in the first place, but she was frightened. She had never been in a situation like this before, and she wanted to believe that her best friend could help her. She didn't want to think that her only chance to be saved was to rely on her best friend's brother.

"You don't think there's any other way to deal with this?" Bria asked.

"Absolutely not," Rosalie replied. "My brother's your only hope."

"*Bene*! Call him."

"Good," Rosalie said, already waiting for her brother's phone to ring. "Because if the chief of police can't help you, nobody can."

CHAPTER 3

Thankfully, Rosalie's older brother, Luca, was nothing like Rosalie. Where Rosalie felt that every person was free to color outside the lines, Luca believed that no one had the right to break rules that were set in place. Despite this fundamentally opposing point of view on how to behave in the world, Luca and Rosalie were extremely close, and there was nothing they wouldn't do for each other. Which was why, as Rosalie had requested, Luca Vivaldi showed up at Bella Bella within five minutes of his sister's phone call, without the usual police fanfare. He arrived without sirens, and he parked at the curve in the hill, not directly in front of the house. However, he did stray from the most important directive Rosalie had given him: he didn't arrive alone.

"What's she doing here?" Rosalie asked the moment she saw Luca's second in command follow him into the house.

"We were on our way to the station when you called," Luca said. "I thought it was quicker to come right here and not drop Nunzi off first. You did say this was an emergency."

"It is an emergency," Rosalie said. "A *police* emergency."

"Nunzi *is* the police," Luca replied.

"She gives out parking tickets!" Rosalie barked. "This is serious police business, Luca, and *per l'amor di Dio*, I told you to come alone!"

"If it's so serious, Rosalie, why don't you stop acting like a *sorrellina fastidiosa* and tell us why we're here?"

Rosalie glared at Nunzi as if she had been called something far worse and vulgar than an annoying little sister. Her glare lasted a little longer than the ones she usually gave people because she absolutely detested Annunziata Della Monica, but more than that, she knew that the comment was warranted. Bria, fully aware of the animosity that existed between her best friend and Luca's best cop, knew she had to intervene if they wanted to focus on the real reason the police had been called.

"There's a dead body upstairs," Bria announced.

In unison Luca and Nunzi snapped their heads in Bria's direction, and together they shouted, "What?"

"Right up there," Bria said, pointing at the upstairs bedroom in question.

Bravo led the way, and Luca and Nunzi followed, with Bria and Rosalie close behind. When Luca opened the door, he gasped and stopped moving, so Nunzi had to do a quick side step to the right not to bump into him. After a moment, Luca entered the room with the women right behind him. Quietly, he took in the scene, studying the dead man's body, not gasping, commenting, or showing any real emotion. Nunzi wasn't as restrained.

"This man is hardly dead," she declared. She then cast a glare at Rosalie that was even deadlier than the one Rosalie had employed. "He's been murdered."

"Bravo, Nunzi!" Rosalie said. "We've already figured that out."

Upon hearing his name and the harsh tone that accompanied it, Bravo quickly retreated downstairs. Bria wanted to race after him to make sure he understood the angry shout wasn't meant for him, but she knew she needed to explain the situation to the humans in the room first and why she had handled it so poorly. Calling Rosalie first had been an emotional impulse, and now that the shock had worn off about seeing a corpse where there shouldn't have been a corpse, she realized her actions could not be perceived as rational. Especially to two police officers.

"I'm sorry, Luca," Bria started. "I know I should have called the police first, but I panicked."

"I understand," Luca said gently.

"I don't," Nunzi added with no gentility whatsoever.

"Nunzi," Luca said. "What did I tell you about your bed-side manner?"

"*Scusa,*" Nunzi replied. "When I'm at the side of a bed with a bloodied corpse lying on it, my manners go right out the window."

"Nunzi is right, Bria. You should've called one-one-eight to report a medical emergency," Luca said.

"There wasn't a medical emergency," Bria replied. "I checked his pulse. I knew he was dead."

"Then you should've called one-one-three for the police," Nunzi said. "That's correct procedure. Every Positanese knows that's how the system works and the only way that we can help you."

Bria understood that Nunzi's use of the word *Positanese* was deliberate and a subtle way to remind her that she was not yet considered a local.

"You're right, Nunzi, and I apologize," Bria said. "*Perdon-ami*. I don't usually react like such a fool, but I guess finding this dead body brought back memories, and I immediately wanted my friend by my side instead of the police."

"Bria, why don't you tell us exactly what happened?" Luca instructed.

She stared at the two police officers and, for the first time since their arrival, actually understood that she was in the presence of two police officers.

She had known Luca almost as long as she had known Rosalie. Since he was eight years older than Rosalie, he had always been more of a distant relative who floated in and out of their lives. Even still, Bria had known him to be only kind, respectful, and always smiling.

Now seeing Luca in his crisp light blue short-sleeved shirt, thick white belt, and black pants with the red stripe down each leg, the de rigueur outfit for the *capo della polizia,* and Nunzi in her all-black outfit, with POLIZIA MUNICIPALE stenciled on the back of her shirt, she realized she was in the presence of the police and not her friends. She needed to stop pretending this was a social visit and take it for the very serious matter that it was.

As she had done with Rosalie, she explained her morning routine and then what she discovered when she returned home. As she was relaying her story a second time, she remembered she had forgotten an important piece of information. It was true what she had heard: eyewitnesses were sometimes completely unreliable because their emotional state made them remember important details incorrectly or forget them completely. Bria was living proof that this was true.

"I think there might have been someone else in the house when I returned," Bria said.

"You didn't mention anything about that when you told me what happened," Rosalie replied.

"I forgot," Bria said, then directed the rest to Luca and Nunzi. "After I found the body, I heard a noise downstairs. I searched but didn't find anyone, but I did notice that the front door was open, and I know that I closed it when I came home."

"You think that someone was hiding downstairs while you were here, and then escaped when you went upstairs?" Luca asked.

A shiver raced down Bria's spine at the thought of some unknown person hiding in her home while she was blithely making a floral arrangement. "I don't have proof," Bria said, "but that's the only explanation."

"Maybe you forgot to close the door when you entered," Nunzi said. "Just like you forgot that there had been an intruder."

"Stop badgering the witness!" Rosalie cried.

"*Sta' zitta*," Luca said.

"Don't tell me to shut up!" Rosalie shouted.

"Rosalie!" Bria shouted back. "Nunzi's doing her job, and she's right to question my memory, but I do remember that I closed the door. I let Bravo in first, because I was holding the bowl that I bought at Paloma's and I didn't have a free hand. I pushed the door closed with my foot, and I distinctly remember hearing it click."

"*Bene*, you closed the front door when you entered and then noticed it was open when you came back downstairs," Luca said. "The question now is, where was the person hiding?"

Bria walked out of the room and stood on the landing. She looked down to the main floor and immediately pointed to the utility closet next to the entrance to the kitchen. Rosalie, Luca, and Nunzi joined Bria in the hallway to see what she was pointing at.

"He had to be in there," Bria said.

"Why do you say that?" Rosalie asked.

"Because she's right," Luca replied.

"It's the only place where he could see that I had gone upstairs without me seeing him," Bria explained. "If he was in the bathroom or in the closet next to it, he would just see the downstairs if he stepped out into the main room. The only way he could see upstairs is if he was hiding in this closet here and peeked out when I wasn't looking."

Luca smiled. "That's the Bria I remember. You're thinking logically now."

Bria smiled back. "Better late than never."

Without saying a word, Luca walked down the stairs while putting on a pair of latex gloves Nunzi had given him. Bravo watched Bria, Rosalie, and Nunzi follow Luca to the closet door, but he remained curled up in a corner of the kitchen, on the cool tile floor, not quite convinced that he liked what was taking place. When Luca's hands were completely enveloped in latex, he tried to open the closet door, but it wouldn't budge.

"Is the closet locked?" Luca asked.

"No, it sometimes sticks," Bria said. "You have to fully twist the doorknob and pull it hard."

On Luca's second attempt, the closet door opened, and Luca saw that it was a standard utility closet split into shelving on one side, next to an open space that was large enough to hold brooms, a vacuum cleaner, or a person. He did a quick visual survey but didn't find anything unusual. The closet didn't hold any clues, but Luca wanted to see if it could hold up to Bria's theory.

He stepped into the closet and closed the door behind him. After a few moments, he opened the door and peeked out. Bria was right: all he had to do was raise his eyes, and he could see that the door to the bedroom that currently housed the dead body was open. He lifted his head and stood on his tiptoes and could see directly into the room. If there had been someone hiding in Bria's home who had snuck out without being seen, this was the most likely place where they would have been hiding.

"Looks like you're right, Bria," Luca said. "It doesn't look like they left any clues behind, but we'll do a more thorough check later. In the meantime, is there anything else that you remember?"

"No, that's it," Bria said before going on to give an encapsulated version of the morning's events. "I came home, Bravo was barking, I saw the man in the bed, I shook his ankle, and he rolled over to reveal his bloodied shirt. I screamed, and then I heard a noise downstairs. I searched but didn't find anything. I noticed the door was open. I looked around outside but didn't see anyone, and I came back in and ran up here."

They had been following Bria around while she delivered her monologue, and just as she finished, they all wound up back in the upstairs bedroom where they had started. "That's when I panicked, asked Bravo for advice on what to do next, and called Rosalie."

"I always knew Bravo liked Rosalie better than me," Luca declared.

"*Everyone* likes Rosalie better than you," Rosalie replied.

"Not everyone," Nunzi said as she shoved her hand into a latex glove, the same kind Luca had used.

Bria swallowed hard to prevent herself from laughing, which she knew would be highly inappropriate. She thought she saw a trace of a smile appear on Luca's lips, but if it had ever existed, it quickly disappeared, and he commandeered the conversation and steered it into more suitable territory.

"You don't recognize the man?" Luca asked.

"No, I've never seen him before," Bria replied. "I assume he's a tourist."

"Probably," Luca said. "We know all the locals and most of the business owners, but so many people come in and out of town, it's impossible to keep up."

"Even now, before the season starts?" Bria asked.

"The season never really ends in Positano," Luca replied, this time allowing himself to smile, his brown eyes, a few shades darker than his olive skin, twinkling. "It grows the last weekend in May and dies down in late October, but there are always new faces walking up and down our famous hills."

"You sound like you work for the tourism board," Rosalie said.

"We all do," Luca replied. "The tourists keep us busy."

"Even the dead ones," Nunzi said. She held the toe of the deceased man's shoe and angled the sole so everyone in the room could see it. "These are Antonio Meccariello loafers. Exquisite craftsmanship and very expensive."

"Our dead man was rich," Luca said.

"Or had expensive taste and lived beyond his means," Bria added.

Once again Luca smiled. "That's very true. I stand corrected."

"May I continue?" Nunzi asked.

Ignoring the sarcasm that flowed so naturally from Nunzi's speech, because he had become used to it and because he did rather enjoy it, Luca replied, "*Prego*, Nunzi. Please continue."

"*Grazie, Capo*," Nunzi said. "There are traces of dirt and sand on his soles, meaning he possibly spent the morning walking on the beach or had been there recently, which is not at all uncommon."

"His suit looks expensive, too," Bria shared.

Nunzi lifted the jacket of the man's royal blue suit and saw the label of a familiar and expensive Italian manufacturer. "You're right. It's Brioni."

The policewoman checked the inside pockets of the jacket and then the pockets of his trousers but didn't find anything. She held the fabric of the right side of the jacket in between her gloved hands and slid them down the full length, then repeated the process on the other side. Nunzi then slid her hands down the man's thighs and shins and then down the underside of his legs, as well. Bria watched in fascination; she was witnessing in person the type of preliminary detective work she had only read about or seen on television procedurals. She knew Nunzi was checking to see if the man was carrying identification or other items that might give them a clue as to who he was. Despite the effort, the result was disappointing.

"Nothing," Nunzi announced.

"That can't be right," Rosalie said. "Did you check him properly? Like a real cop?"

"Rosalie, I'm not going to ask you again," Luca said. "Treat Nunzi with the respect that she deserves. She protects this village, and her actions mean that you don't have to be afraid living by yourself on your boat."

"But God forbid I go walking in the morning, or I might wind up dead in one of Bria's beds," Rosalie said.

Luca dropped his professional persona and became an older brother. He rolled his eyes and threw up his hands, mumbling something that Bria thought compared Rosalie to a porcupine or a rusty nail. Either way, both could inflict pain.

"I don't know how he got here just yet," Nunzi said, "but he must have had his ID stolen. No one travels that light."

"Especially when they're all dressed up," Bria said. "He looks like he was going to a business meeting or the office. He's not dressed for a leisurely day in the sun."

"He could have been dressed up for a night on the town and is still wearing the same clothes," Luca added.

"How do you explain how a complete stranger with no identification winds up in a bed in Bria's B and B and gets himself killed?" Rosalie asked.

"We can't explain it just yet," Luca said. "But we will."

"No, you won't," Bria stated. "Because that's not what happened."

"What do you mean?" Luca said. "That's exactly what happened."

"I don't know the specifics, but he didn't get killed here," Bria declared.

"*Stai scherzando*?" Rosalie said. "You can't possibly know that, Bria."

"Yes, I do!" Bria replied. "And I can prove it."

CHAPTER 4

Three curious faces stared at Bria, waiting for her to enlighten them. She knew it was a ridiculous feeling, but she felt as if she were on trial. She knew they didn't think she had anything to do with the murder. Could they? *No! Assolutamente no!* she told herself. That didn't explain why she felt as if her life depended on convincing them that she was right.

"Look at what's in his hand," Bria said.

"Which one?" Luca asked.

"His right one," Bria replied.

"There's nothing in his hand, Bria," Rosalie said.

Nunzi was about to agree, but then she peered closer at the dead body and saw that Bria was right. Even though the expression on the cop's face was far from a happy one, Bria was thrilled that the police had inadvertently proven her right. Maybe she would survive this nightmare, after all.

"What is it?" Luca asked.

Nunzi held up the crumpled piece of bloodied white cloth, and as she started to spread it out to its original size, Bria informed them that it was a soccer banner from Marco's room.

Luca frowned and shook his head. "Why would he go into Marco's room to get a banner?"

"He didn't," Bria said. "Marco and Bravo were playing with

it this morning. We were running late, so I didn't ask Marco to put his things away like I usually do, and it was left at the bottom of the stairs. I didn't notice it was missing until I saw it in his hand just now."

"Even if this guy picked up the banner, how does that prove he wasn't killed in the house?" Rosalie asked.

"He must've gotten shot or stabbed outside, came in here to seek shelter, and used the banner to stop the bleeding," Bria announced.

"You have a good eye, Bria, but that doesn't completely prove he was murdered outside," Luca said. "That could still have happened right down there."

"But there's no evidence of a struggle," Bria protested. "Not a thing was out of place when I came home except—now that I realize it—the banner."

"If the guy got shot in here, wouldn't there be blood splattered all over the place?" Rosalie asked.

"That only happens in the movies," Nunzi answered. "But you do have a point."

"I do?" Rosalie said, truly shocked.

"If the man was killed outside—and it looks like he was stabbed, because no one reported hearing gunshots—then why isn't there a trail of blood from the front door to the bedroom?" Nunzi said.

"She's right," Bria agreed. "I noticed dirt and some stains, which I guess could be blood, only on the stairs, but nothing anywhere else."

"It's because he's left-handed," Luca said.

The only woman in the room who didn't look at Luca as if he was crazy was Nunzi. "That makes sense," she said.

"To a cop maybe, but would you care explaining it to the rest of us?" Rosalie asked.

"All the information you need to know is right there on the bed," Luca said. "He's putting pressure on his wound with his left hand because that's his dominant side. He must have been doing that outside, which means he used his right hand, the hand without any blood on it, to open and close the front door. He saw the banner, picked it up, and used that as a makeshift bandage."

"When he started to climb the stairs, maybe he got light-headed and stumbled, causing his left hand to drop and some blood to spill onto the floor, along with the dirt," Bria added.

"I think that's exactly what happened," Luca said.

"*Scusami*," Nunzi said. "You left your front door unlocked?"

"*Sì*," Bria said. "All the bedroom doors have locks, but I always leave the front door unlocked."

"*Scusami ancora*," Nunzi said. "That's stupid."

Dramatically, Rosalie threw her hands up toward the sky. "Finally, me and the cop lady agree on something! I've been telling her that for months, but does she listen to me? No! She only calls me when there's a dead man in her bed. Now that there *is* a dead man in your bed, maybe you'll take my advice!"

"You really should, Bria," Luca said. "Positano is a very safe village, the whole Amalfi Coast is, but there are always exceptions. You have to be careful."

"*Bene*, yes, I will," Bria agreed.

"I have one other question," Luca said.

"What is it?" Bria asked, worried because Luca looked even more serious than he had before.

"Marco's favorite team is really Bologna?" Luca asked.

"I think it's because he likes bologna sandwiches," Bria said. "My father is trying to get him to root for Roma, but so far Marco is sticking with Bologna."

"Juventus is the best," Nunzi said. "But what do I know? I'm just the dumb cop lady."

"You're not dumb," Bria said. "And I promise I'll do as you ask and keep the front door locked and not just closed."

Nunzi suddenly looked at the bedroom door. "You said that this door was closed, too, when you got home, right?"

"Yes. Bravo was barking and trying to get in, probably because he smelled the banner and thought Marco might be home," Bria replied.

"If the guy was clutching his wound and was exhausted from climbing up a flight of stairs, would he really take the time to close the door behind him?" Nunzi asked.

"He didn't," Bria said. "Whoever followed him did."

"After he took the man's identification and fled the room when he heard you and Bravo come home," Luca explained. "He closed the bedroom door and then hid in the utility closet when he realized he couldn't escape without bumping into you."

"Whoever did all of that probably killed him, too," Bria said.

"That fits the scenario we're building," Luca replied.

"*Aspettate*," Nunzi said. "I found something."

"What is it?" Luca asked.

Nunzi bent down in front of the nightstand that was next to the bed and reached into the narrow space between the table and the wall. When she pulled out a brown leather wallet, they all gasped. When she opened it up to reveal its empty contents, they all groaned. But when Nunzi slid a latex-clad finger into the opening of a hidden compartment on the inside of the wallet and pulled out a piece of paper, they all shrieked with excitement. It was like Nunzi was performing a magic show, but this one had much higher stakes.

"What is it?" Luca asked.

"A five-hundred-lira note," Nunzi replied.

They were stunned again, because the lira had been obsolete since 2002, when the euro became the official currency of Italy. People still kept some old notes as souvenirs of the past, but no one they knew carried them around in their wallets. The lira was a relic, its power and relevance as dead as the man lying before them.

"Why would anyone carry around lire?" Rosalie asked.

"It could've had sentimental value," Luca said. "Maybe it was his lucky lira note."

"Like Papa," Rosalie said. "He carried a piece of Mamma's wedding veil in his wallet from the day he got married. He was buried with it, too, God rest his soul."

"Maybe this man's wife or someone important in his life gave him that lira years ago, and he carried it with him for luck," Luca said.

"I hope it served him well, because today was definitely not his lucky day," Rosalie added.

"It definitely isn't mine," Bria said. "You're going to have to call an ambulance to pick up the body, aren't you?"

"Yes, I'm sorry," Luca replied. "We'll be as discreet as we can and won't turn on the lights or the siren, but an ambulance is going to have to pick up the body and bring it to the morgue in Amalfi."

"So much for trying to keep this quiet," Bria said.

"Not in this village," Nunzi replied.

"My forensics team is also going to have to come here and dust for fingerprints and do a thorough search for clues," Luca said. "Anything that can help us find out who this man is and who killed him."

"Is there any chance you'll be done by three?" Bria asked.

Luca glanced at his watch and saw that it was almost ten. "Probably, but I can't guarantee it. Why?"

"That's when Marco gets out of school," Bria said. "I'd like to avoid him seeing anyone here."

"The body will definitely be out by then, and I'll have the team get to work immediately," Luca said. "We'll do our best."

"*Grazie*," Bria said.

"You can bring Marco by me if we need to kill time," Rosalie said. "I mean *stall* for time, not kill. There will be no more killing for the rest of the day."

"I'll go out to the car and call it in," Nunzi said.

"Thank you," Luca replied. "I'll wait here."

They stood in awkward silence until they heard the front door close and knew Nunzi had left. The moment that happened, it was as if Bria snapped back to reality and realized her bed-and-breakfast was the scene of a murder investigation. She knew that she was being selfish, she knew that a man had lost his life in a horrific way, but all she could think about was what this was going to do to her business, which was much more than a business and was supposed to be the fulfillment of the dream Carlo had for their family: to live in this beautiful village and welcome visitors from all over the world, hear their stories, and share their lives with strangers who would become friends. Before it had even started, it was about to end in disaster. Bria had to do something to prevent that from happening.

"Luca," Bria said. "We need to keep this quiet."

"We'll do the best we can, but this is a small village. Word is going to get around," Luca replied. "I bet Annamaria is already asking around to find out why the *polizia* are parked down the street."

"*Uffa!*" Bria groaned. "I forgot about Annamaria."

Annamaria Antonelli owned Caffè Positano, Bria's favorite coffee shop in the village. And even though Annamaria was one of the nicest people Bria had met in Positano, she was also the biggest *pettegola*. She was affectionately known as the Gossip of the Amalfi Coast, which was an impressive title considering the coast was 54,717 meters long. Even when that length was converted to the customary American measuring system, thirty-four miles was still quite a distance.

"I bet Annamaria has already given Signor Bombalino a tip for tomorrow's headline," Bria exclaimed. "I can see it now. OMICIDIO OMICIDIO AT BELLA BELLA."

"It does kind of write itself," Rosalie said.

"*Ehi!* You're not helping," Luca said. "But she is right, Bria. I'm sure *La Vita Positano* is going to cover this homicide. It is the town's paper, after all, and maybe that's a good thing."

"How can negative publicity possibly be a good thing?" Bira asked.

"The more people who know the truth, which is that you had nothing to do with this murder, the more they'll know that Bella Bella lives up to its name and is a beautiful place to stay," Luca said.

Bria was so excited she wanted to hug Luca, but one look at his police uniform helped her restrain herself. "You really don't think I had anything to do with killing this man?"

"As Luca Vivaldi, I know you're innocent," Luca said. "As the chief of police, I can't officially rule you out."

"I think I like Luca better than the chief," Bria said.

"I haven't decided which one I prefer," Rosalie added.

"*Basta*, Rosalie," Luca said. "As someone who's known you for decades, Bria, I know you're essentially an innocent bystander."

"That is such a relief!" Bria cried. "I've felt like I have to prove my innocence to you and Nunzi this entire time."

"I know Nunzi can come off as hard edged, but why would you ever think such a thing?" Luca asked.

Bria was about to tell Luca that she thought he might consider her a suspect only because that was exactly what his sister had told her, but then she realized it would only cause the siblings to bicker. She had herself to blame: she loved Rosalie and truly trusted her with her life, but she knew she possessed a wild imagination, which had served them well as kids but wasn't always helpful now that they were adults.

"I've been under a lot of stress lately, and I think this pushed me over the edge," Bria said. "I wasn't thinking clearly, but that's all in the past. I am going to trust that you and your team of professionals will solve this crime in record time."

"We'll do our best to wrap this up as quickly as possible," Luca said.

"In the meantime, why don't I make us some coffee?" Bria suggested. "I think this is going to be a very long day."

Rosalie remembered that she had a boat tour booked in an hour for a group of retired French judges and needed to get back to the marina in order to change into something that would make her look more like a captain and less like a fan of their former president's wife. Nicolas Sarkozy was well-known to judges for all the wrong reasons.

"I'll be back from the tour before three p.m.," Rosalie assured Bria. "If you and Marco need to spend a few hours or the night, just come over."

"I will," Bria said, giving her friend a heartfelt hug. *"Grazie mille."*

"And thank you, big brother, for your help, even though you disobeyed me and brought Signora Frankenstina with you," Rosalie said, giving her brother kisses on both cheeks.

After Rosalie left, the space all around Bria and Luca became quiet, in the way that silence can be welcomed after commotion. Luca sat at the dining room table as Bria went to the kitchen for their coffee. She knew that Luca liked a twist of lemon in his espresso and still couldn't resist Sapori's crunchy almond biscuits, which also happened to be one of Marco's favorites. Bria put the cups of espresso, Luca's with the lemon twist, hers with a splash of heavy cream, and a plate of cookies on a tray and brought it out to the main room. She was pleased to see that Luca's eyes lit up when he saw the cookies.

"Che dolce. Reminds me of my childhood," Luca said, grabbing a cookie before the tray hit the table. *"Grazie."*

"I'm the one who should be thanking you," Bria said, sitting in a chair across the table from Luca. "If any other officer was handling this, I'm sure I would be down at the station right now being interrogated."

"The police aren't that intimidating," Luca said. "Are we?"

Bria took a sip of her espresso and tilted her head back and forth. "Until you're in a situation where you need the police or you think the police are going to accuse you of a crime, you don't realize how incredibly nerve-racking it is to be in their presence."

"It isn't an easy job," Luca said. "But it is my life, which is why I need to ask you some more questions, ones I didn't want to ask in front of Rosalie."

Suddenly, the silence turned awkward. What could Luca possibly want to ask her that he couldn't ask in front of Rosalie? He knew they were best friends and didn't keep any secrets from each other. But Luca was still a man, and men, try as they might, never fully understood the bond between two women.

"Just so you know for the future, you can ask me anything in front of Rosalie," Bria said. "What else do you want to know?"

"Until we learn otherwise, it's realistic to think that this man chose this place to seek shelter randomly," Luca said. "Maybe he tried another door first, and it was locked. Or the bright pink exterior stood out and drew him in. But can you think of any reason why he would have deliberately chosen Bella Bella—your home—as a place to hide?"

"You think he was hiding from someone?" Bria asked.

"Absolutely," Luca replied. "If not, he would have simply screamed for help. He would've knocked on every door he came to, asking for someone to take him to the Red Cross. But he didn't do that. He came here."

Bria couldn't think of any reason why this man would have chosen her bed-and-breakfast instead of another house. She also knew that Luca was asking—by not explicitly asking—if she really did know this man. Bria imagined that Luca, as a police officer, was used to people lying to him, telling him they didn't commit a crime when they did, telling him they didn't know a victim when they were having an affair with them. That was the question he was trying to ask. Had she been involved with the dead man upstairs? It was such an absurd thought she almost burst out laughing. She hadn't been having a romance with him or any man. Other than Enrico and some other business owners in the village, Bria hadn't met any new men since she came to Positano.

When the front door opened and Nunzi pushed a man with long blond hair inside, Bria knew that everything she had just thought was a lie. She did have a new man in her life, a man she instinctively trusted, but when she stopped to think about it, he was a man she knew very little about. Maybe she was more involved in this murder than she had thought? Maybe the man she had hired to work with her—the same man who was not at all happy to be standing next to a policewoman and in front of the chief of police—was not at all the man she had thought he was?

"Giovanni Monteverdi," Luca said. "Been a while since we've had a reason to chat."

Maybe the reason there was a dead body in Bria's bedroom was because of the one new man she had let into her life.

CHAPTER 5

Bria saw something in Giovanni's eyes she had never seen before: anger. She understood that standing in between the police and your new employer in your new place of business wouldn't make someone happy, but Giovanni was positively seething with fury. It looked like he was having a hard time maintaining his composure, and Bria was having a hard time rationalizing her new hire. Did she already make a colossal mistake before she even opened up for business?

When Bria and Carlo first moved into Bella Bella and started to transform it into the bed-and-breakfast of their dreams, they set about to turn the building from an ordinary structure—albeit with an eye-catching paint job—into a destination that would create memories that would last a lifetime. They wanted it to be a place where people could feel like they were being nuzzled in the heart of an Italian village. They would still be working together had Carlo's life not been cut so short.

After Bria buried her husband and the funeral was behind her, there were some lonely nights when she was tempted to give up on their dream, say good-bye to Positano and Bella Bella, and move back to Ravello to be with her parents. Her father, Franco, adored his firstborn daughter and his only grandson and told Bria at the wake that she could stay with them for as long as she wanted, until she was ready to move on. Her mother did not extend the same invitation.

It wasn't that Fifetta loved Bria and Marco any less than her husband did; it was that as a woman, she knew better. She knew that Bria couldn't wilt from the weight of widowhood. She had to become stronger; she had to dig deeper into her faith and continue the journey that she and Carlo had started. Fifetta also knew that Marco needed his mother now more than ever; she was the one person he would have to look to for solace, for direction, and for love. If Bria and Marco moved in with Franco and Fifetta, that would lessen the relationship between mother and son and would make Marco feel as if his father could be substituted by his grandparents. Fifetta would not allow that to happen. It was not the traditional Italian way of thinking, but Fifetta Claudine Fontana D'Abruzzo was not the traditional Italian.

Born in Grenoble, France, Fifetta was the fourth child to a Parisian mother and a Milanese father. The Fontanas lived an intercontinental life, shuttling back and forth between Grenoble and Milan. Fifetta's father was an art dealer and a devoted family man who would often take his family on his business trips to Nice, Monaco, and Austria, filling Fifetta's childhood with numerous cultural experiences, which showed her there was a huge world outside her home. It was the same perspective she later shared with her own children, especially Bria, her eldest.

Fifetta understood the complicated journey a woman had to take in life, and had navigated her own path from daughter to grandmother without ever losing the spirit of an independent woman. Her family would always come first, but Fifetta knew that if she lost herself, she would be no use to her family. When Bria contemplated returning home after Carlo's death, Fifetta advised her daughter that it wasn't a healthy decision for her or Marco. It wouldn't be easy, but Bria had to find her way on her own.

Which was exactly what she did and exactly why she always followed her mother's advice. Fifetta was always right. Or was she?

Once Bria decided to move forward with the plans she and her husband had devised, she wondered if she'd be able to take care of Marco's needs while taking care of her guests and the inevitable issues at Bella Bella that would need to be fixed. Carlo and Bria had thought it would be an invaluable, enlightening experience for Marco to be surrounded by strangers, foreigners who would share with him bits and pieces of their own lives thousands of miles away. They would plant seeds in his young mind that would grow in unknown directions. Their stories would introduce him to worlds and occupations he never knew existed. Bria still felt that way, but she also knew Marco had immediate needs as an eight-year-old boy. She and Carlo had planned on splitting their duties, so while one tended to the needs of Bella Bella, the other would attend to Marco. No matter what happened with the business, Marco would never feel like he came in second. All that changed when Carlo was no longer in the picture.

"You need a new man in your life," Fifetta had said one morning, while visiting.

Bria couldn't believe her mother was suggesting she find a boyfriend so shortly after Carlo's death. Fifetta explained that while men did make wonderful boyfriends and husbands, they were also suitable for many other roles, like chef, plumber, electrician, and lifter of heavy things. Bria needed someone to help her run Bella Bella, make minor repairs, carry luggage up and down the stairs, cook meals, and on occasion babysit Marco. Fifetta wasn't suggesting Bria needed a man; she was suggesting she needed a handyman. Enter Giovanni Monteverdi.

The day after Bria placed an ad in *La Vita Positano*, looking to hire an all-around assistant for the grand opening of a new bed-and-breakfast, Giovanni was the first person at her door. She was instantly taken by his good looks, as was Fifetta, who had joined her for the interview process. And who wouldn't have been? Giovanni could have served as Michelangelo's model: he was a modern-day *David* with longer hair and a beard.

Standing at six feet, three inches tall, Giovanni was muscular, had a mass of wavy dark blond hair, which threatened to break free from the rubber band that held his ponytail in place, and had high cheekbones and a square chin accentuated by a thin layer of stubble. Shimmering green eyes and a long Roman nose finished the masterpiece that was his face. Bria thought he should be on the pages of fashion magazines and not standing in her living room. Giovanni confessed that he had done some modeling when he was younger, but that kind of life wasn't for him. He wanted a simpler life here in his hometown of Positano.

After seeing several other candidates, Bria and Fifetta couldn't get Giovanni out of their minds, and it wasn't because of the way his jeans hugged his thighs or how his loose-fitting T-shirt made his body only more enticing. It was because of his spirit. Bria sensed that he was gentle and patient, which would be necessary when dealing with guests, who would frequently be demanding. Fifetta agreed and liked the fact that he was sturdy and strong, which meant he wouldn't be deterred by manual labor, like some of the other, less physically fit candidates might be. It was only when Bria told Rosalie that she was considering hiring Giovanni that she hesitated.

"He's got a bit of a reputation," Rosalie said.

"An *imbroglione*?" Bria asked.

"No, not a hustler really, but *grezzo*, rough around the edges," Rosalie explained. "Not necessarily a grifter, but a drifter."

"You think he'll work for a few weeks and run off?" Bria asked.

"I don't know him that well, and I know that people in this town like to spread rumors," Rosalie replied. "But my brother doesn't trust him."

"Giovanni did tell me he was arrested as a teenager for vandalism and shoplifting," Bria shared. "Has he been convicted of anything more serious?"

"No, but Luca's questioned him a few times in connection to crimes," Rosalie explained. "Giovanni has a tendency to flirt with danger."

Despite the warnings, Bria and Fifetta sensed goodness in Giovanni. Bria also had the feeling that the man needed a chance to start over, like she did, so she offered him the job. Up until now he had been the perfect employee, diligent, prompt, and incredibly helpful. Now he had been dragged into Bella Bella by the police as a potential murder suspect. She couldn't jump to conclusions; she needed to stand by her employee and find out the truth.

"What's going on?" Bria asked.

"I found him sneaking around in the alleyway," Nunzi replied.

"That's because he works here," Bria said. "He's my employee."

Nunzi smiled for the first time since she had arrived. "What exactly does he do for you?"

Smiles on some people don't work, Bria thought. She much preferred dour, grim-faced Nunzi. "I don't like the tone of your question."

"*Calmati*," Luca urged. "Nunzi, did you ask Giovanni why he was on the premises?"

"I tried to, but he started to run," she explained.

"Vanni, why would you run?" Bria asked.

"Vanni?" Nunzi said, her smile growing. "I didn't know the two of you were so familiar."

"It's a nickname, Annunziata," Bria replied.

"Giovanni, answer your boss," Luca said. "Why'd you run?"

Giovanni raised his eyes from the floor and stared directly at Luca. "I think you know the answer to that," he replied. "After all these years, no one ever believes a word I say, especially *la polizia*."

"But, Vanni, you have no reason to run," Bria said. "You work here. You have more of a right to be here than they do."

His gaze shifted from Luca to Bria, but the intensity didn't waver. "*Grazie*, but not everyone is like you. You see what's there. They see what they want to see."

"Spare me your existential *rifiuto*," Luca said, "and give me an explanation as to why you ran when a police officer asked you a simple question."

"The questions are never simple, Luca, and you know that. You've asked many of them yourself," Giovanni replied. "I like this job, and I need this job, I didn't want to get caught up in an interrogation in front of where I work. My new boss is understanding, but even good people have their limits."

"You ran because you didn't want to cause a scene?" Luca asked. "You realize that's ironic, *comprendi*?"

"It was my impulse," Giovanni replied.

"A criminal's impulse, if you ask me," Nunzi muttered under her breath.

"No one asked you, Nunzi," Bria said very clearly and out loud. "He was protecting Bella Bella, which I appreciate. It's the same thing I tried to do by calling Rosalie instead of the police. If you're going to question him, you should question me, too."

Bria was not one to defy authority, but she was one to protect those she felt were being mistreated, and that was what she felt was happening to her employee, a man she trusted, even though she had no reason to.

"Unless you're going to accuse Giovanni of murder," Bria declared, "I suggest you back off."

"Murder?" Giovanni said, shock filling his voice.

At least the rumors hadn't spread like wildfire just yet. Maybe it would take some time before the residents of Positano found out a murder had taken place in their village.

"You sound surprised," Luca said.

"*Certo* I am surprised," Giovanni replied. "Who was murdered? Is Marco okay?"

"That's a nice touch, asking about Bria's son," Luca said. "I'm sure that'll score points with your boss."

Now Bria was the one who was surprised. While Luca was talking to her about the murder, he was respectful, kind, and very professional; now, as he was questioning Giovanni, he was the complete opposite. There was definitely some kind of history between these two men.

"Marco's fine, Giovanni. He's at school and knows nothing about this," Bria explained. "Thank you for asking."

Bria could tell that Giovanni was visibly relieved by the news, which caused Luca's otherwise pleasing face to turn into a scowl.

"You still haven't explained what you were doing lurking on the side of the house," Luca said.

"I wasn't lurking. I was measuring a slab of limestone that I need to replace because it's cracked," Giovanni explained. "If your henchman goes out and looks down the path on the side of the house, my tape measure will be found where I dropped it."

"That's henchwoman to you," Nunzi said.

"Where were you this morning?" Luca asked.

"In my bed," Giovanni said.

"Alone?" Luca asked.

"Yes, I was alone all morning," Giovanni said. "And all night."

"Doing what?" Luca asked.

"Reading a Salvo Montalbano novel," Giovanni replied. "*Prego*, you may want to try one yourself. You might learn a thing or two."

Bria stifled a laugh. Salvo Montalbano was a famous fictional police chief and the star of a successful string of novels and short stories that had been turned into two different television series. By the unhappy look on Luca's face, Bria could tell that Luca was a fan of the famed detective, but not a fan of the comparison.

"Can anyone vouch for your whereabouts this morning?" Luca asked.

"You mean, do I have an alibi?" Giovanni asked rhetorically. "No. I woke up around six, had breakfast, read a little more, and came right here."

"You didn't speak with anyone on your way over?" Luca asked. "No early morning chitchat?"

"No, the morning was unusually quiet," Giovanni said. "I didn't see anyone."

"Luca, you don't think Giovanni had anything to do with this, do you?" Bria asked.

"The investigation's just beginning. I can't rule anyone out," Luca said. "I am curious to know if Giovanni recognizes the victim. Follow me."

Bria noticed that Giovanni didn't immediately move. She thought at first it was because he was being stubborn, but then she saw the frightened look on his face as Luca started to walk upstairs. He had just realized the murdered victim was not outside but was actually inside the house.

"Someone was murdered upstairs?" Giovanni gasped.

"No," Bria replied. "We think he came in here to hide."

"Giovanni!" Luca called out. "Come up here please."

Reluctantly, Giovanni joined Luca at the top of the stairs, and when he entered the room, his shocked gasp was easily heard. Bria was convinced it was a natural reaction and in no way a cover-up, but Nunzi didn't share her feeling. She agreed with Luca that Giovanni should definitely be on the list of suspects.

"He's a dangerous man," Nunzi said to Bria, her voice not quite a whisper.

Bria knew she wasn't going to change Nunzi's opinion by swaying her emotionally. She tried another tactic, one a police officer should respect.

"Do you have proof of that?" Bria asked.

Nunzi stared off into space, her thin lips pressed firmly together. "No."

"Then may I remind you that a person is innocent until proven guilty," Bria said.

Turning to face Bria, Nunzi replied, "May I remind you that a person is never proven to be innocent, only 'not guilty.' You may find your hunky handyman fun to have around, but I'm telling you it's only going to lead to disaster. If it hasn't already."

Could Nunzi and Luca be right? No, that was impossible. That would mean that Giovanni would have to be a murderer. She hadn't known the man that long, but could she and her mother be that bad at judging someone's character? *Per l'amor di Dio*, he had given her a recipe for ricotta pancakes that was not only easy but also made the most delicious breakfast treats. He had helped her reupholster an old chair she found at a thrift store. She had even watched as he played soccer with Marco in the little field behind the Hotel Royal Positano. Giovanni might not be straitlaced enough to avoid the suspicious glare of the *polizia*, but he wasn't a murderer. Was he?

When he and Luca came back downstairs, she tried to read his expression. Was he in shock because he had just seen a dead body? Or was he in shock because he had seen the aftermath of his own actions? He looked gravely upset, but was it fear that the place where he worked was now a crime scene or fear that his own handiwork might have ventured too close to home?

"Nunzi, take Giovanni back to the station and get his statement," Luca ordered. "I'll stay here until they arrive to take the body out and the forensics team gets here."

"Luca, you can't be serious," Bria said. "You didn't even take my statement, and now you're going to drag Giovanni down to the station to take his?"

"I have enough information from you, but after the body is removed, you'll come down to the station at some point and give your official statement," Luca said. "This is all proper procedure, even if you think I'm not acting at all properly."

Bria wanted to protest, but she had learned that sometimes it was better to keep your mouth shut. For the moment, she would follow the rules and act the way she was expected to act. She was already getting the feeling, however, that this problem wasn't going to be solved as easily as she hoped.

"Don't worry, Giovanni. Go with Nunzi, give your statement, and then come back here," Bria said. "I'm going to need you to watch over the forensics team when they do their job, so they don't break anything."

Bria smiled, and she was grateful that Giovanni did the same in return. She could tell he was doing it only for her benefit, but she hoped he understood that she believed in him and did not consider him a murderer. She didn't know why that was so important to her, but it was.

She watched Nunzi and Giovanni leave, and when she was alone with Luca, the atmosphere around them was completely different than it had been just a few minutes earlier, when they had shared espresso and biscuits. Before she had felt like she was sitting with a friend; now she felt like she was sitting with a stranger. Could this be the real Luca? Maybe harsh, judgmental, and slightly vengeful were his real attributes, and the kindness and manners merely pretext?

Bria was hardly a crusader of justice, but she did believe in truth. She had inherited that from her mother. Both women had agreed that despite the echoes of gossip they heard about Giovanni, they believed they saw his truth. And in Bria's heart, she believed the truth was that Giovanni had nothing to do with the dead man in her bedroom.

She made the sign of the cross and closed her eyes. *Per favore, Dio, don't let me be wrong*, Bria thought. *Our lives may depend on it.*

CHAPTER 6

Precisely one minute and forty-five seconds after the ambulance and Luca's police car left, Annamaria burst through the front door, which Bria hadn't even had a chance to lock. She looked like a dog after it had been held at bay on its leash by its owner and was finally free to run through the park but didn't quite know which direction to head in first. Her chubby cheeks were decorated with red splotches, her forehead was glistening, and her ample bosom was rising up and down as she tried to catch her breath. She was practically rabid.

"Bria! *Dio mio! Grazie* God in heaven, above!" Annamaria cried. "You're not dead!"

She shrieked and made the sign of the cross, kissed her fingers and offered them up to heaven, then repeated the gesture without the shriek twice.

When Bria was rather certain Annamaria was finished, she asked, "Is that the word in the village? That I'm dead?"

"*Metà e metà*," Annamaria replied. "Half of the people think a strange man was murdered, and the other half think a strange man murdered you."

It was Bria's turn to make the sign of the cross. "Look at me. I'm fine."

"Then who was murdered?" Annamaria asked.

There was no way Bria was going to be able to deny it; the truth had already traveled down the jagged edges of the mountain and sprinkled itself among the villagers. If she lied, it would only make her look deceitful and would plant doubts in their minds. Bria had wanted to keep the terrible events of the morning a secret, but that had already proven impossible. Instead of trying to conceal the truth from the villagers, maybe Bria should share it with them in order to control the narrative. That way, she'd be seen as part of them and not as the intruder who had brought death to Positano.

"We're not sure who the man is," Bria confessed. "But yes, I found a dead man in one of my guest rooms."

Involuntarily, Annamaria's face lit up like she had just found out she'd become a grandmother for the first time. She quickly checked her emotions as the gravity of Bria's words hit home. As much as Annamaria was thrilled to be right, she was also horrified that someone had lost their life.

"I can't believe there's been a real murder in our little village!" Annamaria cried. "Is it really possible?"

Bria glanced up to the second-floor bedroom door now decorated with yellow DO NOT CROSS police tape. "I can assure you it's more than possible."

Annamaria followed Bria's gaze, and her black eyes grew wide. She looked like she was the first person to gaze upon the Holy Grail, and not the remnants of a police investigation. "This changes everything, Bria."

"What do you mean?" Bria asked.

"Nothing in Positano will ever be the same," Annamaria proclaimed. "From now on, we'll be able to separate everything into before and after *the murder*."

Even though Bria knew that Annamaria's comment was an exaggeration, she also knew that it bore a kernel of truth. Today was not just another Tuesday; it was a day that would be remembered for years to come. Bria had to make sure that it was remembered correctly. That it would be known as the day the new woman in town found a dead body in her house, and not the day that a murder took place at Bella Bella. Bria needed to prevent false information from becoming legend.

"This can't be the first murder in Positano," Bria said coolly. "There must have been others."

"None that we can remember," Annamaria said. "But we'll remember this one."

"*Come mai*?" Bria asked. "Why is this one so special?"

"Because it's happened to one of us," Annamaria replied, as if it was something Bria should automatically know. "When something happens to one of us in the village, it happens to all of us."

Instinctively, Bria reached for the chair behind her for support. Had she heard Annamaria correctly? Bria *wasn't* an outsider; she was one of them, already a piece of the fabric that made up this village. It was all she and Carlo had wanted, a place to call home.

"*Grazie*, Annamaria," Bria said, fighting hard to hold back her tears. "That's a very kind thing to say."

"*Aspetta*!" Annamaria replied. "It isn't kind. It's the truth."

As if to prove her point, the door burst open to reveal yet another excited Positanese.

Enrico was speaking so quickly and so excitedly that Bria had no idea what he was saying. He was Sicilian, and in moments of extreme emotion, he reverted to using the colloquial dialect of his native land, a version of Italian that Bria didn't fully understand, especially at the rapid speed Enrico was speaking. It was like an American straining to comprehend what a fast-speaking Brit from the east side of London was saying. Same language, different words.

"Bria!" Enrico cried. "*Grazie Dio*! You're breathing!"

"And standing up," Paolo added.

Paolo Vistigliano had entered right behind Enrico, but since Paolo was half the size of Enrico, Bria hadn't seen him until he spoke. Paolo owned the largest parking lot in town, and since parking was extremely difficult throughout much of the village, thanks to its slender, serpentine roads, it meant Paolo was one of the most important and influential people. Despite his status, he was a quiet, soft-spoken man who could sometimes be overshadowed by his peers.

"I'm fine," Bria said. "Well, no, *mi dispiace*, I'm not fine, but thanks to your support, I'm already feeling better."

"It must have been devastating to find a dead body in your own home," Enrico said. "Thank God Marco was at school."

"Yes, *grazie Dio!*" Bria cried. "That is a blessing."

"You were alone, then, when you found the, uh, corpse?" Paolo asked.

"No, I was with Bravo," Bria replied.

"Poor Bravo!" Annamaria cried. At the sound of his name, Bravo came running out from wherever he had been hiding and ran right into Annamaria's outstretched arms. Bria knew that he was hoping for a treat, but like all good Italians, he felt the next best thing to a meal was a hug. "You were so brave for your mamma."

Bravo barked in agreement and licked Annamaria's face. She was proving to be much more than a gossip. But based on how the others were reacting, if she ever decided to keep her mouth shut, there would be a line of people ready to take her place.

"I heard he was missing an arm," Enrico said.

"I heard he was covered in blood from head to toe," Paolo said.

"I heard he was still alive when you found him."

Bria turned around and saw that the third voice belonged to Paloma, who was standing next to Mimi, a retired librarian from Venice who owned A Word from Positano, the local bookstore.

"No, no, and definitely no," Bria replied. "He had blood only on his stomach, he wasn't missing any limbs, and he most certainly was dead."

"Are you sure?" Paloma asked. "I mean, have you ever seen a dead person? I haven't."

An image of Carlo's dead body lying in the morgue flashed through Bria's mind, but she did what she always did when such a visual memory returned: she shut her eyes tight, shook her head, and counted to three. Gone.

"I checked his pulse," Bria replied. "He was dead when I called the police."

"I heard that you called Rosalie first," Annamaria said.

Porca vacca! The locals really know exactly what's going on, Bria thought.

She shouldn't be surprised. Positano was a small village in both population and size. About three thousand residents lived there year-round, but that number swelled to almost twelve thousand during the height of tourist season. Roughly eight and a half kilometers in area, or a little over three square miles, the village, like the rest of the municipalities on the Amalfi Coast, was essentially a cluster of homes and stores stacked on top of each other and built into the side of a vertical cliff. No matter where you lived, you were always in close contact with someone, which made the locals not just neighbors but more like extended family. Information—good or bad—made its way to every family member with lightning speed.

"I knew that the man was dead, so there was no reason to call for an ambulance, and honestly, I panicked," Bria confessed. "I was scared, and Rosalie is my oldest friend, so she's the first person I called."

"*Naturalmente*," Enrico said.

"If I ever find a dead man in between the bookshelves in my

store, I'd call Rosalie, too," Mimi said. "She's very resourceful, she is."

"Once she got here, we called the police," Bria said. "In fact, Luca and his team just left a few minutes ago."

"With Luca on the case, they'll definitely find out who killed that poor man," Enrico said.

"First, they have to figure out who that poor man was," Paloma added.

"How do you know that they don't know who he is?" Bria asked.

"If one of us had been killed, it would be written on everyone's face in this room," Paloma said. "We wouldn't be having a discussion. We'd be in mourning."

One of us. Once again, despite the horror she had witnessed and the lingering uneasy feeling that clung to her, Bria felt happy. She, and by extension Marco and Bravo, was part of the village. No matter what happened, she would have the community on her side. Sadly, not every member of the community could say that.

"Did you hear about Giovanni?" Paolo asked. "They think he may have done it."

The group erupted when they heard Giovanni's name. They all had an opinion about Bria's employee, and none of them were very good. They thought of him as they would a wayward child, a cousin who was always asking for money instead of finding a job, or a relative who was spoken about only in whispers. Bria didn't have memories of Giovanni, but she still felt that the immediate negative reaction toward him and the assumption that he must have played some part in the murder were unwarranted. Now that she was finally considered a part of the in-crowd, she didn't want to appear like an outsider, but she couldn't remain silent, either.

"I don't believe Giovanni had anything to do with this," Bria said.

"You wouldn't be the first one to be taken in by his good looks," Mimi said. "I thought he was misunderstood until I caught him shoplifting."

"*Aspetta*, who else wants to read Giuseppe Ungaretti?" Enrico asked. "Anyone who would risk prosecution to read Italian modernist poetry can't be all bad."

"You know about Italian modernist poetry?" Mimi asked, not at all trying to conceal her surprise.

"Do you think I just sell flowers all day long?" Enrico replied.

"No," Mimi said. "But I didn't think you were reading poetry in your spare time. I assumed you were chasing the ladies around the village."

"Mimi Lanacelli!" Enrico cried. "There's a lot you don't know about me."

"*Vedi*! All men have secrets," Bria said. "Giovanni is no different than Enrico."

"Except he's taller, skinnier, and better looking," Mimi quipped.

"I like Giovanni, I really do," Annamaria said. "I knew his parents, and they were good people, but not . . . *amorevoli*."

"Giovanni was left to fend for himself more often than not," Paolo added.

"That couldn't have been easy," Bria said. "To have a family, but not really be part of one."

"*Questo è corretto*," Annamaria said. "But you, Bria Bartolucci, do not have to worry about that. You are surrounded by family wherever you turn."

Thirty minutes later, after everyone had left, Annamaria's pronouncement was proven true.

"Mamma!" Bria cried.

In her mind she was surprised to see her mother; in her heart she wondered why it had taken so long for her to arrive.

"What are you doing here?" Bria asked.

"Rosalie called me," Fifetta replied.

"She shouldn't have done that."

"*Non essere sciocca*," Fifetta said. "Of course she should have called me. She knew you wouldn't."

"I didn't want to worry you and Papa."

"What do you think we do all day long?" Fifetta asked. "We worry about you. And your sister and your brother. We worry about him a lot *quindi aiutami Dio*. And Marco. Where is *mio angioletto*?"

"At school," Bria replied. "I didn't think it was necessary to interrupt his day."

"*Questo ha senso*," Fifetta replied. "From the look on your face, I can see it was a good thing that I interrupted your day."

Discovering the dead man had brought Bria back to when she first saw Carlo's dead body. It was a sight she wanted to push from her memory and, at the same time, a sight she never wanted to forget. He had been her husband, in sickness and in health, for better or for worse. And nothing could be worse than when Bria saw him after the plane crash.

She didn't know if she was crying for Carlo, the unknown dead man, the problems this was causing for her business, or some combination of all three. It didn't matter why. All that mattered was that her mother was here.

Fifetta held out her arms, and her daughter ran to her. Despite the tears that wouldn't stop flowing, Bria instantly felt at peace. Being wrapped in her mother's embrace was like being held by love.

Neither woman had to say a word. Bria didn't have to explain; Fifetta didn't need to console. They only needed to be. They were one.

When Bria finished crying, Fifetta pulled out some tissues from her purse and handed them to her daughter. Bria dried her tears, and silently thanked God for the most wonderful mother any child could imagine. She also asked for the wisdom and grace so her son would someday say the same prayer.

Bria shook her whole body as a way to break free from the heavy emotions that had taken hold of her. She didn't like to wallow in self-pity or give in to feelings of sorrow. She preferred to take action. She took after her mother.

"Do the police have any idea who this man is?" Fifetta asked.

"No," Bria replied. "He's as much of a mystery as how he was murdered or why he was found upstairs in one of my guest rooms."

Fifetta gazed up at the door covered in police tape and looked defiant. "You'll figure this out."

"Me?"

"It happened here, and it affects your life, so who else is going to solve this mystery?"

"The people who get paid to do it," Bria replied. "The police."

Fifetta tilted her head back and forth and grimaced. "They'll help, but you'll uncover who did this."

"Mamma, *ti amo*, but you're talking crazy. How am I going to figure out who killed that man?"

"Because you have a sharp mind, good instincts, and an open heart," Fifetta replied. "Put them all together, and they'll lead you to whoever did this horrible thing."

Bria wanted to dismiss everything her mother had just said, but Fifetta had the uncanny ability of always being right. She also knew when to change the subject.

"What do you want me to make you for lunch?" Fifetta asked. "I'm famished!"

Somehow, Fifetta whipped up a scrumptious meal of apricots, strawberries, and burrata over a bed of arugula and spinach, sprinkled with croutons, sunflower seeds, and balsamic vinaigrette. While they ate, they talked about anything but the murder.

"I can't stay very long," Fifetta said. "We have a big wedding tomorrow, and I need to get back to help your father."

Fifetta and Franco D'Abruzzo owned Mondo dei Sogni—Dreamland in English—a banquet hall in Ravello, tucked away in the mountains above Amalfi. The lush setting and exquisite views made it a popular destination for weddings, birthdays, anniversaries, and retreats. Bria didn't realize the business had become so popular that they had started to have midweek nuptials.

"A big wedding on a Wednesday?"

"The groom is an opera singer and will be performing in Tokyo over the weekend," Fifetta explained. "This was the central point for both their families and a location that will still get Rodolfo onstage with the least amount of jet lag by the time they raise the curtain."

"Is the groom named Rodolfo or is he playing Rodolfo in *La bohème*?" Bria asked.

"Both!" Fifetta exclaimed. "Someday I'm going to write a book about all our guests. No one will believe the things we've seen."

When the front door opened, Bria couldn't believe what she was seeing.

"Marco! What are you doing home so early?"

Sister Benedicta, who was standing behind Marco, explained. "*Ricorda*? School got out early today. Mother Superior and the nuns on the budgeting committee had a meeting with the mayor and town council."

"*Uffa!*" Bria cried. "I completely forgot."

"Nonna Fifi!" Marco cried. "What are you doing here in the middle of the day?"

Fifetta swooped Marco up in her arms and turned him so his back was facing the upstairs bedroom door covered in yellow police tape. "I had to run some errands, and I wanted to say hello to my favorite grandson."

"I'm your only grandson," Marco squealed.

"You're still my favorite *principino*," Fifetta replied, hugging Marco tightly.

Marco squirmed in Fifetta's arms, but his giggles belied his struggle: he loved being held almost as much as his grandmother loved holding him.

"I told Sister B I could walk home by myself," Marco said. "But she wouldn't let me."

Bravo ran in from the balcony just in time to distract Marco, so Bria and Sister Benedicta could speak without being overheard.

"*Grazie*, Sister," Bria said, grabbing the nun's hands.

Sister Benedicta squeezed Bria's hands tightly and looked her directly in the eyes. It was obvious to Bria that the nun had heard the news. "Are you all right?" the nun whispered.

"Yes, *grazie*," Bria said. "Would you like some coffee?"

"I should really get back to the school," Sister Benedicta said. "*Prego*, unless you'd like me to stay and pray with you."

Bria's breath caught in her throat. *Pray?* The thought had never occurred to her, and suddenly Bria felt overcome with shame.

"*Grazie*, Sister," Bria said. "That would be very comforting."

"Bria," Fifetta said. "Should I take Marco and Bravo for a walk?"

She was grateful her mother was giving her the option to avoid the inevitable, but her mother had also taught her that procrastination never solved a problem or made a situation easier. It only prolonged the pain. Bria had to tell Marco what had happened, and better to tell him with some of people he loved most in the room.

"Marco, bambino, come sit with me," Bria said as she walked to the dining room table.

She sat down and patted the chair next to her so Marco would be sitting with his back to the door with the police tape. Bria didn't think she would be able to get rid of the offensive, but necessary decoration before Marco saw it, but she still felt it was better that it wasn't in his direct line of vision. Dutifully, Marco sat next to Bria as Fifetta and Sister Benedicta sat on the other side of the table. Not to be excluded, Bravo plopped on the floor next to Marco's feet.

"Did I do something wrong, Mamma?" Marco asked.

"No, *piccolo amore*," Bria replied. "You haven't done anything wrong, but something has happened that wasn't good."

"Did Bravo eat your shoes again?" Marco said. "He just does that when he's hungry."

"No, Bravo didn't do anything, either," Bria replied. "What happened is . . ."

Bria searched for her next word, but it was out of reach. She didn't know how to convey to her son what had transpired only a few hours ago. He had already experienced such a great loss when his father died. How could she bring death into his life yet again? It was because she was focusing only on the tragedy.

"Marco, remember what we talked about in school yesterday?" Sister Benedicta asked.

"About heaven and hell?" Marco replied.

"Yes. And what did you tell the class?"

"That my papa was in heaven because he was a good man," Marco said. "He's with God and looking down at me and my mamma."

Bria didn't have to look at her mother to know that tears were sliding down her cheeks, as well. She had been afraid to talk about death with her son, and here he was, sounding wiser than the adults in the room.

"That's right," Sister B said. "Today a man was found here who also went to heaven."

Marco turned to Bria, his blue eyes wide and curious. "Is that true, Mamma?"

"Yes, bambino. I don't know who the man is, but he needed a place to sleep, and he found it upstairs," Bria explained.

Eyes wide, Marco turned to look upstairs and saw the police tape covering the bedroom door. "*Figo.*"

Only an eight-year-old boy would think police tape on a bedroom door was cool, Bria thought.

"The man was found in there?" Marco asked.

"*Sì mio angelo*," Bria said. "He died, and now he's in heaven with Papa and the rest of the angels."

Bria had no idea where the man's spirit was now, but if she was wrong and the man had led a life that would not guarantee entry into heaven, she knew God would understand.

"That means Bella Bella is a special place," Marco said.

"What do you mean by that, Marco?" Fifetta asked.

"If the man came here to die, that means there are angels nearby that can take him up to heaven," Marco explained.

Bria smiled. Her son's explanation was as good as any that she or the police had come up with, so she wasn't going to argue with him. Neither was his teacher.

"*Molto intelligente*, Marco," Sister B said.

"Thank you," Marco replied. "Can I go play with Bravo now before dinner?"

"Of course," Bria said, kissing Marco on the forehead. "Go play and I'll call you when dinner's ready."

Marco hugged and kissed his grandmother and said goodbye to Sister B before running outside with Bravo. Marco had taken the news far better than Bria had expected, but it was reassuring to know she had the support of others in the room. She wasn't ready to let them go.

"Sister," Bria said. "Do you have time to lead us in a prayer for the deceased?"

"Of course," Sister B replied.

The three women took out the rosaries that each of them kept on them at all times or within arm's reach. Fifetta's was a

Lucite rosary given to her by her grandmother, Bria grabbed a pink rosary she had bought on her first trip to the Vatican, and Sister B's was wooden and smelled like roses. They were just about to start the second decade of the rosary when they were interrupted by the ping of Bria's cell phone. It took one glance at Luca's text message for Bria to know that they had another reason to pray.

We're holding Giovanni on suspicion of murder.

CHAPTER 7

The view from Rosalie's boat almost made Bria forget about the past twenty-four hours. Almost. The murder, Giovanni spending the night in jail, having to tell Marco that a dead man had been found in their home, it was unnerving. The scenery, however, was acting as a tonic.

She leaned back in the lounge chair on the aft deck and took in the spectacular landscape of Positano. From where the boat was docked, in a slip about fifty yards from the shoreline, it looked like a child had stacked colorful boxes one on top of the other in a slightly haphazard design and then had placed them all on a pile of jagged, misshapen rocks. It was a famous sight, but one that couldn't truly be captured in postcards or photos taken with a cell phone. It needed to be seen in person. It needed to be experienced.

Growing up in nearby Ravello, Bria had come to Positano many times, but as often was the case with children, she hadn't appreciated her surroundings. She had been too involved in her own world to notice the world around her. When she got older and went to high school in Amalfi, she became more interested in intellectual and artistic pursuits and wasn't one to loll around at the beach. She saw the view but never really took it in.

The first time she truly looked at Positano's panorama with more than just her eyes was from the very same deck she lounged on now, although the circumstances were quite different. Rosalie had met Bria and Carlo in Naples and had taken them to Positano on her boat, *La Vie en Rosalie*, to show them where she was going to set up her business and live. None of them had had any idea it would be the start of a whole new adventure for all three.

Nothing much had changed since that first trip. The natural landscape was still framed by the clearest soft blue sky imaginable. The rugged vertical drop from the mountains' apex to the beach still defied reason—how could a town be built in such an inhospitable setting? Rising above it all was an imperfect but dominating circle of light, a bright yellow sun that was slightly fuzzy around the edge and allowed the sunlight to bleed into the blue sky.

The blue and caramel Byzantine design of the dome on top of the church of St. Maria Assunta still popped out from the mauves and yellows of the square and rectangular houses, not demanding attention, but making you feel helpless to turn away. Legend had it that twelfth-century Saracen pirates had felt the same. According to the myth, they stole a painting of the Black Madonna from the church, and as they fled in their ship, they were caught in a life-threatening storm. The painting of Mary spoke to them, crying, "*Posa, posa!*" They did as they were told and returned the painting to where it belonged.

The combination of complex shapes, multiple colors, and three-dimensional levels of the town created a distinct view, one that, like the pyramids or Mount Rushmore, seemed impossible to achieve but somehow existed for all to enjoy and marvel at. For some lucky people, like Bria and Rosalie, it was called home. Sometimes, however, home felt less like colorful childhood drawings and more like jagged rocks. Even the beauty of Positano couldn't keep away heartache.

She took a sip of the limoncello spritz that Rosalie had made for her, and allowed the sweet yet strong flavor to heat up her throat and float throughout her body. It was far too early for an alcoholic beverage, but she was glad she had made an exception. She didn't realize how much she needed this soothing elixir until it started to flow through her veins.

"Am I a poor judge of character?" Bria asked.

The question floated on the warm breeze for a few seconds while Rosalie chewed the prawn that she had just dipped into cocktail sauce. It was a questionable breakfast, but Rosalie had questionable taste. After she swallowed, she replied.

"No."

Bria waited for more sage words to emerge from her friend's mouth. None came.

"That's it?" Bria asked. "No more reassurances, no more passionate statements about how wrong I am to think such a thing?"

"You have every reason to doubt yourself," Rosalie said. "You may have hired a murderer."

"Rosalie!"

"I warned you about Giovanni. I told you he had a shady past, but you said you felt in your gut that you could trust him."

"I did trust him," Bria replied. She then quickly corrected herself. "I still do."

"But you're questioning that trust, and you should," Rosalie said. "Look, I don't think Giovanni killed this man—I've never known him to have a history of violence—but I do think that he's somehow involved."

"Being involved and being a murderer are two different things," Bria said. "Would Luca arrest him just for being involved?"

"Maybe they're holding him in hopes that he'll confess something that will lead them to the real murderer," Rosalie mused before popping another shrimp into her mouth.

"How long do you think they'll keep him in jail?"

"*Non lo so.* Ask my brother."

"He hasn't answered any of my texts. I think he's ghosting me."

"That isn't true."

"Now that he's investigating a murder at my place of business, I'm no longer a friend," Bria said. "I don't think he's going to talk to me until this case is solved."

"*Ecco!* There's only one way to find out."

"What's that?"

"Turn around and ask him," Rosalie said. "He's walking up the plank."

Bria turned and for a moment couldn't see anything because the sun was shining in her eyes. When she regained her vision, she saw Luca dressed in his tight-fitting police uniform flanked by the golden rays of the never-ending sun, looking more like an action hero than a regular cop. The miracle of backlighting. That, and the limoncello was starting to go to her head.

"Annamaria told me I could find you here," Luca said, climbing aboard the boat.

"I swear that woman could make money as an investigative journalist," Rosalie said. "She knows everything about everybody."

"*Io desidero*," Luca said. "If she knew who the dead man was and exactly who killed him, she'd make my life a lot easier."

"You're not making Giovanni's life any easier," Bria said. "How can you keep him in prison *overnight* if he didn't kill this man?"

"Technically, we can't keep him for that," Luca said.

"Luca!" Rosalie cried. "The chief of police is breaking the law?"

"*Ovviamente no!*" Luca replied. "More like *bending* the law."

Bria felt a heat grow in her stomach. It wasn't the limoncello or a new sensation. She had experienced it many times since she was a teenager. Whenever she or someone she cared about was threatened, she'd feel as if a match had been struck on the other side of her belly button. The feeling had occurred during fencing matches in college, confrontations with her mother-in-law, Imperia, but she had never thought she'd experience it with Luca.

"You need to explain yourself, Luca," Bria said, her words more of a demand than a statement. "Why are you holding Giovanni prisoner?"

"First, he ran from a police officer and resisted arrest for loitering," Luca said.

"He wasn't loitering. He works for me," Bria countered.

"Nunzi didn't know that when she called for him to stop," Luca replied. "Second, he has four unpaid parking tickets on his Vespa. We can hold him for up to forty-eight hours for questioning, and after that he'll be released, once he pays his fine, of course."

"That's very clever," Rosalie said.

"That's very cruel," Bria added. "You know Vanni had nothing to do with this."

Luca took a deep breath and sat on the gunwale next to Bria. He exhaled slowly, gripped the side of the boat, and finally appeared ready to respond to Bria's comment.

"He's an employee of the business where the dead body was found," Luca said. "Given that there were no other witnesses, the murder must have taken place nearby, which limits the number of suspects considerably. Add to that your handyman's not-so-respectable past, and it makes him a definite suspect and, at the very least, a person of real interest."

Luca paused briefly to let Bria and his sister digest that information, then added, "And seriously, when did you start calling him Vanni? Nobody does that."

"When you think about it he really does look so much more

like a Vanni than a Giovanni, with his man bun, the scruffy beard, and those muscles, *caro Signore*!" Rosalie said. "I'm not sure why somebody didn't start calling him that years ago."

"Maybe because he's drifted in and out of this village for years without forming any real relationships," Luca said. He then turned to face Bria and added, "Until now."

"He's trying to change," Bria said. "Can't you see that?"

Maybe Luca can't, Bria thought.

She realized that it might take someone who was also in transition, someone who was trying to move their life in a different direction to be able to recognize someone else who was trying to turn their life around. Someone like her.

"I think it's wonderful that you can see the good in people," Luca said.

"I think it's terrible that you can only see the bad," Bria replied.

Luca smiled, which disarmed Bria. She had just told him that he looked only for darkness, and his eyes lit up? And why did he look so handsome standing on the deck of Rosalie's boat, his hair blowing in the wind, and his lips spreading to expose two rows of incredibly white teeth?

Enough, Bria! Concentrate on the matter at hand.

"You find this funny?" Bria asked.

"No," Luca replied, still smiling. "I do find your position entertaining, because ignoring facts is a luxury I had to give up when I started my career in law enforcement."

"That's quite a loss," Bria said.

For a moment she noticed that Luca's smile faded, but it quickly returned. "I promise you that if we can't find any hard evidence incriminating Giovanni and if he doesn't share some information that will help us with the investigation, we will let him go."

"I'd like to see him," Bria stated.

"Not until he's released," Luca said.

"*Fratello*, do you have any good news to share?" Rosalie asked.

"As a matter of fact, I do," Luca replied. "It's about the dead man."

While Bria focused on a flock of birds flying in and out of the glare of the sun in single file so they resembled a *nastro arricciato,* a ribbon twirling like a corkscrew, Luca explained that according to the medical examiner, it looked like the man had died from a knife wound that punctured his kidney. It meant that their original assumption as to the cause of death was validated.

Their instincts about the time of death were right on target, as well. The man had most likely died within thirty minutes after being stabbed and within thirty minutes before being discovered. Whoever had killed him did it near Bella Bella, because it wasn't long after his arrival that Bria came home and discovered him. They also needed to tag on time for the killer to follow him, steal his identification, and hide in the downstairs closet. The window of time from assault to discovery was about forty-five minutes.

"That isn't very long, but it fits my timeline," Bria said. "I was out of my house for no more than twenty-five minutes, and then it was probably another ten minutes after I got home that I discovered the body. Is any of this information helpful?"

"Violent crime throughout the coast is virtually nonexistent, so our department doesn't have as much experience as they do in the big cities," Luca explained. "But it's very helpful that you found the corpse so quickly."

"Has anyone reported a crime or made an anonymous phone call?" Rosalie asked.

"No, none of the business owners reported a robbery or a break-in, nor has anyone called the police to report being attacked."

"Then it was premeditated?" Bria asked.

"It appears to have been," Luca replied. "Whoever killed this man wanted him dead."

"Did you look to see if a man of his description has been reported missing?" Bria asked.

"We did," Luca replied. "There aren't any missing persons reports that would be a match."

"What about fingerprints and DNA?" Bria asked.

"Who are you?" Rosalie asked. "Giuseppe Dosi?"

"Who?" Bria replied.

"You've never heard of Signor Dosi?" Luca asked.

"Is he famous?" Bria replied.

"Only the most famous Italian detective and disguise artist who ever lived," Luca said.

"He's kind of my brother's idol," Rosalie said. "When we were kids, he would be Dosi and I'd be his sidekick. Together we'd make up crimes and solve them."

"If you were the ones who made up the crimes, there would be no mystery to solve," Bria said.

"We were kids, Bria!" Rosalie cried. "We were playing a game!"

"Well, this isn't a game," Bria said.

"No, it isn't," Luca added. "We're running his prints and DNA in the Interpol system, but so far there haven't been any matches. And before you ask, we also checked trash cans."

"I was not going to ask that," Rosalie said.

"I was," Bria said.

"Why?" Rosalie asked.

"Because they may have thrown the dead man's identification into a trash can to get rid of it," Bria said. "Isn't that right, Luca?"

"*Esattamente*," he replied. "We didn't find anything, so whoever took the ID kept it or got rid of it someplace where we haven't looked yet."

A feeling of hopelessness threatened to overwhelm Bria. She

had learned from experience that she could not give in to the feeling, as it served no purpose and never proved helpful. Once again, her mother was right, and what always helped was taking action. She needed to become an active participant in order to find out who had killed this man. The police department had no experience solving a murder, and although neither did Bria, she was more motivated to find the killer. Before she could start investigating, however, she needed to get rid of the investigator.

"Thank you so much, Luca, for telling us this in person," Bria said.

"My pleasure," Luca said. "You're not angry with me any longer about detaining Giovanni?"

"No, I'm still angry, but I've learned that anger alone doesn't solve any problem," Bria said. "Action does."

"*Hai ragione*," Luca said as he got up to leave. "I'll keep you posted if Giovanni tells us anything."

"*Grazie*," Bria said.

"*Ciao*, big brother," Rosalie said, giving Luca a kiss on his cheek.

"*Ciao*, little sister," Luca replied, kissing Rosalie's cheek.

The women watched Luca walk down the plank, and the moment Bria knew he was out of earshot, she turned to Rosalie.

"Are you ready to be a sidekick again?" Bria asked.

"What are you talking about?" Rosalie replied.

"You and me," Bria replied. "I'll be that Italian detective, and you be my sidekick."

Rosalie glared at Bria, her eyes half-closed and her nose turned up. When she saw Bria's eyes light up, she knew her friend had made her an offer she wasn't going to be able to refuse.

"Let me finish my drink," Rosalie said.

"We don't have time for that," Bria chided. "We have work to do."

* * *

Ten minutes later, once they knew Luca was taking care of police business elsewhere, Bria and Rosalie started walking toward Bella Bella to begin phase one of Bria's plan.

"What do you mean, we're going to reenact the crime?" Rosalie asked. "You're going to stab me in broad daylight so I can stumble to your house?"

"*Basta*! Don't be a fool!" Bria cried. "We're going to start at my front door and walk for fifteen minutes, which is approximately the amount of time the man had after he was stabbed."

"That's smart, Bria!" Rosalie cried. "But how do we know what direction he went in?"

"We don't," Bria said. "We'll have to make the trip a few times to see which direction leads us to a location that could be the crime scene."

"We'll do it as many times as it takes," Rosalie declared. "Whatever's necessary to find the killer."

When they got to Bria's front door, Rosalie's passion had waned. She was hot, she wasn't wearing the proper shoes, and she had forgotten to put on sunblock. She was not acting like the trusting, enthusiastic sidekick she had agreed to portray.

"Could we do this little experiment later on, when it isn't so hot out?" Rosalie asked, sucking on her inhaler.

"*Uffa*! It's always hot in Positano!" Bria cried. "Now come on. We'll start by walking east."

"East is uphill," Rosalie said. "Let's go west."

"Fine!" Bria cried. "Let's just go."

"I need a bottle of water," Rosalie said, turning to go inside the bed-and-breakfast.

"Will you stop stalling!" Bria cried, pulling Rosalie's arm.

When Bria tugged on Rosalie's arm, her friend lurched to the left and stepped on one of Marco's toys, a wooden Pinocchio he must have dropped on the front step, and lost her footing. Rosalie slipped out of her sandal and fell toward Bria. While Rosalie was able to reach out and grab the windowsill to prevent herself from falling, when Bria extended her arm, all she grabbed on to was air. After breaking through the thick bush underneath the window, Bria landed with a thud when her back smashed into the hard ground.

A spasm of pain shot through her body, and for a moment she didn't move. Impersonating a detective was not getting off to a great start, and she made a mental note to exercise more to get back some of the agility she had had while fencing. But when she rolled over onto her stomach to push herself up to her feet, everything changed. She was so excited, she couldn't contain the scream that emerged from her throat.

"Did you hurt yourself?" Rosalie asked.

"No!" Bria shrieked. "I found our first clue!"

Triumphantly, Bria emerged from the bush and presented the reward for their morning's efforts. The long silk scarf dangled from Bria's fingertips and swayed in the breeze. Its intricate gold and navy paisley design was still visible, even though most of the material was covered by a huge bloodstain.

CHAPTER 8

Rosalie moved the large artichoke bowl, a bunch of dried flowers, a roll of twine, several issues of *La Vita Positano*, and a crumpled-up juice box to one side of the dining room table to make room for the scarf. Bria laid it out on the table, making sure not to touch any piece of the fabric except for the two edges she was already holding. It was time for the amateur detectives to detect.

"This has got to be connected to the dead man," Rosalie said. "But how?"

"He must've used it to try and stop the bleeding while he was walking here," Bria deduced. "And somehow dropped it."

"But how did it wind up almost buried in the dirt?" Rosalie asked.

They were abruptly interrupted when Bravo scampered into the room with one of Marco's old *Calimero* dolls hanging from his mouth. The black chicken, a legendary animated character in the history of children's television in Italy, was still wearing its broken eggshell hat, but its left leg was missing, presumably chewed by Bravo and hidden somewhere, never to be found.

"That's it!" Bria cried. "Bravo found the scarf in the bushes and buried it. He does that all the time with things he finds."

"If the killer followed the guy here and took the time to steal his ID, he wouldn't leave the scarf lying around," Rosalie surmised. "He would have taken it with him to dispose of it."

"Bravo did that for him," Bria said.

At the repeated sound of his name and the looks of joy on the women's faces, Bravo wagged his tail a few times and then rolled over onto his back, clearly looking for some belly rubs. Bria didn't disappoint him. She knelt on the floor and rubbed his belly vigorously. Bravo's tongue fell out of his mouth and lolled back and forth while Bria continued to inform Rosalie of what else the scarf helped explain about the murder.

"Since the man was using the scarf to stop the bleeding," Bria said, "that explains why there wasn't any blood outside."

"And why he had to use the banner once he got inside," Rosalie added.

Bria gave Bravo one last rub, then stood up and walked back to the table. Bravo remained on the floor for a few more seconds, hoping she was going to return. Once he realized she wasn't coming back, he rolled over, stood, shook his whole body, and sauntered off to the kitchen. He would get his belly satisfied one way or another. Meanwhile, Bria needed to satisfy her curiosity.

She ripped off a piece of the newspaper and used it like a makeshift glove to lift all four sides of the scarf. When she was finished, she dejectedly crumpled up the paper and tossed it onto the table.

"I thought it might have a tag on it, to tell us where he bought it," Bria explained. "I don't see the name of the designer, either."

"Which means this scarf could've been bought anywhere?" Rosalie said.

"Unfortunately, yes," Bria said. "I don't recognize the pattern, do you?"

Rosalie shook her head. "It looks a bit like Chanel's chain-link design, but probably only because they're both gold."

"I thought that, too," Bria said. "This looks expensive, but it could be a knockoff."

"I don't think this is a cheap imitation," Rosalie said. "It looks like a luxury scarf, but who knows where he got it."

Bria stepped back from the table and ran her fingers through her hair. She massaged her scalp the way Carlo used to when he washed her hair. It was a romantic gesture and one that always made her feel loved and secure. It was the kind of special thing a man would do for a woman, like buying her an impromptu gift.

"He bought the scarf to give to someone," Bria said.

"How do you know that?" Rosalie asked.

"It's a woman's scarf," Bria replied. "He must have bought it before he got to Positano, because there's no bag, and he couldn't have bought it the morning he died, because none of the stores were open yet."

"He could have bought it the day before," Rosalie suggested. "Or during another visit."

"I've shopped at every store in the village, and I don't ever remember seeing this scarf or one like it being sold anywhere," Bria said.

"Take a picture of it," Rosalie suggested.

"Why?"

"Because if you're shopping and see a scarf, you can then compare it to the photo to see if it's a match," Rosalie explained.

"*Buona idea*," Bria said before running to another part of the house.

"Where are you going?" Rosalie asked as she watched Bria race to her bedroom.

When Bria came back, she was holding something that looked oddly familiar but strange at the same time.

"Why do you have a Polaroid camera?" Rosalie asked.

"Don't you remember?" Bria said. "It was Carlo's."

Rosalie threw her hands up. "*Dio mio*! Of course. He loved all those old things. Cameras, typewriters, telephones."

"Somewhere in one of the boxes that has all his stuff, there's an eight-track cassette recorder, which I don't think I'll ever be able to throw away," Bria said.

"I might be able to use that Polaroid camera," Rosalie said.

"Why? The cameras you have are top of the line."

"It would give a retro feel to the weddings I shoot."

In addition to running a tour boat, Rosalie was also a professional photographer. She could officiate a wedding at sea and also take photos of the blessed event. On occasion she worked with Bria's parents at Mondo dei Sogni and photographed their events.

"*Brillante*! My parents will love it. Carlo would, too."

"I hope the thing still works," Rosalie said.

"It does," Bria replied. "I just used it."

The moment Bria heard her words float into the air, she knew she had said too much.

"When did you just use it?" Rosalie asked.

Bria looked at Rosalie with the same sheepish expression she had worn when she had to confess to her friend that she had accidentally ruined her maid of honor dress two days before her wedding and they had to go shopping for something new for Rosalie to wear.

"I used it to take a photo of the dead man after you left yesterday," Bria confessed.

"You did what!" Rosalie screamed.

Bria explained that while Luca had used the bathroom a few minutes before the ambulance arrived, Bria had snapped a photo. Since she didn't recognize the man's face, there was a very good chance she wasn't going to remember it. If she was going to help solve this mystery and clear her name and the name of her business, she was going to need help. Her first instinct, of course, had been to take a photo on her cell phone, but she'd realized that it would live there forever even if she deleted it, and she didn't think Luca or the rest of the police force would appreciate the fact that she had photographed a corpse. Carlo's old Polaroid camera was the perfect solution: it would provide her with a photograph that wouldn't be able to be traced back to her.

"Except that no one else in this village has a Polaroid camera," Rosalie said.

Bria opened her mouth to form a rebuttal but promptly shut it closed. "I'll just have to make sure that no one sees the photo of the dead man unless absolutely necessary."

Bria took a photo of the scarf with the Polaroid and was transported back to a time before she was born. She listened to the sounds of clicks and hums that indicated the camera was generating an image on the film that would soon slide out of the tray. When she saw it emerge, she grabbed on to it when it was completely free, and she shook it a few times, like she had seen Carlo do. She lay it on the table, and she and Rosalie watched the black film slowly metamorphose into an image of the bloodied scarf.

"To think that this was once the height of technology," Rosalie remarked.

"I think it's nice to be able to take a photo and have it be tangible, not just an image on a screen. There's something more permanent about it," Bria said.

"I'm not sure I'd want to have a permanent reminder of a murder," Rosalie said.

"It isn't like I'm going to put these Polaroids on the *frigorifero* alongside Marco's drawings," Bria cried. "*Dio mio*, Marco!"

"What about him?"

"I almost forgot to ask if you could babysit him for a few hours tomorrow afternoon?"

"I have an early evening cruise with a family. He can be my first mate," Rosalie assured her. "Where are you going?"

Bria made the sign of the cross. This time not for an un-known dead man, but for herself. *"Nella bocca dell'inferno."*

The next morning Bria dropped Marco off at school, much earlier than usual, and gave him an extra-long hug because she wouldn't see him until later that night. She wasn't literally em-barking on a journey into the mouth of hell; it only felt that way. She was going to visit her mother-in-law.

Imperia Stalazito Bartolucci was aptly named because she was domineering, haughty and, yes, imperious. To make mat-ters worse, she didn't approve of Bria, not that she would have approved of any woman who married her son. Ironically, it was only because of her son that Bria was making the trip.

Imperia had business documents that Bria needed to sign on Marco's behalf. Thanks to the success of Bartolucci Enter-prises, Marco would never have any financial worries. Despite Imperia's animosity toward her, Bria was grateful that Imperia was turning over many of the documents that had been in Carlo's name to Marco's, even if it meant that Imperia still held the strings in the family. That was the only reason Bria was driving up the Amalfi Coast at 7:00 a.m. on a Thursday morn-ing to get to Rome.

One look to her left, however, and all thoughts of Imperia, murder, and bloodied scarves went out of her head. All she could focus on was the view.

Breathtaking, gorgeous, idyllic were some of the adjectives used to describe the view off the Amalfi Coast, and even though this was a road Bria had traveled numerous times be-fore, it was not one that she took for granted. While having Im-peria as a mother-in-law sometimes felt like a curse, the road she had to take to meet with her was a blessing.

Like most every morning, the sun shone brightly and magni-fied the beauty of what lie below. The sea looked like a swatch of textured fabric, deep blue, that undulated slowly, as if the material was being pulled from all ends. The sky was several shades lighter, a cornflower blue, and at certain points on the drive, when the road curved, it became lighter and blended into the haze of the sun. Behind her, the village of Positano looked almost mythical, like it was an enormous, jagged creature that had emerged from the sea to bask in the magnificent light of the sun.

Expertly, Bria gripped the steering wheel tighter as she entered a curve on Via Gennaro Maresca, and she felt the wheels of the car turn underneath her from the right and then the left in a smooth, fluid motion, like that of the sea bass and bluefin tuna that swam in the Tyrrhenian Sea several hundred feet below. Which made sense because the car, like the nearby fish, was native to the land.

Bria's bright yellow Fiat Dino convertible was a refurbished 1970 model that had been Carlo's father's prized possession. It was the only thing Carlo wanted after his father had died. Because it was the only thing Carlo remembered that had made his father smile.

Guillermo Bartolucci, unlike most Italian fathers, wasn't demonstrative toward his family. He didn't steal kisses from Imperia in public, he didn't scoop his only son up in his arms, and he didn't show affection. He worked hard, built an empire, and left his family wanting for nothing, except, of course, his love. The only time Carlo remembered his father smiling was when he would take his son out for drives on the coast or through the countryside. As a young boy, Carlo believed the Fiat was a magical car, and after Guillermo died, all Carlo wanted was that magic.

As Bria drove onto the A24, the Autostrada dei Parchi, she felt some of that magic. It wasn't yet 10:00 a.m.; she might even have time to have a cappuccino before her meeting. Then again, the extra caffeine might make her even more nervous than she already was. Whatever time she arrived, she'd arrive in style.

Bria had covered her head with a white scarf tied at the nape of her neck, her long black hair billowing in the breeze behind her. She wore the pair of vintage La Giardiniera black-and-white, oval-shaped sunglasses she had found at a flea market while she was pregnant with Marco. The combination made her look like Claudia Cardinale taking a morning spin on the road after a night of parties with the jet set instead of like a mother on a trip to ensure her son's future.

Bartolucci Enterprises was located on Via Antonio Stoppani in Rome's main financial district. Bria didn't think it was the nicest section of Rome, but the building did have its own underground parking lot. That alone made the location desirable.

A tall, achingly thin young man with a sour gaze and a bush of curly red hair ushered Bria into her mother-in-law's office. He immediately closed the door behind her and disappeared. No matter how many times she was alone in Imperia's presence, Bria always felt the same. She was in awe. Carlo used to call it the Sophia Loren factor.

Born into poverty like the movie star, Imperia saw one way out of the *catapecchia*, the slum that she lived in with her parents and five siblings outside Florence, and that was her beauty. At fifteen, she lied about her age and entered a local beauty pageant to be the face of Aldi, a local supermarket. That initial victory was the start of a career that would take Imperia all throughout Italy, winning pageant after pageant and collecting scholarship after scholarship to use toward her college education. Even as a young woman, she knew that intelligence lasted far longer than physical beauty.

At each contest, she would receive either a marriage proposal, a modeling contract, or a role in an upcoming film, sometimes all three at one stop. She turned them all down because she was determined to control her life. And, unabashedly, she wanted her own fortune.

She started as an Avon Lady, using her good looks to persuade middle-aged housewives and widows of any age that it was acceptable to use products to enhance their inner beauty. She graduated at the top of her class from the University of Milan with a degree in business, climbed the ranks of Avon, left to open her own cosmetics firm with her earnings, sold that firm to a competitor, and married the CEO only after he promised—in writing—that she would be the COO of the company and a member of the board of directors for the rest of her life. Imperia had fallen in love with Guillermo Bartolucci, but she had also fallen in love with power. She refused to give up one for the other.

The next three decades were spent building a business empire that had a presence in the cosmetics, fashion, pharmaceutical, and real estate industries, collecting admirers and enemies in both her personal and professional lives, watching helplessly as her parents and siblings died off one by one, celebrating her twenty-ninth wedding anniversary at the bedside of her dying husband, giving birth to and burying her only child, and celebrating the life of her only grandson. Without Marco, Imperia and Bria would have no bond; with him that bond was unbreakable.

Imperia sat at her oversized white marble and glass desk, in a white leather and chrome swivel chair, wearing an ensemble of head-to-toe red. The office walls were painted black, the flooring was gray oak, the couch and two armchairs in the sitting area were black leather, and the artwork was a series of black-and-white photographs and ink illustrations, all depicting facets of the industrial revolution. The only pops of color in the room besides Imperia were the two bouquets of red roses that were in the Baccarat etched glass vases on either side of the desk. Imperia wasn't taking any chances: anyone who walked through her door was going to be drawn to her as quickly as a lazy fly would be drawn into a spider's web.

The only competition Imperia faced was from the view. On

the wall to her left were three floor-to-ceiling windows that looked out onto the city and, in the distance, the Vatican. The Pope's enclave was commanding, but so was Imperia.

When Bria entered the room, Imperia was staring out the window, so Bria could only see her stately profile. Imperia's long aquiline nose was tilted up, and her manicured, red-painted fingernails framed her chin, giving her the appearance of a woman deep in thought. Feeling like a schoolgirl standing in the shadow of the principal, Bria cleared her throat to make her presence known. Imperia, seeing her daughter-in-law's reflection in the window, already knew she was there.

"*Ciao*, Bria," Imperia said, her smoky voice sounding like a rough whisper. "I see that you decided not to dress for a day in the city."

When she left her house, Bria had thought she looked chic; now she wasn't so sure. A navy cardigan sweater over a matching V-neck T-shirt, paired with tan capri pants and navy slingbacks. Italian *Vogue* touted it as the current look for the modern woman on the go.

"I wanted to be comfortable for the long drive," Bria said. "And I'm meeting my sister for lunch at a place near the marina, so I didn't want to get too dressed up."

"You succeeded," Imperia declared, turning to face Bria. "Did you make plans with Lorenza to avoid having lunch with me?"

Yes, Bria thought. "No," she said out loud. "You didn't say anything about lunch."

"It was going to be a surprise," Imperia said. "But you've ruined it."

"I . . . I could change my plans," Bria stuttered.

Imperia didn't respond but held up a finger like Bria did to Bravo when she wanted him to remain quiet. Like her dog, Bria obeyed while Imperia pressed a button on the phone console. A young man's voice immediately responded to Imperia's touch.

"*Sì, signora*?" the voice said.

"Cancel my lunch reservation," Imperia ordered, then pressed the button before the man had a chance to respond. She sat at her desk and, without looking up, said, "Let's get down to business."

As Bria signed the final document, she realized with utter fascination that she had no idea what she was signing. She could be giving over her parental rights to Imperia for all she knew. Carlo had had no interest in his family's business and had rarely spoken of it to Bria. He had studied economics and business management at Bocconi University in Milan, but only to make his parents happy, not because he had any desire to climb the ladder of Bartolucci Enterprises. Understanding his need to distance himself from his family's more capitalistic endeavors, Bria had rarely asked for details. Now she wished that she had.

"What exactly am I signing, Imperia?" Bria asked.

"Quarterly financial statements allowing money to be deposited in Marco's trust," Imperia explained. "And this is the certificate to a new stock that I bought in his name."

"Marco owns stock?" Bria asked.

"Your son has quite a diverse stock portfolio," Imperia said. "Thanks to me."

Bria was thankful that despite Imperia's many, many flaws, she doted on Marco and was ensuring that he would lead a financially worry-free life. Still, she had so many questions she wanted to ask Imperia. What kind of stock? How much money was really in there? Could he lose all the money if the stock market took a bad turn? But with Giovanni still in jail, the police no closer to finding out who the dead man was, and desperately hoping Imperia hadn't heard anything about the murder just yet, she didn't want to prolong the conversation. So she signed the final document and thought she'd be able to make a quick exit. She thought wrong.

"Are you going to tell me?" Imperia asked.

Bria knew exactly what she meant, but she stalled. "Tell you what?"

"I know you aren't highly intelligent, Bria," Imperia said. "But I also know you're not stupid."

From Imperia, those words were to be taken as a compliment.

"The police are investigating the matter and have concluded that the man was stabbed near Bella Bella and came into my house seeking shelter," Bria shared. "But they still don't know who he is, who killed him, or why he was killed. It's a mystery."

"Your obstinance is a mystery," Imperia declared. "Isn't this proof that you and Marco don't belong in Positano? You belong here with your family."

"We've been through this before," Bria began. "I'm making a life for myself and Marco in Positano because that's what Carlo and I wanted."

At the mention of her son's name, Imperia's face softened, but only momentarily. When she spoke, she was as statue-like as she had been since Bria arrived.

"Carlo is no longer here," Imperia said. Bria thought she was going to continue speaking, but she didn't. Either she had nothing more to add or, Bria hoped, Imperia didn't want to risk a display of emotion in her presence. Not once since Carlo died had Bria seen her mother-in-law shed a tear. She prayed Imperia gave in to her feelings during moments of privacy.

"We'll be fine, Imperia. Don't worry about us," Bria said.

"Why should I worry?" Imperia asked rhetorically. "It isn't like there's an *assassino* on the loose."

Bria wanted to respond with a witty comment to make light of the situation, but how could she? Imperia was right. There was a murderer on the loose. And here she was, making awkward small talk. She needed to leave, meet her sister, and then head back home to her son.

"If there's nothing else for me to sign," Bria said, "I should go."

Instead of answering, Imperia focused on the papers on her

desk and waved her hand dramatically in circles over her head. "You go on and meet your baby sister," Imperia said. "I have appointments."

Once again, Imperia pressed a button on the phone console.

"*Sì, signora?*" the same male voice responded.

"Get my driver," Imperia ordered. "I'm going to Milan."

All of a sudden she's going to Milan, Bria thought.

"What's in Milan?" Bria asked.

"Dr. Frangi," Imperia replied.

Bria almost laughed out loud. Only Imperia could question someone's deep-rooted life choices in one instant and plan a trip to the plastic surgeon in the second. Imperia was off to get a touch-up.

When it came to cosmetic surgery and other nonsurgical treatments to make a face look younger, more refreshed, and wrinkle free, there was no one better in all of Italy than Dr. Edoardo Frangipani. Or, as Imperia and the rest of his dedicated clientele called him, Dr. Frangi. He didn't believe in the drastic facial reconstructions that doctors in Beverly Hills, on Park Avenue, and in Mexico City were fond of performing; he believed in a more subtle approach. Smaller, less invasive surgeries and procedures starting at a younger age. It was the speculated rumor that thanks to Dr. Frangi's technique a certain celebrated Italian American soap opera legend was able to maintain her youthful ingenue quality during her entire fifty-year acting career. And it was Dr. Frangi's talent that made Imperia Bartolucci look much younger than she should at sixty-two years old.

"Are you sure you wouldn't like to come with me?" Imperia asked. "I can see that the stress you're under is making you look . . . haggard."

Reluctantly, Bria touched her cheek. Was that face flab? No, she was only thirty-two; all she needed was a good night's rest and a day in the sun.

"Thank you, Imperia, but I think I'll pass," Bria said. "My sister is waiting for me."

That was a bit of a lie, and Bria had to wait almost forty-five minutes before Lorenza arrived, but it was hardly a burden to sit on board a boat that doubled as a restaurant called Barca per Gamberi, which translated into English, meant Shrimp Boat. Bria felt the warmth of the sun on her face as she nursed her Hugo Spritz and dipped shrimp into a creamy lemon-garlic sauce. She embraced the carefree attitude that wafted in with the sea breeze, and she felt like she didn't have a care in the world. She was so lost in her mini-vacation from reality that she didn't hear her sister call her name until Lorenza shouted.

"Bria!"

Startled, Bria wrestled herself from her daydream and almost spilled her drink. Luckily, she saved her cocktail from overturning, but when she stood up to embrace her sister, the contents of her purse scattered onto the deck.

"*Uffa!*" Bria cried.

"*Scusami!*" Lorenza said.

"It's my fault," Bria said, bending down to pick up the fallen items. "I was daydreaming."

"Of a life without any murder?" Lorenza asked, kneeling to help her sister to literally clear the deck of debris.

"How do you know about that?" Bria asked. "I told Mamma that I wanted to explain it to you in person."

"Fabrice told me," Lorenza said.

"How did your boyfriend find out?" Bria asked.

"He's Annamaria's cousin," Lorenza said. "She's got the biggest mouth in all of Italy."

"It must run in their family," Bria said. "Fabrice is a *chiacchierone*, he is."

"*Vero*, very true," Lorenza agreed, putting a lipstick and compact back into Bria's purse. "My friend Kayla, who sometimes works on my flights, is from Iowa in the States and calls him a Chatty Cathy. We all call him Chatty Fabrice now. He's flying a new Mediterranean route today, so the news of your dead body could actually reach Athens by this afternoon."

"*Spaventoso!*" Bria cried. "That's all I need. You need to tell your boyfriend to keep his mouth shut."

Lorenza's scream startled Bria as well as the other diners. Bria didn't think her comment was harsh, but her sister was the emotional one in the family and often interpreted innocent comments incorrectly. When Bria saw what Lorenza was holding in her hand, she realized this was not one of those times. She was holding the Polaroid photo of the bloodied scarf.

"I'm sorry. Give that to me," Bria said. "I know that's shocking."

"It isn't shocking. It's familiar," Lorenza said. "I've seen this scarf before."

CHAPTER 9

Little sisters were always full of surprises.

First, Lorenza had told their parents that she didn't want to go to college and instead wanted to travel the world. They'd compromised, and Lorenza had become a flight attendant. Then she'd announced that she hated garlic, which they considered sacrilege. Now she claimed that she recognized the bloodied scarf.

"What do you mean, you've seen this scarf?" Bria asked. "In a store, in a magazine?"

"On a passenger," Lorenza replied.

"You saw someone wearing this?" Bria asked. Maybe it was a woman traveling with the man who got killed. "What did she look like?"

"It wasn't a she. It was a he," Lorenza replied. "I saw a man wearing that scarf."

So much for old-fashioned gender rules when it came to fashion. "A man was wearing this scarf?" Bria asked.

"As an ascot," Lorenza explained. "Which is not something you see on a man under seventy."

"This is really important, Renza. I found this scarf covered in blood half buried in the dirt right outside my front door, which means it's a clue to solving this murder," Bria said. "When did you see this man?"

"Just the other day," Lorenza said. "On a short flight from Milan to Naples."

The waiter arrived at the precise moment Bria threw her arms overhead and shrieked, almost making the man drop his tray on their table. He adeptly avoided colliding with Bria's limbs and placed a Hugo Spritz and a shrimp cocktail in front of Lorenza. He was most likely used to the demonstrative way Italians talked, because he didn't acknowledge the outburst in any way.

"For the woman who thinks garlic is *il diavolo*," the waiter said, placing a sauce cup filled with traditional cocktail sauce in front of Lorenza.

"Garlic *is* the devil," Lorenza replied. "But how did you know about my . . . What does Papa call it?" She turned to Bria, who shrugged her shoulders, either not recalling or refusing to share the memory. Lorenza remembered and turned back to the waiter. "Oh yes, he calls it a betrayal of my heritage."

"Your younger sister ordered for you and informed me of your *peccatuccio*," the waiter explained.

"Did she also tell you to describe her as my *younger* sister?" Lorenza asked.

"Yes, ma'am, she did," the waiter replied without a change to his expression.

"And did she tell you to address me as ma'am?" Lorenza asked.

"Yes, ma'am, that was her final request," the waiter confirmed. "Do you have any other questions, ma'am?"

"No," Lorenza replied. "You can go now and leave me to attend to my infantile sister."

"*Certo*," the waiter replied with a little nod of the head, and then the slightest smile appeared on his face. "Ma'am."

"I'm glad to see that you still have your sense of humor after death literally took a holiday at your B and B," Lorenza said.

"It's the only thing keeping me sane," Bria said. "Now

back to the scarf. Are you sure that you saw this on a man the other day?"

Lorenza took a sip of her Hugo Spritz and savored the crisp, citrusy taste. "Yes, he was about forty-five years old, handsome, but not like Fabrice."

"No one's as handsome as Fabrice," Bria said.

"No one knows that more than Fabrice," Lorenza said. "The man was well dressed, expensive shoes, and wore this scarf as an ascot. I thought it was so peculiar, I asked him about it."

"What did you say?" Bria asked.

"I asked where he got it from," Lorenza replied. "And he smiled, leered almost, and said it was a gift."

"Did you talk about anything else?" Bria asked.

"No, we had turbulence, and I had to calm down some nervous passengers in economy," Lorenza explained. "I didn't get to spend too much time in first class."

Bria placed her forearms on the table and leaned closer to her sister. "Do you know what this means?"

Lorenza leaned in as well, the ends of her long, straight black hair dangling perilously close to her shrimp. "Men's fashion rules are changing?"

"No! That man wearing the ascot could be the man I found dead in my bed," Bria said. Her enthusiasm was quickly replaced with a heavy sigh of frustration. "But there's no way to be sure. It's a coincidence, but not proof."

"I can get proof," Lorenza declared, dipping one of her shrimp into the cocktail sauce and then plopping it into her mouth.

"How?" Bria asked.

"Fabrice," Lorenza replied.

"How can your pilot boyfriend get proof?" Bria asked.

"I'll get him to pull the passenger list, and we can cross-check it against all the passport photos of male travelers to see if the man with the ascot is the same man you found dead in your bed," Lorenza explained, then chuckled. "That sounds a little dirty, doesn't it? The man you found dead in your bed."

"It sounds brilliant!" Bria shrieked; then a look of concern grew on her face. "Will Fabrice do it? It doesn't sound entirely legal."

"I don't think it is completely legal, but Fabrice will do whatever I ask him to," Lorenza said. "He may be movie-star handsome, but he's also well trained."

Bria stood up and leaned over the table. She grabbed her sister's hands and kissed her on both sides of the cheek. "My baby sister, *la mia sorellina* to the rescue!"

Without getting up, Lorenza mimicked taking a regal bow and replied, "As thanks, I'm going to let you pay the bill. Now, where's that waiter? This ma'am is hungry."

On the drive home, Bria called Rosalie and told her that she would return just in time to pick up Marco, so she wouldn't have to babysit. She also filled her in and told her that Lorenza had identified the scarf and soon they might identify the corpse. After she hung up, Bria took off her kerchief and let her hair fly freely in the breeze. She felt more alive than she had in a long time, and it was all thanks to a dead man.

Once they found out the mystery man's name, the investigation would accelerate, and Luca would be able to find out if the man had any enemies, what kind of business he was involved in, if that business was shady, and this nightmare could end. She could get back to the preparations surrounding the opening of Bella Bella, and life could go back to normal. But was that what she wanted?

Despite the fact that a man had died and her employee was being held behind bars, Bria felt more energized than she had in months. She maneuvered the Fiat skillfully around some curves in the road that would have frightened a nonlocal and caused them to hit the brakes, and barely took notice of the cars and motorcycles whizzing by her in the other direction, and contemplated this unanticipated feeling. Where exactly was it coming from?

Her commitment to open Bella Bella was not manufactured; it was real. Yes, part of it was honoring Carlo's memory, but the new life she was about to embark on was her dream, too. If that was true, then why was she getting a rush playing amateur detective? Why was some unknown man's unexpected death making her feel so alive? As she saw Mount Vesuvius in the distance, she found her answer.

The ancient geological predator was to her left as she drove home and took up a huge expanse of land. Gray, imposing, and violent, it was a source of wonder, humility, and fear. Bria didn't feel that she shared any of those qualities, but she did feel connected to the gigantic remnant of nature's past. Something inside both of them had lain dormant for long periods of time, until it couldn't be suppressed any longer. For Mount Vesuvius, it was lava, and in 1944 the volcano erupted for the first time in centuries; for Bria, it was her love of a good mystery, which she had kept at bay since she was in college.

While Bria loved to paint and draw, her mediums of choice being watercolor and charcoal, she also loved delving into the history of art. What made her heart race was finding out the stories behind great works of art. Was Mary Magdalene truly part of the tableau of *The Last Supper?* Who was the real Mona Lisa? And what had prompted Artemisia Gentileschi to defy tradition to become one of Italy's greatest female painters?

Bria had married Carlo right after college and had become a wife and mother in quick succession, roles she treasured and never regretted for a moment. But in exchange she had given up her pursuit of uncovering the mysteries behind some of the world's greatest paintings and even bringing lesser-known works to the forefront by learning about their histories. Even though she had abandoned her passion for digging into the past, the desire to explore the unknown had never left her. With the arrival of a new mystery, almost literally left on her doorstep, she realized that it had been ignited once again. Her strong urge to solve this mystery wasn't solely based on a self-serving desire to clear her business's name; she also wanted to reignite a long dormant desire to seek the truth.

Maybe it was connected to the fact that she was beginning to come out of her mourning period. She would never stop aching for her husband, and she would never not wake up hoping against reality that she would roll over and see Carlo's face staring at her or peacefully dreaming, but she had to keep moving forward, and she had to keep challenging herself and exploring the world. Figuring out the identity of the dead man was a good start. First, she had to pick up her son.

Bria preferred not to drive down the narrow streets due to the traffic, both from pedestrians, scooters, cycles, and other cars, but if she drove home to park and then walked to St. Cecilia's, she would be late. Instead, she pulled up to the school and was greeted by Marco and Sister Benedicta. As always, Marco was delighted to see his mamma, but the sister matched his enthusiasm. She wasn't as excited to see Bria, but her car.

Marco ran to Bria and jumped into her arms before she was fully out of the car.

"Mamma! Mamma!" Marco cried. "I didn't think I'd see you today."

"My appointment finished earlier than I expected," Bria replied, kissing Marco's warm neck. She could smell the salt on his flesh and figured he had been running around with the other boys as they waited to be picked up after school. The collar of his uniform was already stained with sweat, and Bria made a mental note to use extra bleach when she washed his clothes. "I raced home so I could pick you up myself."

"I'm sure you raced right past everyone else on the road in that car," Sister Benedicta said.

Bria had seen the look in the nun's eyes before and suddenly realized that it appeared only when she arrived in the Fiat. Sister Benedicta was a vintage sports car lover!

"It was my husband's car," Bria explained. "He inherited it from his father, and if I take good care of it, Marco will be able to drive it when he passes his test."

"My papa and his brothers were all mechanics, and where I come from in Apulia, no one has the money to buy a new car. Everyone has a relic from the past," Sister Benedicta explained. "I guess we're the same in that way. Old cars remind me of my papa and where I came from, and this car reminds you of your Carlo and his family."

More truth. Bria paused because she had never considered Marco's teacher in any capacity other than a religious figure and an educator, had never viewed her as a real person. *Ignorante*, Bria silently called herself. Just because a person devoted themselves to God and helping others didn't mean they gave up their human qualities. In fact, it was those threads of humanity that made them serve so well. Bria and Sister Benedicta were probably very similar women, despite their obvious differences in terms of wardrobe.

"If you'd ever like to take it for a spin, let me know," Bria said.

Sister Benedicta smiled a nearly naughty smile. "I would have to seek Mother Superior's permission, but I'll contemplate it."

"Whenever you're ready to sit behind the wheel, let me know," Bria said. "*Andiamo*, Marco. We're late."

Marco chattered on ceaselessly during the short drive, and Bria marveled at his energy and thrilled that he was still at the age where he willingly conversed with his mamma. She knew in a few years that his eagerness might transform into a more evasive attitude.

"Mamma," Marco said. "When is that store going to open?"

Bria looked to the right, where Marco was pointing, and saw that he was asking about the wine and cheese store that still looked the same as it did months ago, when it was bought by some out-of-town businessman. The blinds on the windows were still drawn, no light emanated from inside, and even the flowers and bushes in the front looked like they were dying from neglect. She was as curious as Marco.

"I don't know, *mi topolino*," Bria said.

Marco laughed. "I'm not a mouse."

"You're my little mouse," Bria said. "Marco, *il topolino*. Do you want some cheese?"

"No, but Bravo loves cheese," Marco said. "I'm waiting for the store to open so I can buy him some."

"He does love his mozzarella," Bria said. "We can pick some up at the market until the store opens."

"I think he's having some right now," Marco said as the car pulled in front of Bella Bella.

Bria turned away from her son and looked straight ahead to see Enrico feeding Bravo something out of his hand that looked distinctly like strips of mozzarella cheese. Bria turned to pull into the small space next to the house that served as a makeshift parking spot when she didn't feel like parking the car in Paolo's lot. Before she turned off the ignition, Marco had already jumped out of the car.

"Marco!" Bria cried, following him to the front door. "How many times do I have to tell you not to do that? You might hurt yourself."

"I haven't hurt myself yet," Marco replied.

"Can't argue with logic like that," Enrico said.

"My logical son is going to break his arm one of these days," Bria replied.

"I stopped by to bring you some fresh mozzarella," Enrico said. "But Bravo was guarding the place and wouldn't let me pass until I gave him a taste."

"I was just telling Mamma that Bravo loves mozzarella," Marco said. "So do I."

"Would you like some?" Enrico asked.

"Mamma!" Marco cried.

But Bria didn't answer.

"Mamma, may I have some?"

Bria didn't hear her son, because she was too focused on the text Lorenza had just sent. The simple message read, **Here's your dead man**, and it was followed up with a passport photo. The man in the picture looked exactly like the corpse she had found in her bed except that the eyes in the photo were open and not closed. When this photo was taken, the man had been alive; now he was lying on a cold metal slab in the morgue.

Bria still didn't know the reason why he had been killed, but at least she now knew who he was. The man who had taken his last breath in Bria's B and B was a forty-seven-year-old resident of Milan named Vittorio Ingleterra.

CHAPTER 10

Bria had lived in Positano almost a year and had never had a reason to enter the police station until now. By the look on Nunzi's face, Bria should have waited a bit longer to visit.

"What are you doing here?" Nunzi asked.

"*Prego*, I have to see Luca," Bria replied. "I have information on our case."

"*Our* case?" Nunzi asked.

"Yes," Bria said and then lowered her voice so the rest of the men and women in the station wouldn't overhear. "You know, the dead man that I found."

Nunzi stared at Bria, but the cop didn't say a word. Just when Bria was going to ask her if there was a problem, Nunzi turned to her left, to where Luca was suddenly standing, and tilted her head toward Bria. Rosalie was right. Nunzi really was the strong, silent type. Before Bria could advise Luca that his team should brush up on their verbal communication skills, another strong, silent type was ushered into the room.

"Vanni!" Bria cried. "*Grazie Dio*! Are you all right?"

Giovanni nodded. Bria couldn't tell from his blank expression what he was really feeling, but she could see by the bags under his green eyes and the more-than-usual rough sandy stubble on his cheeks and chin that he hadn't been able to shower or freshen up since he'd been dragged into the station. How could anyone be all right after that?

The cop who had led Giovanni into the room gave him a little shove toward the front desk. Giovanni's lips pressed together tightly, and he let out a long breath through his nose. His hands were rolled into two fists at his sides, and his shoulders were slightly hunched. He looked like he was about to explode.

Bria turned to face Luca and watched him whisper something to Nunzi, an order most likely. He looked composed and every inch the man in charge. She imagined that the combination of his crisp uniform, his square jaw, and his slightly upturned chin would intimidate most people; she was not one of them.

"Luca, you better tell me that you're releasing Giovanni," Bria said.

"We are," Luca replied.

"And you better tell me that you aren't pressing any ridiculous charges against him," she added.

"We aren't," Luca confirmed. "Giovanni has been more than helpful and has answered all our questions to the best of his knowledge. He's free to go."

"I can't believe you held him here for three nights for absolutely no reason," Bria said, trying hard to keep her voice calm.

"You may not have liked it, Bria, but we had every right to detain Giovanni," Nunzi said, without raising her eyes from the paperwork she was sorting.

"*Senza senso!*" Bria shouted. "He told you he had nothing to do with Vittorio's murder, and yet you refused to believe him!"

When every head in the station, including Giovanni's, snapped to face Bria and stared at her with expressions of shock and confusion, she knew had said something wrong. But what? All she had done was tell the truth. Giovanni couldn't possibly know anything about Vittorio's murder. *Oh cavolo!* She had said the V word.

"Come into my office," Luca said. *"Per favore."*

Bria could tell by the tone of his voice that the *per favore* was essentially meaningless and his request was a command. As Bria started to walk into Luca's office, the chief turned to Giovanni and added, "Both of you."

Bria didn't turn around, but a chill ran down her spine when she heard the door slam shut. She felt the strong desire to shout, "Mussolini!" but didn't think Rosalie would hear her shout their safeword down at the marina.

Luca's heels clicked on the hardwood floor as he walked from the door to his desk. As much as she wanted to speak, Bria remained quiet in order to give Luca time to calm down. It also gave her time to relax and realize she hadn't done anything wrong. She wasn't hiding evidence; in fact, she had just found out the identity of the dead man and was here to share it with the police. Once she explained the timeline of the events to Luca, he would understand.

She sat down next to Giovanni in one of the two black leather club chairs facing Luca's desk and glanced over to him. He was looking at her as curiously as everyone else had been. He wanted to know how Bria knew the dead man's name as much as Luca did. So much for the employee/employer bond.

"I can explain," Bria said.

Luca sat down and replied, "The stage is all yours."

"*Grazie.* It's really very simple," Bria began. "It's all thanks to the bloody scarf I found next to my front door."

Mucca sacra! She did it again.

"What bloody scarf?" Luca yelled.

No doubt about it, Bria was *una grossa, grassa bugiarda.* How could she have forgotten about the scarf? Neither she nor Rosalie had meant to keep that from the police. They just hadn't had the time to inform them, as things had been progressing so quickly. In the eyes of Luca—and the rest of the police force, once he told them—that wouldn't matter. Bria would indeed be known as a big, fat liar.

"Answer me, Bria!" Luca yelled again. "What's this about a bloody scarf?"

Bria opened her mouth to speak, but Luca topped off his shouting by slamming his palm onto his desk, causing Bria to flinch. She composed herself and opened her mouth once more, but before her lips could form words, there was a knock on the door. The door opened to reveal Nunzi sporting a very concerned expression.

"*Tutto a posto, Capo*?" she asked.

"Yes, everything's fine," Luca replied, sighing heavily. "Why don't you join us, Nunzi, and close the door behind you."

Nunzi followed her boss's orders, then made a strategic move and picked up the only remaining chair in the room, an armless wooden side chair with a simple gray leather seat and carried it from the door to the other side of the desk. When she sat down on Luca's left, she had cleverly staged an "us vs. them" design. Luca and Nunzi on the side of the law, and Bria and Giovanni on the opposite, unlawful side.

"Bria, I suggest you tell us everything you know, and don't leave anything out this time," Luca said.

She stole a quick glance over at Giovanni, hoping to get some moral support, but the way he was looking at her made her feel even more anxious. Vanni might be sitting right next to her, but she felt that he'd rather be sharing a chair with Luca. Knowing how he felt about the chief of police convinced her she was on her own. She decided to stick to the facts of the story, like she did whenever she had to explain something complicated to Marco.

"Rosalie and I tried to reenact the crime to see if we could determine where the man was killed," Bria started. "Rosalie wanted some water, but I said no, because we were running out of time, so I pulled her arm and fell into the bushes. You know, the ones next to my front door?"

She looked from one expressionless face to the other and realized she sounded just like her son when he would go off on tangents instead of sharing data. "*Scusate*," she said. "I found a bloody scarf that someone had tried to bury in the dirt. We thought the killer had tried to hide it, but then I realized Bravo must have found it outside and buried it, like he does with things that he finds."

"What did you do with the scarf?" Luca asked.

"I took a photo of it," Bria replied.

"Are you creating a photo album of stolen police evidence?" Nunzi asked.

"Of course not!" Bria said. "I was going to bring it to you here. I just wanted to take a photo of it because I didn't want to rely on my memory to remember what it looked like. That's the same reason I took a photo of Vittorio's face."

This time Bria knew she had said the wrong thing well before Luca screamed.

"You took a photo of the corpse! Give me your phone," Luca ordered.

"Why do you want my phone?" Bria asked.

"To delete the photos that you took," Luca said. "I can't have you snapping photos at a crime scene."

"I didn't use my phone to take the photos," Bria said.

"Then whose phone did you use?" Nunzi asked.

"I didn't use anyone's phone," Bria replied.

"Then how did you take the photos?" Luca asked.

"I used Carlo's Polaroid camera," Bria explained.

While Luca and Nunzi looked stunned at the comment, she could see Giovanni smiling out of the corner of her eye. He looked down at the floor and shook his head, but the smile never left his face. She didn't have the time to ask him what he thought was so funny. That would have to wait. Most impor-

tant was making sure that Luca and Nunzi understood she had
taken the photos to cooperate, not to interfere.

"I put the photos in my purse yesterday and forgot about
them, honestly," she said. "Then I had to drive to Rome this
morning to meet Imperia." She turned to Nunzi and added,
"She's my mother-in-law."

"I know who Imperia Bartolucci is," Nunzi said.

"Really?" Bria asked. "How do you know her—"

"Continue your story please," Luca interrupted.

"After I met with Imperia to sign some documents for
Marco, I met my sister, Lorenza, for lunch," Bria said. She
turned to Nunzi and added, "Do you know her, too? Lorenza
D'Abruzzo?"

"No, I do not know Lorenza D'Abruzzo," Nunzi replied.
"Now please do as the chief says and finish your story."

"Of course," Bria replied. "Lorenza knocked my purse over.
She's *una ragazza goffa* that one, always knocking things over
and spilling things. Anyway, everything in my purse fell out,
and she saw the photo of the bloody scarf and recognized it.
She said she saw it on a passenger on a trip from Milan just the
other day." Again, she turned to Nunzi to make sure she had
enough information to keep up with her story. "Renza's a flight
attendant, and her boyfriend, Fabrice, is a pilot."

"I don't care about her boyfriend," Nunzi said.

"You will," Bria replied. "He's the reason we know the murdered man's name."

Tension filled the silent air after Bria spoke. She became
aware of it and wasn't sure if she should continue speaking,
but Giovanni turned to her and nodded his head, long strands
of wavy blond hair dangling in his face. She took it as a sign
that she should continue.

"Lorenza asked Fabrice to pull the passenger list and cross-
check all the men's names to their passport photos," Bria ex-

plained. "He did that because he does anything Renza tells him to do, and she recognized the man who had worn the scarf as an ascot, of all things, which is weird in this day and age, don't you think?"

She paused, but when no one responded, she continued. "Okay, well, then, Lorenza texted me his passport photo." Then she squealed in delight. "Which I have on my phone!"

Bria took out her phone, found the text, and touched the photo so it enlarged to fill up the screen. She placed her phone down on Luca's desk triumphantly. "That's how I know the man who was murdered is Vittorio Ingleterra!"

Luca picked up her phone and typed in some information. Seconds later she heard a ping, and both Luca and Nunzi picked up their phones to see Vittorio's passport photo show up on their screens. Nunzi rose and headed for the door before Luca could speak.

"Run his name through the database and get me everything you can find," Luca said.

Nunzi simply nodded and left the room, closing the door behind her. Luca picked up his phone and turned it to Giovanni so he could see Vittorio's face.

"If you know this man, you should speak now," Luca said. "If we find out later that you lied to us, it won't be good."

Involuntarily, Bria held her breath as she watched Giovanni look at the phone. She was psychically willing him not to recognize the face, because she understood that no matter how much you trusted someone, there was always a small chance that trust would be betrayed. She prayed this would not be one of those times. When Giovanni spoke, her prayers had been answered.

"I've never seen him before in my life," Giovanni said.

"You're sure?" Luca said.

"*Sì, assolutamente*," Giovanni replied.

His voice was soft and rough, a bit gravelly, like it always was, but Bria could hear something else in his tone, something he was trying to conceal. She wasn't sure if it was anger, fear, or a combination of the two, but the sound of it made her feel guilty. He had not been treated fairly, and it was because of her.

"Luca, please let Giovanni go," Bria said. "I know that you're only doing your job, but he's done nothing wrong. You have to stop treating him like a criminal and find out who really did this."

When Luca gazed over at Bria, she thought he looked much more like Rosalie's older brother than the chief of police. His eyes looked kind, and he nodded his head. "You're free to go, Giovanni," Luca said. "We thank you for your cooperation."

Giovanni responded, not to Luca, but to Bria. "Would you like me to wait for you outside? I could walk you home."

"*Grazie*, Vanni," Bria said. "But I don't want to keep you any longer than necessary. I'll see you bright and early tomorrow morning."

Finally, Giovanni smiled. Wide and grateful. "Yes, you will."

No other words were spoken until he had left the room, and when Bria and Luca were alone, the exchange was between old friends, not new enemies.

"Bria," Luca said, "if you want us to find who did this, you can't keep evidence from us."

"I swear to you, Luca, on my grandparents' souls," Bria declared, "I wasn't trying to keep evidence. I'm just not used to playing amateur detective."

"Then leave the police work to the professionals," Luca said.

"I can't!" Bria protested. "Not when my reputation is on the line, as well as the future of Bella Bella."

Luca exhaled a deep breath very slowly. "Where's the scarf?"

"It's home," Bria replied. "I'm sorry. I'll bring it in first thing in the morning, when I walk Marco to school."

"Kids have school on Saturday now?" Nunzi asked.

"They have to make up for some of the days they lost when the school was closed during the torrential rainstorms we had back in February," Bria explained. "I'll drop Marco off and come here and drop off the scarf."

Luca leaned forward and stared right at Bria. "We have to work together, people like us."

Did her passionate rebuttal land her on the police force now?

"What do you mean?" Bria asked. "People like us."

"*Chi ha e chi non ha,*" Luca said.

Bria laughed because it was exactly what Carlo used to say about Positano: it was the haves and the have-nots. A lot of beautiful, wealthy people came to the village for fun and escape, but the locals, the people who made the village what it was, they were different. To them, Positano wasn't a place to visit and leave behind; it was the place where they lived, and they all had to stick together.

On her walk home, Bria thought about what Luca had said, and he was right. People came from all over the world to Positano to grab some joy from this exquisite place. If the local villagers didn't band together, there wouldn't be any joy left for them.

She picked up a loaf of bread and a large piece of branzino. She remembered that she had some broccoli rabe and carrots at home, and she could serve the fish over a bed of rice. That would make for a healthy, quick meal after a long day. The day got longer when she saw Paloma closing up her shop.

"I didn't know you sold scarves," Bria said.

Startled, Paloma turned around, holding some pillows she was going to bring inside the store. "They actually sell themselves. I usually run out of my whole stock in a day," Paloma said. "Women love them because you can wear them in so many different ways. As a kerchief, as a belt, around your neck.

I kept one for myself, in orange, my favorite color, to wear if I can't dry my hair after I go swimming."

"You're still doing that?" Bria asked. "You know, my mother was a swimming champion when she was in school."

"Yes, you told me," Paloma said. "Remember I told you that your mother and I should compare trophies. I won many when I was younger."

Bria looked at the scarves that now hung from hooks on the wall, and while they were all beautiful, none of them looked like the scarf she had found. However, they were silk, and they did appear to possess the same luxurious quality. If she wanted to be an amateur sleuth, she might as well start sleuthing.

She shifted the bag she was carrying and then balanced it on her left hip as she dug into her purse to find one of the Polaroid photos, which she hadn't admitted to having in her possession. No one had asked if she had the Polaroids, so it was only a lie of omission. She'd say an extra Hail Mary at confession to make up for it just in case.

Bria held up the Polaroid in front of Paloma, and before she could warn her friend about the blood, Paloma gasped and tears filled her eyes. The scarf was bloody, sure, but enough to make a grown woman cry? Bria looked at the Polaroid and realized she hadn't shown Paloma the photo of the scarf but of the corpse.

"*Dio mio!*" Bria said. "That's the wrong photo. Forget that you saw it."

"Was that the dead man?" Paloma asked, wiping her eyes.

"Yes, I'm so sorry," Bria said. "I didn't mean to shock you, but now this photo won't scare you at all, despite the blood."

Bria looked at the Polaroid of the scarf before showing it to Paloma to make sure she hadn't made the same mistake twice.

"Was that found on the dead body?" Paloma asked.

"It was found nearby," Bria replied. "He must have dropped it."

"*Madonna mia*!" Paloma said. "That's an awful lot of blood."

Bria turned the photo around to look at it. "I guess I'm getting used to it."

"I could never," Paloma said. "I hate the sight of blood. I run the other way whenever I see it."

"Did a man buy a scarf like this from you?"

"No," Paloma answered.

"What am I thinking?" Bria said, more to herself than to Paloma. "That would be too much of a coincidence."

"But not impossible," Paloma said.

"What do you mean?" Bria replied.

"I have sold a scarf like that," Paloma said.

"You have?" Bria cried. "This exact design?"

"Yes," Paloma replied. "But not to a man. To a woman."

"*Davvero*?" Bria asked. "You really sold this exact scarf to someone?"

"Not just one, but two," Paloma said. "I remember because I only had two of that pattern left. It's very popular . . . I think because the gold links are like Chanel."

"That's what Rosalie said."

"This woman bought the last two."

"In case she lost or ruined one," Bria said. "That's very smart."

"No, she wanted one for her and one for *il suo drudo*," Paloma explained.

"Her paramour?" Bria asked. "That's an odd way to explain a boyfriend."

"I thought so, too, which is why I remember it," Paloma said.

"Could you describe the woman?" Bria asked.

Paloma stopped for a moment and closed her eyes, presumably trying to conjure up an image of the customer, but after a few moments she opened them and shook her head. "She wore a big hat and sunglasses, so I couldn't really see her face. She could've been thirty, or she could've been sixty. I'm sorry I can't be any more help."

"Are you *pazza*?" Bria shrieked. "You've been a great help! Now we just have to find the woman who bought this scarf."

"Why do you care who bought it?" Paloma asked.

"Because whoever bought this scarf could very well be the murderer."

CHAPTER 11

Bria remembered what Sister Caterina had told her before she received her first Holy Communion: "*Più risposte portano sempre a più domande.*" And the nun had been right. Whether exploring religion or investigating a murder, more answers always led to more questions.

Bria took Marco to school and brought the scarf to Luca at the police station like she had promised. When she got home, she made herself an espresso and went over the few facts that she had collected. She now knew the name of the man who had taken his last breath under her roof—Vittorio Ingleterra. She knew Vittorio was from Milan and that he liked wearing classic accessories. She also knew that he was some unknown woman's lover. An unknown woman who had bought them matching scarves. But why? Did she want them to be linked when they weren't together? Did she feel the man was a part of her, a yin to her yang, and the scarves were symbolic? Or was she trying to buy his love?

An older man often secured his relationship with a younger woman by buying her expensive gifts. Perhaps this was the reverse situation: Vittorio was the younger man an older woman was bribing. Paloma had said the woman who bought the scarves was wearing a big hat and sunglasses, not uncommon in Positano, where the sun rarely was hidden by clouds, but it was also a tactic of an aging woman to ward off wrinkles. Bria took a sip of her espresso and gazed out at the mountain peaks and clouds from her backyard hideaway, a self-satisfactory smile on her lips. She had no idea who the scarf-buying woman was, but she had a strong suspicion that the woman was close to sixty years old, if not older.

Bria finished the rest of her espresso and went into the kitchen to make another cup when she saw Giovanni at the dining room table, his hair not pulled back, like he typically wore it, but hanging loose around his face. He was leaning forward, staring intently at his laptop.

She glanced at her watch and saw that it was only quarter past eight. Giovanni didn't start his day until 9:00 a.m., and Bria had assumed that after spending several nights in jail, he'd want to sleep in his own bed for as long as possible. While she was delighted to see that he wasn't avoiding her, she was curious to know why he was early and what was commanding his focus.

"*Buongiorno*, Giovanni," Bria said.

Startled, Giovanni finally looked up. "Bria, *buongiorno*."

"I didn't hear you come in," Bria said.

"I didn't want to wake anyone up on a Saturday," Giovanni explained.

"A Saturday is like any other day," Bria replied. "I've already dropped Marco off at school and I'm about to have my second espresso. Would you like one?"

"*Prego*, please," Giovanni said. "Then I want to show you what I found out about our mystery man."

"Vittorio?"

"Who else?"

Bria's eyes lit up. "The espresso can wait!"

She sat down next to Giovanni and was about to tell him to start sharing the information he had uncovered when she noticed a plate of croissants next to the laptop.

"Where did these come from?" Bria asked.

"I got up early and baked them this morning," Giovanni replied. "I wanted to try out a recipe and see if you might want to include it on the menu."

You got up early? Bria thought. *Madonna mia, Giovanni, after spending a few nights in jail, I would think you'd want to sleep in for days and not get up and bake.*

Bria took a bite of the croissant, then another, and closed her eyes in culinary ecstasy. *"Delizioso."*

Giovanni blushed and tucked a wayward curl behind his ear. "I'm glad you like it."

"I don't like it. I love it!" Bria squealed. "I would have never thought to make a citrus croissant."

"I sprinkled the dough with lemon and orange juice," Vanni explained. "Tart, but fresh."

"Vanni! You can unclog gutters, you can repair a dishwasher, you can even hang curtains, and now this!" Bria exclaimed. "Is there anything you can't do?"

"Plenty," Giovanni replied with a bittersweet grin. "Just ask my father."

Normally, Bria would have wanted to know more about Giovanni's relationship with his father, but she could sense he wasn't in the mood for introspective conversation. Bria not so subtly switched gears to safer territory. "Tell me what you found out about the murder victim."

"Quite a bit, actually."

Giovanni moved the laptop between them so that Bria could see the website for Dolce Vita Real Estate. The name of the company was written in beautiful black script, and the photo depicted an Italian villa in the countryside. Giovanni's fingers flitted over the keyboard again, and the lush landscape was replaced with Vittorio's photo.

"That's our dead man!" Bria exclaimed.

"And his bio," Giovanni replied, scrolling down a bit so Vittorio's photo was almost out of the screen's frame and replaced with one small paragraph of text.

Bria quickly read the bio and was confused. Giovanni couldn't possibly have learned a lot about the man from the four sentences Bria had just read. All she gleaned from the bio was that Vittorio specialized in selling private dwellings and vacation homes, he worked out of the Milan office, and was born in Frascati, outside Rome. According to the final bit of info in the bio Vittorio had been a certified real estate broker for the past twelve years. Doing quick math, Bria determined he'd become a Realtor when he was thirty-five.

"Vanni," Bria said. "Did you find out what he did before becoming a Realtor?"

"No," he replied. "His LinkedIn profile lists Dolce Vita as his one and only job."

"*Molto strano*, especially for a forty-seven-year-old man," Bria said.

"Maybe there was a gap in his work history," Giovanni suggested. "He could have been taking care of a sick parent or child."

"He could have been traveling, going to school . . ."

"Or he could be independently wealthy," Giovanni added.

"What makes you say that?" Bria said.

"This," Giovanni replied.

He typed on the keyboard, and once again, the screen changed. This time Vittorio's Pinterest page appeared, and it was filled with photos of magnificent homes in Italy and all throughout the world, followed by countless images of high-end luxury items. An original Patek Philippe watch was followed by a mid-century Egg Chair, and there was one whole subfolder dedicated to vintage Hermès scarves.

"This is the only social media he used," Giovanni explained. "And it's all about luxury items and lavish homes."

"Now I understand why he was wearing his scarf as an

ascot," Bria said. "He had expensive taste and cherished items that had old-world appeal."

"It also suggests that he may have had something to hide," Giovanni said.

"What do you mean?"

"According to his Pinterest account, he liked flashy things, and a huge aspect of his job was networking and marketing," Giovanni explained. "Why wouldn't he have posted photos of all the houses he sold or was trying to sell on as many sites as possible to reach as many buyers as possible?"

Bria thought it over and realized Giovanni was right. Either Vittorio was really good at his job and didn't need any more exposure or he was really bad at this job and didn't know how to leverage the widest market of potential buyers. She shared her thoughts with Giovanni, and he said his instinct was that Vittorio wasn't successful, but there was no way to prove that just yet. When Bria's phone rang and she saw that she was getting a FaceTime call from Fabrice, her heart beat a bit faster. Maybe Lorenza's boyfriend had found out some information about Vittorio that could be used to prove Giovanni's theory.

"*Ciao*, Fabrice," Bria said.

"*Ciao*, Bria Bria," Fabrice replied.

Ever since she had told her family—and as Lorenza's boyfriend for the past five years, the handsome Fabrice Belragasso (whose last name literally meant "Pretty Boy" in English) was considered a part of the D'Abruzzo family—that the name of the B and B was Bella Bella, Fabrice had always referred to Bria as Bria Bria. Lorenza had said it was a dad joke, which had made their parents almost pass out, thinking the comment was a creative way to announce that Lorenza was pregnant and Fabrice would soon be a dad. Turned out it was just a joke, even though no one but Lorenza had laughed at the time. Bria found Fabrice's nickname for her to be a sweet endearment and one that always made her smile. Even when she had nothing but murder on her mind.

"Did you find out more about Vittorio?" Bria asked.

Fabrice's violet eyes sparkled with excitement. "Yes! For a man who doesn't work in the airline industry, he travels almost as much as I do. I mean *traveled*, *scusami*. There's no more travel in Vittorio's future. Vittorio doesn't even have a future, now that he's dead. Well, murdered, which seems almost more permanent than dead, which isn't really possible, but you know what I mean, don't you, Bria Bria?"

After five years of listening to Fabrice ramble, Bria had learned how to follow what she and Lorenza affectionately called "Fabrice speak." Whereas Carlo had always liked to be direct and straightforward when he spoke, Fabrice preferred to speak in curlicues and tangents. They got to the same end result, but Fabrice arrived several minutes later.

"I do know what you mean, Fabrice," Bria said, smiling at a very amused Giovanni. "How did you find out that Vittorio was a frequent flyer?"

"I pulled the passenger lists for the past six months and cross-referenced them with Vittorio's name," Fabrice explained. "Ingleterra is a very common name, did you know that? I didn't. I had never heard of it before, but I found four other Ingleterras who flew in the same time period. Rocco, Mauro, Silvia, and Yee Han, who interestingly isn't from China or Italy, but Sweden. Isn't that *pazzo*? Would you have ever guessed Sweden, Bria Bria?"

"No, Fabrice, I would not," Bria replied. "Finland maybe."

"Finland?" Fabrice questioned, then realized his girlfriend wasn't the only jokester in the D'Abruzzo family. "Bria Bria is trying to be funny funny!"

I'm trying to find out about Vittorio, but you're not making it easy.

"Can we get back to the dead man?" Bria asked.

"*Sì, certo*," Fabrice said, getting back on track. "Vittorio took eleven trips in six months, and that's just with my airline. He flew to Naples four times, took three trips to Rome, one trip to Venice, and three trips to Sarno."

Bria looked at Giovanni, and they both had the same expression of disbelief.

"Sarno?" Bria asked.

"That's such a small town," Giovanni replied. "Not a business center, like the other cities."

"Is that Giovanni?" Fabrice asked. "I thought he was still in jail."

Bria turned her phone so Giovanni could talk directly to Fabrice. The men were barely acquaintances, but thanks to Fabrice's gregarious nature, he greeted Giovanni like they were best friends.

"I got sprung last night," Giovanni replied.

"*Eccellente*!" Fabrice cried. "I told Lorenza that Luca was *pazzo* to arrest you, just crazy in the head. I mean, I've heard that you've done some things, Giovanni, that could have landed you in jail before, but I mean, who hasn't? There was this one time years ago, when I had just started flying solo, I met this woman . . . Oh, don't worry, Bria Bria. It was before I met Lorenza."

"I'm sure it was, Fabrice," Bria said. "And I'm sure it is a wildly entertaining story, but my phone battery is going to die soon, so could you get back to Sarno?"

"*Certo, certo*," Fabrice said. "Sarno, small town, nothing much going on there, in the southeast of the country, and all three of his trips there were quick ones. He returned to Milan either that night or early the next morning."

"Maybe that's a clue," Bria said.

"It could be, but I'll leave that for you two to figure out," Fabrice said. "I have to go now, Bria Bria. Your sister is waiting for me, and we both know how angry she gets if I'm late."

"Thank you so much for this information, Fabrice," Bria said. "You've been so helpful."

"My pleasure," Fabrice said. "*Ciao* to you, *mi amore*, and *ciao* to you, too, Giovanni. PS Stay out of jail!"

Bria ended the connection before he could say anything further. Giovanni appeared to be amused by Fabrice, but there was only so much jail talk that a recent guest of a jail cell could take. Such guests didn't like to be reminded of what had led them to be incarcerated, even if it was only for a few days. And they definitely didn't like the police showing up at the door unexpectedly.

"Nunzi!" Bria cried. "What are you doing here? And why aren't you in uniform?"

Nunzi stood outside the screen door, looking much less intimidating in a yellow V-neck T-shirt, khaki pants, and the most unattractive sandals Bria had ever seen in her life. Had ugly and unfashionable decided to have an open-toe baby, the result would have been more visually appealing. Bria forced herself to remain quiet about Nunzi's footwear and focused on the Tupperware container she was holding.

"What do you have there?" Bria asked.

"A peace offering," Nunzi replied.

Bria turned to Giovanni, and she could tell from his body language—straight back and clenched fists pressing firmly on the dining room table—that he wasn't in the mood to be on the receiving end of any offering from the police, no matter whether the messenger was in uniform or not.

"I'm going to put up those blinds in the upstairs bedroom," Giovanni said.

He quickly went upstairs, taking the steps two at a time, as Bria walked to the front door, unlocked the screen, and let Nunzi in.

"I didn't think Giovanni would be here," Nunzi said. "Which is stupid on my part, because he works here."

"Don't worry about it," Bria said. "He was helping me do some research, but we do have work for the opening that needs to get done."

"I brought you my famous *ribollita* soup," she said, handing the Tupperware container to Bria. "I always make too much, and Primavera, my cat, doesn't care for beans and vegetables, so I thought you might like some."

"*Grazie*! That's very thoughtful of you, Nunzi. Thank you," Bria said, placing the container on the dining table.

"Because I've been thoughtless," Nunzi replied. "Luca often has to remind me that I'm not what can be considered a 'people person,' and with you and Rosalie, I was a *donna male-ducata*."

"You were hardly a rude woman," Bria said. "You were doing your job and dealing with a meddling citizen."

"A citizen who is continuing to meddle," Nunzi said, glancing over at the computer screen. "I see you've been doing some research into Vittorio, as well."

"Yes," Bria said. "We also found out that he'd been doing quite a bit of traveling the past six months. Rome, Venice, Sarno."

"We found that out, as well," Nunzi said. "I'm not going to ask how you know, but have you made any connections yet? Or figured out why he'd been making those trips?"

"I assume it all has to do with his real estate business," Bria said.

"We're trying to find out if he was selling properties in those cities," Nunzi said. "Luca is going to take a trip to see the owner of Dolce Vita Real Estate tomorrow because they haven't been as helpful as we'd like."

"Maybe he'll find out what Vittorio had been doing and why he was in Positano," Bria said.

"That's what we're hoping," Nunzi said.

Bria took a good look at Nunzi and thought she was far less

threatening out of uniform. She was the type of woman who didn't rely on make-up to enhance her features and wore clothes that were utilitarian, not fashionable. The women were not alike on the surface, but Bria sensed Nunzi's brusque attitude was armor. It couldn't be easy being a female cop in Italy, even if the members of the Positano carabinieri weren't oozing with toxic machismo.

"Can I make you some coffee?" Bria asked.

"*No, grazie*," Nunzi replied. "I have to get back to Primavera. Unlike me, she is a people person, and she gets very upset when she doesn't have company, especially when she knows I have the day off."

"Thank you again for the soup," Bria said. "You saved me from having to make dinner tonight."

Bria's phone rang again, and the screen indicated that another FaceTime call was coming through, this time from Imperia.

"Could you save me from my mother-in-law?" Bria asked.

"I'm sorry, but you're on your own there," Nunzi said. "Imperia frightens me, and I carry a firearm."

Bria was grateful for the disclosure, because to her Imperia always looked upset—except, of course, when she was with Marco. She said good-bye to Nunzi, sighed heavily, forced herself to smile, and answered the phone.

"*Ciao*, Imperia," Bria said. "How are you?"

"Not good," Imperia replied.

Translating Imperia's two-word response, Bria understood that it meant she had done something to ruin Imperia's day.

"What did I do this time?" Bria asked.

"Nothing," Imperia replied. "Which I know must come as much of a surprise to you, as it did to me. I'm the culprit this time. I'm the cause of my problem."

More disclosure? From Imperia? About something that she did wrong? Bria fought the urge to run to the window to see if the sky had fallen.

"What's going on?" Bria asked.

"I have to go out of town again unexpectedly. I'm leaving at nine in the morning, so I won't be able to visit Marco tomorrow, like I said I would."

Is that all? Bria thought.

That was fine with Bria, though she knew Marco enjoyed spending time with his nonna and Imperia truly loved being with Marco.

"What time will you get back?" Bria asked. "You could come in the evening if you can't get here earlier."

"I have a lunch meeting that I fear will go on forever," Imperia stated. "My associate and I have much to discuss."

"Marco will be disappointed, but he'll understand," Bria said.

"Tell my angel that Nonna will make it up to him," Imperia said. "I can see him next weekend."

"That'll be fine. We'll be here," Bria said. "Where do you have to go?"

"A little town that you probably never even heard of," Imperia said. "Sarno."

Sarno!

The moment the call with Imperia ended, Bria called Rosalie.

"Rosalie!" Bria shouted into the phone. "Cancel all your plans for tomorrow. We're going to Sarno."

"*Come mai?*" Rosalie asked. "There's nothing in Sarno."

"Oh yes there is," Bria said.

"What?"

"Our next clue."

Chapter 12

At 7:00 a.m. the following morning, Bria was in full-on working mother mode. Her movements and her vocabulary were efficient, controlled, and minimal. She had already showered, taken Bravo out for his walk, pulled the Fiat from the lot and parked it in front of the house for easy access, woken Marco, answered his questions about the solar system (which he was currently studying), and made sure he brushed his teeth and got dressed for church. While he ate his oatmeal with strawberries and Nutella, Bria focused her attention on the other man around the house.

Since she didn't know how long she was going to be away, she made a list of all the things Giovanni needed to take care of, including a reminder to take Marco to church, drop him off at his Bible study group, and then pick him up again to take him to soccer practice. Another reason Bria had hired Giovanni was that he was a man, and she had felt it would be good for Marco to have a male influence around the house. Luckily, the two got along incredibly well, and Marco brought out Giovanni's playful side, which he usually hid from others. It was still a mystery to her why everyone acted as if Giovanni was the village pariah, but she had known him only for a short period of time. *People have pasts*, she reminded herself, *and reputations cling to a person long after they no longer fit*. She also believed that people changed, and no matter what secrets there were in Vanni's past, Bria felt that he had changed for the better. If she didn't, she would never leave her son in his care.

"Do you think Vanni will show us how to do the Rivelino?" Marco asked.

Bria thought what Marco said sounded Italian, but she had no idea what it was.

"Is that a new dance move?" Bria asked.

"No, it's a soccer move," Marco replied, laughing. "None of us can do it right and Vanni is better at soccer than Signor Malagusto."

"If you ask Vanni nicely, I'm sure he'll show you boys how to do the Rolevino thing."

"Rivelino," Marco corrected.

"*Qualunque cosa*," Bria said. "Just don't tell Signor Malagusto that Vanni is better than he is. Coaches don't like to hear things like that. And remember Vanni has a lot of work to do today even though it's a Sunday."

"That's okay," Marco replied. "I know his boss and she won't mind if he goofs off for an hour."

"Really?" Bria said, trying not to laugh. "I hear his boss can be one tough cookie."

"Nah, she's a softie," Marco said. "Especially around Vanni."

Bria was startled by Marco's comment and wasn't entirely sure what he meant by it. She didn't get a chance to further contemplate its implications, because she had to iron out a wrinkle in her meticulously plotted plan. Before she could move forward with spying on her mother-in-law, she had to deal with the unexpected arrival of her mother.

"Nonna Fifi!" Marco squealed. "What are you doing here?"

"Yes, Mamma," Bria said. "What are you doing here? Unexpectedly. Again."

"I will answer your questions on one condition," Fifetta said.

"What's that?" Bria asked.

"That I get a big hug from my grandson," she replied.

Marco ran to Fifetta and threw his arms around her. Fifetta accepted his embrace with a joyful smile, and for a moment Bria forgot that she was on a strict timetable and relished the undeniable display of the unconditional love that her mother and her son shared for each other. She felt the same way about her mother, and on any other day she would have welcomed the impromptu visit. Today was about a different type of family reunion, and Fifetta was definitely not invited.

"Now I feel better," Fifetta said, releasing her hold on Marco. "Every time I see you, *angioletto*, you're bigger than before."

"That's because I'm a growing boy," Marco said. "Right, Mamma?"

"That's right," Bria said. "A growing boy who has to get to church."

"Well, let's go, then," Fifetta said. "We don't want to keep Father Roberto waiting."

"He doesn't mind," Marco said. "He holds mass for us sometimes. Just like Sister Benedicta waits for us because we're usually late for school."

"Bria!" Fifetta cried. "You don't get Marco to school on time? Tardiness is not a good trait, *carino*. You must always be on time for your appointments."

"I know. That's why we're rushing this morning," Marco said. "Mamma has lots of appointments."

"She does?" Fifetta said. "Funny, your mamma didn't mention anything to me about having appointments. Then again, your mamma doesn't mention a lot of things to me lately."

"*Uffa, Mamma!*" Bria cried. "Don't be so dramatic. We talked the other day. I think you know from our conversation that I've been busy lately."

"Because of the dead man," Marco said.

Bria and Fifetta cried, "Marco!" at the same time.

"This is exactly why I came," Fifetta said. "After such an incident, the family needs to come together. Marco needs his nonna Fifi more than ever."

"Marco always needs his nonna Fifi," Bria replied. "But really, we're fine. I don't need help. Giovanni will be here shortly, and he's going to pick up Marco after school in case I don't get back on time."

"*Nonsenso*," Fifetta said. "Giovanni is a good man, but he's a man. Nonna Fifi is here, and she'll take care of everything."

"Mamma, nothing needs taking care of," Bria said.

"Then why do you have that face?" Fifetta asked.

"What face?" Bria replied.

Marco looked up at his mother and then turned to his grandmother. "That's Mamma's regular face. She looks like that all the time."

"It's the face you have on when you're nervous and need help," Fifetta said. "I know that face like my own. My instincts were right, so let me help."

Bria knew two things for certain. The first was that once her mother was convinced that she was right, there was no convincing her that she was wrong. The second was that her mother was always right, so there was no use trying to convince her that she was wrong. Bria *was* nervous, and even though she had taken care of things, there was nothing like having your mother as backup.

"You're right, I could use your help," Bria said. "If you could take Marco to church, Giovanni can pick him up for soccer practice."

Fifetta spread her arms wide and looked up to the ceiling. "*Grazie Dio!*" she shouted. "Marco, this is proof that you should never doubt your nonna Fifi. Because as God as my witness, I am always right. Now, go wash your hands and let's go to church."

Marco ran to the bathroom, which gave Bria a few moments alone with her mother.

"Thank you," Bria said.

Fifetta waved a hand in front of Bria's face and threw her head to the side. It was the universal body language every Italian mother had employed since 753 B.C., when Rome was founded. Even then, a mother did what a mother always did without any desire to be thanked. Her only request? To be kept informed.

"Now, what's going on?" Fifetta asked. "Why are you running off and not telling me? Does it really have to do with that dead man? You know, your father and I are very worried."

Bria had learned early on never to try to avoid answering her mother's questions or to lie to her. Fifetta would always learn the truth eventually—either by dragging it out of her or finding out from another source. Lying and evading had always made Bria feel guilty. Regardless of the situation or the consequences, Bria had always told her mother the truth.

"There's nothing to worry about, but yes, it has to do with Vittorio," Bria said.

"Who's Vittorio?" Fifetta asked.

"That's the name of the dead man," Bria said. "Lorenza found that out."

"*Ah Dio mio!* You and your sister are involved with a dead man, and I'm not supposed to worry!" Fifetta shouted.

She had a point, Bria thought. She just didn't have the time to discuss it. It was time for Bria to adopt the same tactics her mother had mastered.

Like a shrewd lawyer, Bria asked a question she already knew the answer to. "Mamma, have I ever lied to you before?"

Fifetta pursed her lips, and Bria knew her mother felt like she had been caught in her own trap. "No."

"Then you have to trust me that I'm not lying now," Bria continued. "Lorenza and I are not in any danger. We're just helping Luca and the police find out who murdered this man, so no one thinks Bella Bella had anything to do with the crime."

"Today you're going in search of another clue?" Fifetta asked.

"Yes," Bria replied and then glanced at her watch. "And if I don't leave right now, I may miss my opportunity."

"Go," Fifetta said, hugging her daughter and kissing her on both cheeks. "I'll take Marco to church, and then I'll fix things up here when he's playing soccer."

"You don't have to. Most everything is in order," Bria said. "Giovanni has some repairs to do upstairs, but I think we're ready for the opening."

"My angel, trust me, this place needs a *woman's* touch," Fifetta said.

"And what am I?" Bria asked.

Fifetta stared at her daughter with a quizzical expression. "You're going to be late if you don't get a move on. We will too. Marco! *Vieni qui*! Let's go."

Dutifully, Marco ran to Fifetta, with Bravo trailing right behind.

"*Ciao*, Mamma," Marco shouted.

Before Marco left the house, Bria ran to him, knelt down, and hugged him. She kissed his cheeks and smelled the faint scent of pears, a remnant of the Paglieri SapoNello soap Marco used every morning when he washed.

"You be a good boy for me today," Bria said.

"I'm a good boy every day, Mamma," Marco said.

Marco grabbed Fifetta's hand and led her to the door. Before they left, Fifetta turned to Bria. "You be a good girl for me today, wherever you're going."

Just as Fifetta was about to shut the door, she turned back and proved that she did indeed have a sixth sense. Whether it was because she was a mother or was somehow gifted with the power to know exactly what to say and when to say it, Bria didn't know. She simply accepted that she'd be lost without Fifetta.

"I spoke with Imperia this morning," Fifetta said. "She always sounds calmer when she's at the estate and not in the city."

"Imperia's not in Rome?" Bria asked.

"No, she's at the country house," Fifetta replied. "She said she had to go out of town this morning and it was easier to travel from there instead of Rome. *Arrivederci, mi amore.*"

Bria knew that her mother couldn't possibly know that the reason she was taking this last-minute trip to Sarno had to do with Imperia. Could she? No! Thankfully, Fifetta believed in saying whatever popped into her head. It might not mean anything to her, but it could be useful to whomever she was talking to. She couldn't have been more right. Bria had planned on driving to Imperia's home in Rome to follow her, surreptitiously of course, to wherever she was going in Sarno. Had Fifetta not informed Bria that Imperia wasn't in Rome, the day's adventure would have been a waste of time.

Bria had barely brought the Fiat to a halt to let Rosalie get in before she was driving down the road again. Before they were even out of the village, Rosalie demanded to know exactly why they were going to spend the day chasing after her mother-in-law.

"Because it's too much of a coincidence that Imperia is going to Sarno," Bria said. "One of the few places Vittorio traveled to in the past six months."

"You think she's connected to the murder?" Rosalie asked.

"*Non lo so,*" Bria replied. "Which is why we need to find out what she's doing in Sarno, so we can rule it out."

"You didn't think to ask her why she was making the trip?" Rosalie asked.

"What good would that have done?" Bria replied. "If Imperia is involved, she wouldn't tell me the truth. The only way for us to find out is to follow her."

"Is that why we're speeding, Maria Andretti?" Rosalie asked.

"We have to get to her before she leaves at nine, so we can trail her all the way to Sarno and find out exactly where she's going and who she's meeting," Bria explained.

Bria took Viale Pasitea to Via G. Marconi and then hopped onto Strada Statale 163 toward Spiaggia di Tordigliano. Once on the highway, she got the Fiat up to 128 kilometers per hour, which was about eighty miles per hour, and thanks to the light traffic, she was able to maintain her speed for most of the forty-five minutes they were on the road.

"This isn't the way to Rome," Rosalie stated, her hair bouncing in the wind.

"No, it's the way to Angri," Bria replied.

"We're going to Imperia's estate?" Rosalie asked.

"Yes. She's leaving from there instead of Rome," Bria explained.

"I think it's so fitting that Imperia lives in Angri," Rosalie said. "The name sounds pretty in Italian, but in English it's such an ugly word—*angry*—though it really does explain so much about her."

"Wait until you see her home," Bria said. "You'll see that my mother-in-law has absolutely nothing to be angry about."

Bria stayed on Strada Statale 145 for about an hour, driving north past Meta Campania, then up the coastline toward Vico Equense and beautiful Scrajo Mare, until she made a right onto the E45 near Pompei. From there it was only another fifteen minutes to Angri. Once Bria exited the highway and got onto the streets in the residential section, the homes got bigger and more palatial, and the landscapes were meticulously maintained.

"I knew Imperia was rich, but I didn't think she was this rich," Rosalie said, looking around the area.

Bria made a left at Via Amerigo Vespucci and parked the car near the end of the street. "You see that house on the left, the second from the corner?" she asked.

"The one with the black wrought-iron gate and the massive cypress trees?" Rosalie replied.

"That's Imperia's home."

"That isn't a home. It's a fortress."

"It's actually Imperia's attempt at downsizing. Now that she's on her own, she doesn't need that much space."

"She lives in that airplane hangar all by herself?"

"With some servants and, I think, an assistant," Bria replied. "But essentially, yes, she lives alone."

"Since the two of you don't really get along," Rosalie said, "do you think she and I could be best friends? I wouldn't mind living behind a gate, with my own private wing."

"You'd hate not being on the water," Bria said. "And you know Imperia well enough to know that you'd last less than twenty-four hours living with her under the same roof. Especially if you had to abide by all her rules."

"It's tempting, Bri," Rosalie said. "You have much more willpower than I give you credit for."

"What do you mean?"

"You haven't taken Imperia up on her offer yet and moved in with her," Rosalie said. "Now that I see what she's offering, it's a hard situation to turn down."

"Not hard at all," Bria said. "I'm living right where I want to." Suddenly Bria sat up in her seat and pointed at the house. "And we have Imperia right where we want her."

The wrought-iron gates began to open and roll away from each other, allowing a car to drive through.

"You see that car coming out of the driveway?" Bria said.

"The gold-plated tank?" Rosalie asked.

"It's a gold Maserati Quattroporte," Bria corrected. "That's Imperia and her driver."

"I cannot believe *that thing* is Imperia's car!" Rosalie exclaimed. "Did she steal it from a James Bond movie?"

"No, but in the eighties the producers borrowed Guillermo's Rolls-Royce," Bria said.

For the next thirty minutes, they drove in relative silence as Bria followed the Maserati at a safe distance, allowing some cars to come in between them, but making sure never to lose sight of Imperia's driver. Just as Bria was starting to think that the driver had spotted them and was taking them on a wild-goose chase through every street in Sarno, the car pulled up in front of Angelina's Ristorante. Bria pulled over and parked on the other side of the street and watched as Imperia's driver get out and opened the rear passenger door. Imperia emerged from the Maserati and for a moment, Bria thought she was going to turn around and shoot one of her steely glares at her, but thankfully, she nodded to her driver and walked toward the restaurant.

Angelina's was attached to a golf course and appeared to be part of a country club. In the distance Bria could see tennis courts. Out of the corner of her eye she saw Rosalie unhook her safety belt and start to open the car door.

"No, we have to wait here," Bria instructed.

"How are we going to see what she's doing in the restaurant if we stay here in the car?" Rosalie asked.

Bria reached behind her and grabbed a pair of binoculars from the backseat. "With these."

"Bria D'Abruzzo Bartolucci, you are a genius."

"I'm also incredibly lucky."

"*Che dolce*," Rosalie said. "Because you have me here, riding shotgun?"

Bria hesitated. That wasn't what she meant, but she didn't want to upset her friend. "Yes, *certo*, but mainly because it looks like Imperia is going to sit outside for brunch, which will make it easier for us to spy on her."

Rosalie leaned forward and saw that Imperia was walking out onto a large patio from the second floor of the restaurant. There were about twelve tables in a semi-secluded area, with trees camouflaging some guests, but thankfully, Imperia greeted a woman who was sitting at a table in the center of the patio, and both she and the woman were in full view.

"Who's she with?" Rosalie asked.

"I don't know," Bria said. "But she kissed her on both cheeks, so she must know her very well."

"Use the binoculars to get a closer look," Rosalie ordered.

Bria was already pointing the binoculars at Imperia and her mystery date and turning the lenses to sharpen the image. Once the women came into view, Bria gasped. Her instincts were correct, and she had made the right decision to follow Imperia. She didn't recognize the woman or know her name, but Bria knew exactly who she was.

"The woman that Imperia is with is Vittorio's paramour!"

"How do you know?"

"She's wearing the same scarf that Vittorio was wearing," Bria explained. "Except hers isn't covered in blood."

CHAPTER 13

Despite knowing that the scarf the woman was wearing implicated her in the murder of Vittorio, Bria couldn't help but admire the woman's fashion sense. The scarf complimented her outfit beautifully.

She wasn't wearing the gold and navy scarf as an ascot like Vittorio had, but she'd wrapped it around her shoulders in a more traditional way, over a white blouse with full, flowing sleeves and tight three-inch cuffs. The scarf was fastened to her blouse on the left with a gold pin that resembled a sunburst: it had a round gold center, from which sprang gold pins of varying length. Bria could only see a portion of the woman's legs, but she seemed to be wearing navy blue pants with a flared leg.

The scarf, of course, could have been purchased anywhere, and there was no way of knowing if this woman had bought this scarf—as well as Vittorio's—at Paloma's store. The scarf was not a one-of-a-kind item and most likely had been manufactured, meaning potentially thousands of them had already been sold at hundreds of stores, and they were possibly available online. But there were two pieces of evidence that made Bria conclude that this woman had been a customer of La Casa Felice, Paloma's little boutique, which was only a few minutes' walking distance from Bella Bella. Both evidentiary elements were circumstantial, but to Bria, they amounted to one indisputable result: the woman sitting across the table from Imperia was the first real suspect in the murder of Vittorio Ingleterra.

The initial piece of evidence had to do with their location. Sarno was not a business center, nor was it a major Italian city. There was nothing here that could explain why Imperia had made this trip other than to meet with this woman. The only other link to Sarno was that Vittorio had flown here very recently. Bria knew that this line of thinking had more holes in it than *groviera* cheese, and yet for some reason, she believed both Imperia and Vittorio had traveled to Sarno to meet with this woman, whoever she was.

The second piece of evidence was more ironclad. Paloma had described the woman who bought the two scarves as being of an indiscriminate age, but wearing a wide-brimmed hat and sunglasses. The woman sitting across from Imperia was wearing a white wide-brimmed woven hat with a band of navy material and black sunglasses the same round shape as the ones Bria wore when she drove. In her heart, Bria knew this woman was connected to Vittorio, but she had to figure out how to prove it.

"*Un'immagine vale più di mille parole,*" Bria muttered to herself.

"What did you say?" Rosalie asked.

"A picture. I need to take a picture of this woman so Paloma can confirm it's the same woman who bought the scarves," Bria said.

"Didn't you say that Paloma admitted she didn't get a good look at the woman?"

"Yes, but a photo might jog her memory."

Rosalie peered over to look in the backseat of the Fiat and found what she was looking for. "Here you go," she said, handing the Polaroid camera to Bria.

"We're too far away. You can't zoom in with a Polaroid," Bria said. "I'll have to take a photo with my cell phone."

Bria aimed her phone at the woman, enlarged the image, and just as she was about to take the photo, the woman stood up.

"No!" Bria cried.

"What's wrong?" Rosalie asked.

"She's moving."

"Are they leaving already?" Rosalie asked. "Imperia just got there."

After a few seconds, Bria saw that they were only switching seats, but when the woman sat down in Imperia's seat, she positioned the chair so all Bria could see was the back of the woman's head.

"They switched seats," Bria said. "Now I can't see the woman's face."

"Do you think Paloma would be able to identify the woman from behind?" Rosalie asked.

Bria looked at Rosalie with the same side-eye glance that Sophia Loren had once given Jayne Mansfield. "You're not helping, Rosalie."

"Neither is Imperia," Rosalie replied. "She's leaving."

Bria turned around and saw that Imperia was indeed walking away from the table. Rosalie was half-right: Imperia was leaving the patio, but not the restaurant. Bria had just been given the perfect opportunity.

"Imperia left her purse on her chair," Bria said. "Looks like she's only going to the ladies' room, which means this is my only chance to get a photo of Vittorio's girlfriend."

Bria grabbed her sunglasses and the Polaroid camera and got out of the car. She slammed the door shut and ignored Rosalie's protests and questions and ran toward the front of the restaurant, with an exasperated Rosalie chasing after her. En route, Bria put on the sunglasses, hoping that they would prevent anyone from being able to clearly identify her. She knew that if she bumped into Imperia, there would be no chance of remaining incognito, but she wanted to make sure that if the woman with the scarf saw her taking her photo, she wouldn't later be able to identify Bria in a police lineup. She shuddered at the thought of getting arrested, because she was planning on making Marco's favorite dinner later that night, homemade meat lasagna with ricotta and mozzarella, but she had come here with a purpose, and she needed to see it through. If, for some reason, the woman had her arrested for invasion of privacy or some other fabricated charge, Fifetta would be able to whip up a lasagna, plus some bruschetta and tiramisu for dessert, quicker than the police could collect Bria's fingerprints.

As Bria entered the restaurant, she saw that she had been right, and watched Imperia walk into the ladies' room. The door to the ladies' room was located in the hallway that led to stairs leading to the outdoor patio, so in order for Bria to take the woman's photo, she would have to pass the door twice, once on her way in and once on her way out. She didn't know if she had enough time to avoid Imperia, but she had no choice.

Bria turned and saw Rosalie enter the restaurant, and put her hand up, indicating that she should stay put. No sense in both of them getting caught. Bria speed-walked down the hallway, up the few stairs, and when she entered the patio, she felt as if all eyes were on her. It made sense. She was carrying a camera that had gone out of style about four decades earlier, making her look like some old-fashioned photographer who took strangers' photos for a few dollars. That was it! If she wasn't going to blend into the surroundings, she'd make the surroundings blend in with her motive.

Turning to the left, Bria saw a young couple who looked like they had just stepped out of an ad for the California Tourism Bureau. Suntanned, beautiful, blond, and oh so photogenic. Bria aimed the Polaroid in their direction and snapped. When the photo emerged from the film eject slot, she grabbed it, shook it a few times, and then handed it to the surprised couple.

"*Divertitevi!*" Bria cried.

With no time to spare or to think fully about the implications of her next move, Bria walked to the center of the patio, spun around, and took a photo of Imperia's mystery guest. The woman was not nearly as inviting as the couple from California, and she waved her hand at Bria in an attempt to shoo her away. Perfect. Bria hadn't figured out beforehand how to keep the photo for herself and not give it to the mystery woman. Now that she had been rebuffed, Bria bowed apologetically, grabbed the photo before it fell to the floor, and started to speed-walk back off the patio just in time to see Imperia exit the ladies' room.

Luckily, her mother-in-law was looking down at her skirt and was picking at a loose thread. Bria didn't even have to lock eyes with Rosalie, who was still standing guard at the front entrance. Her best friend immediately knew what to do and sprang into action. The two women had found themselves in various adventures all throughout grammar school and then through college—they had attended Rome University of Fine Arts together—which meant they shared a long, and sometimes rambunctious, history. This wasn't the first time Rosalie had helped Bria escape a sticky situation.

With a combination of fear and utter delight, Bria watched Rosalie race down the hallway, grab a glass half-filled with water from a tray that had not yet been brought to the kitchen, and bump into Imperia, causing the water to slosh out of the glass and drench the front of Imperia's outfit.

"*Goffa idiota!*" Imperia cried.

"*Mi dispiace così tanto,*" Rosalie said in a voice that Bria didn't recognize but that sounded very similar to that of Topo Gigio.

As Imperia tried to brush away the water with her hand, Rosalie crossed in front of her to block her view as Bria faced the opposite direction and scurried past them. Bria didn't stop running until she got to her car. She placed the camera onto the backseat but clung to the photo as she started the car and drove toward the restaurant's entrance just as Rosalie came running out, screaming, "Mussolini!" much to the horror of everyone within earshot.

Bria didn't bring the car to a full stop but slowed down just enough so Rosalie could open the front passenger door and jump in with only minimal risk of severe bodily damage.

"Drive!" Rosalie screamed.

Bria did as she commanded and sped away as Rosalie sat in the passenger seat, puffing on her inhaler. Bria watched a waiter raising a fist in the air in the middle of the street grow smaller and smaller in the rearview mirror, until he disappeared completely when she turned right at the corner. They had escaped. She wouldn't be part of a police lineup—at least not today—and she had captured the proof that she needed.

As Rosalie jabbered on about almost getting caught and how in order to escape from the restaurant, she had to kick in the shins a waiter who was trying to detain her. Bria could only focus on the photo in her hand. She had to find out who this woman was and what kind of relationship she had with Imperia. For the moment, it was all speculation, but something in her gut told her that this woman had played a key role in Vittorio's murder, which meant Imperia was also somehow involved.

With one ear she listened to Rosalie continue to describe exactly what had happened while Bria was running out of the restaurant, but the thoughts in her head were grabbing all her attention. Bria had thought she knew her mother-in-law, but there was a lot about Imperia that was a mystery. Bria didn't know anything about Bartolucci Enterprises, and she knew only the broad strokes about Imperia's personal life. For years she had thought it was because Imperia didn't have a personal life, other than attending and throwing business parties, and she had never heard her speak of any friends. She had assumed it was because Imperia didn't have any. The woman had never been voted Miss Congeniality in any of the beauty pageants she entered, and she could often be dismissive and rude, which didn't make her a magnet for friendship, but perhaps Bria didn't know anything about Imperia's personal life because the woman wanted to conceal that part of her life from Bria. Perhaps it was because that part of her life was less than friendly and nefarious and included people who had the potential to commit murder.

Bria shook her head vigorously and shifted in her seat. Those were heavy accusations she was contemplating, and she forced herself to remember that Imperia was not only her mother-in-law but also Marco's grandmother. No matter how difficult Imperia could be to deal with, she had always been good to Marco. She couldn't possibly be having brunch with a murderer.

"Could she?"

It took a second for Bria to realize Rosalie had uttered the same question, and it wasn't only the voice in her head that she had heard but Rosalie's voice, too.

"Could she what?" Bria asked.

"Could the woman Imperia was sitting with have murdered Vittorio?"

"I don't know," Bria replied. "But the first thing we need to do is find out if she really is the woman who bought those scarves."

Paloma's scream was the response Bria was hoping for. Luckily, La Casa Felice was empty, so no customers were given a reason to run out of the store empty-handed. What was even luckier was that it meant Paloma recognized the woman in the photo.

"Are you sure this is the woman who bought the two scarves from you?" Bria asked.

"It's the same hat, it's the same glasses, it's the same woman," Paloma replied.

Bria could feel her heart race and a rush of adrenaline almost devour her body. She had been right. This was what happened when she trusted herself. Paloma had identified the woman, but they still didn't know who she was. Of course, she could ask Imperia, but in doing so she would implicate herself and reveal that she had followed her from Angri to Sarno because she thought she was involved in the murder. Which was what Bria believed, but she didn't want Imperia to know that just yet. It would be much better if she could identify the woman on her own.

"Did she mention her name?" Bria asked. "Introduce herself to you in conversation?"

"She talked quite a bit about her boyfriend and wanting to get the scarves for the two of them," Paloma said. "But she never mentioned her name or the boyfriend's, and I was so busy that day I didn't even think to ask."

"There might be another way to find out her name," Bria said. "Did she use a credit card to pay for the scarves? Or a debit?"

"No, she paid in cash," Paloma confirmed.

"Are you sure?"

"She gave me two one-hundred-euro bills. Few people do that," Paloma explained. "I remember that because most everyone pays by card these days."

"Well, at least we know that this is the woman connected to Vittorio," Bria said.

"How in the world did you find her?" Paloma asked. "Was it at a restaurant in Positano? Is the woman still here?"

Bria hesitated only slightly and hoped that Paloma didn't pick up on it. She knew that Paloma wasn't the gossip Annamaria was, but she couldn't trust her—or anyone other than Rosalie—to keep quiet about something as juicy as this, especially since the entire village was dying to know more about the murder. She didn't want to mention Imperia's name, in case Paloma couldn't resist sharing the information, as it would inevitably reach Imperia's ears.

"I was having lunch with Rosalie while we were doing some shopping in Naples, and as we were leaving, I saw her," Bria lied. "I thought it was probably nothing more than a coincidence, but I figured I'd take a photo and let you be the judge."

Paloma nodded and seemed to buy Bria's slightly fictitious story, but then she asked a question Bria had not anticipated.

"Do you always carry your Polaroid camera around with you?" Paloma asked.

Startled, Bria couldn't immediately respond; she merely smiled. Well, if one lie worked, why not two?

"Carlo gave it to me, and I like to do things with Marco to remind him of his father," Bria started. "We had taken some photos of Bravo, and I had left the camera in my bag."

Bria could tell by the way Paloma was looking at her that she wasn't convinced. She hoped it was enough to keep her quiet and would not send her running to Bombalino's office to give *La Vita Positano* its next scoop, but she thought it best not to prolong the conversation. Bria was just about to ask Paloma about the still-unopened wine and cheese shop as a way to change the subject when a group of Japanese tourists entered the store. It was the perfect excuse to make a quick exit.

"Thank you so much, Paloma. You've been an incredible help," Bria said. "For now, I'd appreciate it if you could keep this information just between the two of us . . . until I get a chance to inform the police."

"You have my word," Paloma replied. "I won't say anything to anyone about Vittorio's mysterious lady friend."

Just as Bria stepped onto the street, she saw one of the people who absolutely deserved to know the details of Vittorio's love life. And even though Bria had just told Paloma that she intended to tell the police what she knew, she changed her mind.

"Luca," Bria said.

Bria walked toward Luca, making sure that she stopped him before he was in Paloma's line of vision. There might be customers in her store, but if Paloma looked out her window, she'd easily see Luca and Bria talking and might want to join in the conversation. That was not something Bria wanted to happen.

"What are you doing going for a stroll in the middle of the day?" Bria asked.

"I could ask you the same thing," Luca said, glancing at his watch. "

"I had to run some errands, while my mother's taking care of Marco," she replied.

"Fifetta's in town?" Luca asked.

"Yes. She felt I needed some protection," Bria said. "With everything that's going on."

"You told her that I have surveillance on Bella Bella, right?" Luca asked.

"No, I didn't tell her that," Bria replied. "That would only give her more reason to worry."

"Well, I'm glad I bumped into you," Luca said. "I was actually on my way to St. Cecelia's, thinking I'd catch you there."

"Is there a break in the case?" Bria asked. "Did you find out who killed Vittorio?"

"Yes and no," Luca replied. "We found a bag of lire on the steps from Nocelle. Not a huge amount of money, but we think it might be related to Vittorio's murder, since he was found with a lira in his wallet."

"Is there something I don't know?" Bria asked. "Is Italy following in Great Britain's footsteps and leaving the European Union?"

"Not unless it's a statewide secret," Luca said. "But it's definitely odd, and I thought you'd want to know."

"Grazie."

Bria felt pangs of guilt and opened her mouth but quickly closed it. Part of her wanted to tell Luca about her morning escapade and the resulting intel she had gathered from Paloma, but the other part—which was definitely not Italian, because it felt no guilt whatsoever—decided it was better to keep the information private for the moment. She could be wrong about Imperia's relationship with this mysterious woman, and her mother-in-law was still her family. Bria didn't want to get her into trouble or stain her reputation without concrete proof that her reputation was already stained.

Instead, she offered him an invitation. "Would you like to come home with me and say hello to Fifetta? I'm sure she'd love to see you, and Marco gets so excited when you show up in uniform."

"I think he enjoys my company only because I let him beat me at every board game we play," Luca said.

"That might be part of it," Bria replied with a laugh.

"I don't have to get back to the station immediately," Luca said. "It would be nice to see your mother. It's been ages."

Bria hoped Luca didn't notice she started to walk faster when they passed Paloma's shop. She didn't want to risk Paloma seeing them and asking questions about who the mysterious woman could be, since it would be logical for Paloma to think that Bria had shared the information with Luca, given that this was exactly what she had told Paloma she was going to do. When they were in front of the store, Bria glanced through the window and saw Paloma surrounded by the tourists in front of a display of ceramic bowls. Although Paloma was too preoccupied to notice them, Bria was learning that being in control when investigating a crime wasn't always an easy task.

As a mother, however, Bria should have remembered that control was a fantasy.

When she and Luca walked through the front door, it was as if they walked into the center of a three-ring circus. Marco,

Fifetta, and even Giovanni looked at them with three surprised expressions upon seeing Bria's companion. Marco was overjoyed, Fifetta was intrigued, and Giovanni was frightened.

"I bumped into Luca on the way home, and he wanted to say hello to you, Mamma," Bria said. She then caught Giovanni's eye and added, "That's the only reason he came here."

"You didn't come to see me, too?" Marco said.

"*Certo*," Luca said, kneeling down to give the boy a hug. "She just means that I'm here for a friendly visit and not on police business."

"Then you can play Monopoly with us," he squealed.

"You can take my place," Fifetta said. "Franco's been right all these years. I throw a magnificent wedding, but if there isn't a kitchen involved, I have no head for business."

Fifetta embraced Luca warmly and then pulled away to stare into his eyes. "How proud your papa would be to see that you've grown into such a wonderful man. And the *capo della polizia*, keeping this village safe and protected." She glanced to where Giovanni was standing and added, "Even if your motives are somewhat misguided."

"I'm going to check on that loose tile in the backyard," Giovanni said.

"You know there isn't a loose tile, right?" Marco said to Luca. "He's just leaving because he thinks you might arrest him again."

"I'm not going to arrest him," Luca said. "And I didn't arrest him before. We just needed to ask him some questions."

"You could've asked me, and I would've told you that Vanni had nothing to do with that man who died here," Marco said. "Vanni's a good guy, like you. He even lets me win at Monopoly."

"According to this game, my grandson is the richest landlord in all of Italy," Fifetta said.

"I would be," Marco said, "if only my pile of cash wasn't fake money."

Bria felt like she was a schoolgirl again at St. Ann's and Sister Immaculata, who was not as innocent as her chosen name might suggest, had just slapped her across the side of her head for not knowing her multiplication table. Now, like then, the answer had been right in front of her, and she had just needed a little push to find it. Thanks to her son's casual remark, she had just been given the push she needed.

As they all gathered around the table to play another round of Monopoly, Bria pulled Luca aside and whispered in his ear, "It's fake money."

"*Grazie*, Bria, but I already know that Monopoly money isn't real currency," Luca whispered back.

"No," Bria replied, still whispering. "The lire you found on the steps to Nocelle and in Vittorio's wallet."

"What about them?" Luca said, not sure what Bria was getting at.

"I bet you any amount of money—real or otherwise—that every lira you found is counterfeit."

CHAPTER 14

It took forty-eight hours, but Luca was able to prove that Bria's latest hunch was right. According to the Guardia di Finanza, the lira bill that was in Vittorio's wallet and the money that was found in a bag hidden on the 675th step of the steep stairway that connects Nocelle to Positano were both fake. Not Monopoly money fake, but made-to-look-real counterfeit money fake. What the Guardia or Luca couldn't determine, however, was why?

Why would anyone go to such trouble to create and produce fake money no one could use? The lira was a currency that had barely made it into the twenty-first century and was no longer legal tender. Tests were being done to determine the age of the paper used to make the fake lire, and if the results showed that the paper predated 2002, it could possibly mean that someone had attempted to filter counterfeit money into the marketplace prior to the switch from lire to euros. They would then have to figure out why the money was still lying around and hadn't been shredded, since it was completely worthless; but as Bria was beginning to learn, when it came to solving a crime, things moved one slow step at a time and never as quickly as you wanted them to. Even when you were friends with the chief of police.

"You really have no idea?" Bria asked.

"None," Luca replied, leaning back in his chair at the police station.

Bria stared at Luca from the other side of his desk and got the distinct impression that he was lying to her. Up until that point, she had believed he was sharing with her all the details of the investigation as they were discovered. In fact, he often came to her home or sought her out to give her an update in person. This time was different, and Bria didn't know why. She stifled a gasp when she realized that he was treating her the same way she was treating him. They were each sharing the information that they wished to share.

She had been an amateur detective for less than a week, and already she was acting like a cop.

Bria still hadn't revealed to Luca that she had found the woman who bought Vittorio's scarf and that she had found her thanks to Imperia. She was keeping those details secret until she knew they would undoubtedly help the investigation. Maybe Luca was doing the same. Maybe he knew exactly why counterfeit money had been found in Positano and on the dead body but didn't want to disclose that data until he knew it would be helpful and not just be a diversion. Or maybe he already knew about Imperia's involvement and was trying to protect Bria. Bria rarely bad-mouthed Imperia in public, but Rosalie most certainly knew how she felt about her mother-in-law, and there was a very good chance she had spoken to Luca about it over the years. Whatever the reason, it was clear that Luca was not going to give Bria any additional information that would help her enter the next phase of her investigation.

Luca might not be helpful, but Nunzi certainly proved that she was on Team Bria.

Just as Bria was about to leave the police station, she overheard Nunzi talking to a colleague.

"Matteo, could you hold down the fort for me?" Nunzi asked. "I forgot to leave fresh water for Primavera."

"Sure," Matteo replied. "But if you paid more attention to me than you do to that cat of yours, we'd be married by now."

Nunzi adroitly sidestepped the misogynistic comment. "I don't think Primavera is ready for an addition to our family."

Outside, Bria slowed her gait to see where Nunzi was really headed, because as a pet owner herself and knowing how seriously Nunzi took her role as a *mamma gatta*, she knew Nunzi would never leave the house without giving her cat several bowls of fresh water scattered throughout her apartment. Bria didn't have to wait too long to find out where Nunzi was headed, because she quickly heard footsteps behind her.

"Don't turn around," Nunzi said. Her voice wasn't quite a whisper, but it was also not loud enough for anyone but Bria to hear.

"Why not?" Bria asked.

"I don't want us to be seen talking together," Nunzi said.

Che eccitazione! Bria thought. "Is this official undercover police business?"

"Make a left," Nunzi ordered.

Bria looked to her left and saw a very narrow alleyway that was almost completely dark, despite the midday sun, and didn't look to have an exit. Was Nunzi trying to trap her?

"I'm not sure I can fit in between those two buildings," Bria said, trying to get her voice to match Nunzi's tone.

"Turn left," Nunzi repeated. "Now."

It could have been her Catholic school upbringing, the dominant tone of Nunzi's voice, or the fact that Bria was more than a little curious why she was literally being forced down a dark path, but she turned left, as she'd been told to do. A few steps into the alley and she was plunged into almost total darkness. The sun, so vividly strong a few feet away, didn't even make an appearance where she was standing. She turned and waited for Nunzi to join her, but no one came.

What kind of game is the lady cop playing? Bria thought. *Is this an elaborate plan to make a fool of me? And after I complimented her on her soup!*

Growing furious, Bria walked toward the light, and just as she was about to emerge from the alley, Nunzi entered and collided with Bria.

"Nunzi!"

"Don't say my name."

"I thought you were playing a joke on me."

"No. I walked down to the mailbox and turned around, in case anyone was watching us."

"Why are you being so secretive? We do know each other. It wouldn't be that odd if people saw us talking."

"I don't want them to hear what I'm going to tell you."

She *was* about to become part of unofficial undercover police business! If Luca wasn't going to spill some official police beans, Nunzi would do it clandestinely and literally in the dark. But why would Nunzi defy her boss to share a secret with Bria? It might not cost Nunzi her job, but it could most assuredly get her into trouble if she revealed information she wasn't supposed to. Only one way to find out.

"What is it?" Bria asked. "I can't imagine something would be so important that it would make you get all cloak and dagger."

"This isn't the first counterfeit money ring to hit the Amalfi Coast."

Bria let the information settle into her brain. If Nunzi was telling the truth, Luca had indeed lied to her. She couldn't be upset with him, because she had done the same, but at least it was proof that he wasn't being honest and she wasn't imagining things.

"When was this?" Bria asked.

"Back in the late eighties," Nunzi replied. "It was a small-time ring and never really got off the ground, but I think they may be connected."

"Luca doesn't share your opinion?"

"No."

"Why not?"

"Because it was so long ago and all the men who were involved have since died."

"Then what makes you think that the old counterfeit money ring and the new lire that have been found are connected?" Bria asked.

"The bag."

"The bag they found the lire in on the steps to Nocelle?"

"Yes."

"What's so special about the bag?" Bria asked.

"It's from Caruso's."

Bria had heard of the name, but it took her a few seconds to recall how. "That was a popular chain of department stores. Everyone shopped there."

"My father worked there," Nunzi said.

"My aunt Carlotta worked there, too. A lot of people did," Bria replied. "She worked in linens and housewares. She would give the most beautiful embroidered tablecloths to everyone for Christmas. Well, the wives. I mean, men didn't care about tablecloths back then. Most don't care about them now."

"Was your aunt Carlotta implicated as a member of a counterfeit money ring, too?"

"She was accused of shoplifting once, but it was a misunderstanding. The crocheted roses on a decorative napkin got caught on her pocketbook." Bria stopped talking for a few seconds to allow her brain to catch up to her mouth. "Oh! Was your father one of the counterfeiters?"

"He was suspected, and it ruined his reputation. After that

he was never the same," Nunzi explained. "He lost his job and found it hard to keep another one."

"You think just because the bag they found the money in is a bag from where your father worked that they're connected?" Bria said.

"I know it's a long shot, but yes."

Bria wasn't ready to confess that she had followed a similar trail and her long shot had turned out to be a bull's-eye. Instead, she simply agreed that she thought it was a possibility. But why was Nunzi sharing this with her? What was Bria supposed to do with the information?

"Find out everything you can about the counterfeit ring," Nunzi said. "The papers called them the Tre Uomini Poco Saggi."

"Three *Unwise* Men?" Bria asked. "That means your father had two cohorts."

"Yes, one man was from Naples, Alessandro Patroni, but I never knew him, and the other was Giancarlo La Costa."

Bria recognized the second name but thought for sure that she had heard wrong.

"As in Dante La Costa's father?" Bria asked.

"Yes, the mayor's father was the leader of the group," Nunzi said. "He was never convicted, but my father told me Giancarlo was the mastermind."

"And Luca doesn't believe any of this is connected to the murder?"

"He said none of the men involved were ever convicted of another crime, and there's no evidence that ties these two events together."

"How can he say that?" Bria asked. "Vittorio was carrying a fake lira note in his wallet."

"For now, Luca thinks it's a coincidence," Nunzi replied. "Maybe if they uncover indisputable evidence that the lira note found in Vittorio's wallet and the stash in the bag were all made in the eighties, he'd change his mind, but for now, he doesn't believe the present is connected to the past."

"If there is any proof," Bria said, "I promise you I'll find it."

Nunzi stared at Bria, and even in the shadowy light, Bria could tell that she was emotional.

"I knew I could count on you," Nunzi replied.

The next second, Nunzi was gone from the alley, and Bria found herself alone in the darkness. This time she wasn't nervous of the shadows or the unknown lurking in the pitch black all around her. She had a purpose. She waited for roughly thirty seconds and then emerged from the alley as if she was stepping out of her own home. If anyone saw her, they wouldn't question what she was doing. They would simply think she was a woman on a mission, which she was.

Bria's first stop was to drop into the office of *La Vita Positano* to speak with Aldo Bombalino, the newspaper's editor. Aldo was a chubby, round-faced man who was always smiling, even when being threatened with a libel suit by an angry resident whose dirty laundry had been exposed in print. Most of the issues of *La Vita*, as the villagers called it, were filled with feel-good stories about the locals and ads touting their services and merchandise, but every so often hard-hitting articles and very opinionated essays were printed, reminding everyone that at his heart, Aldo was an old-fashioned journalist.

La Vita was essentially a one-man operation and always had been. In 1992 Aldo had inherited the newspaper from his uncle Tonio and had decided to write about truth, justice, and the local flower competitions, instead of following in his own father's footsteps and becoming a butcher. Aldo told anyone who would listen, and often stated it in his own editorial column, that becoming a journalist and not a butcher was the best decision he had ever made. Aldo's father never forgave him for such betrayal. Bria was hoping Aldo was true to his word and was more interested than Luca in revealing the truth.

Aldo's office revealed quite a bit about him and looked more like a hoarder's haven than a newspaperman's workplace. There were stacks of old issues of *La Vita* piled onto chairs, the floor was strewn with binders overflowing with unclipped articles, mismatched filing cabinets took up most of the wall space, vintage portable and electric typewriters in a variety of colors lined the tops of the cabinets, and cardboard boxes that looked like they were rescued from a storage unit that was torn down in 1975 occupied the space under Aldo's desk. The backroom housed the printing press where the paper was actually published and it made the front room look like a study in minimalist design.

Bria stood in the middle of the room because she couldn't find a place to sit, the only chair being behind Aldo's desk and being occupied by Aldo.

"I'm looking for articles on the Tre Uomini Poco Saggi," Bria said.

Aldo's eyes lit up. "The old counterfeit ring."

"You've heard of it?"

"*Certo*," Aldo said. "Small potatoes, as the Irish say, but an admirable attempt to strike some fear into capitalism. Show *the Man* who's really the boss! As the Americans like to scream at the top of their lungs! Are you planning on whipping up some fake euros and hoping you might find pointers in the articles?"

She had not been in Aldo's company very often since she moved to Positano, but the man did live up to his reputation. Whenever he thought he smelled a scandal, he got gleeful. She got the sense that he was going to be helpful and that he would keep quiet. All she needed to do was play along.

"If my bed-and-breakfast fails, I may have to come up with an alternative," Bria said.

"You're going to be a success. I can feel it," Aldo said.

"Bella Bella has already made history by being the site of the first murder in Positano anyone can remember. *Complimenti*!"

This was exactly what Bria didn't want Bella Bella to be remembered for. She started to panic about what this could mean for her business's future but forced herself to remain focused on the task at hand.

"*Grazie*, Aldo . . . I think," Bria replied. "*Prego*, do you have any articles on the counterfeiters? Any that are still available to read?"

"What makes you so curious about the past?" Aldo asked.

Luckily, Bria had thought he might ask, and she didn't want to give her real reason, so she had concocted a cover story. "I thought it would be fun to frame some articles or photocopy and laminate them and put them in each room," Bria said. "Highlight a different fun or notorious fact about the village for my guests."

"*Buona idea*!" Aldo bellowed. "I'll make copies of some of the highlights of our village's history. Everyone thinks Positano is just about sun, sand, and limoncello, but I know its secrets."

"Really?" Bria replied.

"I have more history stored in my brain than Oriana Fallaci did, *Dio riposi la sua anima*," Aldo said. "I would kill to have found out the things she knew about Kissinger but didn't print in that *Playboy* interview."

"A woman interviewed a man for *Playboy*?" Bria asked.

"In 1972," Aldo replied. "I have it here somewhere if you'd like to read it."

Bria looked around the room and thought it would be easier to find a needle if someone hid it in Fornillo Beach.

"I think I'll stick to reading the articles you have about Positano's notorious history," she diplomatically replied.

"How far back would you like me to look?" Aldo asked.

Bria was practically giddy in her response, which slightly disturbed her. "I want to see everything you've got."

*   *   *

Long after tucking Marco into bed and giving Bravo his nightly walk, Bria sat on her balcony and read through the stack of articles Aldo had put together for her. Though Bria was engrossed in her reading she couldn't help notice the scent of orange blossoms in the air, the moon a hazy mix of red and yellow, the dark purple sky floating on top of the lights from the village below. Such a romantic setting. She pulled the soft fleece throw around her body tighter and could almost feel Carlo's strong arms around her.

"Stop it, Carlo!" she said out loud. "I can't think of you right now. I've got work to do."

She took a sip of red wine and turned the page of the final xeroxed article Aldo had given her. This one was about a B-movie starlet on the lam from her husband, who happened to be a rich Saudi Arabian prince, and marked the first time a camel had set foot in Positano. The village had a much more colorful history than she had ever imagined. Unfortunately, the story of the Tre Uomini Poco Saggi was not nearly as interesting.

There were only two articles in the paper's archives that focused on the counterfeit ring, both appearing in February 1988. The first told of how the police uncovered the small-time ring working out of a warehouse in Naples, with the goal of introducing fake lire to the Amalfi Coast. The article named Giancarlo La Costa as the ringleader and described Alessandro Patroni and Nico Della Monica, Nunzi's father, as the lackeys who did whatever Giancarlo told them to do.

The second article was shorter and said that all charges against the three men had been dropped because the counterfeit ring, while fully operational, had never been put to the test. None of the money they created had ever found its way into the shops, banks, or restaurants that were the intended targets. From what Bria read, this was a mere blip in Positano's history, with no legal repercussions for any of the men, despite what Nunzi had told her. Based on this information, Bria understood why Luca assumed these past events had nothing to do with the current investigation. But Bria had doubts. She couldn't shake the feeling that there was a connection that needed further exploration.

When she woke up the next morning, her suspicions hadn't changed. Right after dropping Marco off at St. Cecilia's, she and Bravo headed over to the mayor's office. She had talked to the child of one of the counterfeiters. Why not another?

Barging into an elected official's office with the sole purpose of implicating him in a murder investigation would be daunting to most people, but not to Bria. She didn't consider Dante an enemy, nor was she intimidated by his political position. She knocked on his door, filled with confidence and assurance that he wouldn't throw her out, because she knew that Dante had a crush on her.

Bria had been oblivious to his feelings until Annamaria let it slip that Dante had mentioned he found Bria to be the type of girl he could fall for. Rosalie had been less subtle and had told Bria that the mayor had the hots for her. Lorenza had mentioned it several times, and even Fifetta had told Bria that she should keep wearing black after Carlo's funeral to ward off Dante's advances.

"Bria, what an absolute thrill to see you," Dante said as he opened the door to his office. His smile faded slightly when he saw Bravo. "I see that you've brought a chaperone."

"I'm sorry," Bria said. "We just dropped Marco off at school, and I have a busy day today, but I wanted to stop by, so I thought no better time than the present, *vero*?"

"You are absolutely right," he said. "Come in, both of you, and make yourself at home."

Dante's office was not quite as large or luxurious as Imperia's, but it was still impressive. It was also a completely different style. While Imperia's office made a bold, modern statement, Dante's office honored the past.

The centerpiece of the room was Dante's mahogany desk that was so big Bria thought a forklift would be needed to move it. A brown distressed leather couch sat on top of a brown, green, and magenta rug, and a high-backed wooden chair with a needlepoint seat covering depicting the fight between Romulus and Remus anchored the space. Heavy green velvet curtains hung from the eight-foot windows and were held in place with gold braided tiebacks.

On the walls there were oil paintings of Italian landscapes of the north, near a window stood a bronze sculpture of a man who could have been Nero but also bore a striking resemblance to Marcello Mastroianni, and over Dante's desk was a portrait of Dante. Not Dante Alighieri, the poet, Dante La Costa, the mayor. When you looked at him sitting at his desk, you saw double.

"I was starting to wonder why it was taking you so long to come visit me," Dante said.

Bria sat on the leather couch across from Dante's desk and although Bravo valiantly tried to join her, Bria tugged on his leash until he reluctantly sat at her feet. She wished she could trade places with the dog.

"I'm not sure if you heard, but Bella Bella has seen some excitement," Bria replied.

"That's exactly what I'm talking about," Dante said. "Why are you letting the police spearhead this investigation? The mayor's office is ready, willing, and able to help."

"When it comes to murder, and all sorts of crime, for that matter," Bria said, "aren't the police the ones who spearhead an investigation?"

"Theoretically, yes," Dante replied. "But Luca has never solved a murder before."

"That's because there hasn't been a murder to solve in Positano since he became a cop," Bria noted.

"Details, details," Dante said, waving his hand dismissively in the air. "He can't even solve a petty crime," he said. "Someone slashed the tires of my nineteen ninety-four Alfa Romeo Spider and wrote graffiti on the side of this building—a word I shan't repeat in a lady's presence—and do you think Luca and his band of foolish fops ever found the culprit? *No, non l'hanno fatto.* There's a reason that man is single."

"You're a single man, too, Dante," Bria said.

"I am delighted that you've finally noticed," Dante said.

Dante brushed his hair back with one hand like a vain character in a Pirandello comedy. Not that his hair needed taming: it was slicked back with so much oil and pomade that he resembled Dracula. His formal attire resembled the count's, too. A three-piece midnight-black pin-striped suit, a bloodred tie, black patent-leather loafers, and a gold chain hanging from his vest pocket, attached to what Bria could only assume was a pocket watch. Dante cut a very dashing figure. For 1928.

The mayor walked over toward Bria to join her on the couch. Instantly, she felt trapped and looked for an escape. When she turned to the right, she found one.

"Where are you going?" Bria asked, her hand indicating a small black wheelie suitcase next to the couch.

"Milan," he replied. "There's a global warming conference that I feel I should attend. You know what they say. *Pensa globalmente, agisci localmente.*"

"I agree with the 'think globally, act locally' campaign," Bria admitted. "It's very important to focus on local events that are happening today, and especially on things that happened in the past, in order not to repeat the same mistakes twice."

"You are a highly intelligent woman, Bria," Dante said as he sat down on the opposite end of the couch. "We must all learn from the mistakes of the past."

"Like that counterfeit money ring I was reading about," Bria said.

Dante shot up from the couch much more quickly than he took a seat on it, and little red blotches appeared on his cheeks. He glanced at the clock on the wall and turned to Bria.

"I didn't realize the time," he said. "I'm going to have to leave soon to catch my flight."

Ignoring Dante's lame excuse to make an early exit, Bria continued to talk. "Do you remember anything about that time, Dante?"

"What time?"

"The time of the counterfeit money ring."

"Why would you want to know about that time?" Dante asked.

Bria hesitated. She didn't want to give too much away, but she had to make an offer in order to receive a reward. "Because I think the ring might have something to do with the murder. I can't say any more than that, but there is a loose connection to that moment in Positano's history."

Aimlessly, Dante walked around his office, his suitcase following him, but where could he go? The room, while grand, wasn't very large, and Bravo was watching him like the guard dog he was. When he finally stopped, he turned on his heel and asked, "Why do you care?"

"About the connection?" Bria asked.

"About the murder?"

"Because a man died in my home."

Dante's face radiated. He no longer looked at her accusingly, but longingly.

"Beautiful *and* noble," Dante said. "There are reasons to celebrate all that is Bria Bartolucci, whether one gazes upon her face or her soul."

Bria ignored Dante's Felliniesque line reading of a line that sounded like it had been cut from *Romeo and Juliet* for being too *sdolcinato*, or as the Americans say, schmaltzy. She took the opportunity to get back to the reason she was there in the first place.

"Did your father ever tell you anything specific about how the ring operated?" Bria asked. "Considering he was *la mente*, the mastermind, of it all?"

At the mention of his father, all thoughts of flirting, Fellini, and filibustering disappeared, and Dante suddenly became more like his usual self: cocky and caustic.

"My father was many things, but he wasn't *la mente* of any counterfeit money ring," Dante said. "She was."

"She?" Bria asked. "Those involved were dubbed the Tre Uomini Poco Saggi, not the Tre Uomini Poco Saggi and One Wise Woman."

"Yes, *she*," Dante replied. "Don't ask me who she was, because my father would never tell me. He was protecting her, even though she betrayed them all and almost got him incarcerated, which was just like my father. Left his wife, but he protected the woman who almost got him carted off to jail."

"Do you remember anything he might have said about this woman?" Bria asked. "Did he ever describe her? Tell you where she lived?"

"He never shared any facts about her with me or the police," Dante said. "The few times he spoke of her, he would only say that she was voluptuous, imperious, and duplicitous."

"It doesn't sound like he liked this woman very much," Bria said.

"A fine line separates love and hate," Dante said. "My father loved this devil woman, although he had many reasons to hate her."

"Your father sounds like a passionate man," Bria said.

"As my mamma would always say, God rest her soul, my papa was a *complicated* man," Dante replied. He flashed a grin and gave Bria his best come-hither look, which looked more like he had a twitch in his left eye, and added, "It runs in the family."

Before the conversation got more flirtatious, Bria got up to leave. She started to walk to the door, with Bravo right at her heel in case Dante tried to get any closer, and just as she was about to leave, she looked up and saw something over the doorway that made her rethink making a hasty exit.

"That was the first lira Papa ever made," Dante explained. "The first of many millions, I might add. My father had no reason to make counterfeit money. He had too much of the real thing."

Bria could feel Dante staring at her, but she couldn't turn to face him. She kept staring at the framed lira, thinking one simple thought: *I wonder if it's a fake.*

CHAPTER 15

Positano in the middle of the night was just as beautiful as Positano in the light of day. The mountainside village was known for its nightlife, and the amber lights from the night-clubs and late-night cafés cast a shimmery glow onto the sea. The crescent moon hung in the sky like a crooked smile, its light turning the dark sky a deep purple. Mixed together, the yellow and aubergine colors created a scene that looked like a bruise beginning to heal. They also produced just the right camouflage needed to allow Bria and Rosalie to break into Dante's office.

"I cannot believe you talked me into this," Bria said, her voice hushed but excited.

"You think Dante may be involved in a counterfeit money ring, right?" Rosalie asked, her voice also hushed but stern.

"Yes."

"You think the framed lira in his office may be evidence hiding in plain sight, *giusto*?"

"Yes."

"You said Dante is in Milan this weekend, right?"

"Yes."

"Add it all up, Bria, and what does it spell?"

"If I'm adding things up, shouldn't the result be a number and not a word?"

"*Ah, Madonna mia*! Work with me, Bria! In order to connect Dante to any counterfeit money operation, we need to test that framed lira to find out if it's as fake as all the others. The only way to get that lira is to steal it, because if Dante is involved, he's not going to give it to us willingly, and even if he isn't involved, Dante isn't going to give it to us, because he's cheap."

"*Prego*, why is he so cheap?" Bria asked. "He's rich."

"That's how rich people get richer. They don't spend any money."

"I don't think that's true, Rosalie. Dante's always so beautifully dressed. I don't think I've ever seen him in the same suit twice."

"*Apri gli occhi,* Bria!"

"My eyes are open!"

"No they aren't! If they were, you'd see that Dante spends money on himself, but not on others, and whenever he doesn't have to pay, he doesn't," Rosalie explained. "Mimi told me that he goes into her bookstore, jots down the titles of things he wants to read, and then do you know what he does?"

"No, Rosalie. What does he do?"

"He takes the books out of the . . . *biblioteca*," Rosalie hissed.

"Marco and I go to the library all the time."

"Because you're not rich!"

"That's not entirely true," Bria replied. "I'm comfortable, thanks to Carlo, and Imperia is making it so that Marco will never have to worry about money."

"Unless it turns out that Imperia is working with Dante and she's the one who killed Vittorio."

Hiding in the bushes outside the building on Via Guglielmo Marconi that housed the offices of the mayor and several other of the village's employees, Bria froze. Luckily, Rosalie couldn't see her, as she was concentrating on picking the lock to the front door with a safety pin. It was a skill that her brother had taught her when they were kids. She would always forget her key and would always return home after her curfew. To help his sister avoid getting into trouble with their parents, the future law enforcement officer essentially taught her how to break the law. Technically, if Rosalie got caught now, it would be all Luca's fault. But if their sleuthing resulted in Dante and Imperia getting caught for money laundering or possibly murder, then it would all be Bria's fault. She was the one who had started this—she was the one who wanted to solve Vittorio's murder to salvage Bella Bella's reputation—but she hadn't thought it all the way through. Could she live with herself if she exposed not only the mayor but also her mother-in-law as a perpetrator of a vicious crime?

The sound of the doorknob clicking was the moment of truth. If the framed lira turned out to be fake, it would be another strong piece of evidence linking someone she knew to the murder. Could she implicate a respected member of the community and a member of her own family in a horrible crime just because she wanted to save the name of her business before it even became a real business?

Che macello! Bria thought. And it indeed was a mess.

What Bria needed to do might not be pleasant, but it was necessary. Whoever was involved in this murder, whether in large part or just as an unwitting accessory, needed to be exposed. If that person was someone Bria knew, and if Bria played a part in the revelation of their role, then she would deal with the consequences. They would be easier to deal with than the knowledge that she had sat back and done nothing.

"Ready?" Rosalie asked.

Bria looked at Rosalie and didn't see an ounce of hesitation or nervousness, and she admired her friend's sense of adventure. Sometimes that thirst for thrills got Rosalie into trouble, but more often than not, it allowed her to live her life fully and without regret. Bria loved Rosalie for it and couldn't imagine doing any of the things she had done recently without her. Now she was going to add one more crazy caper to that list.

"Let's go," Bria replied.

Once inside, Bria closed the door behind them, and they stood still for a few seconds, allowing their eyes to acclimate to the darkness. They had both been in the building before, Bria just the other day, but their visits had been few, and they weren't intimately familiar with the blueprint of the building. They did know that Dante's office was on the second floor, so they climbed the stairs, tiptoeing on every step to make as little noise as possible, and stopped only when they reached the large wooden door that led into Dante's private office.

Bria assumed that the door would be locked, so she didn't prevent Rosalie from kneeling down, taking out her pin, and trying once again to unlock a locked door. Her efforts weren't required this time, however, because when Rosalie touched the doorknob, it turned with ease. She pushed, and the door opened.

Surprised, Rosalie leaned back on her haunches and grabbed Bria's leg for support and, instinctively, for protection. Bria, in turn, jumped back when she saw the door open, because she expected Dante to appear on the other side, pointing his finger at them and shouting, "Gotcha!" Bria dragged Rosalie back a few feet, until they both realized the only thing on the other side of the door was a dark office.

"Why's his door unlocked?" Rosalie whispered.

"He must figure since the door to the building is locked, he doesn't have to lock his own office," Bria said. "I used to keep my front door unlocked, until I had a dead visitor."

"I expect that from you, since you're trusting, but not from

Dante," Rosalie said. "I would've expected his lock to be harder to pick."

"*Oh, Dio mio*!" Bria exclaimed. "Do you think it's a trap?"

Rosalie listened for a moment. "I don't hear any sirens or any cops running up the stairs to arrest us."

"Let's get the lira and get out of here," Bria said.

They stepped inside Dante's office and closed the door quietly behind them.

"*Sì, certo,* signora. *Ma scusami*, where is the item in question that you're so eager to acquire?" Rosalie asked, sounding as if she were a salesperson at La Galleria Piazza Garibaldi.

"Look up," Bria said.

Rosalie did as she was told and saw the framed lira hanging right over the door.

"It couldn't be on his desk?" Rosalie asked. When she turned to look at Dante's desk, she once again jumped back a foot. "He's staring at us!"

"It's just his portrait."

"It's a creepy portrait," Rosalie said. "I feel like he's spying on us."

"Ignore him and let's concentrate on what we came here for," Bria advised. "You're taller than me. Do you think you can reach it?"

At five feet, nine inches tall, Rosalie was of above-average height for a woman, but even when she stood on her tiptoes and raised her arm, the frame was still almost half a foot out of reach.

The women looked around the office in search of a chair or a stool that they could use as a makeshift stepladder. When Bria saw Rosalie dragging the side chair with the needlepoint seat, she immediately stopped her friend.

"Are you *pazzo*?" Bria asked.

"This is perfect," Rosalie said. "I can stand on the arms of the chair and get the lira."

"You can't do that."

"Are you saying I'm too fat to climb on this thing?" Rosalie asked. "I'll have you know that I lost five pounds on my new limoncello and espresso diet."

"If you stand on the arms of that chair, it'll collapse under your weight."

"You *are* saying I'm too fat!" Rosalie cried. "Bria Nicoletta Bartolucci, if I were in my right mind, I'd walk out of here and leave you to get the stupid thing by yourself!"

"First of all, you're never in your right mind."

"That is a known fact."

"And second, that chair will break if you step on it, because it's from the sixteenth century."

"What!"

"It's an antique. It's meant for showing, not for sitting," Bria explained.

"Then why does Dante have it in his office, next to the couch, where people sit?"

"Because it's a conversation piece. The chair is designed in the Dante style."

"Only Dante would buy a Dante chair," Rosalie said, dragging the chair back to its original position. "I hope this lira is fake, because I never liked him."

"That's not what you said when you told me he has the hots for me."

"I knew at the time you didn't feel the same way, but I didn't know if your feelings would change," Rosalie explained. "Contrary to popular opinion, I do sometimes think ahead and don't always go through life with a rambunctious flair."

"*Uffa!* Is that what you're calling it now? A 'rambunctious flair'?"

"It has a much nicer ring to it than 'hot mess.'"

"Speaking of hot messes," Bria said, "how are we supposed to get that thing down, so we can get out of here?"

"Hoist me up," Rosalie said.

"What?"

"Stick out your hands, clasp them together so I have some-place to put my foot, and then lift me up," Rosalie explained. "And if you say you can't, because I weigh too much, I swear on your dead husband that I will make your life miserable from this day forward."

"Carlo always said if I ever got into serious trouble, it would be because of you."

"Because Carlo was a very shrewd man," Rosalie said. "Now, stick out your hands."

Groaning, but knowing there was no other solution, Bria stuck out her hands and clasped her fingers together, giving Rosalie a semi-flat surface on which to plant her foot. She squatted as Rosalie grabbed her shoulder with her left hand, then placed her left foot in Bria's connected palms, and as if they were psychically connected, Bria lifted her body at the same time that Rosalie bent her knee and rose upward. Rosalie's right arm was stretched high overhead until it grabbed on to the casing that protruded about two inches from the wall. When Rosalie felt secure, or as secure as she possibly could, she lifted her left arm until her fingers reached the picture frame.

"I've made contact with the object in question," Rosalie said.

"You're not traveling to the moon, Rosa. You're just lifting a frame off the wall."

"If you don't keep quiet, I'll send you to the moon!"

Rosalie pressed down on the casing a bit harder to lift her-self until she could firmly grab hold of the frame and not just touch it. Once she did, she lifted until she was sure the picture wire was no longer resting on the nail that it was hooked on. When she was certain the frame was free, she lifted it high overhead like a trophy.

"Got it!" she exclaimed.

Then Rosalie got too excited and raised her right hand victoriously, in a fist, causing her to lose her balance and fall right on top of Bria. Although her knee landed perilously close to Bria's nose, Rosalie kept her left hand raised so the frame didn't break. The women lay still for a few seconds to make sure they didn't break any bones, and when they concluded that their bodies were sore but still intact, they rose to their feet and began to reverse their steps so they could escape.

"*Madonna mia*! I can't believe we did this," Bria said as they climbed down the stairs.

The women held each other tightly, both experiencing a surge of excitement racing through their bodies and feeling the need to celebrate their triumph.

"I told you we could do it, Bri. You really have to learn to trust me more," Rosalie replied. As she opened the front door, she turned to face Bria and added, "I mean, when have I ever steered you wrong?"

"How about right now?" Bria said.

Confused, Rosalie turned around and screamed. Her voice was silenced only when Bria pressed her hand over her mouth. She tried to speak, but her words were indecipherable underneath Bria's fingers. Luckily, Bria had a pretty good idea what she was trying to say, so she responded for her friend.

"Luca, what are you doing here?"

"I could ask you two the same thing," Luca replied.

Rosalie yanked Bria's hand off her mouth so she could speak. "Luca Raffaello Umberto Vivaldi, you almost scared me to death!"

"Your confirmation name is Umberto?" Bria said. "Why did I not know this?"

"It's a well-kept family secret," Luca replied. "Unlike my sister's penchant for getting into trouble."

"That's what Carlo always said," Bria shared.

"That's what everyone always said," Luca added. "Our mamma, our papa, our grandparents, Rosalie's teachers, Father Maximo, Sister Maxima, in fact, all the nuns and clergy at St. Maximus, where we went to high school."

"*Scusatemi*!" Rosalie exclaimed. "I'm standing right here."

"And holding something that doesn't belong to you and coming out of a building where neither of you belong," Luca said.

"You don't belong here, either, Luca," Bria said. "What are you doing here? Have you been following us?"

"No," Luca replied, then pointed to Bria. "Only you."

"*Perché io*?" Bria asked.

"Because a dead man was found in your home, and we still don't know how or why he chose your place as refuge," Luca explained. "Until we do, I'm having you followed either by someone on the force or by me personally!"

Why do men always think they need to rescue a woman!

"I don't need your protection," Bria said.

"Yes you do," Luca replied. "This isn't a fun *avventura*. A man has been killed."

"I'm aware of that," Bria protested.

"Are you also aware that when someone kills once, they find it easier to kill a second time?"

"You think there's going to be another murder?" Rosalie asked.

Luca sighed heavily. From the way he kept looking from Rosalie to Bria, then back again, Bria could tell that he didn't want to have this conversation. Unfortunately, Bria could also tell that he knew he wasn't going to be able to lie to his sister and his friend. He had no choice but to continue talking.

"I think there's a very good possibility," Luca said. "I need both of you to be careful and to stop doing things like this. Who do you think you are? Imma Tataranni?"

"*Dio mio*! I love Imma!" Rosalie cried. She then turned to Bria. "I never thought of it, but we are just like that TV show."

"You know something? We are," Bria said. "I'm Imma, and you're my assistant."

"Why am I Diana De Santis?" Rosalie asked.

"I'm the one who thought of investigating this murder," Bria said. "You're kind of along for the ride."

"Whose idea was it to break into Dante's office and steal this?" Rosalie said, holding up the picture frame.

"I'll take that," Luca said, grabbing the picture frame. "If you were going to go to all the trouble to break into Dante's office, why didn't you steal something valuable?" Luca asked. "What's so important about this?"

"I know you don't agree, but I think the counterfeit money that you found in Vittorio's wallet and on the steps to Nocelle are somehow connected to the murder," Bria explained.

"You've been talking to Nunzi, I presume," Luca said.

"*Assolutamente no!*" Bria said, not wanting to get the cop into trouble.

"I'm going to interpret that as a yes," Luca replied, ignoring Bria's protestation.

"No! This was all my idea," Bria said. "I searched the archives of *La Vita* and discovered that both Nunzi's and Dante's fathers were two of the three men involved in the ring in the eighties."

"Dante's father was the mastermind," Luca confirmed.

"Not according to Dante," Bria said.

"What do you mean?" Luca asked.

"According to Dante, his father and the two other men were pawns. They weren't in charge. They did the bidding of some woman," Bria explained.

"What woman?" Luca asked, his voice filled with a bit more interest.

"He didn't know," Bria said. "Dante said his father never mentioned the woman's name, but he insinuated that he was having an affair with her."

"I could see that," Luca said. "The La Costa family isn't what you'd call moral."

"I don't think the woman was either," Bria said. "He said she was wealthy, powerful, and turned on all the men when the operation was discovered. She let them take the fall, while she remained unscathed."

"That shocked look on your face, big brother, says this is all news to you," Rosalie said.

Luca glared at his sister. "I still don't think that it means anything, but yes, I am surprised to hear that there was a woman involved."

"When are you and the rest of your gender going to learn that there's always a woman involved?" Rosalie said.

"And thanks to these two women," Bria said, pointing to herself and Rosalie, "you have more evidence to test."

"What do you mean?" Luca replied.

"Dante is away in Milan until Monday, attending a global warming summit," Bria explained. "That should be enough time for your people to test this lira and see if it's a fake like the others. If it's real, we'll break in again and put it back on the wall, but if it's a fake, that should be enough for you to bring him in for questioning. It's more than what you had on Giovanni."

Rosalie filled the pause while Luca tried to articulate a response. "Giovanni isn't the mayor, though, isn't that right, Luca?"

"No, that isn't right," Luca said. "If the tests prove that the lira's a fake, I'll bring in Dante for questioning. But I'll have to first get a warrant to search his office to retrieve the lira. You can't just break into a man's office and steal it."

"But we just did," Rosalie said.

"Rosalie Serafina Augustina Vivaldi!" Luca cried.

"That doesn't work, Luca," Bria said, unable to hide her smile. "Augustina isn't nearly as bad as Umberto."

"Let's get out of here," Luca said. "I'm sure you have to get back to Marco."

"He's staying with my mother until tomorrow. The school had off to put in the new altar in the church," Bria said, and then she slapped Luca on the arm, causing him to wince. "Do you really think I'd leave *mio piccolo angelo* alone in the house with a murderer on the loose just to find some evidence? What kind of mother do you think I am?"

"*Scusa*," Luca said. "I wasn't thinking. And that hurt."

"*Bene!*" Bria cried. "It was supposed to."

As they were leaving, Bria was shaking her head—how could Luca think she would abandon Marco in the middle of the night?—when she saw something next to the bushes that she hadn't noticed before.

"Can Dante sell a state building?" she asked.

"What do you mean?" Luca replied.

"Look over there, on the gate next to the bushes," Bria said. "It's one of those locks that Realtors use to show a home to buyers when the owner isn't present."

"Doesn't Dante own this building?" Rosalie asked.

"Yes, it's part of his family's estate," Luca replied. "He allows other departments to rent office space for free, but he can do whatever he wants with the building."

"Seems like Dante is full of a lot of surprises," Bria said.

"Dante isn't the only one full of surprises," Luca said.

Luca looked at Bria and smiled at her. Bria had to catch her breath, because in the moonlight he looked at her the same way Carlo had. She hadn't noticed another man look at her since she became a widow. It was an unsettling feeling, even more unsettling than the feeling she got breaking into a man's home.

Che macello! Bria thought. Things were starting to get messy. Bria had the distinct feeling that this *avventura* was going to bring her into even more uncharted territory.

CHAPTER 16

As long as the sun rises, there's hope that a better day has arrived. Bria almost laughed out loud, lying in her bed, when that phrase popped into her head. It was something Carlo would say, mainly because it made Bria roll her eyes and shake her head in disbelief. She loved her husband, but sometimes she had thought he was an idiot.

She could picture him now, looking at her with his goofy grin that somehow made his handsome face even more handsome, and smiled at the memory. Bria remembered how Luca had looked at her last night and thought, *Ah, Carlo, will anyone ever be able to take your place in my heart?* The answer came to her immediately. *Probably not.* If another man ever became part of her life, he'd have to cohabitate with Carlo in her heart. That was fine, Bria thought. Her heart was big enough to accommodate Carlo having a roommate.

The morning featured the typical controlled chaos. Walking Bravo, making breakfast, dropping everything to greet Marco when he returned with her mother from his overnight visit, avoiding her mother's litany of questions, convincing her mother she could leave and her world wouldn't collapse, and finally dropping her son off at St. Cecilia's. Bria watched Marco run off into the schoolyard to meet his classmates and, out of the corner of her eye, saw Sister Benedicta give Bravo his morning treat. Everyone loved Bravo, and since she'd moved to Positano, he'd become something of a mascot to the village. Just as the children were filing into school, Marco turned to find Bria and waved to her, his smile beaming. Thinking the wave was for him, Bravo barked, and Bria felt her eyes moisten. Despite the whirlwind of turmoil she presently found herself in, God had granted her two good boys.

"Are you all right?" Sister Benedicta said.

Startled, Bria almost didn't hear the nun's question. "Me? Oh yes. Why?"

"For a moment you looked a bit, well, sad," Sister B explained.

"Just the opposite," Bria replied. "Sometimes I'm overwhelmed with gratitude."

Sister Benedicta's smile indicated to Bria that she understood the feeling she was trying to convey. "Marco is a wonderful boy, and this one has the Lord's light shining in his eyes."

Bria watched Sister B bend down and stare into Bravo's eyes as she stroked the fur underneath his chin. Bravo let out a soft groan, almost like a cat's purr. While Bria smiled at the Sister's actions, it was her words that gave her pause.

Having grown up as a Catholic, like the majority of Italians, Bria was well versed in the teachings of the church, its ceremony, its mystery, its language. Her family, friends, and neighbors all sprinkled their conversations with religious phrases and analogies, making God an ever-present companion. Despite her disapproval of how the Catholic Church had conducted itself on some issues over the centuries, she welcomed its presence in her life. But sometimes, like today, she took that presence for granted.

She loved Bravo dearly and considered him part of her family, as most dog owners did, but to hear Sister Benedicta comment that she saw God's light within her beloved pet was profound. It reminded Bria that when life became too crazy, which was almost a daily occurrence lately, it was important to remember that there was something bigger out there, something that was in control of all the chaos. It helped Bria maintain her footing while living in the eye of the storm.

"That's a beautiful thing to say," Bria said.

"It's the truth," Sister B replied. "Children and animals are truly manifestations of Christ on earth. They're joyful, accepting, and they love unconditionally."

Bria nodded and made the sign of the cross. "Thank you for reminding me of that."

Sister Benedicta stood up and smiled. "How are you doing, Mrs. Bartolucci?"

"Please, call me Bria. My mother-in-law is the real Mrs. Bartolucci," Bria said. "And she herself would tell you that."

Sister Benedicta couldn't help but release a hearty laugh, which she tried unsuccessfully to control. "I have been in Imperia's presence, so I don't doubt that is true. But really, are you okay? I know this has been a difficult time."

"As a single mother and a fledgling business owner, I'm used to a certain amount of disarray in my life," Bria said. "This latest . . . snafu, as the Americans would call it . . . has amped things up a bit and not completely in a bad way."

"What do you mean by that?" Benedicta asked.

Bria paused for a moment and wasn't sure she'd be able to convey exactly what she was feeling or if the nun would understand, but she tried. "It's a terrible thing what happened—a man lost his life violently—but at the same time, it's as if his death has given my life purpose."

Surprisingly, Sister Benedicta understood perfectly what Bria was trying to convey. "That's how it works," she replied. "One window closes, and another door opens. God dies for our sins, and we're reborn. It's the cycle of life and death."

"But I didn't even know this man. We have absolutely no connection, and yet he's changed my life, because for some reason, I'm hell-bent on finding out who killed him." Bria reflected on her poor word choice and apologized. "*Scusami*, I didn't mean to say *hell-bent*."

"Don't worry Sister," Benedicta said. "I'm well versed in the concept of hell."

Once again, the Sister's words affected Bria. She had started the day with sweet memories and laughter, and already she was contemplating deep philosophical concepts.

"Who was Vittorio? He's the man who was killed," Bria said. "Was he an innocent victim? Did he deserve to die that way? Is anyone even mourning his death?"

"Don't be so hard on yourself," Sister Benedicta said, reaching out to hold Bria's hand. "You may not realize it or see it this way, but I think you're doing God's work."

"Me?" Bria asked. "No, I'm just trying to get my business off the ground."

"You're doing much more than that," Sister Benedicta said. "You've taken a moment to look inside yourself, into your heart, and you made the decision to seek the truth and bring this man justice. But remember that such unselfish action does come at a price."

"What do you mean by that?" Bria asked.

"You may not like what you uncover," Sister Benedicta replied.

The nun's words stayed with Bria an hour later, when she was placing a final order for groceries that would be delivered next week, just in time for Bella Bella's opening. She had already found out some disturbing information about people she knew and members of her family. What else would her investigation uncover? She knew herself well enough to know that she had already come too far to turn back; no matter the result, she would see this through.

To Bria, she was at a *punto di svolta*, a turning point, like when Carlo died. She had had a choice to bend under the emotional weight of his death and seek refuge in either her parents' home or Imperia's, but she had known—thanks in large part to her mother's advice—that if she wanted to be the best mother Marco could have and if she wanted to become the best person she knew she could be, she had to forge ahead on her own. She felt the same conviction now. If she wanted to teach Marco that you didn't run away from a question simply because you didn't want to know the answer, she needed to continue working toward solving this mystery.

When she heard Bravo barking and saw a strange man at her front door, she didn't immediately realize that another clue had just arrived.

Prior to the murder, Bria had left the front door unlocked at all times, but now, after a scolding from Nunzi, she had gotten into the habit of locking it whenever she left and even when she was alone in the house, without Giovanni. Since her employee was going to all the business owners in town, getting their brochures and coupons for discounts, which would be given to guests in their welcome bags, and she was alone right now, the front door was locked.

She was greatly relieved when she opened the door, because the man standing before her hardly looked threatening. He looked to be in his midfifties, about her father's age, but not nearly as robust, and while her father still had a thick mane of hair, black with some silver at the temples, this man wasn't nearly as lucky. His thinning brown hair was slicked back from his receding hairline, and in some places the amount of scalp that was visible outweighed his hair.

His business suit was bespoke but ill fitting on his slim

frame, and while the pink petunia in his lapel was a pretty decoration, it only served to give this man an overall air of clownishness. Bria thought he should be holding a straw hat in his hands, and she was waiting for him to slip on an imaginary banana peel and take a pratfall.

"*Ciao*, *signorina*," the man said. "May I have a moment of your time?"

The man's voice didn't disappoint or contradict his physical appearance. It was high pitched, and he tried to sound grand, as if he were Roberto Benigni and was trying to finagle his way into an exclusive party without an invitation. The man flashed a smile that would have made Roberto proud, and Bria invited him in but kept the front door open, in case the man turned out to be less like Benigni and more like one of the Corleone brothers and she needed to make a quick exit.

"*Senz'altro. Entra*," Bria said. "We aren't open just yet, but you can make a reservation. Unless you need a place for tonight. Then I can recommend Casetta di Violetta, a very charming hotel, or Le Sirenuse, more expensive, but very elegant, if that's what you like."

"No, *mi scusi*, I don't need a place to stay," the man said, entering the house. "I just need some answers."

Instinctively, Bria felt her stomach burn. This man was more Corleone than Benigni; she just didn't know if he was as ruthless as Michael or as feeble as Fredo. Smiling to hide her nervousness, she replied, "You haven't asked any questions yet."

"*Vero*, you're very perceptive," the man said. "I imagine you can tell me a lot about the body you found upstairs."

Her instincts were right: this man could be a member of the Corleone family. And she could see a flicker of glee in his eye that could be camouflaging malice. The look convinced Bria he was much more of a rival to Michael, Don Corleone's conflicted but ultimately monstrous youngest child. She needed to find a way to get him to leave Bella Bella without making him think that he was being escorted out.

She glanced at the clock on the wall. "*Dio mio*, look at the time," she said. "*Mi scusi*, but I have to leave for a business appointment."

"Dressed like that?" the man asked.

Looking down at her feet, she saw that she was wearing her fluffy red slippers and still had on the lounge pants she had slept in and worn to walk Marco to school. She didn't have to inspect her ensemble any further, because a T-shirt with Minnie Mouse on it didn't exactly scream business attire. Of course, her intruder had to have a sense of fashion.

"I have to change, and I'm running late," Bria lied. "Thank you for stopping by."

"Forgive me. I should have been honest with you the moment I walked through your door," the man said, smiling sheepishly. "I'm a reporter."

"Aldo doesn't have any staff," Bria said.

"Who?" the man asked.

"You work for *La Vita Positano*?" Bria asked.

"No," the man replied. "A small paper. I'm sure you've never heard of it."

"What's the name of it?"

The man hesitated. His smile faded, causing his thin lips to press together, and his soft features hardened. It was a slight transformation, but Bria knew that this man was capable of violence. Despite his benign appearance, he was dangerous.

"*La Notizia di Milan*," the man finally said.

Milan, Bria thought. *Of all the cities in Italy, he just happens to pick Milan, which was one of Vittorio's frequent destinations.* Suddenly, Bria was more intrigued than frightened.

"A reporter all the way from Milan is interested in a dead man in Positano?" Bria asked.

The smile returned to the man's face, but Bria could tell it wasn't authentic. It was a way to hide his growing frustration. "*Prego*, we like to report on all of Italy. It makes our readers feel connected to other parts of the country."

The man walked farther into the house and looked upstairs, at the door to the bedroom where Vittorio had been found. Bria knew that Aldo had included the fact that Vittorio's body had been found upstairs at Bella Bella in his article, but she was certain he had not mentioned in which bedroom. How did this man know exactly where the body had been found? If he was really a reporter, he could have a contact at the Positano police station. Or maybe he was just gazing upstairs, and not specifically at the last door on the right?

"Anything in particular you're looking at?" Bria asked.

Slowly, he turned to face Bria. This time his face was no longer a friendly mask as he tried to hide his feelings. He looked threatening, and when he spoke, his tone matched his expression. "Tell me everything that you know about the Englishman."

Now Bria knew the man was on a fishing expedition. She wasn't convinced that he was a reporter, but she knew he didn't know anything about the murder.

"What Englishman?" Bria asked.

"The man who was murdered," he replied. "The one you found upstairs."

"He wasn't an Englishman," Bria replied.

Slowly, the man started to walk toward Bria. Bravo, who had been watching the scene intently, stood up and just as slowly walked in front of Bria, growling lowly. The man smiled at Bravo's display of chivalry.

"I really wish you wouldn't lie to me," he said.

"I'm telling you the truth," Bria replied, instinctively taking a few steps backward toward the front door. "If you don't believe me, ask my friend Luca Vivaldi. He's the chief of police and is very trustworthy."

At the mention of Luca's name, the man froze. He quickly recovered and made a show out of fixing the flower in his lapel, but it was clear that he was startled by the mention of law enforcement. Not as startled as he was when Bria's next guest arrived.

"What are you doing here?" Imperia asked.

Bria turned and saw her mother-in-law standing in the doorway and had never been happier to have an unexpected visitor grace her doorstep. She then turned to face the man Imperia had just addressed and was surprised to see fear in the man's eyes. She knew Imperia sparked dread and caused others to be filled with anxiety, but she had thought it was only with people who knew her and not with strangers. Clearly, her mother-in-law's powers weren't restricted by boundaries.

"*Grazie,*" the man said. "I've taken up enough of your time."

A few seconds ago, all she had wanted was for the man to leave; now that she had backup, all she wanted was for him to stay.

"Don't you need to ask me more questions for your article?" Bria asked.

"I have what I need, *grazie,*" the man said before scurrying out the door.

Before he left, he glanced backward, looking not at Bria, whom he had come to talk to, not at Bravo, who was now growling much louder, but at Imperia, who was now standing next to the kitchen counter, her fingers alarmingly close to the handle of the ten-inch serrated knife that Bria had used to cut up day-old bread for croutons to be used in her salad for lunch. Why? That didn't make sense. Unless . . .

As if he had been punched in the stomach, the man flinched.

His shoulders arched forward, and Bria heard a sharp intake of breath through his nose. Without another look at anyone, the man ran off, much more frantically than he had arrived.

None of it made sense. Well, it did make sense, which was more disturbing to Bria than being utterly confused as to the man's presence and his actions. For the second time in little over a week, a man whom she didn't know was in her house. First, Vittorio, and now this so-called reporter. She believed Imperia was somehow linked to Vittorio. Was it possible that she was also linked to this man? Bria took a deep breath and spoke before she lost her nerve.

"Do you know that man?" Bria asked.

"*Che cosa*?" Imperia asked.

Bria felt her strength replace any trepidation she had felt about questioning her mother-in-law.

"I asked you if you know that man," Bria repeated.

"Why in the world would you ask me such a question?"

"Because you asked him what he was doing here."

"Because I know you haven't opened yet, and I know everyone in Positano," Imperia replied. "I knew he didn't belong here."

Plausible, but I know she's lying.

"He recognized you," Bria said. "His whole demeanor changed the moment you arrived."

Imperia waved her hand in the air dismissively and tossed her purse on the counter where it landed next to the knife. She walked over to Bravo and tapped him on the head a few times in an attempt, Bria assumed, to make it look like she was petting the dog. The problem was Imperia had never been affectionate to Bravo, not even when they had first brought him home as a puppy. On the few occasions that she had acted cordially around him instead of completely ignoring him, she had never bent down to be on his level. Relinquishing her position of authority was not something that Imperia would ever do, not with family, a business rival, or an animal.

Bravo accepted Imperia's touch cautiously, and Bria didn't blame him. Why offer unconditional surrender to an opponent whom he rarely even encountered on the battlefield? But why was Imperia in fight mode? Why was she plotting? What was she hiding?

"What are you doing here?" Bria asked.

"I need a reason to visit?" Imperia replied.

"No, of course not, but I wasn't expecting you," Bria said.

Not taking her eyes off Bravo, Imperia spoke. "I came to tell you that I ran into Dante in Milan."

"You were in Milan again?"

"I'm often in Milan," Imperia replied. "I run a corporation."

"I didn't know you had any interest in a conference about climate change," Bria said.

Finally, Imperia stood to face Bria, and she looked like her normal self. Controlled, authoritarian, imperious. "As a businesswoman, I have many interests."

"Of course you do, but why would I be interested to know that you bumped into Dante at the conference?"

"Because he told me you were asking questions about his father and that stupid counterfeit money ring from decades ago."

"He told you that?" Bria asked, surprised Dante would want to share such unflattering information.

"I've been a friend of the La Costa family for years."

"Did you know Giancarlo?"

"Very well," Imperia said. "I wanted to assure you that while Dante's father was not nearly the man my husband was, he wasn't a criminal."

"I never said he was," Bria replied. "I was only asking Dante about what happened back then."

"Because you think history is repeating itself."

Bria was going to fill Imperia in on the evidence she had and the counterfeit lire, but she stopped herself. She was in a unique situation, and she had to tread carefully. Imperia was always the first to strike, the first to make a move in business, the first to confront. Now she was scrambling to defend herself; she was deflecting and steering the conversation toward a new topic to avoid answering Bria's original question. She hadn't made Bria question her initial thoughts; she had only strengthened them.

"I was curious about the counterfeit ring, and I went to Dante to get answers," Bria said.

"Did his answers satisfy you?" Imperia asked.

"Absolutely," Bria lied. "The matter is closed."

"Good," Imperia said. "Dante is a dear friend, and I wouldn't want him to think that my family suspects him of foul play."

"Did you really come all this way just to tell me that?" Bria asked. "You could have called."

"I was in the vicinity, so I thought I'd pop in."

Once again, Bria suspected her mother-in-law of lying, and she decided to use that to her advantage.

"I'm glad that you did," Bria said, involuntarily smiling. "I think it's important to clear the air. Misunderstandings that aren't attended to have the tendency to fester and grow into bigger, sometimes unsolvable problems. Neither of us would want that."

In a quick, easy move, Imperia grabbed her purse from the counter, but Bria thought for sure she was reaching for the knife. It was an involuntary thought, but not unwarranted. Her mother-in-law had not gotten what she came for. She had come to put Bria in her place, to remind her that Imperia had friends all over, in every facet of society. All she had done was prove to Bria that she had something to hide.

Unfortunately, her visit had also taught Bria that Imperia had some acquaintances she preferred would remain in the shadows. Imperia could claim that she didn't know the man who had posed as a reporter, the man who had been looking for an Englishman, the man who had asked questions about a murder victim. But no matter what Imperia said, Bria knew that her son's grandmother was lying.

Now all she needed to figure out was the identity of the man who had posed as a reporter and how he was connected to Imperia.

CHAPTER 17

"*Bugiardo!*"

Bria's outburst was so loud that the man sitting next to her at Caffé Positano turned around to eavesdrop and appeared to be more curious about her conversation than the one he was having with the woman sitting across from him at the small table overlooking the sea. His companion, who was several years older than Bria and more than several pounds heavier, leaned over and slapped the man on the shoulder so hard that he teetered on his chair and had to grab the edge of the table to steady himself. The woman sputtered some colorful language at the man that sounded more suitable coming from an inebriated Italian sailor than a caffeinated Italian woman. Bria saw all this action out of the corner of her eye, and while she did find it, on one level, entertaining, she was much more interested in what Luca had just told her—he had proof that Dante was a liar.

"What do you mean, there was no global warming conference in Milan?" Bria asked.

"There wasn't a global warming conference anywhere," Luca said. "Not in Milan, Munich, or Mozambique. We were able to confirm that he did go to Milan, so he didn't lie about that."

Bria took a quick sip of her lemon cappuccino, a house specialty that Annamaria had personally created. As anxious as she was to find out more about Dante, she hesitated a moment to allow the citrus and bitter combination to settle on her tongue before swallowing. Her father had always reminded her never to race past the simple pleasures in life, but to savor them.

"How do you know he really went to Milan?" Bria asked. "Did you plant one of those GPS devices on his car? Or did you implant one of those microchips in his skin, like I've read people do in Denmark?"

Luca stared at Bria, and she couldn't tell if he was amused or perplexed. Had she said something foolish? She had read about the technologically obsessed Danish in the very respectable daily paper *Corriere della Sera*, not some *National Enquirer*–type tabloid published by Generoso Pope. Maybe her instincts were getting too close to the police department's top secret actions? Or maybe the caffeine was making her ramble incoherently? Either way, Luca seemed confused.

"Don't you think that's a smart thing to do?" Bria asked.

"What?" Luca asked in return.

"Putting microchips in our skin so every person's whereabouts can be tracked."

"That would be an invasion of privacy."

"That would also make it much easier to track suspects when they say they're going to Milan for a global warming conference that doesn't exist."

"The conference doesn't exist, but we did track Dante and can confirm he flew to Milan."

"How?" Bria asked again.

"Fabrice was the pilot," Luca explained, squinting into the afternoon sunshine. "He and I were playing racquetball, and he told me."

It was Bria's turn to be confused. "You play racquetball with Fabrice?"

"We've been playing for the past few years," Luca replied.

"Why didn't my sister tell me?"

"Maybe Fabrice didn't tell her."

Bria laughed so hard this time, she attracted the attention of not only the man but also the woman sitting next to her. She turned to them and apologized for her outburst and then resumed her conversation with Luca. When she spoke, she couldn't do so without giggling.

"There isn't anything that Fabrice does that Lorenza doesn't know about," Bria said. "I think *she* might have implanted one of those chips under Fabrice's skin while he was sleeping."

Luca's light brown eyes shimmered in the afternoon sunshine as he joined in Bria's infectious laughter. "*Indossa i pantaloni in quella relazione*," Luca said.

"Fabrice loves to let Lorenza wear the pants in their relationship," Bria added. "She's lucky he loves her so much, otherwise he might get upset with her being so *autoritaria*."

"I'm sure he told her at some point," Luca said. "We play whenever he's in town and has some free time."

"And he told you Dante was on his flight?" Bria asked.

"Yes. Both to and from Milan," Luca said.

Bria took a longer sip of her cappuccino and gazed down at the beach. The blue and white cabanas at Spiaggia Grande lined the shoreline and looked postcard perfect. The sun was making the horizon blur, and it was hard to distinguish where the water ended and where the sky began. The landscape was a swirl of color and light, like a Monet painting, a mere impression of the truth. Like what Luca had just told her. She had learned some factual information but still didn't know what Dante had really done this past weekend.

What was the truth about Dante? Bria wondered. And had he done something that made an impression on Fabrice?

"Did Fabrice tell you as a friend or as a police informant?" Bria asked.

"Great question," Luca replied. "Why do you ask?"

"I know men gossip more than women, although they refuse to admit it, and Fabrice could have simply mentioned it in passing," Bria started. "But was there something that Dante did or said that made an impression on Fabrice and compelled him to tell you?"

"I think it was more gossip," Luca confessed. "He said that on the return flight, Dante wore his sunglasses the entire time and wouldn't take them off. Kayla, one of the flight attendants, told him that."

"That's Lorenza's friend from Iowa," Bria explained. "Which is in America, *tra l'altro*."

Luca flashed a grin. "I know where Iowa is."

"*Scusami*," Bria said. "I didn't know the chief of police was also a world traveler."

"Hardly," Luca said. "I don't like traveling alone."

"You and Fabrice should go somewhere," Bria said. "He's a pilot, so he could fly you anywhere, and I'm sure Lorenza wouldn't mind if he was going with you."

Luca blushed. "Fabrice isn't my first choice for a traveling companion."

"Who is?" Bria asked.

Uffa! The second the words spilled out, Bria wished she could gather them up, sprinkle them into her cappuccino, and gulp. Too late for that. Her words and their implication were out in the world, as bright as the Positano sun, unshadowed and searing into her brain, just as she knew they were searing into Luca's. *Who's your first choice for a traveling companion? Who do you like?* It was a schoolgirl question, as gossipy as anything Annamaria might say, but that wasn't the real problem. Bria didn't want to know the answer.

If Luca said that he wanted to travel with Paloma or Violetta
—when she wasn't running her hotel of course—or some
woman outside the village, that would mean he didn't want to
travel with Bria. But did Bria want to travel with Luca? The
thought washed over her like a sudden wave from the Tyrrhenian Sea. She felt as if the normally tranquil body of water had
inexplicably erupted into a tsunami and smacked her right in
the face. She didn't want to travel with Luca. Did she? Did
Luca want to travel with her? Why was she having these
thoughts when the focus was supposed to be on Dante? Why
wasn't Luca saying anything?

Just when Bria was going to apologize for asking such a personal question, Luca replied by not truly answering the question.

"I . . . haven't really thought about that specifically, but I
prefer not to travel alone," Luca said diplomatically. "I'm so
busy with work I don't have much time for a vacation any way,
especially now that we're trying to solve this murder case."

Ah yes! The murder.

"If Dante wasn't attending a conference, why did he go to
Milan?" Bria asked.

"The local authorities couldn't—or, more likely, *wouldn't*—
keep a trail on the mayor of Positano after he landed, so we
lost him after that," Luca explained.

Bria was going to share that Imperia had also been in Milan
that same weekend, but the city was a large business and cultural center, so there were literally thousands of reasons why a
person would spend the weekend there. The fact that she and
Dante had been there at the same time was just coincidence.
Imperia was a distraction, and the focal point should be Dante.

"If we don't know why Dante went to Milan, do we at least
know if the framed lira is real or counterfeit?" Bria asked.

"We do," Luca replied.

Bria waited for him to continue, and when he didn't, she

thought she was going to explode. "Luca! What did you find out? *Dimmi*!"

"I was pausing for dramatic effect."

"*Dio mio*! Whoever says women are drama queens never met a man!" Bria cried. "Now tell me, is the lira real or fake?"

"It's real," Luca finally admitted.

"*Veramente?*"

"*Veramente.*"

"Really?"

"Really!"

"I was convinced it would be fake," Bria said.

"Don't tell Nunzi," Luca replied, "but I was hoping it was, too."

"I thought you said you didn't believe any of it and you were going along with testing the lira only to prove to me and Nunzi that we were wrong," Bria replied.

"I never said that."

"You didn't have to say it out loud. You insinuated it with your tone and your facial expressions."

"My facial expressions?" Luca said, scrunching his face into an expression that conveyed surprise, amusement, and confusion all in one.

"Yes, your right eyebrow rises whenever you think something or someone is being ridiculous, but you don't want to say they're being ridiculous," Bria explained. "You use body language instead of words."

"You noticed that I do that?"

"Yes. Does that mean I'm right?"

"It's a habit I keep trying to break," Luca said. "Guess I have to work a bit harder."

"That means you think I'm ridiculous."

"Not always. Just in this instance. And the test results reveal that my initial instinct was correct."

"The test could be wrong."

"I had it tested twice."

"*Dannazione*! Crucify me, because I was a little ridiculous, but so was Nunzi."

Luca flashed a dazzling grin, all white teeth and shimmering brown eyes, which seemed to grow lighter in the midday sun. Bria forced herself to sip her cappuccino and turn away, acting as if she was more interested in watching the endless stream of scooters and Vespas whoosh by. Even though Bria was annoyed with Luca, she couldn't help noticing how handsome he was, but she didn't want Luca to notice that she had noticed.

"Neither of you were being ridiculous, but you both allowed your personal feelings to invade the investigation," Luca explained. He leaned forward and lowered his voice. "I don't particularly like Dante, and I do think, like most politicians, he has secrets he'd like to hide and has more than likely been involved in a shady deal or two. These are my personal feelings, and they have no bearing on this case, nor do they make him a suspect."

"That's not how you treated Giovanni," Bria replied. "You hauled him in for questioning simply because of his past."

"That isn't true," Luca rebutted. "I arrested Giovanni because he didn't have an alibi, he ran from Nunzi, he is one of the few people who has easy access to Bella Bella and could have entered the premises without causing any suspicion, and because he has a documented criminal past. Dante might be a con artist, but Giovanni is an ex-con."

A tightness squeezed at Bria's throat, and she had to consciously relax and breathe deep to lessen the pain. It wasn't an unfamiliar feeling, but it was an uncomfortable one. It was the same feeling she used to get when she was forced to realize that Carlo had won a long-fought battle. The truth was that she liked to win—art contests, fencing matches, debates—and she often did. Losing to an opponent she hardly knew was bearable; losing to someone she cared about was an unwanted disruption.

"I have a lot to learn if we're going to have a new relationship," Bria said.

Luca's *left* eyebrow shot up. Bria didn't know what secret meaning his left eye conveyed, but she assumed this was how he reacted when he was startled. She realized her words could be taken very differently than she had meant them.

"*Perdonami*! Not, you know, in a personal way. Not that at all," Bria stammered. "I meant that our new relationship is sort of like colleagues, detectives, you know, now that I'm working on this case."

"You're not working on this case," Luca stated.

"I am, sort of."

"Only as a civilian informant."

"*Informant* sounds like a very official title."

"It just means that you're giving the police force—of which you are not a part—information."

Some information, Bria silently corrected. "Absolutely. Whatever I find out, you find out very, very shortly thereafter. And vice versa, as they say, *giusto*?"

"*Certo*," Luca said. "Which brings me to the last bit of . . . I'm not sure we can call it evidence. But one more piece of information that we uncovered about Dante that does connect him to the murder and indicates why he can't be considered a suspect, but he can definitely be considered a person of interest."

"You have more dirt on Dante?" Bria asked. "How much more do you need to consider him a suspect?"

"Quite a bit," Luca replied. "We need to establish means and motive, and we can't prove either, but we will question him."

"What's this information?"

"He knew Vittorio."

"What! Why wasn't that the first thing you said to me?"

"It's called building a case."

"You build very slowly, Luca!" Bria said. "How does Dante know Vittorio?"

"Dante recently sold his father's house in Perugia."

"That place isn't a house. It's a palazzo."

"It's big, but in need of repair," Luca said. "Dolce Vita Real Estate handled the transaction, and Vittorio Ingleterra was the Realtor. Our murder victim sold Dante's father's house."

"That's incredible!" Bria exclaimed. "That ties Dante to the murder victim."

"Dante and every other person who worked with Vittorio," Luca replied. "Although selling the palazzo was his first significant sale in three years, so he doesn't have many business clients."

"I bet none of those other people also live in Positano. *Ho ragione?*"

"You are correct," Luca confirmed. "Dante's the only one."

"Now who's being ridiculous?" Bria asked.

"Me?"

"Yes! I'm not sure how and I'm not accusing Dante of murder . . . I don't know him well enough to know if he's capable of that," Bria started.

"But you think it's possible," Luca replied, framing the comment as a statement of the truth as opposed to asking a question.

Bria considered her response before responding. She wanted to make sure Luca understood what she really felt, but she didn't want to come off as flighty and as a woman who relied too heavily on female intuition. She didn't want to give him any reason to think she couldn't be as analytical as a man.

"I do," she answered. "Dante is cagey. He lives next to the truth, if you know what I mean. Whenever I've spoken to him, it's always as if there's a whole other conversation going on in his mind that he keeps private. I think that Dante, the one that he keeps tucked away inside his mind, is definitely capable of unprovoked violence. That's how I feel, anyway, which is the complete opposite of my feelings about Giovanni."

"You have feelings about Giovanni?" Luca asked.

"No."

"You just said that you did."

"I didn't mean *feelings*. I meant *feeling*."

"There's a difference?"

"Sometimes you're such a man."

"*Grazie.*"

"It wasn't meant as a compliment," Bria said. "My instinct about Giovanni is the opposite of my instinct about Dante. I know that Giovanni has done things in the past . . . I investigated him . . . a bit . . . But I believe that he has changed and that in his heart, he is incapable of murder."

"What about defense?"

"What do you mean?"

"Do you think Giovanni is capable of defending himself?" Luca asked. "I'm sure you've noticed he's rippling with muscles."

"I wouldn't say rippling," Bria replied. "But yes, he is *nerboruto* . . . muscular."

"In a physical altercation, Giovanni could easily defend himself against an attacker."

"You think Vittorio attacked Giovanni and got stabbed in a fight?"

"It's possible," Luca said. "That would explain why Vittorio was found at Bella Bella. The incident could have happened nearby, and he could have followed Giovanni as he was going to work."

"I never thought of that," Bria replied. "I didn't consider the possibility that Vittorio was the aggressor. I just assumed that if he was murdered, someone attacked him."

"Just an innocent bystander?"

"Maybe not innocent, but not the one who started the confrontation."

"If you want to solve a crime, you have to look at it from every angle," Luca explained. "Even the ones that might hurt your vision. You have to separate your feelings from your instinct. It isn't always easy, but it's possible."

"Is that what you'll do with Dante?" Bria asked.

"Yes," Luca replied. "I'm going to return the framed lira. I'll tell him that we found it in a trash can, that it was stolen, and I'll use the opportunity to question him about Vittorio."

"Which means that Dante is still a suspect," Bria declared.

"A person of interest," Luca corrected.

"*Tu dici patata*," Bria said. "However you say it, the bottom line is that the mayor of Positano could also be its latest murderer."

CHAPTER 18

The next day completely revolved around food, which in Italy was a typical daily routine. Shopping for food, preparing food, cooking food, eating food. Food was simply an integral part of Italian life. Food connected families and friends, food communicated emotions, and food instigated conversation. Bria was hoping it would help her get closer to finding out if Dante, Imperia, or someone else in the village had killed Vittorio.

It started with breakfast.

After she dropped off Marco at school, she came home and fed Bravo, giving him some extra eggs and sausage mixed in with his dog food as a deterrent to keep him from bothering her while she was cooking. She decided to make ricotta pancakes topped with whipped cream and strawberries and a mushroom and pepper frittata. It was a large breakfast and not at all what she ate on a daily basis, but she wanted to make Giovanni linger at the table instead of running off and working, like he normally would. She needed him to talk.

Bria realized that if Giovanni had a morally ambiguous past, perhaps she could use it to her advantage. If Dante had an equally murky past—or possibly even present—their paths had probably crossed. The village of Positano wasn't large. It was stretched out and had many levels on its vertical descent from the top of the Monti Lattari to Spiaggia Grande, thanks to having been built on the side of a mountain, with the beach as its foundation, but its community was small. People knew each other, cared for each other, gossiped about each other. If Dante was involved in something he wanted to keep quiet, chances were that Giovanni would know about it, even if the police didn't. It might be just the clue needed to connect Dante to Vittorio's murder.

"*Porca vacca!*" Giovanni exclaimed standing in front of the smorgasbord. "Now, that's a big breakfast."

"I'm trying to get used to cooking for more than just me and Marco," Bria explained. "*Vieni*, join me."

Like the typical Italian mother that she was, Bria wasn't going to take no for an answer. She had witnessed her mother, her grandmother, and almost every adult woman she knew, except Imperia, serve breakfast, lunch, dinner, or a late-night snack to everyone, no matter if they proclaimed they had just finished eating, weren't hungry or, God forbid, were on a diet. Luckily, Giovanni confessed he had been running late and hadn't had time to eat, so Bria wasn't going to have to convince him to join her at the table. All she needed to do was find out how to wrangle details out of him that he probably wanted to keep secret.

A healthy plate of the frittata and pancakes in front of him, Giovanni started eating with gusto. He stabbed a strawberry with his fork and then punctured a double layer of pancakes before shoving the bounty into his mouth and relishing the taste. He made some sounds that Bria knew all too well: they were the same kind of sounds Carlo used to make when Bria made a special meal. During their marriage she hadn't always cooked. Carlo liked to whip up meals in the kitchen, Fifetta would constantly drop off containers of home-cooked food, or they would eat out at a café. When Bria did cook, however, she always followed her mother's advice: either cook with love or don't cook at all.

"*Delizioso, Bria. Semplicemente delizioso*," Giovanni said.

"*Grazie, Vanni. Mangia, mangia*," Bria instructed, sitting down at the end of the table across from Giovanni.

She let him eat uninterrupted, watching as he scooped up some frittata on his fork and devoured the pancakes. When it seemed that Giovanni's taste buds were making it impossible for him to think of anything else, Bria began her interrogation.

"You won't believe what I heard," she began. "Dante is connected to Vittorio."

Vanni looked surprised by this news but kept on chewing.

"It turns out that Vittorio is . . . well, was, *scusami* . . . the real estate broker who just happened to sell Dante's father's palazzo in Perugia," she explained.

Vanni mumbled something, but Bria couldn't make out the words, because he had spoken with his mouth full.

"What did you say?" Bria asked.

"That makes sense," Vanni replied.

"Why?"

"Because six months ago, on his Pinterest page, the one devoted to real estate, Vittorio posted a series of photos of a huge villa with a sprawling estate," Giovanni explained.

"Was it identified as the La Costa estate?"

"No. It only said that the estate was a recent sale in Perugia," Giovanni replied. He then pulled out his cell phone and started pressing buttons. "*Perdonami, sono un tale stupido*! I also found his ex-wife's Instagram feed."

"Vittorio has an ex-wife?"

"Linda Ingleterra," Vanni replied. "Originally from Spain. Terrassa, near Barcelona."

"Has anyone told her that her ex-husband's been murdered?" Bria asked.

"If they have, she hasn't posted anything about it," Vanni said. "The only mention of Vittorio is indirect. For instance, she thanks V for the alimony payments next to a photo of a new dress."

Giovanni brought a photo up on the phone's screen of a very short, very red, and very silky piece of material that doubled as a dress.

"*Ah, Madonna mia*," Bria said. "That's what Grand-mère Chantal would call *ennuyeux*, which is French for *noioso*, boring."

"I know the French are very opinionated when it comes to their style," Giovanni said, knowing that Bria was talking about her grandmother on her mother's side, who was from France. "But would she really consider this dress boring?"

"Yes, because it leaves nothing to the imagination," Bria explained. "My father's mother, Nonna Josefina, would just call it *classe bassa*."

"Whatever you call it, it proves that the former Mrs. Ingleterra is spending Vittorio's money, if not wisely, in large amounts."

"Is there anything else about him in her posts?" Bria asked.

"No, Linda seems to be consumed with her life in Beverly Hills and the premiere of the new movie *Wave Dancers*."

"She's an actress?" Bria asked.

"No, her boyfriend produced it," Vanni replied. "Her social media is plastered with photos of the cast, a trailer for the movie, even the red carpet at the recent opening."

"*Aspetta*!" Bria exclaimed. "Maybe it was a messy divorce, and she came back to Positano to confront him because she was angry that he had left her or because he wasn't paying her alimony. Then they got into a heated argument, and she killed him."

"Not possible," Giovanni replied.

"Why not?" Bria asked. "Women can just as easily commit murder as men."

"True, but the ex-wife has an airtight alibi," Vanni explained. "She was with Arthur—he's the new boyfriend—at the premiere, along with a thousand other people."

"*Dannazione!*" Bria cried. "Do you know if he has any other family?"

"Only a sister, Julietta, who lives in Switzerland, near the border," Vanni said. "Based on Julietta's social media, it seems that she and Vittorio are estranged. There's no sign of any interaction between the two of them. She hasn't come to Positano to claim the body, which means that she either doesn't know or doesn't care that her brother is dead."

Bria made the sign of the cross, kissed her fingers, and offered them up to God. How could a sister deny her brother? She and Gabrielo were hardly close, but if he needed her, she would go to him, and if he died, she would not disrespect him. Maybe Julietta was Italian only by birth and not Italian by life; maybe she didn't believe in the importance of family. Or maybe she was the one who had killed him.

As if reading Bria's mind, Giovanni said, "The sister has an alibi, too. The photos she took of a wedding she attended in Geneva were date stamped at 4:45 a.m. the morning Vittorio was murdered."

"That's some long wedding."

"*Vera.* And it proves that both women were far too busy to hop a flight and come to Positano to murder the man. His murderer has to be someone else."

"But his ex-wife might be able to point us in the right direction," Bria said.

"How so?"

"If she's living in Beverly Hills, that means she has to maintain a certain lifestyle, one much flashier than when she was

212 / MICHAEL FALCO

living in a little town outside Barcelona," Bria explained, munching on some pancake smothered in whipped cream. "Could you show me her page?"

Vanni nodded, fiddled with his cell phone again, and when he had found what he was looking for, he handed the phone to Bria. What she saw on the screen made her scream.

"*Non posso crederci*!" Bria exclaimed.

"What don't you believe?" Vanni asked.

"Her name!"

Bria turned the phone so Giovanni could see Linda Ingleterra's Instagram page. She hadn't screamed because of the photos she saw; she had screamed because of the name Linda chose as her handle.

"The Pretty Englishwoman!" Bria exclaimed.

"That's the rough English translation of her name," Vanni said. "*Linda* means 'pretty' in Spanish, and *Ingleterra* basically translates to 'England.'"

"Which is why the man with the flower in his lapel asked me about the Englishman," Bria said.

Why is Vanni looking at me like I told him that I made the pancakes from a box? Bria thought. *Oh, of course! I haven't told anyone about the mysterious man who came to visit.*

"I should explain," Bria said.

When Bria finished explaining what had happened, Vanni understood why she had gotten so excited. The man, falsely claiming to be a reporter, knew exactly who had been found dead in the upstairs bedroom. How exactly he knew Vittorio was not clear.

If the Englishman was a nickname, the two men could have been close personal friends. If it was a code name, they could have been illegal business partners or even spies. After a brief discussion, Bria and Giovanni assumed it had to be the latter. If they were friends, the man would have asked about Vittorio by name. The other thing they knew was that the man was definitely not a reporter. Even if Aldo Bombalino had hired a freelance reporter to cover the murder, the man would have been able to provide identification as a member of the press. He also wouldn't have made a hasty exit the moment Imperia arrived.

"You're sure the man recognized your mother-in-law?" Vanni asked.

"Positive," Bria replied. "I believe Imperia recognized him, too, but she denied it."

"Did you tell any of this to the police?"

"No. I didn't want to implicate Imperia if this was all a misunderstanding."

"I understand—family is family—but you should tell Luca about the man who came to visit you and about his reference to the Englishman."

"You think it's that important to involve the police?"

"Bria, the man could be dangerous. If Imperia didn't show up when she did, who knows what he would have done."

"I was starting to get nervous, but I had Bravo by my side, and he would never let anyone hurt me."

At the sound of his name, Bravo came bounding out from Marco's bedroom and sat in between Bria and Vanni, so they both had easy access to pet him, which they both did.

"I'd bet my life on this little guy," Vanni said, rubbing his nose up against the side of Bravo's face. "But despite his courage, he wouldn't have been able to protect you if the man had a gun."

"Okay, *va bene*. I get your point."

"Plus, the Englishman might be a clue."

"How so?"

"It's an odd way to address someone. It sounds like it's out of some old Mafia movie, which means it might have been used a long time ago . . ."

"Like when Dante's father and those other people were trying to pull off their counterfeit money scam."

"*Esattamente!*" Vanni cried. "Maybe Vittorio and Dante and this other guy were trying to resurrect it."

"Don't forget about the woman in charge of the whole thing," Bria said.

"What woman?"

"Dante claims that neither his father nor any of the Tre Uomini Poco Saggi—"

"Three *unwise* men?" Vanni interrupted.

"That's what the papers back then called them," Bria explained. "Dante claims a woman was the mastermind. Someone he described as ruthless and imperious."

Giovanni's eyebrows shot up and looked like two hunchbacked blond caterpillars. "Uhhh, like Imperia?"

Bria squirmed in her chair and threw her hands in the air. It was the first time she had made the connection between the mystery man's words and her ever more mysterious mother-in-law. "That is one option."

"Is there another?"

"Imperia did meet a strange woman one morning in Sarno, the same small town Vittorio had recently visited."

"How do you know that?"

"Rosalie and I followed her," Bria shared. "This was while you were in prison, so there's no way you could have known. I actually took a photo of her, but I don't recognize the woman."

"Let me see it."

"You think you'd know who the woman is?"

Giovanni hesitated enough for Bria to notice. Before she could comment on it, he answered her question. "She might have spent some time in Positano, or she might have been in the papers. Your mother-in-law does travel in more visible circles than we do."

Bria reached across the table for her bag, rummaged through it, and finally pulled out the Polaroid of the woman. She showed it to Vanni, but like Paloma, he found it nearly impossible to identify her, since her face was camouflaged by a hat and sunglasses. She looked like any other high-class Italian woman.

"I don't know who she is, but she does look as imperious as Imperia," Vanni said. "She could be the woman Dante was talking about or just some random socialite."

Bria jumped up, causing Bravo to scatter and Giovanni to flinch. "I have to make lunch."

"Do you need to test more recipes?"

"No! Time is running out if I'm going to clear Bella Bella's name before we open," Bria said. "I need to invite Imperia over and ask her who the woman was that she met in Sarno, without her knowing that I followed her there."

A few hours later Imperia was sitting at a table on Bria's deck, sipping a limoncello spritzer garnished with an orange wedge and nibbling on bruschetta topped with chopped shrimp, basil, and prosciutto and sprinkled with olive oil and lemon juice. Normally, Imperia commented on Bria's cooking, offering advice on how to improve her culinary skills or her presentation, even though Bria was certain the woman had not personally cooked a meal in all the time she'd known her. Today, however, she must have been hungry because she was eating in silence.

Come to think of it, when Bria had called her to invite her over, Imperia had immediately accepted. She hadn't questioned why she was getting a last-minute invite; she hadn't tried to get Bria to travel to Rome by feigning a business matter that needed her immediate attention prevented her from leaving the city. She had simply thanked Bria and told her she would be there by one o'clock. *Cooperation* and *civility* were not words most people would use when describing Imperia. Something wasn't right.

Bria made herself a drink in the kitchen, opting for a glass of nonalcoholic Chinotto soda with a dash of orange juice to cut the bitter taste. She grabbed a tray of olives, chunks of provolone cheese, and rolled-up slices of salami and *soppressata* and joined Imperia on the deck. When Bria placed the tray on the table, Imperia did something she rarely did in Bria's presence: she complimented her.

"What beautiful antipasti," Imperia said.

Her next comment almost made Bria trip over her chair.

"It was very thoughtful to invite me over, especially on a day like today."

Today? What was so special about today? For a moment Bria couldn't even remember the date, but when she did, it bore no significance. It wasn't a holiday, it wasn't anyone's birthday, and it wasn't her and Carlo's wedding anniversary, or anyone else's that she could think of.

She noticed that Imperia was staring at her, but Bria didn't dare speak until she could decipher Imperia's comment. Instead, she sat in her chair, smiled, and raised her glass. To her amazement, Imperia did the same and even clinked her glass with Bria's before taking a long sip of limoncello. Something extraordinary had happened on this day, but what was it?

Bria remembered how her fencing coach had taught her to prepare for a match. She closed her eyes to calm her body and created a blank slate in her mind. When she was competing, she would imagine her opponent was an extension of her mind, their body moving with the same rhythm as hers. It was a mindset that had allowed Bria to trick herself into thinking she was always one step ahead of her rival. She used the tactic now to try to get inside Imperia's mind. If today was a day of celebration, Bria needed to think of all the happy occasions Imperia would consider worth celebrating. She came up empty. But then she realized joyful events weren't the only ones celebrated; unhappy milestones were also remembered. That was it! Someone died. Someone very special to Imperia, who also had ties to Bria.

She opened her eyes and saw Imperia looking off into the distance. Her inner reflection bought Bria a few more moments to search for the answer, but luckily, the playing field had been shortened considerably. There were very few people who had played large roles in both Imperia's and Bria's lives who would be remembered in a way of any importance. The first was Carlo, and the anniversary of his death was months away, which left only Guillermo, Imperia's husband.

Bria was certain that it wasn't Imperia's wedding anniversary because it was part of their family folklore that Imperia was whisked away during a snowstorm to elope. There might be a random spot on earth where it snowed in late May, but Bria was confident enough to take that chance. No, today must be the anniversary of her husband's death.

How could I have forgotten? I'll go to Assunta later and confess. For now, I need to remain in control.

"I can't believe it's been so long since Guillermo passed," Bria said.

Her comment pulled Imperia back to the conversation. "Only six years but feels like sixty. Not a day goes by . . ."

Bria maintained the silence Imperia had created and allowed her mother-in-law the chance to submerge herself in memory. It also gave Bria a chance to figure out how she was going to wedge the Englishman into their talk. She hadn't expected Imperia to be so reflective and, well, *nice*. She had thought Imperia would be her usual combative self, and Bria would just have to drop in the name like a non sequitur and

not care about her mother-in-law's emotional response as long
as she extracted a fact. Thanks to Imperia's more genteel
mood, Bria would have to use finesse as a tactic. Bria the
fencer knew how to spar gracefully; Bria the single mother and
business owner was a bit more clumsy. She did what she always
did when she was feeling insecure in a match: she let her opponent take the lead.

"Do you know what my Guillermo was doing the day he
died?" Imperia asked.

Bria shook her head. She didn't know, but she didn't think
she was supposed to know. The question was merely a segue to
a reminiscence. She kept quiet as Imperia traveled down memory lane.

"He was planning a trip for our anniversary," she said. "He
was going to take me to his favorite place in the world so we
could celebrate our thirty-five years together as husband and
wife. We never got to make that trip."

This was the first Bria was hearing the story. She had always
thought Guillermo had a heart attack while on the golf course.
Maybe Imperia was playing loose with the details. It was a
widow's prerogative.

"Where was he going to take you?" Bria asked.

"St. Ives," Imperia replied, a rapturous smile on her face.

On Bria's face was a look of dismay. She had never heard of
St. Ives, not the place or the saint. "Where's that?"

"On the southwest shore, almost the tip, in fact, of England," Imperia said.

Now Bria felt a rapturous smile start to form on her lips.

"England?" Bria said, trying to make her voice sound calm
and not as excited as it was. She had no idea if the shores of
England were worth visiting; she had never been to the country. All she knew was that Imperia's comment was the verbal
lifeboat she was searching for.

"He visited there while he was studying for a semester at Oxford and completely fell in love with the place," Imperia explained. "He promised that someday he was going to take me there when we were married. He always talked about us going there, but we never did, and now we never will."

What a depressing story! Bria needed to turn things around; she needed to get Imperia to stop being wistful and start giving her the information she needed. She took a page out of Rosalie's rule book about how to live your life and spoke without thinking.

"It must be a sign!" Bria exclaimed.

"*Che cosa?*"

"The man who paid me a visit the other day . . . Remember you met him," Bria said. "The one who was here when you arrived."

"The one you said claimed to be a reporter?"

"Yes, that one," Bria replied. "I don't think he was a reporter, but he was definitely inquisitive, and I think he might have been sending me a message from Guillermo."

Imperia finally looked at Bria in the way Bria was accustomed, with derision and haughtiness. "You think my dead husband is trying to communicate with you?"

"Maybe I was a conduit," Bria said. "He was sending me a message, knowing I would ultimately pass it on to you."

"Because the two of us are so inextricably close?" Imperia asked, sounding so much like her old self that it made Bria smile.

"Guillermo did have a wicked sense of humor."

"That he did," Imperia said, her smile looking just as wicked. "What was this 'so-called' sign?"

"The man referred to Vittorio as the Englishman," Bria said. She paused to see if the name elicited a reaction from Imperia, but none came. Bria continued. "I didn't understand it, because Vittorio is Milanese, but now it makes sense."

"It does?" Imperia asked.

"Yes! Guillermo wanted me to remind you that he was going to take you to England."

"But you didn't remind me," Imperia corrected. "I recalled the memory myself."

My mother-in-law is starting to become like my mother. She is always right!

"Because you and Guillermo share an inextricable bond, but maybe he wanted you to share that memory with someone else."

Imperia's face softened. She was not a woman who believed in the supernatural or ghosts or anything that she couldn't see or touch with her own hands. But when it came to her husband, she was willing to suspend her belief.

"It *was* nice to share that memory," Imperia said. "Even with you."

Ignoring the barb, Bria thanked Imperia, and because she was desperate for more details, she pushed the moment. "And you're sure you don't know who the man is?"

"I actually may know him."

"Really? You recognized the reporter?"

"No, the dead man."

"What? You think you know Vittorio?"

"Possibly," Imperia replied. "I'm sure I'm wrong, but I had brunch with a dear friend recently who had been dating an Englishman, until their relationship abruptly ended."

"Because the man died?"

"She didn't say," Imperia replied. "My friend isn't as open with her feelings as I am."

Grazie, Dio! Thank you for showing me that Imperia is nothing like my mamma and isn't always right.

"All she told me was that things with her paramour had suddenly ended," Imperia said.

"Her *paramour*?" Bria asked excitedly. "You're sure she used that word?"

"Yes, a bit old-fashioned, but so is Daniela."

"Daniela is your friend?"

"Yes, Daniela di Santi."

Grazie, Imperia, Bria thought.

Her impromptu interrogation had taken an unexpected, circuitous route, and Bria hadn't gotten the answer she was expecting about the Englishman, but she had gotten something better: The name of the Englishman's lover.

CHAPTER 19

Now that breakfast and lunch were finished, Bria needed to focus on dinner. Before she could do that, however, she had to figure out how to get rid of her mother-in-law.

After she and Imperia picked up Marco at school, they stopped by Mimi's bookstore, and Imperia let Marco pick out whatever book he wanted to read. Marco chose *Strega Nona Meets Her Match*, one of the books in the classic series about a grandmother who is also a witch. Bria prayed to every saint she could think of, including St. Ives, for confirmation that Marco had never heard her call Imperia a witch. She never wanted her own feelings toward Imperia to compromise or have an impact on Marco. Their relationships were completely different. To Marco, Imperia was a loving grandmother; to Bria, she was much more complicated.

And she continued to prove to be an enigma.

"You're like the witch in the book, Nonna," Marco said.

Instead of being insulted, Imperia appeared delighted. "Then maybe I should put you in the oven and eat you up."

Marco's giggles joined Imperia's laughter to create an infectious and heartwarming sound. Bria watched with amazement as the woman who she suspected could be involved with a murder made her son throw his head back and laugh. After all these years, did she really know the woman?

"*Mi principino*," Imperia said, "tell me, why am I like the witch in the book?"

"Because you love me so much," Marco said. "You make me feel like I have the power to do anything I set my mind to."

The simplicity and honesty of Marco's words rendered Bria speechless, brought tears to Imperia's eyes, and made the woman at the end of the aisle, whom Bria didn't recognize, clutch her heart and make the sign of the cross. They all knew they had witnessed a precious moment, and they all knew that such moments needed to be honored. Unfortunately, Bria also knew that if she was going to get to the bottom of the mystery of who this Daniela di Santi really was, she was going to have to ruin the moment.

"*Uffa!*" Bria cried and then lied. "Look at the time. I completely forgot that I have to meet Rosalie."

"Are you helping her with plans for the party?" Imperia asked.

"What party?" Bria replied.

"My party," Imperia said, recapturing some of the tone Bria had come to expect. "The one for which you have yet to RSVP."

Oh, that party.

"*Perdonami*," Bria replied. "No, she's arranging a tour for some artists who want to paint on the boat, and she asked for my help."

"You're not an artist," Imperia said.

"You said you gave up being an artist when you became a *mammina*," Marco added.

"Can't I be both?" Bria asked. "Anyway, I'm late. Imperia, could you please take Marco home and make sure he eats? I won't be very long."

"On one condition," Imperia replied.

Oh, caro Dio in Cielo, why did you have to taunt me with nice Imperia if she wasn't going to hang around for more than an hour? Bria thought.

"What would that be?" Bria asked.

"Tell me you're coming to my party," Imperia replied. "It's a Bartolucci event, and you are a Bartolucci."

"I'm a Bartolucci, Nonna," Marco said. "Can I come to the party?"

"I'm sorry, *piccolino*," Imperia said. "It's only for adults, but you and I will have our very own party today as long as your *mammina* tells me what I want to hear."

There was nothing Bria was less interested in doing than getting dressed up and going to Imperia's party on her yacht. It didn't matter if she was part of the family; she still felt like an outsider at such events. She had been brought up in a comfortable environment, but one that was firmly stuck in the middle class. Carlo had shielded Bria from having to participate in any of Imperia's posh soirees because he had loathed them as well. Without Carlo around, Bria would have to protect herself, and sometimes protection came with a price.

"I'll put my RSVP in the mail the moment I get home," Bria said.

She kissed Marco quickly on both cheeks, muttered a quick *grazie* to Imperia, and ran out of Mimi's store before anyone could stop her.

Rosalie poured the contents of a chilled bottle of Fiorduva, a local white wine, into two large glasses. She handed one of the glasses to Bria and shoved the bottle back into the ice bucket. As she sat in the lounge chair next to Bria, Rosalie raised her glass and then stretched her legs out. She appeared ready to hear whatever it was Bria had told her she simply couldn't wait another second to tell her.

"I'm all ears, *mia amica*," Rosalie said. "What's so important that it couldn't wait?"

"First, you have to tell me why you're in that getup," Bria answered.

Rosalie looked down at her outfit and said, "This old thing?"

"Yes," Bria replied. "Are you hosting a costume party?"

"Kind of."

Rosalie explained that she was giving a tour to a group who were having a retro birthday party for which they wanted to capture the glamour of early 1970s Italian fashion. Never one to miss out on the fun or appear like she wasn't invited to the festivities, Rosalie had dressed the part. She was wearing a multicolored Pucci-inspired caftan, silver sandals with a platform heel, white plastic bangles and dangling earrings, and circular white sunglasses, which were propped on top of her head. Her normally frizzy hair had been slicked back and manipulated into a ponytail. She looked like Alda Balestra, Miss Italy of 1970, all dolled up and ready to be Gianni Versace's plus-one at a party at Valentino's palazzo instead of sitting on a lounge chair on her boat, ready to hear the latest news about the murder.

"You look gorgeous," Bria said. "Promise me you're not going to adopt this for your everyday look. I don't think I could keep up with you."

"I can make no such promise, Bria," Rosalie replied. "This caftan is outrageously comfortable and slimming at the same time. But enough about me and my gorgeousness. Tell me what's going on."

"I'm ninety-nine percent certain that I found out the name of the woman Imperia was having brunch with," Bria said. "Daniela di Santi."

"That name sounds familiar," Rosalie replied. "Is she famous?"

"I don't know. I've never heard of her, but I think she's some kind of socialite."

"She sure did look the part," Rosalie said. "She didn't look as fabulous as I do right now, but who does?"

"*Zitta*! I have more," Bria said. "Daniela is Vittorio's lover."

226 / MICHAEL FALCO

"Are you sure?"

"Yes! Remember I showed the photo of Daniela—although we didn't know her name at the time—to Paloma?"

"Yes," Rosalie replied. "And Paloma couldn't tell if Daniela was the same woman who bought the two scarves."

"*Corretto*, but she did confirm that the scarf Daniela was wearing was the same kind that the woman bought for herself and her paramour."

"And the paramour is Vittorio?"

"Yes! Imperia told me that her friend, who turns out to be Daniela, told Imperia over a recent brunch that her affair with her *paramour* abruptly ended."

"Because she stabbed Vittorio in the stomach!" Rosalie exclaimed.

"That's what I'm thinking!" Bria replied, equally excited. "Vittorio had to be killed in a crime of passion, something spur of the moment, like in the middle of a lovers' quarrel. He said something that got Daniela furious."

"Like maybe he wanted to break up with her."

"Exactly! Being the spoiled, rich socialite that she is, Daniela is used to getting her own way and refused to accept his rejection. She reached out to grab the first thing she could find."

"A really big knife!"

"And stabbed him," Bria said. "She didn't mean to do it, and maybe she tried to help him, but she couldn't take back what she did."

"The deed was already done."

"All she could do was watch him hobble off and flee the scene," Bria finished.

"That's cold," Rosalie said. "I thought Stefano was heartless when he broke up with me, but this takes cruel to a whole new level."

"Stefano was an idiot and never deserved you," Bria said.

"Not that you deserved being dumped on the radio while he was being interviewed for that book he wrote."

"You mean *A Rosalie by Any Other Name?*" Rosalie asked. "The one about the guy who kills his girlfriend so he can steal her identity to give to the woman of his dreams, who just faked her own death, so they could get married."

"At least he only killed you fictionally. Daniela actually stuck a knife into Vittorio's stomach."

"He got to die quick. I was left to suffer for years," Rosalie said. "But this is amazing. You solved the murder."

"Not yet," Bria said. "I still need to find out if Daniela had the means to kill Vittorio. She might have an alibi."

"Luca will be able to find that out."

"I don't want to tell Luca yet."

"Why not?"

"I want to find out who this Daniela is first and then talk to Imperia," Bria explained. "She's my son's grandmother, and I can't let her be blindsided."

"But your son's grandmother could be a criminal or associated with criminals, whether it's the murder or the counterfeit money ring."

"At this point it's all speculation," Bria said. "The lira in Dante's office is real, so even though he's connected to Vittorio through a real estate transaction, there's no evidence that the counterfeit money ring has been resurrected. And there's absolutely no evidence that Daniela was involved in that years ago."

"The woman could be a murderer *and* a money launderer, right?" Rosalie asked. "Some people don't know how to kick back and relax."

"All I know is that Dante said a mysterious, imperious woman was in charge of the counterfeit money ring when his father was involved," Bria shared. "That could describe Daniela, but it also describes Imperia. The other thing is that Giovanni found out that Vittorio seems to have been living large. He died wearing very expensive clothing, his ex-wife who was living off his alimony payments, and the little social media presence he had celebrated a luxurious lifestyle. But Vittorio didn't have a lot of income. According to your brother, the house he sold for Dante's father was his first lucrative sale in three years."

"Which explains why he'd want to print up fake money," Rosalie said.

"*Sì*, but why print lire and not euros?" Bria asked.

"Seems like you've got a lot of information, but not a lot of answers."

"Which is why I need to dig further before I share everything with Luca," Bria said.

"How much further are you going to dig before you dig yourself a hole you can't get out of?" Rosalie asked.

"What do you mean?"

"If Daniela committed murder and Vittorio was involved in a fake moneymaking scheme, you're . . . What's that phrase I hear people say? Oh! You're poking the bear. That's what you're doing. You're poking the bear, Bria! Do you know what happens when you do that?"

"No, but you're going to tell me, I'm sure."

"The bear eats a nice Italian meal," Rosalie said. "Which reminds me . . . Didn't you promise me dinner along with my undivided attention?"

"I did, but first, I need to call my parents."

"Ask your mother for her stuffed pork loin recipe. I can never get it right," Rosalie said. "Either the pork is undercooked or the spinach and ricotta melt."

"I don't need help with dinner," Bria said. "I need help with Daniela."

Bria propped her tablet on the small table in between the lounge chairs and dialed her mother's number. Seconds later Fifetta appeared on the screen. Specifically, only a portion of Fifetta's body was visible, from her chin to her waist. As usual, Fifetta was having a bit of difficultly with her phone, not because she didn't understand technology, but because she was in the middle of cooking.

"Bria!" Fifetta cried. "How are you, my *bambina*?"

"*Sto bene,* Mamma," Bria replied. "I can't see your face. Move your phone around."

Fifetta positioned her phone so Bria could now see all her mother's face, albeit slanted to the left. She knew from experience that this was going to be as good as it got, so she didn't press her mother to fix the image. She would work with what she got.

"Where are you, Bria?" Fifetta asked.

"I'm with Rosalie on her boat," Bria replied. She moved the tablet to the right so Fifetta could see Rosalie.

"*Ciao*, Fifetta," Rosalie said, waving a caftan-clad arm.

"Rosalie! *Che favolosa!*" Fifetta cried. "Oh! You remind me of my *zia* Gloria when she would go out on the town. Are you going out on the town, Rosalie?"

"No, I'm staying right here on the boat," Rosalie explained. "I have a tour group coming on tonight, and the theme is vintage seventies glamour."

"*Tale divertimento!*" Fifetta cried. "Don't have too much fun. That's how Gloria wound up having her *figlio* Shamus-Pablo. The father was either from Ireland or Spain. She never really knew."

"I promise you, Fifetta, I will not have that much fun," Rosalie assured her.

"Because you're a good girl," Fifetta replied. "Now, why did my good girl call me?"

"*Mamma*, do you know Daniela di Santi?" Bria asked.

"*È la figlia del diavolo!*"

Even though the voice that screamed the response was from somewhere off-screen, Bria and Rosalie knew exactly whom it belonged to.

"Papa?" Bria asked. "Is that you?"

Franco D'Abruzzo's face suddenly appeared next to Fifetta's. In order to fit on the screen, he made Fifetta lean to the right, which finally made her image straighten out on Bria's tablet. What was still off-kilter was her father's response to her question. Clearly, he knew Daniela di Santi, but why did he think she was the devil's child?

"Papa, you know this woman?"

"I know the whole family," Franco said. "They're *tutti malvagi*! No good, not one of them."

Bria knew that her father, like many Italian men of his generation, could be considered a *testa calda*, a hothead. She had never seen him become physical with anyone, not with a family member, friend, or stranger, but if any non-Italian ever heard him screaming and yelling, they would think his next move was to punch a wall or a face.

Most of the time he was comical, loving, gentle—especially with Marco—but when he felt strongly about something, he did not hold back. He let his feelings be known. Like now. Bria needed to find out why he harbored such ill will toward Daniela and her entire family.

"What did the di Santis ever do to you, Papa?" Bria asked.

"They never did anything to me or my family, because I didn't let them," Franco replied. "I stayed far away from them, and so should you."

"Your papa's right, *mio amore*," Fifetta added. "That family lives by their own rules, and let's just say that God would not approve."

"Are they mafiosi?" Rosalie asked in a hushed voice, even though the seagulls were making so much noise, no one within three hundred feet would be able to hear their conversation.

"I'd rather deal with the mafiosi," Franco said. "At least with them, you know what you're getting. With the di Santis, you never know, because they'll lie to each other's face if it means they'll come out on top. All they care about is money and winning."

"Are they involved with Dante's family?" Bria asked.

"The La Costas and the di Santis are related," Franco said.

"Not closely, but they are family," Fifetta added.

"Dante's grandfather, Patrizio, is cousins with Daniela's father, Ruperto," Franco explained.

"Third cousins," Fifetta corrected.

"They're still cousins," Franco said.

"*Certo*," Fifetta said. "I'm just pointing out the distinction. A third cousin isn't like a first cousin. A first cousin is like a brother or a sister, a third cousin is more like a friend you bring home from school because their mamma doesn't know how to cook."

"Like me," Rosalie said.

"*Aspetta*! Never!" Fifetta cried. "You are *famiglia*, Rosalie Vivaldi."

"Like a second daughter!" Franco added.

"Papa! Lorenza is your second daughter."

Franco paused for a moment. "That one is always flying around the world I forget what she looks like!"

"Rosalie," Fifetta said, "you're our third daughter."

"Don't ever consider yourself a third cousin!" Franco shouted. "Like someone we don't really like!"

"I won't, I promise," Rosalie said. "I consider the two of you my second parents. I love you both dearly. I was just making a joke."

"No more joking like that!" Fifetta scolded. "You're not like a guest who'll come to Bella Bella."

"If I have any guests," Bria said.

"What do you mean?" Franco said. "Aren't you booked up for the summer?"

"That was before a dead body was found in one of my bedrooms," Bria replied. "I'm afraid that once word gets out, people are going to start canceling their reservations."

"*Ah, Madonna mia*!" Fifetta cried. "If people are going to

refuse to sleep in a bed where someone died, they should never come to Italy."

"Especially Sicily," Franco said. "Which is where the di Santis are from."

"What did they do that makes you hate them so much?" Rosalie asked.

"I'm not going to go into details. I don't like to dredge up the past," Franco replied. "All you need to know is that there isn't one di Santi, young or old, male or female, who can be trusted not to stab you in the back."

"Would they also stab you in the stomach?" Rosalie asked.

"They'd stab you in the left eye if they wanted to prove a point!" Franco cried. "You stay away from them."

"Isn't Daniela a friend of Imperia's?" Bria asked.

"The daughter is worse than the mother," Franco said. "And I didn't think anyone could be as bad as Carlotta."

Fifetta stopped chopping whatever vegetable she was cutting up and glanced at Franco. He sighed deeply and held his hands up, palms to the camera.

"Imperia's world is very different from ours," Franco said. "I'm not saying it's wrong or bad. Just different. Same goes for Dante. They have chosen to do business with the di Santis and families like them. We chose different."

"Sounds to me like you chose the right path, Signor and Signora D'Abruzzo," Rosalie said.

It was a lovely comment, but one that made both Fifetta and Franco raise their voices so loud that Bria had to turn down the volume on the tablet.

"Since when do you call us that!" Fifetta screamed.

"What did we just tell you, Rosa!" Franco screamed.

"Signora?!" Fifetta said.

"Signor?!" Franco shouted. "What kind of way is that to speak to your second father? Papa Segundo, *that's* my name."

"Haven't I always been Mamma Fifi?" Fifetta asked. "All of

a sudden, I'm signora. Is that wine I see? Are you drinking during the day, Rosalie? What kind of people are you letting on your boat?"

"*Perdonami!*" Rosalie cried. "I will never, ever use those words again. I swear on every one of my relatives who's ever died!"

"*Bene!*" Fifetta said. "I don't like nonsense talk like that."

"Don't you go back on your word, Rosalie," Franco added. "Or else all those dead spirits will rise and haunt you every day of your life. Just ask my sister Serafina."

"*Dio mio!*" Fifetta cried. "That poor thing. Never a moment's peace. Always some dead relative appearing to talk to her."

"Mamma, Papa, *grazie*," Bria said. "I swear to you I will not get involved with the di Santis."

"Or their relatives," Franco said.

"I promise, Papa," Bria replied.

"Because you're *una brava regazza*, Bria, a good girl, like Rosalie," Fifetta said. "Now, go have fun at your party."

"But not too much fun!" Rosalie added.

"Arrivederci, *amore mio*," Franco said. "Arrivederci, Rosalie."

"Arrivederci, Papa," Bria replied.

She blew her parents kisses and then turned off the tablet.

"I forgot how talking to your parents works up my appetite," Rosalie said. "What did you bring for dinner?"

"Forgive me, Rosalie, but I need to use this food as a peace offering," Bria said.

She took a long swig of wine, grabbed her bag, and started to leave.

"Where are you going?"

"To defy my parents' wishes."

Bria couldn't tell if Dante was happy to see her or annoyed by the intrusion, because when he opened the front door of his building, he was wearing sunglasses. Bria had expected to be greeted by one of his many assistants, even though it was after business hours. The fact that he looked like he had been out for a stroll on the beach near Hotel Pupetto was a bit more disconcerting. Bria had definitely interrupted something. But what?

"*Scusami*, Dante," Bria said. "Were you on your way out?"

"No," he replied. "I was reviewing the, uh, documents I received from the global warming conference I attended in Milan."

"You weren't at the conference in Milan," Bria said.

You weren't expecting that, were you, Dante? she thought.

"How do you know that?" Dante asked. "Did you bug my office when you stole my framed lira?"

You weren't expecting that, were you, Bria? she thought.

Bria almost fell backward at the news. It was only because she was holding a tray of vegetable lasagna that she caught herself from tumbling down the stairs. She had been taught never to waste food.

"You know about that?" Bria asked.

"*Certo*!" Dante said. "I'm the mayor. I have a security camera in my office to catch common criminals like yourself. But how do you know I wasn't at the conference in Milan?"

"Because there wasn't any conference in Milan," Bria said. "If you're going to lie, Dante, you need to make it plausible."

"If you're going to steal from my office, you should wear a mask!" Dante cried.

"You should be thankful I broke in, because I proved your innocence," Bria declared. "The lira is real and not counterfeit."

"That's what I told Luca when he returned it to me with that feeble story that someone had broken in and thrown it in the trash," Dante said.

"Don't blame Luca," Bria said. "I forced him into testing the lira, and he went along with it only to rule you out as a suspect in Vittorio's murder."

"I had nothing to do with Vittorio or his murder!" Dante shouted. "Now, will you get in here before the entire village overhears our conversation and thinks I need to defend myself against some preposterous and unfounded charges."

Bria entered the building and heard the door slam behind her. She started to walk toward the stairs to go to Dante's office, but his command stopped her halfway to the staircase.

"Stop!" Dante cried. "Where do you think you're going?"

"To your office, so we can continue this conversation in private."

"We are in private right here," Dante confirmed. "All the offices are empty, and I gave my staff the night off."

"Aren't you a wonderful boss."

"Yes, I am. Now, why are you here, and what are you holding?"

"I've come to apologize for breaking in," Bria said. "I was going to confess, and I brought my mother's vegetable lasagna, which you love so much, in case you were angry."

"How do you know that I love your mother's lasagna?" Dante asked. "Seriously, did you bug my office?"

"Annamaria told me. She's better than any bug the AISE could ever invent," Bria said.

"Ssh!" Dante exclaimed. "Are you *pazza*, mentioning the Agenzia Informazioni e Sicurezza Esterna out loud? If my office is bugged, they'll hear you."

"Why would the AISE bug your office?"

"I am a very important political figure, Bria," Dante said, with a surprisingly straight face. "I'm also famished. Set the lasagna down over there. That delicious aroma is making my knees weak. I haven't eaten all day."

Bria set the tray of lasagna on the sideboard as Dante had instructed, and when she turned, he was still wearing the sunglasses.

"Could you take off your sunglasses?" Bria asked. "It's strange talking to you with them on when we're inside."

"I can't," Dante replied. "I have a migraine, and the light is hurting my eyes."

"I can shut the curtains."

"That doesn't help! I need total darkness."

Bria had a memory of Imperia telling her the exact same thing last year, after she had made a similar trip to Milan. That was it!

"You didn't go to a climate change conference," Bria said. "You went to see Dr. Frangipani!"

She whipped off Dante's sunglasses, and as she expected, he had the same yellow-blue bruises under his eyes and the same small pieces of tape at the corners, where crow's-feet should have been, that Imperia had had when she had an eye lift. Dante must have had the same procedure and was still recovering.

"How dare you!"

"You can't deny it, Dante," Bria said. "It's written all over your face! I had no idea that you went to the same plastic surgeon as Imperia."

"*Bestemmia*! Dr. Frangi is not a plastic surgeon! He's a miracle worker," Dante proclaimed. "Thanks to his handiwork, I don't look a day over forty whenever my photo appears in the papers or when I'm on TV."

"You're only thirty-seven," Bria said.

Dante's eyes bugged out so wide, the surgical tape almost popped off his face. "Cameras add ten years to a face!"

"I also don't remember ever seeing you on TV."

"I am interviewed often!" Dante cried. "Now, I insist that you go."

"Not yet. I haven't said everything I came here to say."

"What else is there to say?" Dante asked. "Thanks to the police, who for once proved that they aren't completely incompetent, I am innocent of any implication in this murder."

"The police can't prove that you're involved with the counterfeit money ring they think Vittorio was involved in, but they can prove that you and Vittorio had a professional connection," Bria explained. "He sold your father's house, and your father was involved in a counterfeit money ring decades ago. That might be circumstantial evidence, but it's still evidence."

"*Non è niente!*" Dante said. "There is absolutely no connection between my family and Vittorio."

"How can you say that?" Bria asked. "He's your family Realtor. He can be your family counterfeiter, too."

"He isn't my family Realtor!"

"*Uffa!* Stop lying! You said he sold your house for you."

"I said he sold our house, but he was the Realtor for the buyer."

"Who's the buyer?"

"Daniela di Santi."

CHAPTER 20

The next morning Bria was still so giddy with the news Dante had shared with her that she felt like the *necci* she was preparing for Marco's breakfast. The rolled-up pancakes were usually stuffed with ricotta cheese, but Bria had substituted pureed berries for the ricotta to determine if it would work as a breakfast treat for her guests. Just like the *necci* were bursting with a surprise in their center, so was Bria.

Thanks to Dante, not only had Daniela become the prime suspect, but Imperia had been bumped off the list, as well. There was still the possibility that Imperia knew more than she was revealing and had participated in some quasi-illegal business dealings, thanks to her involvement with the unscrupulous di Santi family, but Bria was convinced that Imperia didn't murder Vittorio. Marco would be spared having to visit his grandmother in prison.

The fresh smell of blueberries, strawberries, and lemon enveloped Bria as she pureed berries in her Klarstein Lucia Rossa food processor in hot pink, of course, her favorite color. The humming sound of the machine blended with the insistent chirps of the family of sparrows living out in the lemon tree on her patio and lulled Bria into a near meditative state.

Marco was sitting on the floor, drinking a smoothie Bria had made for him that was filled with vegetables masked by bananas and a hint of Nutella and watching *Lupo Alberto*, a cartoon that, as far as Bria could determine, chronicled the life of a skinny blue animal. The animal was possibly a rabbit, but also possibly a skinny pig, but it was definitely terrorized in a G-rated way by an overweight dog. Marco loved it, and Bravo, possibly because the cartoon featured a strong canine character, shared her son's enthusiasm. They both sat in front of Marco's laptop—a childproof version of the one Bria used— and laughed, snorted, and barked while Alberto and his anthropomorphic friends cavorted and cajoled each other on the screen.

She heard the faint sounds of a seventies rock band from Australia that had become a sensation in the United States and had ultimately gained international fame coming from the vintage radio Giovanni was listening to upstairs. The radio, part of Carlo's retro collection, was an orange Brionvega radio cube from the late sixties, created by Marco Zanuso, a famous Italian architect, and Bria's son's namesake. Carlo had admired the man and Bria's grandfather, Frederico, was an architect who built Mondo dei Sogni, so they had thought it was a fitting moniker for their son.

Bria herself sometimes felt like she was part of some vintage collection. She loved so many things from yesteryear, most especially the pace of life. Things were slower, more relaxed; people were friendlier and less suspicious. The only time she enjoyed a quick pace and an aggressive opponent was during a fencing match, when it was appropriate. Other times she preferred life to be like it was in the village, which was a haven, a place to breathe and be reminded of what was important in life. Like family, food, and unexpected guests.

"*Ciao*, Enrico!" Marco shouted. "Alberto is getting clobbered by Mosè again!"

"Poor Alberto," Enrico said. "He'll never learn. Dogs are vicious, isn't that right, Bravo?"

At the sound of his name, the hound dog ran to Enrico and accepted the treat that was waiting for him. Enrico bent down and rubbed Bravo vigorously under his chin, making the dog whimper, bark, stick out his tongue, and wag his tail so furiously, it looked like he might take off and become airborne.

Enrico raised his left hand and extended the bouquet of flowers he was carrying to Bria. "These are for you," he said. "You should take them now, before Bravo gets excited all over them."

"Bravo only goes outside to *fare pipi*," Marco said.

Laughing, Enrico replied, "That's because you trained him very well."

"That's what friends do for each other," Marco replied.

"And you, my friend, shouldn't be giving me such beautiful flowers," Bria said. "You can sell these."

"Don't be silly," Enrico said. "These are the extra bits and pieces I cut from other arrangements. They'd wind up in the compost or the garbage. I'd much rather they wind up in a vase on your table."

"In that case, *grazie*," Bria replied. "They're beautiful."

Bria laid the flowers on the counter and took out a tall glass vase from one of the cabinets. Like so many things in her home, the vase had a special meaning. It had been her grandmother's on her mother's side of the family and had always been prominently displayed on a small side table in her dining room. Delicate etchings of feathers and leaves were inlaid around the circumference, and while the vase wasn't expensive, it had great sentimental value.

"That's a beautiful vase," Enrico said.

"It was my grand-mère Chantal's," Bria said.

"The French side of the family," Enrico noted. "Then you have a very international display. Italian flowers in a French vase."

She filled the vase with water and then with the flowers themselves, spreading them out and letting them fill up the space naturally. Roses, petunias, daisies, some other flowers Bria didn't know by name, and some greenery to frame the vibrant colors. She smiled and marveled to herself that such a small gesture could literally brighten up the day.

"*Grazie*, Enrico," Bria said. "They're beautiful."

She pointed to a purple flower that looked like a lily that was bent over, inspecting its stem. "What's the name of this one?" Bria asked. "I've seen them before, but I don't know the name."

"That's an aquilegia," Enrico answered. "It's in the lily family. The one next to it is a mandevilla, which looks just like Positano's petunias that you see everywhere, but its petals are wider and curve to the right at the bottom."

"Just like Petunia Pig's bottom," Marco said.

"Marco!" Bria cried.

"*Che cosa, Mamma*?" Marco replied. "Petunia's a pig. She's supposed to have a big bottom."

Shaking her head and smiling conspiratorially with Enrico, Bria told Marco to wash up and get ready for school. As he ran out of the room to the bathroom, with Bravo right behind him, another unexpected visitor arrived at the front door.

"*Ciao*, Mimi," Bria said.

"*Ciao*, Bria," Mimi replied.

Mimi and Enrico explained pleasantries like the old friends they were. Ever since Bria moved to Positano, she had thought they'd make a cute couple. They were both in their midsixties, both widowed without any children, and they shared the same values and enjoyed the slower pace of life. Bria made a mental note to explore opportunities to push them together once she opened Bella Bella and brought Daniela to justice. Until then, she'd just accept their gifts.

Mimi placed a small bag with the logo of her bookstore on the counter. "I thought I'd drop this off on my way to the store."

"*Che fortuna*!" Bria exclaimed. "Two gifts in one morning."

"Sorry, Bria," Mimi said. "This isn't for you. It's for Marco."

"For me!"

Marco appeared seconds after they heard his cry, a blob of toothpaste still clinging to the side of his mouth. Bria handed him a napkin and told him he had to wash his mouth before he could accept any gifts. And then she wanted to know why Mimi was showering her son with gifts for no reason.

"They're not from me. They're from Imperia," Mimi explained. "She ordered the entire Strega Nona series. It's a new version with leather-bound covers and autographed by Tomie dePaola, the author."

"*Grazie*, Mimi," Marco said. "Can I call Nonna and thank her?"

"You'll have to do that later," Bria said, glancing at her watch. "If we don't leave now, you'll be late for school, and Sister Benedicta said they're having a surprise today."

"What's the surprise?" Marco asked.

"It wouldn't be a surprise if you knew what the surprise was going to be," Enrico said.

"I would still act surprised, so no one would know," Marco said. "I always fool Mamma when I do that."

"I think you may have let the cat out of the bag, *piccolino*," Mimi said.

"Like when you faked being surprised when I gave you that soccer ball on your birthday?" Bria asked.

"You knew I had already peeked?" Marco asked, his blue

eyes widening like moons.

"I think it's time you found out, Marcolo, mammas know everything," Enrico said.

"Papas too," Marco said. "At least my papa, because he's an angel in heaven."

Mimi made the sign of the cross, and Enrico bowed his head, both of them avoiding looking at Bria, who they knew would want to take a private moment to think about the strong impact Carlo had made on his son. Bria was too emotional to speak; instead she kissed Marco on the cheek and hugged him tightly. Marco squirmed in his mother's clutch and shook his head as he looked at Mimi and Enrico.

"Mamma's going to make me late for school again," Marco said.

"Then let's go," Bria said, pulling herself away from her son, although she wanted nothing more than to keep holding him until he was old enough to graduate.

Just as she was about to shout up to Giovanni that she was leaving, two more people entered the room. Bella Bella hadn't yet officially opened, and already it looked like it was the most popular place in the village. Unfortunately, Bria knew that her most recent unexpected guests were not at all the kind of people Giovanni would want to have to greet.

"Luca, Nunzi," Bria said. "Is this an official visit?"

"It is," Luca replied.

Smiling awkwardly, Bria looked at the adults in the room and then at Marco. "We might be a bit late for your surprise today."

"*Senza senso*," Enrico said. "I can take Marco."

"And I can join you," Mimi said.

"*Grazie*!" Bria said. She turned to Marco and gave him a kiss on the other cheek. "You be a good boy."

"Yes, Mamma," Marco said. "Bravo will make sure of that."

"I can bring Bravo back, as well," Enrico said. "I'm not opening the store until later, because I have Giacomo fixing the hydration system."

"That isn't necessary," Bria said. "Bravo knows the way home."

"We can pass by Paloma's and say hello," Mimi said. "She got dumped by yet another boyfriend. She'll appreciate a visit from a handsome young boy like you."

"Another one?" Bria asked. "Is this the third?"

"The fourth," Mimi replied. "But who's counting?"

"You," Enrico said.

"*Aspetta!*" Mimi cried. "I just want her to be happy. Come on, Marco. Let's get going so the officials can talk."

"*Addio*, Mamma," Marco said. "*Ciao*, Luca."

"*Addio*, Marco," Luca said.

The group exchanged pleasantries as they left the house, and once they were gone, all that remained was silence. Until Giovanni came downstairs.

"Bria, I finished all the touch-ups," Giovanni said. "I just want to repaint the floor in the bedroom where Vittorio was found since the police made a mess in there."

"Sorry about that," Luca said. "Bria, send me the bill for whatever repairs you need to do, and I'll make sure it gets repaid."

"I assume you'll hold this against me the next time you need to cart someone off to jail to prove that you're in charge," Giovanni said.

Nunzi was about to speak, but Luca, almost sensing her response, raised his hand to prevent her from escalating the scene to something that could end in them carting Giovanni off to jail for a second time.

"Please understand we were only doing our job to protect this village and everyone who lives and visits here," Luca said.

"We've made it known that you are not under suspicion for Vittorio's murder, but you do know that we had every reason to arrest you."

"Because I ran," Vanni said.

"From a police officer who ordered you to stop," Nunzi interjected.

"I'm sure I'm not the first person to run from you, Nunzi," Vanni said.

"As long as I wear this uniform," Nunzi replied, "you won't be the last—"

"Would anyone like coffee?" Bria interrupted, using her best hostess voice.

Luca replied yes as Nunzi replied no, causing Bria to be unsure how to respond. Erring on the side of caution, she decided to make coffee for all of them.

"I'll take that as a yes to coffee for everyone," Bria replied. "Including you, Vanni."

Reluctantly, Luca, Nunzi, and Vanni sat around the table as Bria prepared the coffee in the kitchen. She shouted innocuous comments to them about the weather, the paint color she had chosen for the upstairs, which was called Florentine Blue but looked more gray than blue, and she revealed that Sister Benedicta's surprise was a visit from a zookeeper in Naples, who was bringing some snakes with him. She told them she was already preparing all the reasons why they couldn't have a snake as a pet for when Marco inevitably asked that question when he got home after school.

She brought in the cups and the pot of coffee on a silver tray that had once belonged to her father's godmother *Madrina* Alda and had originally been part of her grandmother's set that was handcrafted in Florence around the turn of the eighteenth century. Now it was stored with Marco's partition plates and Bria's Tupperware.

"What's so important, Luca, that you had to make a house call?" Bria said as she poured coffee into a cup and handed it to Nunzi.

"Dante paid me a visit and told me that he knows it was you who stole the framed lira," Luca said.

"He told me the same thing," Bria replied, pouring coffee into another cup and handing it to Vanni.

"When did he tell you that?" Luca asked.

"When I paid him a visit," Bria replied.

"When were you going to share that with me?" Luca asked.

"When I thought it would be appropriate for you to know," Bria replied.

"*Quindi aiutami Dio*," Luca said. "Sometimes you are as infuriating as Rosalie."

"*Grazie*," Bria said, handing a cup of coffee to Luca. "That's a lovely thing to say."

"I don't believe he meant it as a compliment," Vanni said to Bria under his breath.

"He also told me that you asked him about Daniela di Santi," Luca said.

"That's not quite right," Bria replied, pouring coffee into the final cup for herself. "He told me that Daniela had bought his father's house."

"How did that come up in conversation?" Nunzi asked.

"Because I thought Vittorio was the Realtor—" Bria started.

"Vittorio *was* the Realtor," Luca interrupted.

"Vittorio was the Realtor for the buyer, not the seller, like we originally thought," Bria explained. "Didn't Dante share that with you?"

"No, he didn't," Luca replied. "He told me that Daniela di Santi bought his father's house, but not that Vittorio was *her* Realtor."

"Why would the mayor lie to the chief of police?" Bria asked.

"He didn't necessarily lie. He just didn't share all the details," Luca said. "A concept I think you might be familiar with."

Luca ended his comment with a smile, but Bria knew that he was not happy that she had concealed information from him. Maybe it was time for her to prove him wrong.

"There's more to the story that Dante didn't tell you," Bria said. "Vittorio wasn't just Daniela's Realtor. He was her boyfriend."

"What!" Luca and Nunzi cried at the same time.

"I guess that's something else that you two weren't aware of," Vanni said.

"How do you know that they were romantically linked?" Luca asked.

"Because I saw a woman wearing the same kind of scarf that Vittorio was wearing, and I took a picture of her, which I showed to Paloma because she had told me that a customer bought two scarves, one for her and one for her boyfriend, and Paloma said the woman in the photo was the customer who had bought the scarves," Bria explained. "Paloma wasn't completely certain it was the woman, because she was wearing a big hat and sunglasses, but she said it could definitely have been her, and Imperia confirmed it."

Luca looked at Nunzi, who merely shrugged her shoulders and tilted her head.

"Do you mind telling me how Imperia is involved?" Luca asked.

"Not anymore," Bria replied.

"What do you mean by that?" Luca asked.

"I didn't want to tell you before, because I thought Imperia was involved in the murder," Bria started. "Now that I know she isn't involved, I don't mind telling you what I know."

"Thank you for putting your civic duty before your family commitments," Luca said.

"No need to thank me. I'm happy to help," Bria replied, ignoring, or not understanding that his comment was sarcastic. "Imperia told me that Daniela had recently ended a relationship with her paramour, and Paloma said the woman who bought the scarves said she was buying one for herself and one for her paramour. Who uses the word *paramour* these days, right?"

"I've used it recently," Nunzi said.

"You have not," Vanni challenged.

"I was doing a crossword puzzle, and the clue was an eight-letter word for 'intimate companion' . . . *paramour*," Nunzi explained.

"Were you doing that crossword on Saturday night?" Vanni asked. "By yourself?"

"No," Nunzi replied. "Primavera always helps me."

"Could we get back to how Imperia is involved with Daniela?" Luca asked.

"They're friends and business associates," Bria replied. "Imperia was having brunch with Daniela when I saw her wearing the scarf. Imperia didn't know I took the photo, because at the time I thought my mother-in-law might be involved in the murder and I made sure she didn't see me."

"You thought your mother-in-law might have killed Vittorio and you never said anything?" Nunzi asked.

"It was only a suspicion," Bria said. "She's still my family, and family always comes first. But I don't have to make any hard decisions now because Daniela is the murderer."

"How did you come to that conclusion?" Luca asked.

"Daniela was linked to Vittorio both romantically and professionally," Bria said. "She's quite possibly the woman who was involved with the counterfeit money ring that Dante's father was a part of and the murder was a crime of passion. Women, more often than not, commit crimes of passion."

"Do you have any idea how powerful Daniela di Santi is?" Luca asked.

"Powerful people commit murder all the time," Bria said.

"Yes, but powerful people and powerful companies like di Santi Enterprises also have strong legal teams, and if we're going to charge her with murder, we need to make sure the charges will stick and she won't be able to wiggle out of them," Luca explained. "Daniela has been involved in some business dealings through the years that haven't been entirely on the up-and-up. There have been investigations, but none have ever resulted in charges being brought against her."

"If she was part of the counterfeit ring from years ago, which is a bit of a stretch, because she would have been very young, she's eluded the police for decades," Giovanni said.

"Thanks for pointing that out, Vanni," Nunzi said. "See how cooperative you can be when you choose to."

"Ahh! I know how we can build a stronger case against Daniela!" Bria cried.

"We?" Nunzi asked.

"My family can help," Bria said. "I can have Lorenza ask Fabrice to cross-reference all Vittorio's trips with Daniela and see how many connect. Luca, you and your team check to see if Daniela has an alibi for the morning of the murder."

Luca looked at Bria, and it wasn't clear to her if he was trying to hide a smile or a shout. "Yes, we will do that immediately," he said.

"And if she doesn't, we'll bring her in for questioning," Nunzi added.

"I know a better way," Bria said. "You can question her at Imperia's party Saturday night."

"The one on the yacht that you told Rosalie you would never go to in a million years?" Luca asked.

"That's the one," Bria admitted. "But that was before I had a reason to go."

"And now you do?" Luca asked.

"Yes," Bria replied. "And you're going to be my date."

Luca, Nunzi, and Giovanni all replied at the same time, "Your date?"

"Yes," Bria confirmed. "We can go together and interrogate Daniela in the guise of yacht party chatter."

"Yacht party chatter?" Nunzi asked.

"It's like regular dinner party chatter, only on a yacht," Bria said. "You talk about incredibly superficial things, like second homes and expensive jewelry and . . ."

"Yachts," Nunzi finished.

"Exactly!" Bria said.

"It's a good way to question Daniela without formally bringing her in," Luca said. "All right, I'll go."

"*Meraviglioso!*" Bria cried. "*Prego*, Luca, this is a black-tie affair. You'll need to wear a tux."

"I have a tux," Luca replied.

This time it was Bria, Nunzi, and Giovanni who all responded at the same time. "Really?"

"Why is it so surprising to find out that I own a tux?" Luca asked, trying not to sound as insulted as he was. "It's vintage Armani, if you must know."

"I have a vintage Armani gown!" Bria cried. "Looks like this was meant to be."

Bria noticed that Nunzi and Vanni didn't seem to be nearly as excited as she was about the prospect of being able to confront Daniela in a setting where she literally couldn't escape. She didn't want to dwell on whatever negative thoughts were filling their heads. Instead, she focused on the fact that this mystery was closer to being solved than she ever imagined.

Another, more frightening thought popped into her head:

this was going to be the first adults-only event she'd be attending with a member of the opposite sex since Carlo died. She would dwell on that aspect of the evening later, as well. For now she wanted to concentrate on business.

"So, it's a date?" Bria said.

"It's a date," Luca replied.

CHAPTER 21

Bria could practically taste the salt water in the air.

On mornings like this, when it rained the night before, the air was rich with moisture. As Bria walked along the narrow stone pathway about seventy feet above sea level, she closed her eyes for a few seconds, and it was as if she was walking on water. Blindly, she took a few steps and was consumed with a sense of freedom and wonder: anything could happen if she just believed hard enough.

A strange clicking sound invaded her reverie, and she turned to find out where the sound had come from. When her right foot tried to touch the flat ground, it stepped on a rock, and her ankle rolled to the side, causing her body to teeter to the left. Finally, her quick fencing reflexes kicked in, and she corrected her body, so it leaned toward the right. She scraped her arm on some thorny bushes, but scratches were a much better alternative to plummeting down the side of the hill and crashing onto the beach.

"And just like that, I almost made my son an orphan," Bria muttered to herself. "Where's my mother of the year award?"

Bria heard the clicking sound again and turned around but didn't see anyone in either direction. She assumed the sound must have been a bird's early morning call, though it had sounded man-made to her. On the rest of her walk to meet Rosalie at Positano, Bria kept her eyes open. She didn't want to risk getting any more scratches on her arms, since she was going to be playing dress-up that evening. She had planned on wearing an asymmetrical gown, sleeveless on the left, but a long sleeve on the right, which would cover the scratch marks from her near fall. If she stumbled into another bush and got marks on her left arm, she'd have to pick out something new to wear. The only other formal gown she owned was her wedding dress, and she didn't want to give Luca the wrong impression on their first date.

"*Dio mio*! Am I really going on a date?" Bria asked herself out loud. "No, you're not going on a date. This is like one of those stakeouts that cops do."

She heard the clicking sound again, and when she saw a couple in the distance walking toward her, a man and a woman holding hands, she realized it was the woman's high heels that were making the sound each time she stepped on a stone. Just as the couple passed her, the woman took a step that was almost her last. She did the same thing Bria had done, and when her ankle rolled, she almost slipped off the path. Both the man and Bria grabbed the woman at the same time, preventing her from falling.

"Thank you!" the woman cried, her accent distinctly American.

The man, visibly shaken, held the woman close and moved her as far from the precarious edge of the pathway as possible.

"Yes, thank you so much," he said to Bria, sounding even more American.

"Not a problem," Bria replied. "I did the same thing a few seconds ago."

He then turned to his companion, and his face was filled with the unmistakable mix of fear and anger so common when a loved one barely escaped a dangerous situation. Bria didn't notice any wedding bands, but they were obviously a couple.

"I told you not to wear those shoes. They almost got you killed."

"I know," the woman replied. "I didn't realize how hard it would be to walk in them."

The woman leaned into her boyfriend and took off one of her shoes, revealing a bloodied foot.

"Ouch," Bria said. "Montefusco's is right around the next bend in the road. It's a *farmacia*, and you can get bandages and some antiseptic."

"Thank you," the woman said.

"Is there any place where she can buy a pair of sneakers?" the man asked.

"No, but if you go to Maestro Sandals, they can make a pair of sandals for you in a few minutes," Bria suggested. "With a nice flat heel."

"What a perfect excuse to buy new shoes!" the woman squealed.

"Have you ever needed an excuse to buy new shoes?" the man asked.

The couple thanked Bria again and hobbled down the path. Bria watched them for a few seconds and was reminded how nice it was to be part of a couple. She definitely wanted that again in her life. For now, she'd settle for one of Annamaria's frothy caffeine-fueled concoctions with a side of almond biscotti.

By the time Bria turned onto Viale Pasitea, Rosalie was already on her second espresso, had devoured a croissant, and was several bites into her lemon–poppy seed muffin. Bria sat down across from Rosalie and saw that her friend had already ordered for her. Before she could say *grazie*, Rosalie started firing off questions to her like a soldier in a skirmish.

"Are you going on a date with my brother?" Rosalie asked.

"Why are you making him wear a tuxedo? You know he doesn't like formal events, and right now he's frantically trying to get his tux dry-cleaned before the party tonight. And why are you even going to the party? You said you hated those things, which is why you've never gone before. What's so special about Imperia's party this year that makes you want to attend? And what in the world are you going to wear? The only gown you own is your wedding dress, and if you wear that tonight, I guarantee you my brother will jump overboard and swim all the way to Gibraltar, no matter how much he likes you. If you haven't already noticed, the Vivaldi siblings are a bit marriage shy."

Bria waited a few moments before responding in case Rosalie wasn't finished. When she watched her friend bite off another chunk of muffin and start to chew, she realized she could speak. She couldn't remember the order of Rosalie's questions, but she did her best to answer them all.

"First of all, I do own another gown, the red Armani that I bought when Carlo and I went to Paris a few years ago, and your brother bragged about owning his own tux. If he's so proud of it, he should make sure it's ready to wear at a moment's notice," Bria started. "Second, we're not going on a date. It's called a reconnaissance mission. Daniela di Santi is going to be at the party, and we thought—well, it was my idea really—that we could ask her about her relationship with Vittorio and hopefully get her to confess to his murder in a more convivial setting than the police station."

Rosalie took a sip of her espresso and peered at Bria, presumably contemplating if what she had just heard was the truth or a rationalization.

"Sounds like you're going on a *reconnadate*," Rosalie said. "A detective's mission in the guise of a date."

"*Basta così!*" Bria cried. "It isn't a date."

"Then why are you nervous?" Rosalie asked.

"I'm not nervous," Bria claimed.

"You are, too! You have that sweat moustache you always get when you get nervous."

Bria froze and realized her friend was right. She could feel the beads of moisture settling on top of her lip. It was warm, as it always was at this time of day, but not unseasonably, and there was a cool breeze coming in from the coastline. Her hair was pulled back, and she was wearing shorts and a halter top, both in a light cotton material. Her outfit was not sweat inducing, but clearly, her thoughts were.

She brought the mug up to her lips and took a long sip of her cappuccino, barely tasting the hint of anisate Annamaria had added. Quickly, she dabbed her mouth with her napkin to remove any hint of moisture her nerves may have produced. Her actions got rid of the evidence but not the inquisitor.

"Do you think I didn't see what you just did?" Rosalie asked.

"What did I just do?" Bria asked, not so successfully feigning innocence.

"*Sei la mia migliore amica*, Bria. You're my best friend," Rosalie said. "But sometimes I don't understand you."

"What's to understand?" Bria replied. "Your brother and I are going undercover on a mission to a party that all our friends and family will be attending. It isn't like we're going out on the town by ourselves."

Rosalie put down her espresso and reached across the table with both hands. Bria didn't fully understand the gesture, but since she knew Rosalie was physically much stronger than she was after years of doing most all the crew work on her boat by herself, she clutched her mug even tighter. It was not the reaction Rosalie was hoping for.

"I'm trying to have a sweet moment with you, Bria!" Rosalie said. "Now, hold my hands!"

With no way out, Bria put her mug down to the side and grabbed on to Rosalie's hands. To her surprise but delight,

Rosalie's grip was tender and not bone crushing. Her words fell somewhere in between.

"I love you, and I love my brother, and if this clandestine affair turns out to be the start of a real affair, no one will be happier than me," Rosalie said. "But . . ."

Bria felt Rosalie's hold tighten, and she knew the old adage was true that nothing someone said before a "but" meant anything. The harsh truth always came after the conjunction.

"If you hurt my brother and break his heart, I will make you pay," Rosalie said.

Bria had heard Rosalie speak in that flat, determined tone of voice before, so she knew her friend was serious. She didn't know, however, if she was *serious* serious or seriously joking.

"How exactly are you going to make me pay?" Bria asked, not entirely sure she wanted to hear the response.

"I don't know!" Rosalie cried, letting go of Bria's hands and throwing hers in the air. "Maybe I'll spray-paint *heartbreaker* on your front door or just a scarlet *H*."

"I think you mean a scarlet *A*," Bria corrected.

"*Heartbreaker* doesn't start with an *A*," Rosalie replied. "Luca's a big boy, and he can take care of himself, but he's not been so lucky in love."

"*Già abbastanza*," Bria said. "Your brother is like—"

"Do not say that he's like a brother to you," Rosalie interrupted. "Because I hate to tell you this—and I'm only repeating your words—your brother, Gabrielo, is lazy, unreliable, and not to be trusted. My brother is none of those things."

"Gabi isn't really lazy anymore. He works as an interpreter all the time," Bria said. "Unreliable and untrustworthy, he still is."

"Which is nothing like my brother."

"Luca is more like a distant relative," Bria said. "A cousin whose parents divorced, and he was raised in the States, and we texted only around the holidays and our birthdays."

"I have absolutely no idea what that means," Rosalie replied.

"Luca is familiar," Bria said. "I've never really looked at him in any other way than as your brother or my friend. In fact, before the murder, we hardly spent any time together."

"How sweet that an ice-cold corpse ignited the fire that flames between you two," Rosalie said.

"You have a sick, twisted mind, *mia amica*," Bria said.

"*Grazie*," Rosalie replied. "To be clear, I'm not going to break your legs or throw you off the side of my boat to feed you to the fishes if Luca gets his heart broken, and honestly, it isn't him that I'm worried about."

"Why are you worried about me?"

"You shouldn't start something you're not ready to start."

This was why Bria considered Rosalie more of a sister than a friend. Her relationship with Lorenza was solid, and they had rarely fought while growing up, but Lorenza's career took her out of town often, and her younger sister did have a tendency to be superficial. Even though she was only a few years younger than Bria, Lorenza sometimes acted like she was a teenager. Rosalie, on the other hand, despite her bohemian lifestyle and laissez-faire attitude toward life, possessed a maturity that made her a much more responsible person and a more dependable friend. She would never do anything that would endanger her relationship with Rosalie, even if that meant keeping her distance from Luca until she felt truly ready to let go of the memory of her husband.

It was Bria's turn to reach out and take hold of Rosalie's hands. "I promise I would never do anything to hurt Luca," Bria said. "And I thank you for loving me so much that you could be honest with me."

"That's why they call me Honest Rosie," Rosalie said.

"No one calls you that."

"But it has a nice ring to it, doesn't it?" Rosalie asked. "Maybe I should rename my boat that."

"God no. People will think you're running an offshore casino or something illegal," Bria said. "You aren't, are you?"

"Would Honest Rosie be involved in something dishonest?" Rosalie asked.

"Who's dishonest?"

Bria and Rosalie both looked up and were surprised to see Annamaria standing by their side, holding a tray of pastries that smelled like they were a gift from Salvatore De Riso's oven. If Sal was the most famous pastry chef in Italy, it was only because Annamaria didn't distribute her culinary creations outside the Amalfi Coast. Thankfully, she was handing out free samples to her customers.

"*Mangia*," Annamaria said. "Take one and tell me what you think."

"*Grazie*," Bria said. "But I shouldn't be eating anything today. I have to squeeze into a gown tonight that I haven't worn in years."

"Bria Bartolucci, you're as skinny as those models who come in here and drink espresso all day long," Annamaria said.

"Like me," Rosalie said, raising her espresso cup and lifting a pastry off the tray.

"And you want to call yourself Honest Rosie?" Annamaria laughed so hard, she almost dropped her tray. "And, Bria, you should talk! Miss I'm Not Going on a Date with Luca."

"We're not going on a date," Bria protested.

"You're wearing a gown, he's getting his tux cleaned, and you're arriving together to a party on a yacht," Annamaria said. "Sounds like a date to me."

Bria knew better than to challenge Annamaria when she thought she was right, so she focused on something that would yield more positive results, like picking out one of the pastries from Annamaria's tray and taking a bite. The immediate sensation was a rush of flavors—citrus, sweet, with a touch of . . . pepper? No, could it be chili? Whatever it was, it was unexpected and fleeting and turned what looked like a traditional puff into a bit of gourmet intrigue.

"What is that spice?" Bria asked. "I can't name it, but it makes the whole pastry taste like nothing I've ever eaten before."

"I need to have another one to make sure I love it as much as I think I do," Rosalie said, grabbing another puff from the tray.

"Don't you have to fit into a gown tonight, too?" Annamaria asked.

"I'm wearing a pantsuit," Rosalie said, then shoved the puff in her mouth. "With lots of sequins to hide the elastic waistband."

"I think the entire village is going to the party," Annamaria said. "I'll be there, along with Mimi, Violetta, Paolo."

"My whole family is going, too," Bria said. "Is Paloma going? I need someone to watch Marco."

"She isn't going, but she told me she has other plans," Annamaria shared. "I think she might have another mystery man in her life."

"I thought she just broke up with someone," Bria said.

"That doesn't stop her," Annamaria said. "Paloma Speranza is a hopeless romantic. *Per l'amor di Dio*, her last name means *hope*."

"What about Giovanni?" Rosalie asked. "Could he watch Marco?"

"I asked him," Bria said. "But he has plans, too."

"Maybe Giovanni is Paloma's mystery man," Rosalie said.

"Never!" Annamaria gasped. "Don't you remember they dated a few years ago, and Paloma thought he was cheating on her with that waitress at That's Amore? I can never remember her name, but she was *voluttuosa*."

"Sì, sì," Rosalie said. "Her name was an Anna, like yours, but not Annamaria."

"Annalisa?" Annamaria asked.

"Annabella?" Bria suggested.

"Annarosa? Annagrace?" Annamaria added.

"No, none of those," Rosalie said. "Marianna! The waitress was named Marianna."

"That's not like Annamaria," Annamaria said. "It's the exact opposite."

"*Scusatemi*, I flipped it," Rosalie said. "Giovanni swore he didn't sleep with Marianna, but Paloma didn't believe him and wouldn't even be his friend."

"She got so mad, she broke up with him right in front of St. Cecilia's," Annamaria said. "I remember because it was one of Father Roberto's best sermons, but no one heard, because they were more interested in what Paloma was shouting."

"I don't mean to interrupt this trip down memory lane," Bria said, "but I still need a babysitter. Any suggestions?"

"Ask Enrico," Annamaria said. "I know he isn't going tonight."

"I thought all the business owners were invited," Bria said.

"We were, but he has a bit of a history with Imperia and her husband, God rest his soul, and he said he'd rather eat dairy-free mozzarella than attend her party," Annamaria said.

"*Dairy-free*?" Rosalie repeated. "*Dio mio*, he must be serious. The man makes his own mozzarella."

"I had no idea that he had a history with my mother-in-law," Bria said. "Was it business or personal?"

"I think it might have been a little bit of both," Annamaria replied. "Enrico does have an eye for the ladies. He makes Silvio Berlusconi look like one of Sister Benedicta's choirboys!" Annamaria blushed slightly at her own comment and took a moment before finishing her thought. "And your father-in-law was a jealous man."

"That he was," Bria confirmed. As she continued to speak,

she texted Enrico on her phone. "This is all news to me, but hopefully, this means Enrico will be free."

Bria got confirmation that Enrico was indeed free ten seconds after she sent her text. Not only was he free, but he'd be delighted to watch Marco and teach him the finer points of bocce. Learning the sport was a rite of passage for all Italian boys and, unfortunately, Carlo had never had the chance to teach it to his son.

"That's settled," Bria said. "Now I can relax."

Instead of leaning back in her chair and finishing her cappuccino, Bria saw something that made her practically jump out of her seat.

"Do you see that man over there?" Bria said, pointing at a man about fifty yards away, walking down Viale Pasitea. "The man in the suit, with the flower in his lapel."

"Is he the one who questioned you about Vittorio?" Rosalie asked.

"Yes!" Bria replied. "The one who said he was a reporter."

"He's not a reporter," Annamaria said.

"You know him?" Bria asked.

"Of course I do," Annamaria replied. "He's Delfino di Santi, Daniela's older brother."

CHAPTER 22

There was nothing more glamorous than attending a yacht party in Positano on a Saturday night in May. There was also nothing more nerve-racking. Bria looked at herself in the mirror and questioned not only her motives but her image, as well.

The woman looking back at Bria was a stranger. She was sultry, exquisitely dressed, and possessed an air of mystery that clung to her tighter than her couture gown. Bria had no idea who she was.

This was the first time since Carlo's death that Bria would attend such an extravagant event. It was also the first time Bria would go out as a woman and not as a widow, mother, friend, or daughter. Tonight she was going out as Bria, and the prospect of having to be herself, and not being able to hide behind a comfortable mask, was beginning to make her question her motivation. Did she really want to confront Daniela and possibly her brother, Delfino, to solve this murder mystery, or was she more interested in exploring a possible romantic entanglement with Luca? The fact that she couldn't formulate an answer even to herself made her knees buckle.

She took a deep breath and closed her eyes, her go-to tactic when the world around her and inside her mind became too overwhelming. She tried as best she could to push all thoughts from her brain and make it an empty shell. An exhale followed by another deep breath, and she tried to allow only the truth back in. What was it that she truly wanted to achieve this evening? The answer shocked her.

I want to live again.

Those were the words she heard as clearly as she heard her son's laugh every morning, and she was as sincere as Carlo had been when he asked her to marry her. The intensity of the moment hit her with such force she had to hold on to the bedpost to prevent herself from crumpling to the floor. She had thought she had been doing well since Carlo's death: she had not wallowed in widowhood but had kept moving forward to be the best mother, friend, daughter, and businesswoman she could possibly be. But no, deep down inside, she knew that something had been missing. Getting things done and checking things off her to-do list was not living; it was existing. And she wanted so much more out of her time on this earth. She didn't think she was ready for a romantic relationship; now was a bit too soon. But she was ready for platonic conversation with an adult man.

Tentatively, she stood up straight and really gazed at her image. She took in each element alone and then the full picture, and the woman looking back at her slowly became familiar. This was who she was. A beautiful, confident, strong woman able to succeed in anything she set out to do, whether that was to uncover a murderer or to flirt with a man. Or not flirt with a man. The choice was hers.

She allowed herself the privilege of acknowledging how incredible she looked. It wasn't vanity; it was the truth. The Armani dress clung to her like a second layer of skin. The deep red, silk and Lycra asymmetrical gown with one long sleeve on the right and none on the left was formfitting, but thanks to the flexible fabric and a mid-thigh-high slit on the left side, walking in the gown was not a hardship. Her shoes, however, presented a learning curve.

Since coming to Positano, Bria had mainly lived in flats, sneakers, and ergonomically constructed sandals with wedge heels, all of which were designed to look pretty but ensure that the wearer could navigate a rough terrain without injury or pain. The Christian Louboutin shoes she was wearing hadn't been on her feet for over a year. But even though she was standing three inches taller than normal, her feet felt like they were being enveloped by soft clouds. They felt cradled, and not crushed. It was the Louboutin effect—footwear fashion that even feet loved.

She inspected her hair and make-up and was genuinely pleased. Her black locks fell naturally in waves to her shoulders. She wore a hair clip on the left side that pushed her hair back a bit, making her hair match the asymmetry of her gown. She smiled because the clip looked expensive but was a cheap knockoff that Marco and Carlo had found for her at some arts and crafts fair. Whoever had made the red and white jeweled barrette was a skilled artisan, because to the untrained eye, it looked like Bria was wearing a gem bought at one of Buccellati's boutiques.

Her make-up was much more dramatic than her everyday application. Matte red lips, layered rouge, and eye shadow that shimmered from deep to pale red, with a slight undertone of gold in the center. Framing her face were dangling ruby and diamond earrings, which, unlike her hair clip, were the real thing and a surprise gift from Carlo. "To celebrate another day I get to spend with you as my wife," he'd told her. Another surprise was that the memory made Bria smile, not bittersweetly but with pride.

Because of the gown's bodice, she didn't wear a necklace. The only jewelry she wore was an Elsa Peretti bone cuff bracelet in yellow gold, which was one of the gifts her parents had given her for her college graduation. A wearable piece of art for an art major. They had picked it out because it was fem-

inine yet strong, and a reminder that the two things could co-
exist and weren't exclusive to each other.

Bria took in her image and smiled. It really was true what
Sophia Loren had once said. *Nothing makes a woman more
beautiful than the belief that she is beautiful.* And Bria believed.

The other thing Bria believed was that by the end of the
night, this nightmare she'd been living would be over. She and
Luca would expose Daniela as Vittorio's murderer and uncover
what role Delfino may have played, and they could all get on to
living life in their village. The night was destined to be eventful.

Bria stood on the deck and watched the guests walk down
the red carpet on the dock at the marina to a narrow plank and
onto Imperia's yacht. She still shook her head in disbelief that
she was related to someone who owned a yacht. Imperia's
lifestyle was so different from Bria's and the kind of life Carlo
and Bria had created that it always came as a shock to her
when she realized just how wealthy Imperia was. As much as
Bria enjoyed a sophisticated evening, she wasn't entirely comfortable in such an extravagant setting.

Bria's mother, however, was a different story. When she saw
Fifetta and her father, Franco, step onto the yacht, she could
tell from her mother's glowing smile that she was deliriously
happy about the evening's festivities. And since Bria's father
was only truly happy when his wife or children were happy, he
was wearing a matching smile. Bria was overcome at seeing
them, and this time when she silently spoke to God, she
thanked Him for blessing her with such loving and good parents. Who were also sometimes a little bit annoying.

"Where's your date?" Fifetta asked.

"What date?" Bria replied.

"*Mio tesoro,*" Franco said, "you don't have to worry. We
think it's good that you're on a date, and we think the world of
Luca."

"*Il capo della polizia* is worthy of *mi figlia*," Fifetta said. "He's a good man, respected, admired, handsome—"

"Not as handsome as Fabrice," Franco interrupted.

"*Oh, andiamo*, Franco!" Fifetta exclaimed. "Have you ever met anyone more handsome than Fabrice?"

Franco opened his mouth to speak, but Fifetta beat him to it.

"No, and do you know why?"

Franco opened his mouth a second time, but Fifetta was once again quicker.

"Because there is no one who is more handsome than Lorenza's Fabrice," Fifetta said. "Though, Bria, I think you should remind Lorenza of that because she's pretty, *mi bambina*, but Fabrice is prettier."

"You want me to tell my baby sister that she isn't as pretty as her boyfriend?" Bria asked.

"Yes!" Fifetta replied. "You can't take a man like that for granted. If Lorenza doesn't treat him right, he'll just move on when he finds someone who will."

"Mamma, Fabrice loves Lorenza and she has him wrapped around her little finger," Bria said. "You don't have anything to worry about where the two of them are concerned."

"Your mamma won't stop worrying until Fabrice proposes and makes an honest woman out of Lorenza," Franco said. "*Mi Fifetta* is old-fashioned. She doesn't understand the modern ways like I do."

Bria's heart warmed as she watched her mother feign insult and saw her father's impish grin. After decades of marriage, her parents teased and flirted with each other like they were still dating. Maybe it was the youthful banter that made them both look years younger than their real ages.

Thanks to playing soccer well into his thirties and then taking up the noncontact sport of tennis, Franco was fit and trim and looked impressive in his tuxedo. His thick mane of salt-

and-pepper hair and his close-cropped beard of the same color only made his black eyes shine brighter and highlighted the fact that his skin was smooth and hardly showed any wrinkles. Her mother had aged even more graciously.

At five feet, five inches tall, Fifetta was the shortest member of their family, and while she had gained several pounds since her children were toddlers, she was still in excellent shape. She joined her husband on the tennis court and was a formidable doubles partner, but she got her main exercise by spending hours each week in the pool at the local university, swimming alongside members of the swim team. She had won some trophies in swimming competitions when she was younger, and her precise strokes and breath control had won the admiration of the college girls. By the way Franco couldn't take his eyes off his wife, it was clear that he was admiring her other assets.

Fifetta wore a simple long-sleeved, navy-colored gown with a boatneck adorned with sequins, which trickled down to her knees and then disappeared. As always was the case with Fifetta, her jewelry was minimal, and she only wore the diamond stud earrings Franco had given her on their first wedding anniversary and her engagement ring, which was still the most beautiful diamond Bria had ever seen. Bria's sister, as always, had decided more was better when it came to accessories.

When Lorenza and Fabrice stepped onto the yacht, a small round of applause was given. Not one to shy away from accolades, Lorenza did a twirl and curtsied, and Fabrice simply stood alongside her and smiled. He didn't move to garner applause. In his perfectly tailored single-button white tuxedo jacket with black satin lapels and his black trousers, wavy black hair falling freely around a face that seemed to have been chiseled by Michelangelo, Fabrice looked like a movie star who had been styled and coiffed by a team of assistants. But to Fabrice's credit, if he understood truly how handsome he was, he never showed it. And by the way he gazed at Lorenza, Bria knew that he believed she was the more alluring of the two. Bria agreed.

Her baby sister was all dolled up, and it reminded Bria of how they used to play dress-up when they were little. Even as kids, Bria would opt for a more refined look, while Lorenza chose a trendier, more provocative style. Nothing had changed.

The yellow taffeta halter top descended into a voluminous skirt that bounced and crinkled with every step. The front hem was a few inches higher than the rest of the dress, creating a showcase for the multicolored sandals with ankle straps and three-inch heels that she wore. The pink, yellow, and blue pattern of the shoes was replicated in Lorenza's many accessories.

On her right hand she wore a cluster of bracelets in all the same colors, and on her left wrist was a watch with a pink satin ribbon tied in a bow as its strap. Her dangling earrings, two balls of multicolored rhinestones, swayed when she walked, and her long hair was swept up into a bun on the top of her head and held together by a dazzling pink hairpin.

"Lorenza! *Mi bebè*!" Fifetta cried. "How I've missed you!"

"Mamma!" Lorenza cried even louder. "You just saw me last week."

"That was six days ago," Fifetta said. "When are you going to stop flying all over the world and settle down?"

"Maybe sooner than you think," Lorenza said.

"Lorenza!" Bria cried and tried to ignore the fact that she sounded an awful lot like her mother. "Are you and Fabrice . . . ?"

"Looking for a house together?" Lorenza said, finishing her sister's sentence, but not in the way her sister had hoped.

"You're going to live together without getting married?" Fifetta asked.

"Fifetta, let them do what they want," Franco chided. "No amount of shouting is going to get them to do anything other than that."

"*Grazie*, Papa," Lorenza said. "But we're not getting married, and we're not living together. I want to find my own place. I'm tired of having a roommate."

"I could kill you right here for almost giving me a heart attack!" Fifetta cried.

"Sorry, Mamma," Lorenza said. "If I wanted to give you a heart attack, I would have told you I'm pregnant. Be thankful, I only want an apartment."

"Let me know if you need help looking," Bria said.

"You don't have any time, what with Bella Bella, Marco, and solving murders," Lorenza said. "Plus, Paloma is helping me."

"Paloma?" Rosalie said. "I didn't know you were close with her."

"She's helping me as a broker, not as a friend," Lorenza said. "She has her real estate license."

"I didn't know that," Bria said.

"Call Signor Bombalino!" Lorenza cried. "There's something my big sister doesn't know."

Laughing, Bria turned, and she saw something else she hadn't been aware of. Just how elegant Rosalie could look.

Even though Bria had told Rosalie over the years that she looked beautiful in dresses and body accentuating clothes, Rosalie, for a variety of reasons, had simply never felt comfortable in such attire. She did, however, look beautiful in a black, sequined, deconstructed pantsuit. Padded shoulders and flowing pants both highlighted and hid Rosalie's frame, but she nonetheless looked striking. It helped that she wasn't wearing a blouse underneath her top and that the only thing keeping the jacket closed was a large rhinestone starburst brooch, which drew attention to her ample cleavage.

Her hair was parted on the side and slicked down; the rest of her mane was woven into a clump of braids that nestled at the nape of her neck. She wore earrings to match the brooch and sultry make-up to bring out her southern Italian features.

Bria thought her look was bold, risk taking, and completely unique, just like her friend.

When Bria looked past Rosalie, her heart skipped a beat. She had forgotten that feeling and was surprised it had returned, but she understood the cause.

Luca was always wearing his police uniform, so she had rarely seen him not looking polished and put together, but there was something about seeing a man in a tuxedo for the first time that told a woman everything she needed to know about him. Did he look comfortable and natural? Was the tuxedo overpowering, and did it make the man wearing it disappear? If so, the man usually lacked confidence and was still more of a boy than a man. In Luca's case, the opposite was true. The tuxedo made him look more sophisticated, more natural, more *manly* than Bria had ever noticed before.

The classic Armani tux cut Luca's body in all the right places. His shoulders looked broader, his waist smaller, and he looked taller, thinner, and simply better than Bria had ever seen him look before. Bria caught her mother staring at her, and her eyes grew wide, but Fifetta quickly smiled and raised her eyebrows. She couldn't chastise Fifetta, since she was only doing what Bria was doing—enjoying the moment.

Unlike his sister, Luca let the waves in his hair fall naturally, but he was clean shaven, so the cleft in his chin wasn't hidden by stubble, as it had been the last time she saw him. When Luca took Fifetta's hand and kissed her on both cheeks, Bria did notice that his fingers and cuticles looked like they had recently been manicured. It was nice to know that some men, like most women, went to the trouble of taking care of their entire appearance.

Luca hugged Franco and Fabrice and told Lorenza how spectacular she looked. When Luca took Bria's hand, they both stood awkwardly for a moment. Bria could feel the eyes of the rest of her family staring at them, and whatever not-so-

272 / MICHAEL FALCO

platonic feelings she felt stirring in her gut immediately disappeared when she realized she needed to say something, or else her family, specifically her mother, was going to faint due to the anticipation.

"You look very handsome for someone not going out on a date," Bria joked.

"I see that you didn't try very hard, either," Luca said.

"Thank you," Bria replied. "Wait! What?"

Luca laughed a full belly laugh before speaking. "You look beautiful every day, whether you're wearing gym clothes or a gown, with or without make-up. But there is something different about you tonight."

"What's that?" Bria asked.

"I'm not sure yet," Luca replied. "But there's something in your eyes. A hunger maybe."

Oh dear, Bria thought. *Am I being that obvious? Reel it in, Bria. You don't want to come off as some desperate woman out on the town for the first time in almost a year.*

She wasn't desperate; she was lucky. Whether or not this was a date didn't matter. What mattered was that she was in the company of a man she liked, and they had a common goal: to solve a murder. Luca bent down to kiss Bria's hand in a show of gentlemanly affection just as an ungentlemanly man came into view.

"Stop!" Bria shouted.

Startled, Luca stood straight up, a frightened expression covering his face. "*Scusami*, did I do something wrong?"

"No, of course not," Bria said. "Turn around. There's the reporter."

Luca whipped around but didn't see anyone. "I thought you said that man wasn't a reporter."

"He isn't, but you don't know who he really is," Bria said.

"Are you going to tell me?" Luca asked.

"Daniela's older brother, Delfino," Bria replied.

"You're not serious?" Luca replied, now looking grave and concerned.

"Yes. I saw him earlier today in the village, and Annamaria identified him as Daniela's brother," Bria explained. "Now he's here on the yacht."

"That's impossible," Luca said.

"Are you calling me a liar?" Bria asked. "I saw him twice with my own eyes, and Annamaria saw him, too, which I guess means you think we're a pair of liars."

"I don't think either of you are liars, but it's still impossible," Luca said.

"*Uffa*! Why is it so impossible that Delfino is on a yacht, at a party thrown by his sister's friend?" Bria asked.

Luca shook his head in amazement. "Because Delfino di Santi is supposed to be in jail."

CHAPTER 23

No party—whether held in a house, in a restaurant, or on a yacht—would be complete without a slight outbreak of pandemonium. That was exactly what happened when Bria and the rest of the group heard Luca's announcement.

"Jail?" Bria cried. "What's he supposed to be in jail for?"

"Embezzlement," Luca replied. "And grand theft auto, because he stole his sister's nineteen fifty-six mint-green Jaguar XK140 roadster."

"*Mucca sacra*!" Fabrice cried. "Now, that's an exceptional vehicle."

"But mint green?" Lorenza asked. "That doesn't sound like a good color for a sports car."

"Normally, I'd agree with you, *bella*," Fabrice replied. "But on the roadster it works. The light color highlights the curves."

"*Veda*!" Lorenza exclaimed. "Like my dress."

"*Esattamente*," Fabrice said before kissing Lorenza on the neck.

"Pretty boy, could you let Luca get back to explaining how Delfino broke out of jail?" Rosalie asked.

"If he broke out, we would have been told," Luca said. "The entire coast would've been alerted, so we could be on the lookout to find him."

"Then the di Santis must have paid somebody off to get him released early," Franco said. "What did I tell you about them, Bria? The entire family is despicable!"

"I understand how you feel, Franco," Luca said. "But we don't have any evidence that Delfino was released thanks to a bribe."

"I don't need any evidence to know the truth," Franco declared. "Fifetta, come on. We're leaving."

"Leave our children alone with a dangerous escaped criminal?" Fifetta asked rhetorically. "We're not going anywhere."

"Do you think he's dangerous, Luca?" Rosalie asked.

"He doesn't have a history of violent crime, but when a man is pushed far enough to the edge, there's no telling how he'll react," Luca stated.

"What do you mean by that?" Bria asked.

"He means that Delfino could kill us all as easily as he killed that man who wound up in your bed," Lorenza said.

"Vittorio was found in a guest room, not in my bed, and we don't know that Delfino is the killer," Bria clarified, then turned to Luca. "Or do you know something else that you're not telling us?"

"No. Up until this point, I thought he was behind bars for another six months," Luca confessed. "But he must have gotten released early due to good behavior."

"My money still says that the di Santis paid someone off to get their spoiled little boy out of jail," Franco spat. "Has anyone seen that miserable mayor? I bet he knows what happened."

"I haven't seen Dante yet," Bria said. "Has anyone?"

They all replied that they hadn't seen Dante, although Luca reminded them that he could have arrived early and could be somewhere on one of the three levels of the yacht. Now that they thought about it, they realized they also hadn't seen Imperia, but since she was the hostess, she was most likely going to make a grand entrance after everyone arrived. One person they had never thought they'd see tonight was Sister Benedicta, who walked onto the yacht looking like a child walking into a candy store for the first time.

"Sister Benedicta!" Rosalie cried. "What in the world are you doing here?"

When the nun saw people she recognized, her face lit up like the candy store owner had just told her she had carte blanche to fill her bags with as much candy as she wanted.

"Familiar faces," the nun gasped. "I'm so happy to see you. I was afraid I wouldn't know anyone, and I don't think you'll be shocked to hear that I've never been on a yacht before or to a party this glamorous."

"It's lovely to see you," Bria said. "And please don't take this the wrong way, but what are you doing here?"

"Didn't you read the invite?" Fifetta asked.

"I had no intention to come until—" Bria stopped when she realized there was someone in her company who didn't know her true motives for attending the soiree. She smiled and turned to Sister Benedicta. "Until I changed my mind and thought it would be good to get out for the night. Luca had the same thought, and we decided to come together."

The nun smiled at her, but Bria couldn't tell if she approved of her connection to Luca or thought that for a widow, it was an unchristian act. She'd dwell on that later. At the moment she was more interested in the nun's reason for being at such a swanky nonreligious ceremony. That reason, according to her mother, was most likely printed on the invitation, which Bria had never taken the time to read.

"The party is in honor of the FAI, the Fondo Ambiente Italiano," Sister Benedicta explained. "It's an organization based in Sarno—"

"Sarno?" Bria interrupted.

"Yes," the nun replied. "It supports the arts in schools and institutions all throughout Italy, and one of those lucky schools that benefits from its generosity is St. Cecilia's. I'm here as a representative to, well, collect our check."

Bria looked at Rosalie and saw that her friend was just as surprised as she was to hear that Imperia and Daniela really did have a reason to be in Sarno. That explained where they had met and why, but it still didn't clear Daniela of her connection to Vittorio. Madame di Santi remained their prime suspect.

"Arts education is vitally important," Fifetta said. "Children need to be able to express themselves creatively before they grow up and forget what it's like to create. Isn't that right, Bria?"

Bria knew her mother wished she would start painting again and Bria wanted to as well. She would pick up a paintbrush once she had some free time.

"It's the biggest mistake adults make," Sister Benedicta said. "That God doesn't want them to play and experience joy, when the truth is that He wants us to do that until our last breath on earth."

"It's how I live my life," Fabrice said.

"I tried to get them to do the same thing, approach their life with a sense of joy and wonder," Sister Benedicta added. "They nodded their heads in agreement, but I don't think they really meant it. No one ever really wants to disagree with a nun."

"Who did you say that to?" Luca asked.

"Daniela and Imperia," Benedicta replied. "They came to tell me that St. Cecilia's had been chosen to receive funding from the FAI. I was very thankful, of course. We can always put new donations to good use. But I noticed there was a seriousness about them. It could have been a great sadness that they shared."

"Or it could be that they're just not friendly people," Franco said.

Fifetta slapped Franco on the chest. "Don't talk about Marco's grandmother like that!"

It's because Daniela was mourning Vittorio's death, and Imperia was consoling her friend, Bria thought. *It's hard to smile when you just killed your boyfriend.*

Marco's grandmother may be too serious most of the time and not overly friendly, but she did know how to turn an entrance into a photo opportunity. Standing on the deck, Imperia didn't have to say a word to make every head on the yacht turn to face her and stop all conversation. Her presence was enough to turn the party silent.

Despite the complicated feelings Bria had for Imperia, she did love the woman. Mainly because she knew that Carlo had loved her. It was an unconditional love, and Carlo had admittedly acknowledged all his mother's shortcomings, both large and small. He would also say that everyone had flaws, and Imperia just didn't care about hiding hers. Which was true. Imperia Bartolucci felt that if God accepted her the way she was, the rest of the world should, too.

As Imperia stood in front of the large group of people gathered, a combination of family, friends, social climbers, business associates, and one bemused nun, Bria could feel energy pouring out of the woman. Imperia was in her element. Commanding, imperious and, Bria happily admitted, strikingly beautiful.

Her jet-black hair was styled basically the same way as she always wore it, but it had been given some additional height, and one side was tucked behind her ear to show off the huge diamond and sapphire earrings she wore. Her long-sleeved gown was dark blue, with a deep V-neck. The back of her gown was made of lace all the way to the waist, and then additional lace filled out the back, creating a small train that followed her wherever she walked.

The rest of her accessories—a few rings, a bracelet, and a spectacular necklace—were all variations on the diamond and sapphire theme and were all outrageously expensive. Bria knew how much every item Imperia was wearing cost because Imperia had told her. Her mother-in-law believed that price tags, when containing at least five digits, should be made public.

"*Signore e signnori*," Imperia said in a strong, clear voice that commanded attention, eliminating the need to shout. "Thank you for coming to my little party."

She paused until the applause, which she knew her introduction would elicit, had subsided.

"My husband, Guillermo, started a tradition decades ago to celebrate each year with the friends, family, and colleagues who helped make Bartolucci Enterprises a success, as a way to give thanks," Imperia said. "Originally, the party was in our offices, but as we grew, so did the festivities, which is why we find ourselves here today on my yacht."

Another round of applause interrupted Imperia's speech, and she paused. A smile emerged on her lips and Bria couldn't tell if it was organic or manufactured. Probably a little of both.

"After my beloved husband died, I decided to make this party more about a celebration of the company's success and a way to give back to the community we couldn't survive without," Imperia said. "Each year Bartolucci Enterprises joins forces with the FAI to make a charitable donation to a worthy organization, and this year I am proud to announce that I have chosen St. Cecilia's right here in Positano as the recipient."

The applause this time was much louder, and Imperia let the adoration wash over her.

"There will be a more formal ceremony later tonight, but for now, *mangia, bevi, e divertiti*," Imperia said.

By the time Imperia made her way over to Bria and the rest of the family, the applause had finally ceased. All they could hear was the chatter of the guests and the sounds of the string quartet, which was playing something by Verdi or Puccini. Bria couldn't identify the melody and couldn't determine if the sound conveyed delight or despair. She felt the same when Imperia spoke.

"I see that you are true to your word and finally decided to join the party."

"I told you I was coming," Bria said.

"At the last minute," Imperia replied. "And without RSVP'ing."

Bria smiled through clenched teeth. "I'm here as promised."

"I'm glad you're here," Imperia said without a trace of sarcasm or clenched teeth. "And I see you've brought . . . company."

"I received my own invitation," Rosalie declared.

Finally, Imperia clenched her teeth. "I was referring to Bria's . . . date. I'm honored that a member of the carabinieri has the time to celebrate with us, what with a murderer at large."

"My team is working on finding Vittorio's murderer," Luca declared. "And so am I."

"And Luca is not my date," Bria interjected.

"Your personal life, dear daughter-in-law, is none of my affair," Imperia replied. "Luca, are you on duty right now?"

"I'm the chief of police. I'm never off duty," Luca said, meeting her glare without backing down or displaying defiance.

"The guest list is large and varied," Imperia said. "Who knows? Maybe the murderer is on board with us right now."

Sister Benedicta let out a gasp at the prospect of being on board a moving vessel with a murderer. Most of those assembled were used to hearing Imperia's melodramatic comments and didn't give credence to every word she uttered, but Bria knew she was right. If their suspicions were correct, they were partying with a killer.

Bria needed to switch the focus of the conversation to a

more appropriate subject matter, one that would also meet Imperia's approval. Fifetta beat her to it.

"Imperia, you look stunning, as usual," Fifetta said. "Did Concetta make this for you?"

"She's the only seamstress I trust," Imperia replied. "I don't know who I'll use when she retires."

"Pay her more money and she'll never retire," Franco said.

"Spoken like a true businessman," Imperia said. "There's a reason Guillermo always respected you."

"Likewise," Franco said.

"You all look beautiful, as well," Imperia said. "Worthy accessories to the sunset, the landscape, and my breathtaking three-story yacht."

Bria laughed out loud with the rest of the group. Imperia was many things, but modest was not one of them.

"I thought Dante might arrive with you, Imperia," Franco said. "We haven't seen him."

"As the mayor, he's as busy as Luca," Imperia said. "He may have been detained."

"By the police?" Rosalie asked.

"What could the police possibly want with Dante?" Imperia chided. "Unless it was a political matter. More funding perhaps? A better time-off policy?"

Bria was happy to see that Luca didn't take the bait and merely laughed at Imperia's absurd assumptions.

"Who would say no to a little more time off?" Luca remarked. "Not me."

The rest of the group laughed along with Luca, although Bria suspected none of them thought what he had said was particularly funny.

"Sister Benedicta," Imperia said.

"Yes, Mrs. Bartolucci?" the nun replied.

"Please come with me. I'd like to introduce you to some of the members of the board of the FAI."

"Of course," the nun agreed.

The other guests watched them leave, and when Imperia was completely out of earshot, Bria looked around the deck and could tell by looking at each person's eyes that they all wanted to say something about their hostess. Bria's mother wouldn't allow it.

"If anyone says anything bad about Imperia, *che Dio mi sia testimone*, they will suffer my wrath for the rest of the year," Fifetta said. "She is our family, and none of you should ever forget that."

No one said a word, not in agreement or in jest, because they all knew that when Fifetta got that Scarlett O'Hara tone in her voice, she was not to be contradicted or challenged. She and Imperia were vastly different women, and Bria knew that Fifetta didn't approve of everything Imperia did or said as a businesswoman or socialite, but she knew that Fifetta considered Imperia to be a good mother and an exceptional grandmother. Those two qualities outweighed almost everything else Imperia had or may have done. No amount of arguing would ever change that, so Bria had never tried to change her mother's opinion.

"*Mi amore*," Franco said, extending his hand to his wife, "come have champagne with me."

Fifetta blushed slightly. "*Scusatemi*. I seem to have caught a gentleman's eye."

As Franco and Fifetta walked toward the bar, Fabrice pulled Lorenza away from the group, whispering something about having some privacy. Rosalie then announced that she wanted to find the yacht's captain and ask him some nautical questions only the captain of a yacht could answer. That left Bria and Luca alone.

They stared at each other for a moment, and just when it was about to get awkward, they both started laughing. The release felt good and reminded them both that regardless of where things would lead, they were and always would be friends. Luca held out his arm, bent it at the elbow, and Bria hooked her arm with his.

"Shall we get this non-date started?" Luca suggested.

"I thought you'd never ask," Bria replied.

They walked into the main salon and accepted glasses of champagne from strolling waiters, who looked so classically Italian, Bria thought they had jumped out of the paintings in one of the Vatican Museums. Bria was in the middle of a mental search to find an innocuous topic to discuss when she once again saw Delfino di Santi. He was standing near a doorway that led to the upper deck, having a conversation with someone unseen. Bria gasped, and Luca turned around just in time to see Delfino's companion step into view. It was Daniela.

Luca grabbed Bria's hand and tilted his head in the direction of the di Santis, indicating to her that they were going to confront their prey. Or was it their predator? They pushed through the crowd, which seemed to thicken and grow larger with each step they took, and by the time they got to the doorway, the di Santis were gone.

"Do you think they saw us and ran?" Bria asked.

"I don't know. I lost sight of them halfway over here," Luca said. "Why don't we split up? I'll take upstairs, and you go through that door over there."

Bria looked to her left and saw a door that she hadn't noticed before. She didn't know where it led, but she'd soon find out.

Just before Luca let go of Bria's hand, he said, "Be careful."

"You too," Bria replied.

She felt a rush of adrenaline surge through her body as she pushed through the door. She didn't know what she'd find on the other side, but she wasn't expecting to see Daniela leaning against the railing, the fabric of her silver chiffon, Greek-inspired gown flowing all around her, making her appear to be floating. Her blondish-brown hair was swept up into a sophisticated

284 / MICHAEL FALCO

and complicated hairdo reminiscent of what women wore in the sixties. Bria thought she should be wearing white gloves to complete the outfit, but instead her hands were bare, except for one ring on her right hand with an incredibly large amethyst stone. It was square and outlined in diamond chips, and Bria thought it was so big that Daniela could use it as a life preserver if she fell overboard.

But Daniela wasn't going anywhere.

"I've been waiting for you, Bria," Daniela said. "It's about time we had a chat."

CHAPTER 24

Bria felt like Pinocchio. The little wooden boy wanted to be human so badly, but when he got his wish, he didn't know what to do. Now that she was face-to-face with the woman she believed had killed Vittorio Ingleterra, the woman she had been desperate to confront, Bria had no idea what to say to her.

She remained silent and took in the view, allowing it to calm her. The sunset was an artist's creation, a base of orange layered with ascending shades of purple, each one darker, until the sky became a deep midnight blue. The lights from the many hotels, homes, and businesses in Positano behind them created a shimmering haze and gave the surroundings an ethereal presence. The gentle rocking of the boat, more prominent to Bria as she stood next to the railing than when she was among a group of people in the yacht's interior, gave her the sensation that she was existing outside her body and in some kind of dream state. The feeling was unnerving, just like Daniela's stare.

Seeing the woman's face fully for the first time and not behind dark sunglasses or camouflaged by a large hat, Bria was struck by how forceful she looked. Daniela possessed the same poise and confidence that Imperia did, but whereas Imperia was always ready to fight if provoked, Daniela looked ready to strike first. Anger helped shape her face; vengeance was etched into her skin. Bria knew very little about the woman, but with one look, she felt like she knew exactly who Daniela was and what she was capable of doing. And it made her afraid.

Ignore the fear, Bria told herself. *She's only a woman, just like you.*

And all women had one thing in common: a desire to be loved.

"Was Vittorio your boyfriend?" Bria asked.

She expected many responses, but not a howl of laughter.

"Boyfriend?" Daniela repeated. "*Mia cara*, adult women don't have boyfriends. They take lovers."

"Or paramours?" Bria asked.

The ice that comprised Daniela's face softened, and Bria knew she had to continue.

"Was Vittorio your paramour?"

"He was," Daniela confirmed.

"Until you killed him?"

Daniela gripped the railing so tightly that her knuckles whitened and the skin around the amethyst reddened at the sudden pressure. She smirked at Bria and shook her head.

"Imperia was right about you," Daniela declared. "You're as common as a pigeon in Piazza Navona."

"At least I'm not a murderer."

"You think I murdered my Vittorio?"

"Yes, I do," Bria replied.

"Can you back up this unfounded and preposterous accusation with an ounce of proof?"

"What's in your Balenciaga bag?"

With her free hand, Daniela grabbed the silver satin bag hanging from a thin chain draped over her shoulder. "All the usual things a woman carries with her when she goes out alone. Lipstick, aspirin, a handgun."

"You're carrying a gun?"

"When you become an adult, you'll understand it isn't just a woman's prerogative to be armed. It's a necessity."

Bria felt a chill run up her spine, and it wasn't the breeze; the air was still and warm.

"Funny that you didn't use your gun to kill Vittorio but knifed him instead."

Daniela let go of the railing, but not her handbag, as she took a few steps toward Bria. Self-preservation kicked in, and although Bria tried to maintain her stance and not retreat, she felt herself walking backward. She would have kept walking as far as she could if her back hadn't hit a pole that was part of the stairway that led to the upper deck, the same stairs Luca had taken to chase after Delfino. Bria thought that if she screamed loud enough, maybe he would hear her and come running to her rescue.

No! Bria heard herself scream inside her head. *I don't need a man to come to my rescue. I can get out of this situation on my own.*

Bria took a step forward and was now mere inches away from Daniela. The woman's skin was flawless, pale, and nearly wrinkle free, but Bria didn't know if that was the result of good genes and moisturizing or frequent visits to Dr. Frangi in Milan. Maybe she and Imperia had got a two-for-one discount? Whatever the reason, she could understand how Daniela would attract a younger man like Vittorio even if she wasn't a wealthy woman. The fact that she was rich made her even more appealing to a financially challenged man of any age.

"You claim that you're an adult woman, but you bought matching scarves for you and Vittorio to wear," Bria said. "That's something a schoolgirl would do to let the world know she has a boyfriend."

"Vittorio and I shared the same sartorial style," Daniela replied. "He understood the importance of having a smart wardrobe."

"Unfortunate that he couldn't afford it on his own," Bria said. "He looked like he belonged in your circle, but the truth was that he lived several stations lower. If I were to use the vocabulary of the common, I'd say he was broke and you were his meal ticket."

Daniela waved a finger in Bria's face. "That isn't true."

"You mean *wasn't* true," Bria corrected. "Your paramour is dead. I'm sorry, murdered. And here you are, all dressed up at a party, without a care in the world."

"Vittorio loved me!"

"Did you love him?" Bria asked. "Enough to kill him?"

"*Sei stupido o cosa?*" Daniela asked.

"If I were stupid I wouldn't have uncovered enough clues to know that you killed Vittorio," Bria replied.

"I swear on my mother's soul, if you say that one more time, I *will* commit murder!" Daniela shouted. "And you'll be the dead body some *idiota* finds!"

"I just want to end this and find out who killed the man I found dead in my home!" Bria cried.

"Then you need to look somewhere else because I loved Vittorio. I wanted to marry him. Why in the world would I kill him?"

"Maybe he didn't want to marry you."

Bria's comment wasn't shouted, but the impact on Daniela was great. Bria couldn't tell if this was something that the woman had never contemplated or if it was something that had gnawed at her spirit, something that had made her question the very validity of her relationship. If it was something that had bothered Daniela, then perhaps their relationship hadn't been as secure as Daniela wanted to believe. Maybe Vittorio would have ended things with Daniela had he not been killed. If he were alive today, would he be standing beside her right now as her date?

Bria felt a fire in her stomach, and she knew that her instincts were right—Vittorio had been killed in a flurry of passion. He had done or said something that Daniela didn't like, and she had stabbed him. Daniela didn't agree with Bria's line of thinking.

"I've tolerated your snooping," Daniela said, "but I'm warning you to stop saying and accusing me of things you cannot prove."

"How do you know that I've been snooping?"

Daniela smiled a very satisfied smile. "You caught that, did you? I guess you're smarter than I thought."

"Don't flatter me. Answer my question," Bria said. "How do you know I've been trying to find out who killed Vittorio?"

"Because when you're a wealthy *adult* like I am, you have friends everywhere," Daniela said. "Even in the police force. I'm telling you for the last time, watch your tongue when you speak about me."

"Or what?" Bria asked. "You're going to cut it out with the same knife you used to kill Vittorio?"

The look of venomous rage that appeared on Daniela's face frightened Bria, and she didn't know if the woman was going to pull out her gun and shoot her dead, ignoring the fact that she would be arrested and thrown into jail for the rest of her life. Daniela looked like a woman who didn't care what consequences her actions produced. All she cared about was getting rid of the woman standing in front of her.

Just as Bria thought she might actually need to scream "Mussolini!" to get Rosalie to rescue her, she was saved by an even louder voice—Imperia's.

Her mother-in-law could be heard over the loudspeaker asking Daniela di Santi to come to the stage in the main dining salon. Imperia had to ask twice before Daniela composed herself and was ready to leave. But before she turned to go, she whispered to Bria, "This isn't over."

No, it isn't, Daniela, Bria thought. *Not by a long shot.*

Bria gripped the railing and leaned forward. She breathed in the sea air, and after a few moments the sound of applause could be heard. Daniela must have stepped onto the stage. Bria walked toward the yacht's main salon to get a better look and to keep the woman in her sight. Before she made it to the salon, however, she crashed into Luca, who had rounded a corner and slammed right into Bria. She had to hold on to the chief of police tightly, or else she would've toppled to the deck, with him on top of her.

"*Perdonami*!" Luca said. "Are you all right?"

Frazzled but upright, Bria found herself thinking that Luca's body was much harder than she ever would have imagined. He wasn't muscular like Giovanni. He had more of a lean frame, like that of a long-distance runner. Whatever he did for exercise, it worked, because the parts of his body that she was holding on to—his upper back and waist—felt like slabs of granite.

"I'm fine," Bria said, reluctantly releasing Luca's body from her grip. "I spoke with Daniela."

"I spoke with Dante," Luca said.

"You couldn't find Delfino?"

"No, he scurried away, but he's somewhere on this yacht," Luca replied. "What did Daniela say?"

"She was involved with Vittorio romantically, though I didn't get a chance to find out if they had a business relationship, as well," Bria recounted.

"That's okay," Luca replied. "A lover has just as much motive to kill as a disgruntled business partner, especially if the romance is troubled."

"That's what I think, but she didn't make it sound like they had a tumultuous relationship or that either one of them had broken up with the other," Bria shared. "I have to admit that I got the feeling that she did love him."

"That's not so great," Luca replied. "But it does give me enough reason to bring her in for further questioning."

"Did you get anything out of Dante?"

"He confirmed that Delfino was let out of prison early for good behavior," Luca reported. "Which means that your father is right and his family paid somebody off, because Delfino hasn't exhibited good behavior since *scuola dell'infanzia*."

"I remember when Marco was in kindergarten," Bria mused. "He couldn't pronounce *scuola* and kept saying *gola*. The nuns all thought he had a sore throat."

Luca smiled and Bria recognized the smile as one of indulgence.

"I'm sorry. I hear my son's name and I go off on a tangent," she said.

Luca's smile turned into a laugh. "I didn't mention Marco's name. You did."

"It doesn't matter who says Marco's name. When I hear it, all I can do is think about him in his little school jacket and tie walking up to the gate at St. Cecilia's." Bria stopped herself and apologized for rambling. "*Scusa*, no more mother talk. I'm back to being your partner."

"The chief of police doesn't have a partner," Luca said.

"The chief of police might not have a partner, but Luca Vivaldi does," Bria corrected. "Did Dante say anything else about Delfino? Where's he been since he got out of jail? Is he trying to restart the counterfeit money ring?"

"Dante wouldn't come clean, but he's covering for Delfino," Luca said. "He was acting more *cauto* than usual."

"Dante's always acting cagey. He's a politician," Bria said. "Do you think he's working with Delfino or just protecting him?"

"With Dante, you never know," Luca said. "He's always had money, and since he's become the mayor, he has power. The combination of the two can be dangerous."

"Because he thinks he can get away with anything?" Bria asked.

"Yes."

"Even murder?"

"Possibly," Luca said.

Their conversation was interrupted when the voices from the main dining salon grew louder. A commotion was brewing, and shouting could be heard, but Bria couldn't make out what they were saying or what they were arguing about. The only words she clearly heard were Daniela's when she spoke even louder into the microphone as a way to control the situation.

"The FAI is a cherished organization in the di Santi family," Daniela said. "My father was a fierce supporter of the arts."

"Your father was a fraud!"

Bria recognized the thin, high-pitched voice, and as she and Luca rushed into the dining salon, her suspicion proved right. The voice belonged to Delfino. And his tone meant that he didn't agree with his sister's assessment of their father.

"Our father was a great man!" Daniela shouted. "You should be ashamed!"

The iron maiden had softened. Bria hardly knew Daniela, but she didn't think public emotional outbursts were the norm for her. Hers was a more rigid, guarded character, and she wasn't the type of woman who would reveal her inner thoughts and feelings except behind closed doors in a hermetically sealed room. This explosion did not seem typical.

Imperia grabbed the microphone from Daniela and in a voice that was even more commanding than her usual tone but at the same time filled with amusement, glossed over the situation.

"*Liti familiari*," Imperia said. "We all have been involved in family squabbles. You can't live with them, and you can't live without them."

The audience, anxious for a diversion, laughed gratefully. They knew they were being manipulated, but that was what they wanted. They had come here for a night of fantasy and frolic, not for a family frenzy. Whatever problems Daniela and Delfino had, they would have to sort them out on their own.

All the guests wanted to do was eat more shrimp wrapped in prosciutto and oysters *al forno* and drink limoncello when they grew tired of champagne. Bria and Luca had other plans.

"You follow Daniela," Luca said. "I'll go after Delfino."

Bria saw Dante yank Delfino by the arm and push through the crowd to exit through a door at the yacht's stern. She turned and just caught Daniela as she walked through an archway at the bow. Bria lifted up her gown so she could run faster, and once again was thankful that she had spent the extra money on her Louboutins. The pope should designate the designer a saint, because it was a miracle that you could run in these heels.

Running after Daniela, Bria couldn't believe how large the yacht was. There were so many passageways leading to different parts of the vessel that she felt like she was in a maze. When she came to a private deck at the bow, she saw Daniela pacing back and forth and got the eerie premonition that Daniela was a caged mouse and Bria was the cheese.

"It seems that you and your brother have different opinions of your father," Bria said.

Daniela turned abruptly, practically swiveling on her heel, hands on hips, and glowered at Bria. The look she gave Bria was worse than the stare Barbara Fusar-Poli gave her ice dancing partner, Maurizio Margaglio, after he dropped her a few seconds before their free dance skating routine ended at the Torino Olympics. The way Daniela looked at Bria, it was clear she wanted to drop her off the side of the yacht.

"My brother, like you, is small minded and petty and can't think about things that he can't see," Daniela said.

Bria didn't know what Daniela was referring to, but she knew that she had to keep her talking to find out.

"What is it that your brother can't see?" Bria asked.

"That our father only did what was best for his family, and not to spite our mother or his children."

Quickly translating Daniela's comment into useful information, Bria remembered that Imperia had told her Daniela was a powerful businesswoman. She also recalled that Luca had told her Delfino was Daniela's older brother. Traditionally, in Italian families—as in families in most countries—the firstborn child inherited any family company, especially if that child was a boy. How angry and jealous would Delfino be if his younger sibling, a sister at that, was given full reign of di Santi Enterprises?

"Delfino thinks that you got what was rightfully his," Bria said. "He's just a jealous big brother."

"He's an idiot," Daniela said. "Just like my father."

Wait a second. Didn't Daniela just praise her father in public? Now, in private she was maligning him as well as her brother. Was she powerful or just ruthless?

"Like father, like son," Bria said. "Who's the bigger idiot of the two?"

"They're both *tontos*!" Daniela cried. "My father was given everything and almost destroyed it. If it wasn't for my mother hovering over my father, we'd be penniless. Carlotta di Santi is the reason we still have a lira to our name."

A lira to their name? That was an odd choice of words. And if Carlotta di Santi was the family savior, that meant she had to be domineering and imperious, like the woman Dante had said was the real ringleader of the old counterfeit money ring. It also fit in the timeline better, as Carlotta would be roughly the same age as Dante's and Nunzi's fathers. Bria wanted to grill Daniela about her mother, but the woman only wanted to talk about her father.

"The one sensible thing Papa ever did was to leave the company to me," Daniela said. "As much as he wanted to leave everything to his precious bambino, he knew that Delfino would destroy it, and the di Santi name would mean nothing. We would be a laughingstock, a cautionary tale."

"But Delfino still thinks he's the rightful heir to the throne," Bria said.

"It doesn't matter what my brother thinks or does," Daniela said. "My father didn't even trust him with his own inheritance. If my brother wants to withdraw one euro from his account, he has to ask me first."

"You pull the strings on Delfino's money?"

"*Certo*! If I didn't, he'd spend it all in a day."

"I can't imagine he likes having to do that."

"He doesn't get to have a say because I run the business and I will do whatever it takes to protect my family's legacy."

"Even if it means killing your lover."

Daniela didn't get angry at Bria's comment; she didn't attack her. She laughed out loud and threw her hands up in mock despair.

"Dear God, will you listen to this little girl!" Daniela shouted. "Imperia was right about you."

"Did she say that I was clever? Tenacious?"

"She said you were a pain in the ass!"

Daniela's words stung harder than any slap across the face. Imperia had said that? Really? Bria knew she could be aloof and distant when it came to her relationship with Imperia, but that was because she just didn't feel the two of them got along. Bria knew that she wasn't an annoying person or a pest or someone who bothered Imperia constantly, which could only mean that Imperia hadn't been referring to her as Bria, her daughter-in-law, but as Bria, the amateur detective. That was it. Imperia thought Bria was a pain because she wouldn't give up until she discovered who had killed Vittorio, and by the way Daniela was reacting, the woman was inching closer with every second to being announced the culprit.

"Those who are guilty usually consider those of us trying to uncover the truth to be painful thorns in their side," Bria said.

"I will tell you one final time, I did not kill Vittorio," Daniela said. "I loved him, and I am mourning him."

"When you're in mourning, you usually don't attend parties on yachts."

"Wearing black and wailing in a church pew after your husband was killed isn't the only way to mourn," Daniela seethed. "How can you possibly say you want to know the truth when you're unwilling to open your eyes and see it? You want to live in your little shell and think the world doesn't exist beyond your four walls, go ahead, but remember, not all women act in the same way. Don't make the same mistake men make all the time."

A cold breeze swept over Bria, and she wasn't sure if it was the air or something she conjured up when Daniela brushed past her and left the deck.

For a few moments, Bria stood motionless and contemplated Daniela's words. Did she have the woman all wrong? Could she have loved Vittorio even though she wasn't acting as if her lover was recently murdered? Some women might think what Bria was doing—getting all dressed up to spend the evening with a man on a yacht less than a year after she had buried her husband—was also wrong. It didn't matter if it wasn't an official date; Bria was, in fact, starting to have feelings for Luca. Would those feelings lead anywhere? She had no idea. That didn't matter because she had still allowed another man into her heart, where previously there was room only for Carlo.

"When will this be over?" she muttered aloud to herself.

"I'm ready to go if you are."

Bria spun around and was grateful to see a friendly face. And another full glass of champagne. She took the champagne, downed half the glass, and then looked at Rosalie.

"Let's find your brother and get out of here," Bria said. "I've had enough of these people to last me a lifetime."

"What did that witch say that got you so rattled?" Rosalie asked. "She practically knocked me down when she passed me."

"I'll explain later," Bria said. "Let's go."

"Where are you going?"

Luca stood there, breathing heavily. He had undone his bow tie and it was hanging from his neck, the top collar of his shirt was unbuttoned, and beads of sweat had formed on his forehead. Bria thought he looked even more attractive now than when the night started.

"We're leaving," Bria said. "I wasn't able to get Daniela to confess. She continues to profess her love for Vittorio. I'm sorry, but this whole evening was a waste of time."

"Were you able to find the brother?" Rosalie asked. "I saw you run off in his direction."

"No. He must be hiding somewhere," Luca said. "This yacht has more secret compartments and passageways, it's like it was built by Houdini."

"The food was good at least. I have to give Imperia credit for that," Bria said. "On our way out, if you see a waiter with those shrimp and scallop skewers, throw a few in your purse."

Rosalie patted the black sequined purse hanging from her shoulder. "I've got so much seafood in here, I'm surprised every cat in the village isn't clamoring at my feet."

Just as the three of them began to exit the private deck single file, they heard a sound that made them stop. At first, Bria thought Imperia was putting on a fireworks display, but then she heard a woman scream, "No!" She knew it wasn't in reaction to a burst of color in the sky.

"That was a gunshot," Luca said.

"Are you sure?" Rosalie asked.

When they heard another sound, it was unmistakable. Someone had pulled the trigger of a gun. Twice.

As they turned the corner and stepped onto the balcony off the main dining salon, it took them a moment to take in the scene. Daniela was lying on the floor, a pool of blood pouring out of her chest, while her brother, Delfino, was straddling the railing. When he saw them, his face registered fear, and it was obvious that he knew Luca was the chief of police and Bria was the woman he had spoken with at Bella Bella.

"Don't do it, Delfino!" Luca shouted.

But Delfino didn't listen, and he jumped overboard.

Thankfully, when Luca told Dante—who was standing over Daniela's dead body, a gun dangling in his hand—not to move, the mayor listened.

Chapter 25

"Drop the gun, Dante," Luca commanded.

Slowly, Dante pulled his gaze from Daniela's dead body and looked up at Luca. He looked like he was in shock, like he had woken up from a deep sleep and still thought that he was in a dream, floating on an iceberg or sliding down a rainbow into a pot of gold, only to see that his world had changed in an instant. One second he was the mayor; the next a murderer.

"Don't make this worse, Dante," Luca said. "Put down the gun and raise your hands."

"It's my gun," Dante said, his voice a throaty whisper.

"Don't say another word. Just put the gun on the floor," Luca said.

"What's my gun doing here?" Dante asked.

"Dante."

Bria didn't shout, but her voice, for some reason, captured Dante's attention. Maybe he did have strong feelings for her. Maybe her voice reminded him of his mother. Whatever the reason, Bria needed to use it to her advantage.

"*Prego*, place the gun on the floor and kick it over to me," Bria said. *"Per piacere."*

This time Dante followed orders and did as he was told.

When the gun stopped moving a few inches from Bria's foot, Luca crossed over, pulled a silk handkerchief out of his pocket, and used it to pick up the gun by its trigger to avoid getting any fingerprints on it.

"Since when do you carry a silk handkerchief?" Rosalie whispered.

"I was going to use it as a pocket square but thought it would be too much," Luca explained.

"You made the right decision, *fratello*," Rosalie said.

"Nunzi, do you see anyone in the water below?" Luca asked.

"Nunzi?" Bria asked.

"Where'd you come from?" Rosalie followed up.

"I've been here all night," Nunzi replied. "I don't see anyone, Chief, but I'm calling in the coast guard."

"Tell them Delfino di Santi jumped overboard," Luca said.

Nunzi called in the distress call, while Rosalie and Bria still questioned if Nunzi was telling the truth or not.

"Did you see her before now, Bri?" Rosalie asked.

"No, and I've been all over this boat," Bria replied.

Nunzi finished her call and then directed her next comment to the ladies. "You must not have recognized me."

They hardly recognized her now, and she was standing right in front of them. They had seen Nunzi out of her uniform before but never dressed like this. She looked like a completely different person. Fit and toned, her broad shoulders tapering to a tiny waist that gave way to long legs, she had the body of an athlete. Her uniform didn't fit her nearly as well as her simple jersey gown did.

High necked and sleeveless, the emerald-green gown showcased her body in all the right places. She didn't wear any jewelry and let her hair fall naturally to just past her shoulders. The personality the gown conjured was youthful and carefree, the complete opposite of Nunzi's authoritarian, strict persona when on duty. But despite the upscale outfit, Nunzi proved that her no-frills attitude toward her outward appearance wasn't a pretense.

"Your gown is beautiful," Rosalie said. "Where'd you get it?"

"Someplace online," she replied.

"*Ah, Madonna mia*! I buy a T-shirt online, and it doesn't fit me right," Rosalie griped. "She buys a gown, and it fits her like a glove."

"Rosalie, *basta*!" Luca chided.

He flicked his head in Daniela and Dante's direction to remind his sister that they were in the presence of a dead body and the person who had caused that body to be dead.

"This is a crime scene," Luca said. "Not a joke."

He didn't have to repeat himself because no one was laughing. Not even when Nunzi pulled out a pair of handcuffs from her purse and instructed Dante to put his hands behind his back as Luca told him he was under arrest for the murder of Daniela di Santi and read him his rights. Dante obeyed but still appeared to be fighting his way out of a haze. Others were fighting their way in.

"It sounds like an angry mob out there," Bria said. "What are you going to do?"

"Control the situation," Luca replied.

"How can we help?" Bria asked.

"I need the two of you to stand at the entrance and do your best not to let anyone through," Luca instructed. "Nunzi, I can handle Dante. Go ask the captain to return to the dock and see if he has a loudspeaker so I can talk to the guests without opening these doors."

"There might be a loudspeaker inside one of these benches," Rosalie said. "They're usually used to store extra equipment."

There were two benches on either side of the balcony that

served as cushioned seating. When the lids were lifted, they revealed that the benches were also used as storage.

"Voilà!" Rosalie cried, pulling out a loudspeaker and handing it to her brother. "Here you go."

"*Grazie*, Ro," Luca said.

"I'll go talk to the captain," Nunzi said before exiting the balcony to go to the upper deck.

Luca turned on the loudspeaker and tested it by blowing into the mouthpiece. A loud whooshing sound filled the air, followed by a piercing wail, the sound that occurred when the speaker's mouth got too close to the microphone.

"May I have your attention please," Luca said, his voice booming into the night. "This is Luca Vivaldi, your chief of police. There has been a fatal shooting, but there is no need for alarm. The shooter has been apprehended and is no longer a threat. The yacht is returning to shore, but do not try to leave once we dock. I need you to remain where you are until further notice. *Grazie*."

The banging on the door that separated the dining salon from the balcony stopped, and it seemed that everyone understood the need to follow Luca's command. All but one passenger, anyway.

"Imperia, you can't come in here," Bria said.

"Get out of my way," Imperia ordered.

"Please trust me, you don't want to go out there."

But Imperia did want to go out on the balcony, and Bria understood why: she didn't want her friend to die alone. It didn't matter that she might already be gone. If there was any chance that her spirit, her soul, was still in her body or hovering nearby, Imperia wanted to make sure that Daniela didn't leave this earth without a friend by her side. Despite Luca's command to protect the balcony from intruders, Bria couldn't deny Imperia the right to comfort her friend.

"Daniela!" Imperia gasped when she saw the woman lying on her side, her silver gown discolored and soaked in blood.

Before she could get next to the body, Luca blocked her way. "I'm sorry, Imperia. You can't get close to the body."

"You mean my friend," she corrected.

"*Perdonami*," Luca replied. "*Sì*, your friend. Please understand that if you get too close or touch Daniela, you could destroy any evidence."

"Evidence? What more evidence do you need!" Imperia yelled, gesturing toward Dante. She looked at him with frenzy. "Why, Dante? Why would you do such a thing? Daniela was your friend!"

Finally, Dante seemed to emerge from his somnambulistic state, and when he spoke, he sounded like his true self. Defiant, dismissive, and definitive.

"I didn't kill anyone."

"I told you, Dante, you have the right to remain silent," Luca said.

"I'm not going to remain silent and let everyone think I'm a cold-blooded murderer," Dante said.

"That's what you are!" Imperia shrieked.

"How long have you known me, Imperia?" Dante asked. "Have I ever done anything violent?"

"A man only has to act once to be violent," Imperia said. "And it looks like you've acted twice."

"What are you talking about?" Dante asked.

"First, Vittorio, now Daniela," Luca said. "Once you get yourself a lawyer, you can explain to the world why you did it."

"I didn't do anything!" Dante shrieked.

Before Luca could stop her, Imperia slapped Dante across the face. He stumbled a few steps to the right, and Luca had to run to steady him, otherwise Dante may have hit the railing and accidentally fallen overboard. A search party was already going to have their work cut out for them trying to find one body in the dark water below. A second body would have taxed all their resources.

Bria was stunned by Imperia's actions. Never before had she seen her raise her hand to anyone, not even in jest. She had also never seen her so distraught before, not even at her husband's funeral or Carlo's. At those sad events, Imperia had been poised and in control of her emotions. She may have broken down behind closed doors when she was alone, but in the company of family and friends, she'd been heartbroken yet dignified. Here, she was acting as if she had lost her only friend. Bria felt like all the air had been knocked out of her when she grasped that that may have been what had just happened.

A safe distance from Daniela's body, Imperia knelt down, the seam of her gown splitting from the tension across her thighs, but Imperia didn't notice. She opened her purse and pulled out a rosary that Bria instantly recognized as the one that was given to everyone who attended Marco's christening. Mother of pearl beads held together by a gold chain and ending in an opal crucifix. It was an extravagant gift, but she and Carlo had felt it matched the importance of the ceremony and was a way to bond the family together forever.

Imperia quietly prayed at Daniela's side as the rest bowed their heads. Well, almost all the rest.

"You have to listen to me. I didn't do this," Dante stated.

"Be quiet," Luca barked.

Bria was torn, because her heart swelled from the knowledge that Imperia was in such despair at the sudden death of her friend, but her heart also hardened because Imperia had not shown this much outward grief when her own son died. She was about to turn and leave the balcony when she saw Nunzi walking down the passageway, followed by her parents.

Fifetta and Franco embraced their daughter and Bria nodded her thanks to Nunzi for bringing them to her. She was certain her parents had refused to take Nunzi's word for it and had demanded to see with their own eyes that their daughter was alive and well. When Fifetta pulled away, she saw Imperia kneeling by herself. Bria watched as her mother did not hesitate, but immediately walked over to Imperia, knelt down beside her, and joined her in prayer.

This is what family does, Bria thought. *It's what my mother has always said and always done. It's time I followed in her footsteps.*

Bria walked over to the other side of Imperia and knelt beside her. Her mother-in-law didn't immediately respond, but when she finished a Hail Mary, she reached out to grab Bria's and Fifetta's hands. The three women stayed like that until they had finished saying their rosary. Bria had no idea if they had made a difference in Daniela's death, but she knew for certain that on this night she and her mother had made a difference in Imperia's life.

The next morning it seemed the entire world had changed.

The headline of *La Vita Positano* read MAYOR/MURDERER and was accompanied by stock photos of Dante and Daniela. Dante was smiling, and Daniela wasn't drenched in blood. Bria, however, was still unsettled.

Despite seeing the words in print, despite having seen Dante standing over Daniela's lifeless body and holding a gun, she wasn't convinced he was the murderer. Not Daniela's or Vittorio's. Unfortunately, no one agreed with her.

Her parents, Lorenza, and Fabrice had spent the night at Bella Bella. Franco had already taken Marco and Bravo out for breakfast and a long walk along the shore, and Fifetta was making a frittata for the rest. Bria had extended an invitation to Imperia to spend the night with them, and while she had appeared moved, she had chosen to sleep on her yacht as she had planned. Bria hadn't thought her mother-in-law should be alone, but she hadn't pushed. As Daniela had pointed out, every woman grieves differently.

"I knew it was Dante. He has beady little eyes," Lorenza said. "They teach us in flight attendant school that if you look someone in the eyes when they board a plane, you can tell what kind of person they are."

"I can see that," Fabrice said. "He's a politician. Being shady is part of the job description."

"I've known Dante for years," Fifetta said, mixing cut-up vegetables into the egg batter. "I never would have thought he could take a life. He's frightened by life, not angered by it."

"What do you mean, Mamma?" Bria asked. "I never thought of Dante as scared."

"Because he hides it behind his bravado, his machismo," Fifetta explained.

"Mamma, Dante is not macho," Lorenza said.

"He tries to be," Fifetta corrected. "He's *falso, fasullo*, not because he's a politician, but because he's scared to reveal his true self to the world. He's like a little boy pretending to be a man."

"I never thought of looking at it that way," Bria said.

"The easy answer isn't always the right answer, *mi amore*," Fifetta said. "Fabrice, are you still staying away from onions?"

"Yes, Mamma Fifi," Fabrice replied. "My doctor doesn't think it's wise."

"You mean Dr. D'Abruzzo doesn't like the smell of onions on your breath," Bria joked. "Isn't that right, Lorenza?"

"That is absolutely *coretta*," Lorenza replied. "The onion has a vile smell."

"No onion for Fabrice, no garlic for Lorenza," Fifetta said. "You two are making me cook like an Irishman."

"It's better for our jobs," Lorenza said. "If we smothered everything we ate in onions and garlic, we wouldn't be able to work with the public."

"That's it!" Bria exclaimed. "That's why I don't think Dante killed Daniela!"

"Because he doesn't smell like garlic and onions?" Lorenza asked.

"No, because she was killed in public," Bria said. "If he killed Vittorio, he did it in private, there were no witnesses, and that murder was most likely spontaneous."

"Why do you say that, Bria?" Fifetta asked as she transferred the frittata from the pan to several plates.

"Because I believe it was a crime of passion, like an explosion. The emotions got too hard to control, and the killer stabbed Vittorio," Bria explained. "Once they saw what they did, they stopped and probably panicked."

"I think you might be right," Fabrice said. "If it was premeditated, the killer would've stabbed Vittorio several times to make sure he was really dead."

"Exactly!" Bria cried. "One stab and then Vittorio was able to escape. That's not the actions of a person who is determined to kill."

Fifetta put a plate of frittata in front of Lorenza, Fabrice, and then Bria. "What does all of this have to do with Dante?"

"If Dante did kill Vittorio, why would he take the complete opposite approach to kill Daniela?" Bria asked the group. "Even if Daniela's murder wasn't premeditated, he was close with Daniela, which means he'd had ample opportunity to be alone with her and kill her in private, without any risk that there would be a witness to his actions."

"It had to have been premeditated," Lorenza said. "Dante brought his gun to the yacht party."

"He told me that as mayor, he needs to have protection,"

Bria shared. "I thought it just meant in his house, but maybe he meant that he carries a gun with him all the time."

"Can a person do that?" Fifetta asked.

"Daniela was carrying a gun, too," Bria said. "Mamma, this is delicious. *Grazie*."

"Even without the onions, *è buona*!" Fabrice added.

"You went a little heavy on the salt, Mamma," Lorenza said.

Fifetta rolled her eyes. "*Sta' zitta! Mangia*," she replied. "Salt is all you've left me to use as seasoning! And, Bria, stop tugging your earlobe like that, you'll wind up lopsided."

"She's thinking," Lorenza said. "She's tugging her earlobe, like she used to do whenever she studied for a test."

Fifetta then noticed Bria had stopped eating as well. "What are you thinking about, *tesorina mia*?"

"Despite how it looks, I don't think Dante killed Daniela, or Vittorio, for that matter," Bria said.

"Have you signed up to work with your boyfriend as his newest detective?" Lorenza asked.

"Luca isn't my boyfriend," Bria protested.

"Yet," Lorenza said.

"*Polpetta*! *Basta*!" Fifetta cried.

"*Polpetta*?" Lorenza replied. "Why am I a meatball and Bria's your little treasure?"

"I think the nicest explanation would be that you're being a little spicy," Fabrice explained.

"Your sister took a big step last night, and it wasn't easy," Fifetta scolded. "You should show some respect and compassion, instead of making a joke out of it."

"It's all right, Mamma," Bria said. "I know Lorenza was only kidding."

"Sometimes, Mamma, I forget that you're half French," Lorenza said. "Those people have no sense of humor."

"*Ah, Madonna mia*!" Fifetta cried. "I don't know what I'm

going to do with you. Fabrice, if you don't marry my daughter, she's going to wind up an old spinster, all by herself, with no one to laugh at her so-called jokes."

"Don't worry, Renza. I'll still come visit you and laugh at all your jokes," Fabrice said. "And pick up after you."

"Pick up after me?" Lorenza cried.

"*Polpetta*," Fabrice said. "You know I love you, but you are a slob."

"And Dante isn't," Bria said.

"Again with the Dante!" Lorenza cried. "Bria, I'm not joking now. You have to stop this. The mystery is solved, and the killer has been revealed."

"No, Dante is fastidious . . . how he keeps his house and his style," Bria said. "Nothing is out of place, and he's always impeccably dressed, like Fabrice."

"*Grazie*," Fabrice said.

"Tell me, Fabrice," Bria started. "Would you ever put your cell phone in your front pants pocket?"

"*Mai*, never," Fabrice replied. "It would ruin the line of my trousers."

"Trousers?" Lorenza asked. "Sometimes I think I'm dating an old woman."

"Did you see the size of Dante's gun?" Bria asked. "It was big, and his tuxedo jacket was tight. There was no way he could hide it in his jacket. The material would bulge."

"His pant legs were very narrow, too," Fabrice added. "There's no way he could strap a gun onto the side of his leg like they do in the movies."

"But in order for him to have shot Daniela, he must've brought the gun with him to the party," Lorenza said.

"Unless he didn't and someone else brought the gun instead," Bria said. "The real person who killed Daniela."

"I hate to admit it, but you may be right," Lorenza said.

310 / MICHAEL FALCO

"The evidence against Dante is still damning, but there is doubt."

"Not according to Luca," Bria said.

"What do you mean?" Lorenza asked.

"He just texted me and said he's holding Dante without bail."

As expected, the entire village was abuzz with the news that their mayor had a side hustle as a murderer, having successfully completed not one, but two projects. Bria was practically the only one who thought Dante was innocent; the court of public opinion had agreed on a swift guilty verdict.

She took Bravo for a walk down to the beach to clear her head, and although they took the long way, avoiding the village center, she still managed to bump into several people, who wanted nothing more than to express how happy they were that the killer had been found and life could get back to normal. Annamaria and Mimi were both surprised to hear that Dante was a two-time murderer, but they agreed with the newspaper's declaration. Paolo and Paloma also agreed that Dante would probably have been voted "least likely to commit homicide" a month ago, but they felt it was obvious that he had done the two nefarious deeds.

"First, he uses a knife, and then he shoots someone," Paolo said. "I didn't think killers used different methods."

"I would've thought Dante would have one of those fancy handguns with a decorative handle, not the huge piece he used," Paloma said. "*Mamma mia,* that was one serious gun."

"Dante has always been full of surprises," Paolo said.

Bria was about to head back home when she saw Enrico carrying a large bouquet of flowers to his car. Bravo ran ahead and greeted the man warmly, jumping on his leg and barking.

"*Bravo! Fermati!*" Bria called out. "Leave Enrico alone."

"He's a good boy, aren't you, Bravo?" Enrico said, petting the dog with his free hand. "He and Marco were both angels last night."

"Thanks again for watching them," Bria said. "At least you missed all the drama."

"I'll say," Enrico said. "I can't believe Dante shot that woman."

"I don't think he did," Bria said.

"The way the paper made it sound, Dante was caught red-handed with the gun," Enrico said.

"He was and I was one of the people who caught him," Bria said. "But no one saw him pull the trigger."

"You think it was someone else?"

"I do, but Luca doesn't agree with me."

"Which doesn't mean you're wrong," Enrico said. "If you're right, Bria, I'm sure you'll prove it."

"Thanks for the vote of confidence," Bria said. "Those are beautiful flowers, by the way. Are you taking them home for yourself?"

"No, I'm delivering them to the owner of the new consignment shop in town. Vintage clothing and décor," Enrico explained. "The business owners' association usually delivers flowers as a way of welcoming the new owner to the village."

"Of course! I remember when you brought them over for me and Carlo. It made us feel right at home," Bria said. "But what do you mean, *usually*?"

"We try to do it for every new owner, but sometimes we don't know who the owner is," Enrico said. "Like the wine and cheese store."

"The one that still hasn't opened?" Bria asked.

"That's the one," Enrico replied. "We still don't know who bought it or when it's going to open."

"I think it's time that we found out," Bria said.

* * *

When they arrived at the police station, Bria and Bravo were greeted with Nunzi's typical poor people skills.

"Dogs aren't allowed in here," Nunzi declared.

"Bravo isn't a dog," Bria stated. "Bravo's Bravo."

Nunzi thought about it for a second and then tilted her head back and forth and shrugged her shoulders. "I'll buy that."

"I need to see Luca," Bria said.

"He isn't here. He's at the courthouse, making sure Dante's lawyer doesn't successfully appeal the judge's no-bail ruling," Nunzi explained. "Is this a professional or personal visit?"

Bria saw the faint trace of a smile on Nunzi's face but chose to ignore the insinuation that she and Luca had something personal to discuss.

"Professional, but maybe you can help me," Bria said. "Who owns the wine and cheese store that still hasn't opened in the village? It's been vacant for so long, and the tourist season is about to start."

"I was thinking the same thing," Nunzi said. "I did a trace on it a few weeks ago."

"Who owns it?" Bria asked.

"It was registered by a Nome Falso."

"It was registered by someone named *Fake Name*?"

"I thought that deserved a bit more attention, so I searched every database I could, and no one exists with that name," Nunzi explained. "I couldn't find the name or a *codice fiscale* number associated with the sale, which you need when you buy property."

"What about trying to do a reverse search to find out who sold the property?" Bria suggested.

"Damn you, Bria Bartolucci!"

"What did I do now?"

"You always come up with really good suggestions, which makes it very hard to dismiss you as just another *ficcanaso*."

"Carlo used to always call me a busybody," Bria recalled. "But when he met Annamaria, he changed his mind and just considered me curious."

Nunzi started typing on her computer, and after a few seconds a report appeared on her screen that made both women shriek. They couldn't believe the names they were reading on the screen and what their connection implied.

As Bria suspected, Vittorio Ingleterra was the Realtor who had sold the building. However, she would have never guessed that he had sold it to Giovanni Monteverdi.

CHAPTER 26

Nunzi had immediately called Luca to fill him in on the discovery of their latest clue, so he was already waiting for them when they arrived at the wine and cheese store.

"You really don't think we should contact Giovanni first?" Bria asked.

"Why?" Nunzi replied. "If we let him know that we found out he's the owner of the store, the only thing he'll do is run."

"That's assuming something illegal is taking place behind these closed doors," Luca added.

"Only one way to find out," Nunzi said.

"What's that?" Bria asked.

"We break in," Luca replied.

Bria watched as Luca expertly picked the lock with a thin piece of metal that looked like something you'd find at an antique store, in the section devoted to vintage burglary tools. Bria couldn't believe how deftly and quickly Luca was able to unlock the padlock and then open the door. He was even better at it than Rosalie. If the chief of police could perfect such a criminal act, a criminal would have no problem mastering the technique. Bria made a mental note to put a large piece of furniture in front of her locked door whenever she and Marco were home alone.

Luca pushed open the door and identified himself as the chief of police, in case anyone was lurking inside. They didn't have to worry about that, because the room was completely empty: no people, no furniture, no fixtures, nothing. They weren't expecting to find a wine and cheese shop, but they were expecting to find the bare bones of some kind of store.

"Why would Giovanni buy a store and then keep it empty?" Bria asked.

"Didn't you tell me that Giovanni told you he was rebuilding his life and he desperately needed a job?" Luca replied.

"He didn't use those exact words, but yes," Bria said. "He shared that he had made mistakes in his past and he hadn't always been smart with his money."

"Then where'd he find the money to buy a store?" Nunzi asked.

"Guess we'll have to go straight to the source and ask him," Luca said.

They walked toward the door, and as they were about to leave, Bria realized Bravo wasn't with them. She turned around and saw him sniffing at something near the back wall.

"Bravo, *mi cucciolo*," Bria called out. "Come. We have to go."

Uncharacteristically, Bravo ignored Bria and started scratching the wall and brushing his paws against the floor. He was acting the same way he had right before Vittorio's body was discovered. It was as if he smelled or heard something inside the wall and was trying to break through the plaster to reach it. Maybe a wild animal had got caught in the wall and had died and Bravo could smell the decay? Or maybe the wall was hiding even more clues?

Luca tapped on the wall several times in several different places and came to a very quick conclusion.

"It's a fake wall," he announced. "Nunzi, help me break it down. Bria, take Bravo and stand over there."

Bria grabbed Bravo by the collar and took him to the other

side of the store. She knelt down and held Bravo tightly against her body. She didn't know exactly what Luca and Nunzi were going to do to break down the wall, but she knew it was going to be loud, and Bravo, like most dogs, was not a fan of loud noises. If Bria didn't hold him tightly, he'd try to break free. Bravo knew his way around the village better than most of the longtime residents, but Bria didn't want him running scared through the streets.

Luca pulled out a small blunt instrument that had been clinging to his belt. It looked like an ordinary black tube, but Luca twisted it to reveal there was a second layer, which made the tube double in size. He twisted it again until it clicked, indicating that both pieces were locked into place, making it a sturdy weapon.

Nunzi had a regular billy club hanging from her belt. She unlocked the club and was ready to use it when Luca had finished. They stood next to each other and raised their weapons. Luca tapped on the wall again, and it made a hollow sound. He nodded, and they both rammed their clubs into the wall, easily breaking through the plaster and creating a small hole.

The noise they created wasn't thunderous, but it was enough to make Bravo bark and squirm in Bria's arms. She whispered to him that everything was all right, but he wasn't convinced. And who could blame him? Luca and Nunzi didn't look like they were having fun or playing nice with the wall. They kept bashing it until the opening was large enough for them to walk through.

"You were right all along, Bria," Luca said.

"I was right about what?" she asked.

"Come and see for yourself," Luca replied.

Bria let go of Bravo, who had stopped barking, and joined the others at the opening in the wall. She saw a small room that contained what looked like xerox machines and one large rectangular table in the middle of the room on top of which were stacks of money. They would have to have the money tested, but they were certain they would find that the lire and euros piled high on the table would turn out to be fakes.

"These are counterfeit machines," Luca said. "This one is a relic and was designed to produce lire. It's the one that might have been used decades ago."

"The one my father ran," Nunzi added.

"I don't know how Dante is involved, but this must be where Vittorio and Delfino were printing out the money," Luca said. "Probably testing out the lira machine first to get a handle on how to operate the machinery before moving on to the more expensive current models."

"Can we prove Delfino was really involved, though?" Nunzi asked.

Before Luca could respond, Bria did. "Absolutely! Look at these flowers."

She pointed at a vase of petunias on the table surrounded by a few piles of euros, and the red flowers, though a little wilted, added quite a bit of color to the otherwise drab and undecorated space. How it proved Delfino was part of this operation was a mystery to both police officers.

"When Delfino came to me posing as a reporter, he was wearing a petunia in his lapel," Bria said. "And Enrico told me a man would often stop by the flower shop and buy petunias by the bunch and he saw him walk in here."

"That's a very strange clue and hardly conclusive," Luca said. "But it makes a believer out of me."

"Me, too, actually," Nunzi said. "It would be better if we could talk to Delfino and get him to confess."

"Has there been any sign of him since he jumped off the yacht?" Bria asked.

"None," Luca replied. "The coast guard couldn't find him, which means either he swam to another boat and is hiding or he drowned."

"Based on what Daniela told me the night of the party, Delfino has the motive to make counterfeit money," Bria said. "He doesn't have access to his own inheritance and has to ask Daniela's permission to make a withdrawal."

"No man would want to have to do that," Nunzi said.

"Especially someone who looks at his sister as the enemy," Bria said.

"Daniela said that?" Luca asked. "I know that there's bad blood in the family, as there is in most very wealthy households, but I didn't think he considered her an enemy."

"Their father left everything to his daughter instead of his eldest son," Bria explained. "Any ambitious brother is going to be infuriated by that."

"If the brother is also egotistical and not the smartest kid on the block," Nunzi added, "that brother may venture into unscrupulous territory."

"But what's Vittorio's motive to become a counterfeiter?" Bria asked. "Is it also simply greed?"

"Greed is never simple, Bria," Luca said. "It pushes people to do things they never thought they were capable of doing. Like getting involved in a fake money scam."

"And murder," Bria added.

"Yes," Luca said. "And murder."

"Where does this all leave Dante?" Bria asked. "And how do you think Giovanni's involved?"

"The answer to both those questions is that we don't know yet," Luca said. "Dante could easily be involved, especially if that old machine turns out to be one his father used. If Vittorio wanted a bigger cut, he and Dante could've gotten into a fight that resulted in Dante plunging a knife into Vittorio's stomach."

"Maybe Dante didn't even think he killed Vittorio," Bria said. "Maybe they got into a fight, Dante stabbed him out of fury, immediately regretted it, but when Vittorio left to get help, maybe Dante thought he was okay and was just running from the argument."

"If Daniela was keeping such a tight grip on Delfino, she

must have known he was involved," Nunzi said. "Maybe she was trying to talk Dante into cutting ties with Delfino the night of the party and Dante killed her to stop her from interfering."

Luca shook his head and winced. "I don't see that happening."

"Me either," Bria said. "Daniela wasn't afraid of Delfino. If she had found out the truth, she would have told Delfino to stop it or she would have called the cops on him."

"The only thing that makes sense is that their business deal went sour, and Dante set out to kill both his partners," Luca said. "First, Vittorio and then Delfino. But Daniela got in the way and took the bullet that was meant for her brother."

"Do you think Dante deliberately killed them in different ways to make it look like there were two killers?" Bria asked.

"Possibly," Luca replied. "Serial killers usually have one method of killing, but people who kill more than once, the ones who get caught up in a cycle of killing to cover their tracks, don't necessarily act the same way a dedicated assassin would."

"I guess that could explain Dante's involvement," Bria said. "But I still think something's missing."

"You believe Dante is innocent of both murders, don't you?" Luca asked.

"I do," Bria replied.

"What about Giovanni?" Nunzi asked. "Do you still think he's just misunderstood?"

Bria let out a breath. "I think he has some explaining to do."

"Is he at Bella Bella now?" Luca asked.

"Yes," Bria said. "He's paying some invoices."

"Is he watching Marco?" Luca asked.

"No. Marco is on a field trip with Sister Benedicta to see a production of *Carmen* in Naples," Bria explained. "They won't be home for another hour."

"*Carmen* isn't what I'd call second grade material," Nunzi commented.

"It's a kid-friendly version," Bria said. "They're not going to

understand a bit of it and will come away thinking that everyone sang really loud, and have a sudden desire to become a
bullfighter."

"Let's go back to your place and question Giovanni while
he's alone," Luca said. "I can't wait to hear how he talks his
way out of this one."

When they arrived at Bella Bella, part of Bria was hoping
that Giovanni would have already left. All this time she had
been adamant that Giovanni had nothing to do with the murder, that he couldn't possibly have been involved with Vittorio.
But he was; his name was on the deed. Which meant that Bria
had been wrong about her handyman assistant all along. He
was nothing but a criminal and maybe, worse, a murderer.

But when she saw him at the dining room table, typing on
his laptop, a glass half-filled with chocolate milk and a plate of
cut-up carrots and celery at his side, she couldn't believe that
someone who ate so healthy could be mixed up in anything illegal. Bria knew that was a stupid thought, but she couldn't
help herself. Maybe she just hated to be wrong. Maybe she
thought a man so physically attractive wouldn't feel the need to
resort to criminal behavior. Maybe she would be really disappointed if she had to open up Bella Bella while Giovanni was
sitting in a jail cell, serving a prison sentence.

Giovanni looked up from the table, and when he saw Luca
and Nunzi standing behind Bria, a flicker of recognition flashed
across his face. Could he know why they had come? Did he
suspect he'd at some point be caught?

"We'd like to ask you a few questions, Giovanni," Luca said.

"Here or down at the station?" Vanni asked.

"That would be up to you," Luca said. "If you're in the
mood to cooperate, we can have our talk here. If you're feeling
ornery, we can escort you to the police station."

Luca stared at Giovanni, who stared right back at him.

Standing in the middle of the two men was Bria. Her position was almost symbolic, as she felt that she was being pulled in both directions, with each man trying to get her to be on his side. Should she be Team Luca or Team Giovanni?

Where is this coming from? Bria asked herself. *Why am I making this all about me?*

"*Basta!*" Bria cried. "Can we just get on with it?"

"Yes," Vanni said, closing his laptop. "What do you want to know?"

Luca walked toward the dining room table, and Nunzi and Bria followed. Bravo ran around the other side, sat at Giovanni's side, and laid his head on his thigh. Vanni started petting Bravo's head without looking down. He maintained eye contact with Luca, who sat down across from him at the table. Nunzi took a seat next to Luca, and Bria made a split-second decision to sit next to Giovanni. She told herself it wasn't because she was choosing sides; she just didn't want it to be three against one.

"Did you know Vittorio Ingleterra before he died?" Luca asked.

"No," Vanni replied instantly.

"Did you know that he was a real estate broker?" Luca asked.

"Not until I did an online search about Vittorio and saw that he worked at Dolce Vita."

"Then how do you explain the fact that Vittorio sold the wine and cheese store in the village to you?" Luca asked. "Unless you're going to tell us that there's another Giovanni Monteverdi in Positano?"

"No, I'm the only one."

"Which makes you the owner of the wine and cheese store that's been sitting there empty for months?" Luca stated.

"Yes."

"Vanni!" Bria exclaimed. "How?"

"Bria, please," Luca said.

"I can explain," Vanni said.

"I hope you can," Luca replied.

"I owed someone a favor, and he collected," Vanni said.

"You need to be much more specific than that," Luca said. "Who did you owe and why?"

Giovanni stopped petting Bravo and brought both his hands up to his face. His palms pressed into his eyes, and Bria thought Vanni might be trying to prevent himself from crying. But no, he just needed a moment to disappear. When he folded his hands together and placed them on the table, Bria knew he had returned.

"My past is no secret to anyone in the village," Giovanni started. "I've done things that I'm not proud of. I've paid my dues, I served my time, and I swear on my parents that I've done nothing to jeopardize my freedom. I'm a changed man, but that doesn't erase the fact that I used to be a man I am not proud of."

Giovanni stopped speaking and finished the rest of the chocolate milk. No one interrupted him; they all remained quiet and patiently waited until Giovanni resumed his speech.

"When I was barely twenty, I stole a woman's purse," Giovanni said. "There wasn't much in it, but the purse belonged to Carmelina San Turino."

"Who's that?" Luca asked.

"Delfino di Santi's godmother."

Bria, along with the others, gasped. It wasn't the most professional reaction, especially from two seasoned police officers, but like Bria, they were shocked to learn that Giovanni wasn't connected to Vittorio, like they had suspected, but to Delfino.

"Delfino found out you were the thief and promised that no one would press charges against you if you returned his godmother's purse with all its contents," Luca surmised.

"*Corretto*," Vanni said.

"Then he made you promise that if he ever needed a favor, he would ask you and you couldn't refuse," Luca added.

"*Corretto di nuovo*," Vanni repeated.

"Is Delfino the real owner of the store?" Luca asked.

"I think so, but he never said that to me," Vanni replied. "He told me a transaction was going to be made, but the buyer couldn't have his name on the deed, so I needed to sign some papers."

"Did Delfino wire money into your bank account to cover the sale?" Nunzi asked.

"Yes," Vanni said. "Once I signed the papers, the money was withdrawn and, I assumed, went to the seller."

"You never knew why the store was bought?" Bria asked. "Haven't you wondered why it hasn't opened and has just been sitting there empty for months?"

"I have no idea why they wanted the store or what they were using it for," Vanni said. "I assumed the deal fell through and the buyer ran out of money to renovate or get a liquor license. These things happen all the time."

"Why should we believe that you didn't know they were running a counterfeit money ring out of that store?" Luca asked.

"Because I'm telling you the truth, like I did before," Giovanni stated. "I had nothing to do with Vittorio's murder. I didn't know he was the broker who did the deal on the store, and I didn't know Delfino was involved in a counterfeit ring." Giovanni paused to take a breath, but he had more to say. "Does this mean Dante's involved, too?"

"We don't know," Bria said.

Luca shot Bria a quick glance, and she instantly realized she shouldn't have spoken. She might feel like she was part of the police force, but she wasn't an official member. She needed to remember her place.

The hell with that! Giovanni was her friend and her employee, and she'd tell him whatever she wanted. That was what she thought. Out loud she said she was sorry.

"Do you have an alibi for the night Daniela di Santi was killed?" Luca said.

"Yes," Vanni said. "I was on a date."

"A date?"

The only reason Bria knew she said that out loud was that both Luca and Nunzi turned to face her. They looked like two kids in school who had just heard the most unexpected gossip. So did Bria.

"Sorry. I'm just surprised," Bria said. "You never mentioned you had a girlfriend."

"She isn't my girlfriend," Vanni said. "It was just a date."

"Does your date have a name and a telephone number, so we can contact her?" Nunzi asked.

"Toni Ann Casamento," Vanni said.

Bria didn't recognize the name, which meant the woman probably didn't live in Positano, but in one of the neighboring villages. A surge of heat started to rise from Bria's neck to her cheeks. She knew it was a symptom of a much larger problem. Bria was jealous of whoever this Toni Ann Casamento was.

"I can text you her phone number," Vanni said.

"Thank you," Luca said. "And thank you for telling us the truth."

Giovanni looked shocked by this statement. "That means you believe me?"

"For now," Luca said. "We'll speak with Toni Ann to see if she corroborates your story, but regardless of the outcome, don't leave town."

"How can I?" Vanni said. "Bella Bella is set to open at the end of the week."

The end of the week! Bria thought. *How am I ever going to open up this bed-and-breakfast if I'm right about Dante being innocent? If I am right, that means there is a murderer still out there.*

The hot flash Bria had just experienced evaporated and turned into a cold sweat. She had experienced a panic attack only once before in her life, but she could feel one coming on. She couldn't sit there for another second longer and listen to them interrogate Giovanni or talk about Vittorio, Delfino, or Dante. She needed to get out of there so she could breathe.

"Scusatemi."

That was all Bria could mutter before she ran out of the house. She didn't stop running, not as she went through the village, then down the narrow, curving stairway to the beach, not until she got to water on the far end of Fornillo Beach and could feel the cool water rush over her feet. She inhaled and exhaled, taking in the fresh, clean air and throwing out the anxiety, stress, and fear that were threatening to consume her.

Unfortunately, there was another threat looming in the distance. Bent over, her hands on her knees, Bria looked up and took a gulp of air, and when she saw the body float toward her, she almost choked. Another wave and the body was at her feet.

It was Delfino.

He rolled onto his back, and Bria couldn't tell if he was alive or dead. She knelt down to him and put her ear to his mouth to see if she could hear him breathing or feel air coming out of him. She didn't hear breathing, but she heard his final words.

"She did it."

CHAPTER 27

Sometimes ugliness could be found in the most profound beauty. Evil intentions lurking behind the most exquisite face. Poison within the sleek, vibrantly colored body of a snake, just waiting to be discharged. Or a dead man's body on the pristine sand of one of the most beautiful beaches in the world.

Bria had been trying to clear her mind and get away from the whirlwind of drama she had unwittingly plunged herself into and now she was in even deeper. She felt like she was standing in quicksand, and each time she thought she had grabbed on to a branch to pull herself to safety, what she was really doing was sinking deeper and deeper into the heart of a murderer. She was getting closer to figuring out who the killer was, and her instincts were right. It wasn't Dante; it was a woman.

"Are you sure that's what Delfino said?" Luca asked.

This time when she'd found a dead body, she'd done as she had been told to do. Well, almost. She had still called Rosalie first, but she'd called the police very quickly after she and her best friend hung up. Her conversation with Rosalie had been quick and to the point.

"Rosalie!" Bria had cried. "I found another dead body."

"Of course you did," had been Rosalie's immediate response. Then snark had given way to sympathy. "Was it someone we know this time?"

"Delfino di Santi."

"First, the sister, and now the brother. Those are some odds."

"The odds get even better," Bria said. "He told me something right before he died."

"Did he confess to killing Vittorio and Daniela?"

"No. He said, 'She did it.' "

"She who?"

"I don't know. He just said, 'She,' but that means Dante's innocent."

"Only if Delfino was telling the truth."

"Why would a dying man lie?" Bria asked.

"Haven't you figured out that not everyone's motives are pure, even if they're about to take their final breath?" Rosalie replied.

"*Ah, Madonna mia*! Must you always be so cynical?"

"Just looking at the situation from both sides. Where are you?"

"On Fornillo Beach, directly east of your boat."

"I'm on my way."

"Okay. I'm calling your brother now, but if he asks, tell him I called you second."

"*Certo*. And I'll walk slow, so maybe he'll show up before me."

When she ended the call with Rosalie, Bria called Luca and told him a little truth and a little lie. She informed him that she had discovered Delfino's body washed up on the shore and that he was the first one she contacted. There was always the chance that he or, more likely, Nunzi would check her cell phone records, but she thought it was a slim possibility and a calculated risk that would result in her favor.

When Luca showed up with Nunzi in tow, they were both more concerned with dealing with the surprise return of Delfino than with the question of whether Bria had followed protocol. Nunzi knelt beside Delfino to examine the body as Bria explained to Luca how she had stumbled upon yet an-

328 / MICHAEL FALCO

other dead body. Well, an almost dead body since Delfino had still had enough life in him to whisper a clue in Bria's ear.

"His last words were, 'She did it'?" Luca asked.

"Yes, that's what he said before he died," Bria replied.

"*Capo!*" Nunzi cried. "That's wrong."

"Nunzi, I know what I heard," Bria said. "He told me, 'She did it.'"

"That might be what he said, but it isn't what he said before he died," Nunzi corrected. "Delfino's still alive."

"What!" Bria cried.

"He has a faint pulse and very shallow breath," Nunzi said, holding Delfino's wrist. "He may have lapsed into a coma."

Luca immediately instructed a medical transport team to arrive at the beach to transport Delfino to Ospedale Evangelico Villa Betania, and while they waited, he and Nunzi pumped Bria for more information. They wanted to know exactly what had happened and why she had run from Bella Bella. She explained that the interrogation of Giovanni had become too much for her and she'd needed some fresh air. The revelation that Giovanni was connected to Vittorio before he was found dead, the possibility that Giovanni was lying about not knowing about that connection, and the fact that he was the owner of the wine and cheese store that was merely a cover for the counterfeit money ring, had made her head spin and she had felt faint. Learning that Giovanni was dating some woman named Toni Ann hadn't helped, either. Bria didn't want to be known as the woman who fainted when she became overwhelmed, so she'd run.

"I wanted to chase after you," Luca said, "but I wasn't finished questioning Giovanni."

"What about Giovanni?" Rosalie asked as she ran toward the group.

"You called Rosalie first, didn't you?" Nunzi asked.

"No!" Bria and Rosalie protested at the same time.

"At least you remembered to call the police quicker this time," Luca said.

"There's a learning curve when attending the police academy," Rosalie said.

"What did you do with him?" Bria asked. "Did you put Giovanni back in jail?"

"Nunzi briefly spoke with Toni Ann, who vouched for Giovanni and supported his alibi," Luca said. "I did advise him not to leave town because I'm going to need to talk to him further about the lease that he signed."

"Maybe Delfino will be able to fill in the blanks," Bria said.

"If he survives."

Luca's comment reminded Bria once again just how serious this situation was. It wasn't just a game; it wasn't an adventure to clear her reputation and lift any air of suspicion from her new business venture. It was real life, and people were getting killed. Vittorio, Daniela, and now possibly Delfino, all in a few short weeks. That was unheard of in the quiet village, which was known for fun and frolic and as an escape from the harsh reality of everyday life. It wasn't where people met their demise.

Before Bria could say another word, the beach filled with paramedics, who went into action, lifting Delfino's body onto a stretcher and hooking him up to an oxygen machine. Luca advised that Nunzi would go with them on the boat to Naples and would stay at Delfino's side until a guard could be posted outside his hospital room. The medics understood and assured Luca that his orders would be followed.

When the medics and Nunzi had left the beach, Luca spoke to the small crowd that had gathered, a combination of local fishermen, some residents, and tourists. He assured them that the situation was under control and that the man who had been discovered, whose name would be kept silent until the next of kin could be notified, was being taken to the hospital.

The group bombarded him with questions that Luca spent the next several minutes answering, until he finally put his hands up to quiet the crowd and told them that he had no more information to share and needed to get to the hospital.

When Bria knew they were out of earshot and their conversation wouldn't be overheard by anyone, she started pummeling Luca with her own barrage of questions.

"Daniela must be the killer," Bria said. "She's the *she* Delfino was talking about."

"We don't know that for sure," Luca replied.

"Who else could he be talking about except his sister?" Bria replied. "Plus, it fits the profile."

"What profile?" Luca asked.

"The profile of Vittorio's killer," Bria said. "As Vittorio's girlfriend, Daniela may very likely have committed a crime of passion."

"I see that as an extremely strong possibility," Rosalie agreed.

Luca shot her a glance that only a big brother could throw to his younger sister.

"Unfortunately, we haven't been able to prove Daniela was in the village at the time of the murder," Luca said. "Maybe when Delfino wakes up, he can help us with that. Even if she did kill Vittorio, we know that she didn't kill herself. That means Dante is guilty of murdering only one person, not two."

"There's another possibility that I think you're missing," Bria said.

"What's that?" Luca asked.

"That Dante didn't kill anyone."

"If Dante is completely innocent, then who killed Daniela?"

"Delfino."

The cries of several seagulls filled the silence Bria's comment created. Luca appeared to be mulling her observation over in his head, but Bria couldn't wait for him to come to a conclusion. She was too anxious, too excited, not to share what she was thinking.

"Daniela told me that she would do anything to protect her family's legacy," Bria said. "Making sure the counterfeit money ring Delfino was spearheading never saw the light of day would fall under that goal. If Delfino knew Daniela was trying to shut his operation down, maybe he decided to shut her down first."

"Then how does it wind up that Daniela is dead at the yacht party and Delfino jumps overboard?" Luca asked.

"Because Dante unexpectedly comes onto the scene," Bria began. "Dante sees Delfino shoot Daniela, and maybe Dante attacks Delfino and in their struggle, Delfino drops the gun."

"Dante picks it up, and Delfino decides to jump off the yacht to avoid getting shot," Luca finished.

"Do you think Dante would really have shot his business partner?" Bria asked.

"Why not?" Luca said. "If history has repeated itself, these business partners are probably not so different from the partners the first time there was a counterfeit ring. More like nemeses than friends."

"I still find it hard to believe that Dante is a killer," Bria mused. "Though I have no problem seeing Delfino pull the trigger at his sister."

"There's only one problem about that theory," Luca said.

"What's that?" Bria asked.

"There was only one set of fingerprints on the gun, according to forensics," he shared, "and they belonged to Dante."

"Delfino could've worn gloves," Bria said.

"He wouldn't have had enough time to shoot Daniela, take off the gloves, shove them into his pocket or hide them somewhere before we arrived to find him straddling the railing," Luca explained.

"Don't forget that he would have also had to leave the gun by Daniela's side, try to run, and get caught by Dante," Bria added.

"I know you want Dante to be innocent, but that scenario seems implausible," Rosalie said.

Bria shook her head and searched for a reason to dispute what her friend had just said, but she couldn't find one. "*Uffa!* Try as I might to come up with another explanation, it really does look like Dante shot Daniela."

"If that's what happened, we'll prove it," Luca said. "For what it's worth, I'm confident we've gotten both killers off the streets of our village."

"Thank you, Luca," Bria said. "I can't believe this nightmare is almost over."

"It is," he said. "And we couldn't have done it without you. You should be proud of yourself."

"I hope you're proud of yourself."

An hour later, basically the same sentiment took on an entirely new meaning.

Imperia stood in the doorway at Bella Bella and looked at Bria with an expression that could only be described as filled with hatred. Bria knew the reason. Imperia blamed her for Daniela's death. It wasn't based on fact, but it was how she felt. If Bria hadn't persisted in finding out what was going on between Daniela and Vittorio, Daniela wouldn't have gotten shot at the yacht party. It helped Imperia channel her anger at her friend's death to another individual.

"If you had let the police do their job, instead of confronting Daniela at my party," Imperia said, "none of this would have happened."

"I know that you're angry with me," Bria said.

"I am furious!" Imperia shouted. "It's because of you that my best friend is dead and Dante is being held in jail."

"Imperia, that's ludicrous! I never wanted anyone to die. I just wanted to find out who killed Vittorio and move on from all of this. If the police uncover that Daniela did kill Vittorio and Dante was the one who pulled the trigger, none of that is my fault."

"Daniela loved Vittorio! She wouldn't have killed him. She was heartbroken that he was seeing someone else."

"Vittorio was cheating on Daniela?"

"No, but there was another woman who was in love with Vittorio," Imperia explained. "Vittorio swore that Daniela was the only woman for him."

"Is that what she told you when the two of you had brunch in Sarno?"

"How do you know that?"

Funny how something that had previously felt so difficult to confess now seemed trite in comparison to the latest events.

"Rosalie and I followed you," Bria said. "Rosalie was the woman who spilled her drink on you so I could get out without you seeing me. Daniela figured it out. I thought she would've told you."

"No, she didn't," Imperia replied. "All she did was tell me how much she missed Vittorio."

"Did she also confess that she murdered him?"

"No. We weren't there to talk about him. I was meeting her to discuss the di Santi family's donation to the Museo Archeologico Nazionale della Valle del Sarno as part of the FAI," Imperia explained. "How could you possibly think that I would be involved with something like this?"

"I never really did, Imperia, not in my heart," Bria said. "That's why I didn't go to the police when I had my suspicions."

"What suspicions? That I was a murderer?"

"No! That you might have partnered with some unscrupulous people and gotten mixed up with something illegal."

"You amaze me, Bria. I know that you don't like me very much, but I thought you understood me," Imperia stated. "I am a very wealthy woman, but I have no husband. I've lost my only son, and all I have left in this world is Marco. Why would I risk everything to join forces with people who could land me in jail and take the chance of never seeing my grandson again?"

Bria felt smaller than she had ever felt in her life. Those thoughts had been circling in her brain. They had popped up, but each time they had, she got sidetracked by a new clue or a new piece of evidence or a new trail to follow. She had never spent the time to really think if Imperia would do something to jeopardize her relationship with Marco. Bria was ashamed of herself, and she realized she had lost sight of what was important.

"Forgive me, Imperia," Bria said, choking back tears. "*Per favore, perdonami*. I was so caught up in trying to find Vittorio's murderer to salvage my business that I forgot how much you love Marco and how important family is to you."

"*La famiglia* is the *only* thing that's important," Imperia replied. "Without it, the richest woman in the world has absolutely no reason to live."

"You're right," Bria said. "I have absolutely no excuse for the way I treated you, except that I've been trying to fulfill Carlo's wishes and make Bella Bella a success."

"At least we have one thing in common," Imperia replied.

"What's that?"

"We both want to see Carlo's dreams come true."

After Imperia left, Sister Benedicta brought Marco home. Once again, Marco's teacher had come to the rescue when Bria failed to fulfill her parental duties and pick up her son after school.

"*Mi dispiace molto!*" Bria exclaimed. She bent down to hug Marco and kiss his cheeks. "Mamma was very busy today, but I will never forget to pick you up again, I promise."

"Remember what Papa said, Mamma," Marco replied.

"What's that?"

"Don't make a promise you can't keep," Marco said. "I know you're busy, and even if Sister B couldn't take me home, I know the way."

Bria sat on her haunches and stared at her son. She forced herself not to cry.

"My little boy is growing into a little man," she said.

"Mamma, I'm only eight years old," Marco replied. "I won't be a man until I'm at least ten."

Bria threw her head back and laughed, deep and hearty. It felt so good to feel happy. It had been a long day.

"Marco, go and wash up, and I'll have supper ready soon," Bria said.

"*Si*, Mamma," he said. "*Grazie*, Sister B, for walking me home."

"It was my pleasure," the nun replied. "I'll see you tomorrow morning and remember we're having a spelling test in the afternoon."

"I'll study right after supper," Marco said. "And that's a promise I intend to keep. Come on, Bravo."

Marco ran into the bathroom, followed by Bravo. Bria got up and thanked the nun.

"*Grazie*. My head has been all over the place today," Bria said.

"I can imagine," Benedicta replied. "I left the party early, but I read about what happened. I can't believe someone was killed . . . that poor woman. The mayor is the murderer, and that man who fell overboard . . . ! He must be an excellent swimmer not to have drowned. It's all unreal."

"It's all too real," Bria replied. "And here's where it all started. Right upstairs."

"I'm sorry you've been going through all of this, but at least it seems like it's over," the nun replied. "The paper didn't have many details and said hardly anything about how the woman was killed."

"She was shot."

"Yes, but how did anyone smuggle a gun onto the yacht? I know they make them small these days, but . . . Oh dear, if Mother Superior could hear me talking about guns."

Bria did think it was odd that a nun was asking questions about guns, but the topic of murder had gripped the village for the past few weeks, so it was only natural. And yet there was something odd about her questions.

"I won't say a word."

"I do have something that will change the subject, though."

Sister Benedicta put a hand in the pocket of her skirt, and for a split second Bria thought she was going to whip out a gun. Her imagination really was getting the best of her. Luckily, what the nun gave her had nothing to do with violence and everything to do with chocolate.

"Gianna has decided to close up her shop," the nun said.

"Sogni di Cioccolato?" Bria replied. "What's Marco going to do? He practically dreams of her chocolate."

"I know," the nun replied. "Which is why I bought some chocolates that I know he likes. The ones with the raspberry jelly and the rainbow cookies."

"Grazie, grazie! He'll love them," Bria said. "But I can't believe Gianna is leaving. Did she say why?"

"I think it has to do with her mamma. She's not doing well and she's by herself in Foligno," the nun explained.

"And Gianna is going to take care of her," Bria said. "It's what we all would do."

"At least that's what I heard," Benedicta replied. "It was too loud and busy in the store to have a conversation, but I definitely know she's selling the place, because there was one of those Realtor locks on the little gate in the front, the ones Realtors use to get into your store after hours."

"That's a dead giveaway that she's selling," Bria said.

"Maybe someone will buy the whole store and keep it a candy shop and Marco won't be disappointed," the nun said.

"Let's hope so," Bria replied.

After Sister Benedicta left, Bria sat for a while at the dining room table, thinking about their conversation. Slowly, Bria realized it hadn't been an odd conversation but a successful one. She had started this journey not knowing what she was doing; she had never solved a crime before or a murder, let alone two and maybe a third. But when she placed a call to Luca, she was brimming with confidence.

"Dante didn't kill Vittorio or Daniela, and I can prove it," she said. "Come over at noon tomorrow and I'll explain everything."

CHAPTER 28

Bria felt exhilarated. Her entire body was pulsing with life, which did strike her as ironic, since the reason for her euphoria had everything to do with death. Two deaths, to be specific, and possibly another, although according to Luca's morning text, Delfino was still in a coma and couldn't yet be added to the body count. Still, there was a small part of Bria that felt bad for feeling so good.

She hadn't realized at the time that finding Vittorio dead in her upstairs bedroom would be a turning point in her life. Up until then, she had been going through the motions, and everything she'd done in her daily life was for two people—Carlo and Marco. She had wanted to fulfill Carlo's dream of opening up Bella Bella, and she had wanted to provide a loving and stable home for Marco. She hadn't been living a lie, but she had forgotten that she could also live life for herself.

Not everything she did had to be silently approved of by Carlo. He would always be a presence in her life, but he couldn't be the driving force and the reason she lived. And even though she would spend the rest of her life putting Marco's needs before her own, she knew she couldn't lose herself like she had before. She could be Carlo's widow, Marco's mother, and Bria Bartolucci all at the same time. First, she needed to expose a double murderer.

Rosalie hadn't even asked why Bria wanted her there, but she arrived at precisely 12:30 p.m. As Bria had instructed, she came empty handed, but she was overflowing with questions.

"What's going on, Bri?" Rosalie asked the second Bria closed the door behind her. "This has to do with the murders, right? I thought all that was behind us now that Dante is behind bars."

"This is about the murders, but it has nothing to do with Dante," Bria replied.

At the sound of Rosalie's voice, Bravo came running out from wherever he had been napping and didn't stop until he was rubbing his forehead into Rosalie's knee.

"*Ciao*, Bravo," Rosalie said, greeting the dog enthusiastically. "I love you, but right now I have to make your mamma tell me the truth."

Bravo barked, and Rosalie took this as his full understanding that Rosalie needed to focus her attention elsewhere. Still, she couldn't help petting Bravo all the while she interrogated Bria.

"Are you going to prove his innocence?" Rosalie asked.

"No questions," Bria said. "I need you to act like this is just another meal."

"Haven't I gone along with everything so far and acted as if playing amateur detective came naturally to me?" Rosalie asked.

"It does come naturally to you," Bria said. "Me, too, for that matter, but this is the finale, so it's more important than ever that you don't give anyone reason to suspect they were invited here for any other reason than to have a fun meal before Bella Bella officially opens."

"*Lodate Dio e tutti gli angeli e i santi!*" Rosalie cried. "You're going to reveal who the killer is, aren't you?"

"*Stai zitta!*" Bria cried. "Keep quiet, before someone hears you."

"*Scusami*," Rosalie said. "But this is so exciting! Tell me who did it, *per favore*."

"No," Bria said. "You'll find out when the others do."

"Give me a hint," Rosalie begged. "I think I deserve it."

"Rosalie, *basta*!" Bria exclaimed. "I need you to cooperate and play your part."

"You told my brother, didn't you?" Rosalie said. "Just because he's the chief of police doesn't mean he should outrank the best friend."

"Rosalie! *Lo giuro su Dio*! If you don't stop right now!" Bria exclaimed.

"My brother is going to be *molto geloso* if you solve this case before he does," Rosalie said. "And Nunzi! *Dio mio*! Her head will explode. That one takes her job *very* seriously."

"That's because I took an oath."

Rosalie whipped around and was surprised to see Nunzi standing in the doorway, not looking like a cop but once again like an ordinary citizen. Not dressed in a gown, but in jeans and a simple buttoned-down blouse.

"What are you doing here?" Rosalie asked. "And out of uniform? Again?"

"It's my day off, and Bria invited me to lunch," Nunzi replied, stepping inside. "Here's the salad you requested."

"Thank you, Nunzi," Bria said, taking the tray from the cop and placing it with the rest of the food already on the dining room table.

Bria hadn't had time to prepare an entire lunch with what she had in her refrigerator, and she didn't want to waste food since she knew the spread was primarily for show. Rosalie would definitely fill up her plate, but most of the others would pick at the offering and be more interested in the conversation. At least that was her hope. In case she was wrong, she had asked certain guests to bring extra food. As Fifetta had drummed into her head, it was always better to have more food than to have your guests tell others that you had made them starve.

"Why don't you two have a seat," Bria suggested. "The rest should be here shortly."

On cue, Lorenza walked through the door, chatting with Fifetta, who was carrying a tray of lasagna.

"Sorry I'm late," Lorenza said. "Mamma couldn't decide what to wear."

"*Aspetta*! I was dressed and ready and had to wait twenty minutes for Lorenza to pick me up," Fifetta said. "Let me introduce you to my daughter, *il lumaca*."

"I am not a slowpoke, Mamma," Lorenza declared. "Bria knows I prefer to show up fashionably late. Where's my Bravo?"

At the sound of his name, Bravo left Rosalie's side to greet Lorenza, who immediately started to profess her love for the dog and bury her face in his fur.

"It's disrespectful to arrive late," Fifetta said. "And to come without a gift."

"Thank you, Mamma," Bria said. "Your lasagna is so much better than mine. I'll put this in the oven to keep it warm." Bria took the tray from Fifetta. "You sit with the others and relax."

Lorenza and Fifetta joined Rosalie and Nunzi at the table, and the four guests exchanged pleasantries while Bria worked in the kitchen. They were all curious as to why they had been summoned to Bria's on such short notice, but Bria could overhear that they were keeping the conversation light and free of any mention of murder. When the next guest arrived, Bria wasn't sure the air of levity would be maintained.

"Imperia!" Fifetta cried out. "Come join us."

Imperia stood near the doorway and surveyed the room. She didn't look very pleased to see that almost every seat at the table was occupied. Nor did she appear thrilled with the women occupying those seats.

"I didn't realize this was going to be . . . *un grande affare*," she said, sarcasm dripping from her lips.

"It's just us girls," Fifetta said. "Come join *le regazze*."

Looking like she was being led to an execution and not a lunch, Imperia placed her purse on the counter and sat in the chair next to Fifetta. At Fifetta's prompting, the two women hugged and kissed each other on the cheek. Fifetta didn't stop there but felt the fabric of Imperia's lavender silk blouse.

"This is smoother than a baby's skin," Fifetta cooed. "I don't know how you can wear silk in this weather, Imperia. I live in linen and cotton all summer long, and on hot days like this, I still sweat."

"I've trained myself not to perspire," Imperia said.

"You can train yourself not to sweat?" Rosalie asked.

"If one has discipline," Imperia said, "one can do anything."

"In that case, I'd rather train myself not to gain weight," Rosalie said.

Imperia surveyed Rosalie from head to foot. "Then again, there are things that for some of us remain an impossibility."

Even from the kitchen, Bria could feel the tension rise in the dining room, and so she quickly threw cold cuts on a plate, dumped the chunks of cheese she had cut up earlier on top of them, and then turned the olive jar upside down and ran it along the circumference of the plate so the outer rim was filled with green olives. Her appetizer tray wouldn't win any awards, but it might distract the ladies long enough for them to forget they didn't particularly enjoy each other's company. Or, more specifically, Imperia's.

"This should hold us over until the lasagna is warm enough to eat," Bria said, placing the plate in the center of the table.

"Who else are we waiting for, Bri?" Lorenza asked. "Your invite was cryptic at best."

"Just a few more," Bria said just as the front door opened. "And here they are."

Annamaria entered, carrying a tray of pastries, and was followed by Paloma, who was holding a pitcher of limoncello.

"*Ciao, belle!*" Annamaria squealed.

"I think you mean *belle belle*," Paloma commented.

All the women laughed at Paloma's joke except, as expected, Imperia, who merely smiled.

"Is that everyone?" Imperia asked as Annamaria and Paloma took seats around the table. "Or have you invited the entire female population of Positano?"

"Is Mimi coming?" Paloma asked.

"She had to go to Isernia for a booksellers' convention," Annamaria replied before Bria could respond.

"Now that we're all here, could you please tell us why you've gathered us?" Imperia said. "It can't possibly be to celebrate the opening of this . . . What is it called?"

"A bed-and-breakfast," Bria replied.

"Yes, *that*," Imperia said. "Why are we here?"

"I'll explain everything. We're just waiting on one more person," Bria said.

"Who else is there?" Rosalie asked.

"Here she is now," Bria said.

All heads turned to the front door to see Sister Benedicta standing in the doorway.

"May I come in?" the nun asked.

"*Certo*," Bria said. "Come in and join us."

Before the nun could get to her seat, Bravo bounded over to her, and like she did every morning when Bria dropped Marco off at school, she gave him a treat.

The nun bent down and held her hand out and Bravo scooped up the treat with his tongue. "*L'angioletto di Dio*," she whispered.

Bria smiled, because she agreed that Bravo was God's little angel.

Sister Benedicta took a seat next to Paloma, and finally, all the women Bria had invited were assembled. She knew that her gesture was grand, and she didn't need to be so elaborate, but she wanted to make sure that there were others in the room with her when she exposed the killer, in case they wanted to retaliate. Bria felt she would feel stronger surrounded by friends and family.

She looked at all the women, some curious, some mildly anxious, others, like Lorenza, merely chewing, and Bria knew she couldn't wait any longer. The time had come to see if she was right or if she was about to make the biggest mistake of her life.

"Thank you all for coming on such short notice," Bria started. "I know that everyone is busy, but I promise this won't take very long."

"Take as long as you need, Bria," Annamaria said. "I left Antonio in charge of the café, and the tourists love him. Isn't that right, Paloma?"

Surprised to hear her name linked to Annamaria's employee, Paloma blushed. "That was a long time ago."

"Is Antonio the tall, thin waiter with the pierced ears?" Lorenza asked.

"He got rid of his earrings and pierced his nose," Annamaria said. "He's still thin, though."

"Too bad it didn't work out, Paloma," Lorenza said. "He's handsome—"

"Bria, I think you were saying something about not wasting our time," Imperia interrupted.

"Yes, I did, and I will be true to my word," Bria replied. "I've asked you all here today because I want to tell you who really killed Vittorio Ingleterra and Daniela di Santi."

"Holy moly! No way!" Rosalie shouted a bit too enthusiastically.

"Bria!" Fifetta cried. "What are you talking about? Dante is in jail."

"I know that, Mamma," Bria said. "I can prove that he doesn't belong there."

Fifetta looked around the room nervously. The others did

the same. Slowly, it dawned on the group that Bria thought one of them was a murderer.

"Is this like one of those murder mystery party games?" Annamaria asked.

"This isn't a game," Bria said. "This is deadly serious and a day we'll remember forever."

Bria had hoped her words would hush the group into silence. They had the opposite effect, and they all started to laugh.

"Bria, sometimes you really can get full of yourself," Lorenza said. She then mocked Bria's serious tone of voice. "Today is a deadly serious day that will be remembered for all the days to come."

"Renza!" Fifetta scolded. "But your sister's right, Bria. This isn't La Scala."

"Forgive me, Mamma," Bria said. "But I am trying to set the stage."

"Then start with the plot," Imperia said. "Why do you think Dante is innocent and one of us is the killer?"

"One of us?" Sister Benedicta cried.

"That's why we're all gathered here, isn't it?" Imperia asked. "Bria thinks that one of us killed Vittorio and Daniela."

Bria remained silent and fought the urge to look everyone in the eye to see if she could detect fear rising from the pits of their stomachs and creeping into their pupils, but she remained focused and controlled and didn't look away from Imperia.

"That's correct," Bria said. "I believe that one of you committed murder. Twice."

It was like a bomb had gone off in the room, and all the women began talking at once. Bria could make out only snippets of the conversation, bits of the dialogue. Still, she knew that they were all protesting, claiming their innocence, and sharing how crazy they thought their hostess was. All of them were right except for one.

"*Calmatevi per favore*," Bria said. "Let me explain."

She walked to the head of the table, which faced the front door and stood with her back to the kitchen. She began to lay out her theory and hoped she presented the image of someone who was in control.

"I've always said that Vittorio was the victim of a crime of passion, killed by someone who loved him."

"Daniela di Santi?" Lorenza asked.

"Daniela loved him, but she didn't kill him," Bria said.

"That's what I've been trying to tell you," Imperia said.

"Why not?" Lorenza asked. "Daniela was Vittorio's lover, and a lover is usually the person who commits a crime of passion."

"Daniela didn't kill Vittorio because she had no reason to," Bria explained. "He wasn't going to leave her. He was going to leave Paloma."

A collective gasp erupted, and all heads turned to face Paloma. She sat there for a moment with no expression on her face at all; it was as if she were wearing a mask, one of innocence and not of guilt. When Bria saw her reaction, she knew that she was correct, and Paloma had committed murder. Now she had to lay out the facts for the rest of the group and convince them, as well.

"Bria, with all due respect, that's absurd," Paloma said, her voice controlled and quiet. "I'm not a murderess. I own a home goods store."

"The two vocations aren't mutually exclusive," Imperia said.

"We all knew that Daniela bought the two scarves from Paloma, even though at first, Paloma had no memory of the sale," Bria said. "It was only when I showed her the photo of the bloodied scarf that she remembered."

"*Dammi una pausa*! I sell a lot of merchandise, Bria," Paloma said. "I can't be expected to remember each item."

"True," Bria agreed. "Nor could you be expected to recognize Daniela in the Polaroid I showed you, but when I showed you the photo of Vittorio, you reacted quite strongly."

"Anyone would react strongly if they were shown a photo of a dead man," Paloma protested.

"You had tears in your eyes," Bria said. "That's not how you usually respond to a stranger's death. Fear, empathy, disgust, yes, but deep sadness that provokes instant tears, no. You reacted that way because Vittorio was the man who dumped you, the one Annamaria told us about."

"I didn't know it was Vittorio," Annamaria said. "Paloma never mentioned his name."

"But Paloma did tell you that she was dating someone who broke up with her suddenly," Bria said. "Which is a pattern in your life, isn't it, Paloma?"

Hands clasped in front of her, Paloma narrowed her eyes and looked down at the table. "I don't know what you're talking about."

"Yes, you do," Bria said. "I've been here only a short time, but both Mimi and Annamaria have told me that you are unhappily single and haven't had any luck in the boyfriend department. I even learned that you and Giovanni dated a while back, and you refused to be friends with him because you accused him of cheating on you, even though he denied it."

"That's how a woman acts when she feels betrayed," Fifetta said. "How can you say for certain that woman was Paloma?"

"Because whoever killed Vittorio had to live in the village," Bria replied.

Bria was growing more confident. She was no longer sharing a theory; she was presenting facts. It made the difference between feeling unsure and feeling empowered.

"Thanks to Fabrice and Lorenza, we were able to track down Vittorio's itinerary, and we couldn't find any hotel reservation for him in Positano," Bria said. "Ours isn't the easiest village to get to, and Vittorio landed early in the morning in

Naples and didn't rent a car, which means that someone must have picked him up and given him a place to stay. That person had to be a resident.

"Then there's the matter of how Vittorio was killed and where he actually died," Bria continued. "He had to have been stabbed somewhere nearby in order to have the strength to walk to Bella Bella and not be noticed by anyone milling about in the early morning. There's a shortcut that leads from here to the back of Paloma's store, as well as to some others, that is only a ten-minute walk. It's close and secluded."

"Why exactly would Paloma kill her boyfriend?" Fifetta asked.

"Because he dumped her for Daniela," Imperia said.

"That's right, and I thank you for that information, Imperia," Bria said. "Daniela didn't share that with me, but you told me that although another woman was in love with Vittorio, he chose Daniela."

"When having to decide between someone of Daniela's stature and a shop owner," Imperia said, "there really is no choice."

"Especially if Vittorio was in debt and enjoyed a lavish lifestyle," Bria said. "I'm afraid you never stood a chance, Paloma."

"Stop talking about me like I'm not here," Paloma said. "*Non sono invisibile!*"

"That explains the personal part," Annamaria said. "But what about the professional?"

"The only reason Vittorio was in town was because of the wine and cheese store, which was nothing more than a front for the counterfeit money ring he and Delfino were trying to get started," Bria said. "Daniela was a legitimate businesswoman and was furious that her brother and Vittorio were trying to resurrect an illegal money ring that wasn't successful the first time around. I believe Daniela pressured Vittorio to bow out of the scheme, which left Delfino on his own."

"That's why she was furious with her brother," Imperia said.

"I suspected he was doing something that wasn't aboveboard ever since he got out of jail, but I didn't know what it was."

"So you did recognize Delfino when you saw him here posing as a reporter," Bria said.

"Of course I recognized him," Imperia replied. "I wanted him to leave because I know how dangerous he can be. I knew he'd be scared of me because I would tell Daniela what I had seen."

"The illegal business does seem to be all Delfino's idea, and I believe Dante was helping Daniela by trying to convince Delfino to stop, but Delfino wouldn't listen," Bria said.

"Dante and Daniela were very good friends," Imperia said.

Bria leaned forward on the table and stared at Paloma.

"Is everything I've said correct so far, Paloma?" Bria asked. She continued before Paloma had a chance to respond. "Was Vittorio only using you to stay close to the wine and cheese store? Were you the woman he dumped so he could devote himself entirely to Daniela? Did the two of you argue all the way home on the drive from Naples after you picked him up? And did he finally tell you that the affair that you thought was filled with love, was really just filled with lies?"

By the time Bria was finished, Paloma looked like Mount Vesuvius ready to explode.

"Everything he said to me was a lie! *Tutto quanto*! Do you have any idea what that feels like? To know that the love a man professed to you is fake? That *nothing* he has said to you was the truth? Do any of you have any idea what that's like!"

The person who answered Paloma was the only person no one at the table would think understood.

"No, but I always told you that you were not alone."

Paloma looked at Sister Benedicta, and it was lucky that there wasn't a knife close by, because there was fury in Paloma's eyes.

"What could you possibly know about *men*!" Paloma shrieked.

"I'm sorry I couldn't help you," Sister Benedicta replied.

"But you did, whether you know it or not," Bria said.

When Sister Benedicta didn't answer, but merely bowed her head, Bria knew that the clue the nun had given her had been the result of a deliberate act. It was the nun's way of revealing evidence that otherwise may have gone unnoticed. Bria had always known that Marco's teacher wasn't the typical nun, but Sister Benedicta was even shrewder than she'd thought.

"How did Sister B help you deduce that Paloma killed Vittorio?" Rosalie asked.

"She didn't," Bria said. "She helped me realize that Paloma killed Daniela."

Another outburst erupted at the table, and even Bravo joined in by barking. When everyone had quieted down, Bria continued.

"Sister Benedicta told me that Paloma described Dante's gun to her as quite large," Bria said. "I didn't think anything of it at first, but then I realized that Bombalino didn't describe the gun in any of the articles he printed, and since Paloma wasn't officially on the yacht, there was no way Sister B could know that unless Paloma had secretly crashed the party."

"Bria, even if Paloma snuck into the party and saw what kind of gun was used to kill Daniela, that doesn't mean that she was the one to shoot her," Fifetta said.

"There was also the information that both Lorenza and Sister Benedicta shared with me that proved Paloma had access to Dante's gun."

"What information is that?" Lorenza asked.

"The Realtor's lock," Bria said.

"The one outside Gianna's store?" Annamaria asked. "What does that have to do with the mayor?"

"It reminded me that Lorenza said Paloma has her real estate license, and therefore she had easy access to open those locks, like the ones outside Gianna's store and Dante's office."

"That's right!" Rosalie said. "We saw the one outside his building."

"Paloma was able to open the real estate lock in front of Dante's house, get the key to the house, and break in to steal his gun," Bria said. "I'm sure that when the police look at the surveillance video, they'll see Paloma in action."

"Dante has security cameras?" Paloma screamed.

"Of course he does. He's the mayor!" Rosalie retorted. "Any *stolta* knows that."

Bria glanced at her friend and smiled when she saw that Rosalie was dead serious. Obviously, she had forgotten that they were foolish enough not to realize the mayor had a security camera set up when they broke in to steal his framed lira.

"Dante was friends with that woman, and I knew that he was one of the reasons Vittorio sided with Daniela," Paloma explained. "If I couldn't have Vittorio, neither could she! She deserved to die! She stole the only man I ever loved!"

"Daniela did not deserve to die!" Imperia screamed.

"Yes she did!" Paloma cried.

"You were the one who pulled the trigger at the party and then ran off, leaving Dante to pick up the gun," Bria said. "I assume you dove off the side of the yacht and swam to shore."

"I swam underwater the entire way," Paloma responded, beaming. "I told you I was just as good a swimmer as your mother."

"How many trophies have you won?" Lorenza asked.

"Seven," Paloma replied.

"Ha!" Lorenza cried. "Mamma has ten."

"*Grazie*, Renza," Fifetta said. "But now is not really the time to argue about who has the most trophies."

"Who's arguing?" Lorenza asked. "I'm setting the record straight."

"There is one thing that confuses me, Paloma. I'm hoping you can clear the air," Bria said. "I saw you the morning Vittorio was killed, and presumably, it was right after you killed him."

"It was," Paloma said. "While we were arguing, I stabbed Vittorio. I didn't mean to. It just happened, and he stumbled out of my store. I didn't realize how badly he was hurt until I saw him walking down the shortcut, clutching his side. I was going to follow him, but I saw you coming from the other direction. I had blood on my hands, so I dropped a plant, spilling dirt all over, as a distraction."

"You're a clever girl," Imperia said.

Paloma glared at Imperia but quickly resumed her recollection of the fatal event. "I ran after Vittorio and saw him just as he was going into your house. I followed him and made him go upstairs to hide. By that time, I realized the wound was much more serious than I had thought and I wasn't going to be able to save him. I was about to leave when I remembered he had a receipt from my store in his wallet. If the police found that, they'd link us together, so I took his money and ID to make it look like a robbery. I took the shortcut back to my store, cleaned up, just in time to sell you that artichoke bowl."

"*E fredda,*" Imperia said. "A clever and cold, cold girl."

Paloma scoffed at Imperia's comment. "I even had time to put Band-Aids on the backs of my ankles, where I cut them from running in my heels back and forth from Bella Bella."

"I knew that was odd!" Bria cried. "I saw an American woman walking on a path who had cuts in the same places because she was wearing heels, and I remembered that you did, too. But you never wear your heels through town, so I couldn't imagine how you had cut yourself."

"Now you know," Paloma smugly replied.

"I also know that it couldn't have been you who was hiding downstairs," Bria said. "The person I heard leave while I was upstairs in the bedroom with Vittorio."

"That was Delfino," Paloma replied.

"If you weren't in Bria's house, how do you know it was Delfino?" Imperia asked.

"He came to me the next day and told me he had seen me," Paloma explained. "He was set to meet Vittorio that morning at their fake store, and he saw me stab him. He said he was going to tell the police what I had done, and I told him that if he did, I'd tell them about the counterfeit money ring."

"Stalemate," Rosalie said.

"*Giusto*," Paloma replied. "We both agreed to keep each other's secret."

"Delfino broke his promise," Bria said.

"What do you mean?" Paloma asked.

"He finally told the truth," Bria replied.

"When did he do that?" Annamaria said. "I spoke with Teresa, a nurse at the hospital, who's a friend of my cousin who's also named Teresa, which is funny, and Teresa the nurse told me that Delfino is still in a coma."

"When I found Delfino on the beach, he said, 'She did it,'" Bria said. "I thought he was talking about Daniela, but he was talking about Paloma. He saw you shoot Daniela, didn't he?"

"I should've shot him first, but Daniela was being so smug I had to shut her up for good," Paloma said. "I went to shoot Delfino, but I missed, and then I heard all the commotion. I didn't have time to finish him off."

"Well, two out of three ain't bad, Paloma," Rosalie said.

It looked like Paloma was about to finish Rosalie off, but before she could move, they all heard a noise coming from the closet.

"What's that?" Fifetta asked.

"It's coming from the closet," Paloma said, her voice growing scared. "The same one Delfino hid in."

Immediately, Bravo ran to the door and started barking. The women got up and walked to the closet as the noise grew louder. Someone was banging on the door.

"Bria, the door's stuck!"

"That's my brother!" Rosalie cried.

"The chief of police is locked in the closet?" Fifetta asked.

"Sorry, Luca. I thought Giovanni fixed the door to make it stop sticking," Bria announced.

"It couldn't get stuck when Delfino was in here?" Luca cried from inside the closet.

"Rosalie, help me!" Bria ordered, and she and Rosalie started pulling on the doorknob.

Out of the corner of her eye, Bria saw Paloma start to inch her way toward the front door, obviously hoping she could make a run for it before Luca was set free.

"Stop her!" Bria cried.

Just as Paloma darted for the front door, Sister Benedicta lifted up her skirt and extended her leg, tripping Paloma and sending the two-time murderess sprawling on the floor. Nunzi jumped on top of Paloma, grabbed her wrists, brought them together behind her back, and then hoisted the woman up to a standing position just as the closet door flung open and Luca burst into the main room.

"Paloma Speranza, you're under arrest for the murders of Vittorio Ingleterra and Daniela di Santi!" Luca shouted.

Bria felt a genuine sense of relief wash over her. She heard Rosalie and Lorenza screaming congratulations. She watched as Luca read Paloma her rights. She saw her mother hold Imperia's hand at the table, and she noticed Sister Benedicta bow her head in prayer. So many emotions, so many different responses to the same scene.

"It's over Rosalie. This nightmare is finally over," Bria said, hugging her best friend.

"I have one more mystery for you to solve," Rosalie said.

"*Uffa!*" Bria cried. "Now what?"

Rosalie looked over at Sister Benedicta and said, "Explain to me how a nun has better legs than I do."

For a moment Bria didn't know how to respond, but then

she burst out laughing. It was inappropriate, slightly disrespectful, but it felt so wonderfully good. Bria knew she was going to have to take time to process everything that had happened since this all began, but for the moment, she was genuinely happy. She had set out to restore Bella Bella's good name and find out who the murderer was, and she had succeeded on both counts. As an added bonus, along the way, she had found herself again.

She couldn't wait to reintroduce Bria Bartolucci to the world.

EPILOGUE

The next day the world was ready to greet Bria Bartolucci.

Her photo appeared on the front page of *La Vita Positano*, under the headline LOCAL RESIDENT SOLVES DOUBLE MURDER, and when Bria stepped out of her house, she was greeted by a group of *i locali* and some tourists who were aware of the recent developments. They were cheering, waving Italian flags, and Annamaria and Enrico were holding up a banner that read *BRIA: LA REGINA DI POSITANO*. It was silly to admit it, but Bria did feel like a queen.

From the way Bravo was barking, Bria suspected the dog thought all the hoopla was for him. It took all the strength she had not to break down and cry. *What a dumb reaction*, she thought. But then she changed her mind. *No, this is the most perfect reaction of all.*

Bria may not have saved the town, but she had saved her business, and she had saved the dream that originally brought her here. Bella Bella was going to open, and no one was going to think they were spending the night in a murder house. Instead, they were going to tell their friends that they had stayed at the home of the Queen of Positano. Most important, her friends in this little sun-kissed village had become new members of her family.

After the crowd dispersed, one person remained who, remarkably, had made more of an impact on Bria's life than anyone else.

"I never expected to see you here," Bria said.

"That's because you only *think* you know me," Imperia replied. "I came to thank you."

"I'm almost afraid to ask, but thank me for what?"

"For bringing my friend's killer to justice," she replied. "My life won't be the same without Daniela—I won't have a confidant or a friend I can ask to brunch—but if it wasn't for your tenacity and conviction, her killer would have gotten away with her murder, and the wrong man would've been sent to jail." Imperia stared at Bria as if if was the first time she was seeing the woman. "*Grazie.*"

In all the years Bria had known Imperia, she had never heard her sound more heartfelt and sincere. Her mother-in-law was most certainly a complicated woman, but she was also a woman whom Bria thought she'd like to get to know a little better.

"I'll be a little busy with my B and B," Bria said. "But I always have time for brunch if you'd like a companion."

Imperia looked at Bria strangely and then turned away. Bria thought—no, she was certain—there were tears in Imperia's eyes. Bria looked down to give Imperia a moment to compose herself. A woman knows when another woman needs some privacy.

"I may take you up on that," Imperia said. "But remember, running an empire is much more complicated than running a . . . *guesthouse.*"

Bria waited for Imperia to smile, because she must have intended what she said to be a joke, but when no smile came, it was even better. Laughing hysterically, Bria did something she hadn't done in years. She hugged Imperia. Her mother-in-law didn't hug her back, but Bria didn't expect her to. One miracle in a week was enough.

One by one, all Bria's friends and family called or stopped by to congratulate her on making their village safe again or to wish her luck on the grand opening the following day. Lorenza and Fabrice sent a framed photo of themselves looking stunning on the night of the yacht party, and said that Bria could put the photo in the living room and tell all her guests that she was related to celebrities. Sister Benedicta dropped off a small statue of St. Christopher, the patron saint of travelers that could be put on the table next to the front door so each new guest would be blessed by the beloved saint when they passed by, and Enrico sent the most beautiful display of flowers Bria had ever seen. There wasn't a petunia in the bunch.

Nunzi wrote out her mother's recipe for *ribolitta* soup, which Bria could then give to all the guests as a memento of their stay; her parents gave her two framed pieces of art, which she at first didn't recognize were her own college creations; and Dante even gave her a plaque stating that Bella Bella had received the seal of approval from the mayor's office.

The night before the grand opening, Rosalie gave Bria a gift that was more for her than for her business. It was a photo of Bria sitting at the marina, leaning back, her face, not much more than a profile, staring off at the horizon. Her eyes were bright and wide, and she was smiling.

"I don't remember being that relaxed in ages," Bria said.

"That's why I took the photo," Rosalie said. "So you can remind yourself that you have everything you need to succeed. The future is whatever you want it to be."

"*Grazie*, Rosalie," Bria said. "Promise me my future will have you in it."

"I'll be right here with you," Rosalie replied. "Unless I decide to take my boat and sail around the world."

There was an awkward moment when both Luca and Giovanni showed up at the same time with matching bouquets of pink roses. Bria stood between the two men, both handsome, both possessing strength, loyalty, and solid character, and she was grateful to have both men in her life. She accepted their bouquets and felt triumphant because she didn't feel compelled to act like a fairy-tale princess. She didn't have to choose a prince. She didn't have to choose a man to give her a happy ending because she had already given that to herself.

She thanked Luca and Giovanni for the roses and was genuinely glad they were in her life. Would one of them be part of her future? Only time would tell. For the moment, however, the only man in her life was Marco.

After Luca and Giovanni left, Marco ran out from his room with Bravo in tow, and they both jumped on the couch to join Bria.

"*Ti amo, Mamma*," Marco said, giving Bria a hug.

"*Ti amo anch'io, mio angioletto*," Bria said. "But what was that for?"

"We learned in school today that we should celebrate the simple things in life and not wait until big things, like birthdays and anniversaries, to say I love you," Marco explained.

"That's a good lesson to learn," Bria said. "But tonight is a special night, because it's the last night that we'll be alone in this house for a while. Tomorrow, our first guests arrive."

"I know," Marco replied. "I can't wait to see them."

"Me, too, *amore mio*," Bria said, kissing her little boy on his forehead.

She looked over at the photo of Carlo on the sideboard and smiled back at him.

"It'll be like a dream come true."

POSITANO

A Trip to Remember and Tips to Share

When I started doing research for this book, I realized rather quickly that Positano wasn't like any other place on earth. Visually, it was completely different from anything I'd ever seen in my travels. The architecture; the almost pre-historic landscape; the vibrant colors; the narrow, twisting streets; the never-ending sunshine. I was fascinated.

But the more videos I watched on YouTube, the more my fascination turned to confusion. How could this place be real? I mean, could Positano and the rest of the Amalfi Coast be that breathtaking? Well, there was only one way for me to find out—I had to see it for myself.

I booked myself a two-week trip to the Amalfi Coast with Positano being my home base. And let me just say that seeing truly is believing. This seaside village lives up to its reputation and its many, many accolades. It is spectacular. It is awe-inspiring. It is bewitching. It's a setting that both soothes and stimulates the senses. A place where there is so much to do and nothing at all to do. A village that will play a trick on you because long after you're back home you'll feel as if you've never left.

That's how it's been for me. Months after I had returned home, I was still thinking about Positano. And Capri. And Amalfi. And Ravello, Sorrento, Praiano, Naples. Each of the towns that make up the Amalfi Coast have their own specific charm, their own Italian attitude—or Italiatude—as I like to call it. Each one has given me memories that I will cherish forever and never forget.

Over the course of this new book series, I thought I'd share with you some of those memories to inspire you to take your own trip to the Amalfi Coast or remind you that it's time for you to return. I'll also share some tips I learned from my trip that you can use when you travel. I know that I can't wait to return to my favorite restaurants and cafés, lounge at the beach clubs I missed on my first visit, and explore even more of Positano and the Amalfi Coast. I know there are magnificent treasures that I can't wait to discover.

They're waiting for you too!

Ciao . . . for now!

Michael Falco

Tour de Force

Positano isn't a huge village, but it has a lot to offer. Almost too much to take in on one visit. And definitely too much if you don't know you're way around. The best way to see the town is to see it through the eyes of a local. I got incredibly lucky because I was able to book a last-minute private walking tour with Zia Lucy (http://en.zialucy.com/). Lucy was born and raised in Positano and she is a living, breathing encyclopedia of the village. She's filled with facts, anecdotes, hilarious stories, and helpful tips on the best places to eat. She even helped me find a store that was open late and sold adapters that convert electricity so American plugs can work in Italian sockets.

Lucy's insight into the village, its people, how it has evolved over the years, and about the local mindset, was invaluable. I heard her voice over and over again as I was writing this book and breathing life into Bria and the rest of the characters. Even if you're not writing a book about Positano, listening to Lucy share her knowledge about the village's history is an experience you'll never forget.

You can book a private or group tour of varying lengths and times. But don't do what I did and wait until the last minute. Book early!

His Story Made History

Positano really was a sleepy little seaside village until John Steinbeck decided to write an article about the town for *Harper's Bazaar* in 1953. Written on Le Sirenuse letterhead, it's a must-read for anyone traveling to Positano or anyone interested in what travel was like before the Internet, social media, and Uber. It's a delightful read and will make you ache for yesteryear.

The essay can be easily found in several places online. What might not be as easy is booking a stay at Le Sirenuse. It's a world-renowned hotel, almost always filled to capacity, and very expensive. If there's no room at the inn or not enough extra funds in your wallet to make a stay at the hotel possible, you can still enjoy its elegance by having a drink at Aldo's, the rooftop lounge, or schedule a couple's massage or an anti-aging body wrap at the spa.

If the sirens are calling, just go to https://sirenuse.it/en/ and answer their call.

Up, Up, and Away!

One of the most exciting things that happened to me while I was in Positano is that I got a text from a friend telling me she was also in the area. She's a tour guide for a company that specializes in upscale vacations and her territory just happens to be the Amalfi Coast. Originally, she was leaving the day I arrived, but luckily she had to cover for a co-worker and stayed in Italy for an extra week. That meant we would be able to spend some time together.

We met on the island of Capri, which must be at the top of your list of places to visit when you go to Positano. It's a short ferry ride away and once you arrive you'll feel like you're a celebrity on one of those press junkets to a foreign country where everyone treats you like royalty. I'm not kidding. If there's one thing Italians can do, it's make you feel welcome!

When you arrive, you can explore the port, but that's just the beginning. The fun is up top. Get a ticket to take the funicular up to Capri town. Once there you can shop until you'll need to open up a new credit card. Have a Hugo Spritz (like Bria does!) at Hotel Quisisana. This is where I met my friend and I truly felt like Alexis Carrington having a mid-day cocktail, basking in the glorious southern Italian sun, being doted on by a handsome waiter. Well, that is, if Alexis had any friends, but you get the idea.

We then took a cab ride—in a hot pink cab!—to Anacapri, which is simply the fancy Italian way of saying above Capri. Our driver was funny, loud, and oh-so-Italian. You can pick up a cab at the centrally located transportation hub, which you can't miss, and choose a cab in your favorite color.

Once we got to Anacapri, my friend surprised me with something that I didn't even know existed even though I had done quite a bit of research on the Amalfi Coast before I traveled. It's something that turned into one of the major highlights of my entire trip. The Monte Solaro chair lift. Yup, a chair lift. Like the ones at ski resorts. Only better.

Built in 1952, the lift travels for about fifteen minutes and takes you to the top of the mountain, approximately 589 meters or 1,932 feet. It's high. But it's worth it.

The 360 degree views allow you to see the Gulf of Naples, Mount Vesuvius, the jagged coastline and the Faraglioni, which are oceanic rock formations that jut out from the sea. And do what I did—resist the urge to take photos with your cell phone the entire time. Put the phone away and take in the extraordinary beauty. I promise that it'll be a magical experience.

http://www.capriseggiovia.it/en/impianto.html

When You Get Lemons—Make Limoncello

Lemons are everywhere you look in Positano. There are lemons on trees, lemons on ceramic bowls like the ones Paloma sells at La Casa Felice, lemons on linen skirts, dresses, and blouses in all the boutiques, and lemons on everything from ashtrays to kitchen utensils to magnets in the scores of souvenir stores that are scattered throughout Viale Pasitea. Arguably, however, the most famous and coveted lemon product is the limoncello.

More than a mere libation, limoncello, is *the* drink of the Amalfi Coast. Although its origin is disputed, most agree that it was created in the early 1900s in either Isola Azzurra or Sicily. Wherever it began its life, it is now celebrated all throughout Italy as a digestive, a lazy afternoon cocktail, or just a fabulous drink.

I'm a traditionalist and prefer a limoncello spritz. It's super easy to make and is three parts Prosecco, two parts limoncello, and one part club soda or any type of sparkling water over ice.

Garnish with a slice of orange and you have a refreshing and delightful citrus conflation.

If you're a purist and want to drink limoncello without any bells and whistles, drink slowly and take small sips. Limoncello—especially homemade varieties—are very strong. As I was waiting for my flight home, I ordered a limoncello at the airport thinking I was going to get a spritz like I had been getting during my stay. Wrong. I got straight limoncello in a large glass. I took one sip and nearly burned my throat. Luckily, I thought of a quick Plan B and ordered a Coca-Cola. I poured the soft drink in a glass filled with ice, added the limoncello, and had a surprisingly refreshing limoncocacello. (I just made up that name, but feel free to ask for it the next time you're at a café. Perhaps we can make it go viral!)

You can find limoncello at almost every store in Positano. Small bottles, large bottles, pistachio flavored, melon flavored, and crema di limoncello. There's even a non-dairy version! I bought several bottles of Pallini's non-dairy, gluten free, crema di limoncello. With a name like that it shouldn't be good, but it's delicious. I'll definitely be ordering some more!

https://www.pallini.com/en/products/limoncello-cream#.Y89oOuzMITU

GLOSSARY

Since Bria and the rest of her family and friends live in Italy, they, of course, speak the language of their land. Throughout the book, I've sprinkled their dialogue with Italian words and phrases and I thought it would be helpful to include a list of them so nothing gets lost in translation. I'm Italian and even I picked up a bunch of new words doing my research!

Many of the words are easy to decipher because their spelling is close to how the word is spelled in English, like *avventura*, which means adventure. Or the way the word sounds gives away its meaning, like Bria's catchphrase—*Uffa!*—which I'm sure you figured out means Ugh!

And who knows? If you keep reading every new Bria Bartolucci mystery, you just might learn a whole new language!

Italian/English
addio – good-bye
amica mio – my friend
amore mio/mi amore – my love
amorevoli – loving/affectionate
andiamo – let's go
angioletto – little angel
aspetta/aspett – wait/hold on

assolutamente – absolutely
apri gli occhi – open your eyes

Basta con il tiro alla fune – Enough of the tug of war
Basta cosi – that's enough
beh – well
bene! – fine/good
bestemmia – blasphemy
biblioteca – library
brillante – brilliant
bugiardo – liar
buona giornata – have a good day
buona idea – good idea
buongiorno – good morning

calmati – calm down
canaglia – scoundrel
capo della polizia – chief of police
carciofo – artichoke
carino – cute one
caro Dio in Cielo – dear God in Heaven
caro Signore – dear Lord
catapecchia – slum
certo – of course
Che cosa? – What?
che Dio mi sia testimone – God be my witness
che dolce – how sweet
che fortuna – how lucky
che macello – what a mess
chi ha e chi non ha – the haves and the have-nots
Chi stai cercando di prendere in giro? – Who are you trying
    to kid?
chiacchierone – chatty
classe bassa – low class

Come mai? – How come?
comprendi – understand
cucciolo – puppy/term of endearment for a little boy

dammi una pausa – give me a break
dannazione – darn it
davvero – really
delizioso - delicious
il diavolo – the devil
dimmi – tell me
Dio mio – my God
Dio riposi la sua anima – God rest his soul
divertitevi – have fun
donna maleducata – rude woman
drudo – paramour

eccellente – excellent
ecco – Here you are
esattamente – exactly

falso – false
famiglia – family
farmacia – pharmacy
fasullo – fake
fermata – stop
ficcanaso – a snoop
figlia/figlio – daughter/son
figo – cool
fratelllo – brother
e fredda – cold

già abbastanza – enough already
giusto – right
goffa – clumsy

goffa idiota – clumsy idiot
grazie – thank you
grazie Dio – thank God
grazie mille – thank you very much
grezzo – rough/uncultivated
una grossa, grassa bugiarda – a big, fat liar

ha senso – makes sense
hai ragione – you're right

idiota – fool
indossa I pantaloni in quella relazione – she wears the pants
   in that relationship
imbroglione – swindler
Io desidero – I wish

lampadario – chandelier
Liti familiari – family quarrels
i locali – the locals
Lodate Dio e tutti gli angeli e i santi – Praise God and all
   the angels and saints
Lo giuro su Dio – I swear to God

Madonna mia – my goodness
malagi – evil
mamma gatta – cat mother
la mente – the mastermind
metà e metà – half and half
mi dispiace così tanto – I'm so sorry
molto geloso – so jealous
molto intelligente – so smart
molto vero – very true
molto strano – very strange
mucca sacre – holy cow

necci – Italian pancakes
nella bocca dell'inferno – into the mouth of hell
nerboruto – muscular
no non l'hanno fatto – no, they did not
non è niente – it's nothing
non essere sciocca – don't be silly
non lo so – I can't believe it
non preoccuparti – don't worry
Non sono invisibile – I'm not invisible

oh cavolo – oh boy!
un ospite – a guest
ovviamente no – obviously not

pazza/pazzo – crazy
peccatuccio – peccadillo
pensa globalmente, agisci localmente – think globally, act locally
per favore – please
per l'amor di Dio – for the love of God!
per piacere – please
perdonami – forgive me
perché io – why me?
pettegola – gossip
piantala! – cut it out!
piccolo amore – little love
Più risposte portano sempre a più domande – More answers always lead to more questions
Posa, posa! – Put me down, put me down
prego – you're welcome/please
principino – little prince
polpetta – little meatball
porca vacca – holy cow
punto di svolta – turning point

qualunque cosa – whatever
questo è corretto – that's right
la quiete prima della tempesta – the quiet before the storm
quindi aiutami Dio – so help me God

le regazze – the girls
ricorda – remember
rifuto – rubbish
una rimbambita – a dummy

salve – hello
sbrigati – hurry up
scuola primaria – grammar school
scusa, scusami, scusi, scusatemi – excuse me
sdolcinato – schmaltzy
sei la mia migliore amica – you're my best friend
sei stupido o cosa – are you stupid or what
senz'altro – certainly
senza senso – nonsense
sorrellina fastidiosa – annoying little sister
spaventoso – frightening
sta' zitta – shut up
stai scherzando – Are you joking?
sto bene – I'm fine

tale divertimento – such fun
testa calda – hothead
ti prego – I beg you
tontos – idiots
topolino – little mouse
tra l'altro – moreover
tu dici patata – you say potato
tutto a posto – everything fine?
tutto malvagi – utterly wicked
tutto quanto – everything

uffa – ugh

un'immagine vale più di mille parole – a picture's worth a
   thousand words

va bene – all right

vedi – you see!

veramente – really

vero – true

vieni qui – come here

voluttuosa – voluptuous

zia – aunt

zitta – shut up